PRAISE FOR PATRICIA SCANLAN

CITY LIVES
'A page-turner ... for incurable romantics who love a fairytale ending' *Ireland on Sunday*

CITY GIRL
'Her story of three young Dublin girls, who start their twenties with high hopes and endure various hard knocks along the way, will pull at your heartstrings' *Options*

APARTMENT 3B
'A story of jealousy, love and characters who stop at nothing to achieve their latest thrill, this is the perfect book for those moments when you need to escape'
Woman's Realm (Book of the Week)

MIRROR, MIRROR
'This is perfect summer reading: hearty, humorous and romantic. Be prepared to be bad company, though – it's a compulsive page-turner which keeps us guessing till the very end' *Home & Country*

PROMISES, PROMISES
'Love, laughter and tears' *Candis*

FINISHING TOUCHES
'An intriguing tale that follows the disasters and triumphs of three best friends' *Woman's Realm*

FOREIGN AFFAIRS
'A warm Irish saga of friendship, love and travel' *She*

FRANCESCA'S PARTY
'Her best yet ... Pacy, poignant, entertaining and believable' *Irish Independent*

TWO FOR JOY
'There is heartbreaking authenticity in her observations ... it's a pleasure to get pulled along in the lives of these characters' *Irish Times*

www.book

D0974531

DOUBLE WEDDING

PATRICIA SCANLAN

BANTAM BOOKS

LONDON • TORONTO • SYDNEY • AUCKLAND • JOHANNESBURG

DOUBLE WEDDING
A BANTAM BOOK: 0 553 81401 X

Originally published in Great Britain by Bantam Press,
a division of Transworld Publishers

PRINTING HISTORY
Bantam Press edition published 2004
Bantam edition published 2005

3 5 7 9 10 8 6 4 2

Set in 12/15.5pt Ehrhardt by
Falcon Oast Graphic Art Ltd.

Bantam Books are published by Transworld Publishers,
61–63 Uxbridge Road, London W5 5SA,
a division of The Random House Group Ltd,
in Australia by Random House Australia (Pty) Ltd,
20 Alfred Street, Milsons Point, Sydney, NSW 2061, Australia,
in New Zealand by Random House New Zealand Ltd,
18 Poland Road, Glenfield, Auckland 10, New Zealand
and in South Africa by Random House (Pty) Ltd,
Endulini, 5a Jubilee Road, Parktown 2193, South Africa.

Printed and bound in Germany by
GGP Media GmbH, Pössneck.

Papers used by Transworld Publishers are natural, recyclable
products made from wood grown in sustainable forests. The
manufacturing processes conform to the environmental
regulations of the country of origin.

To my beautiful parents

Acknowledgements

Put your hope in God for I will yet praise Him, my Saviour and my God. Psalm 42

With great gratitude I give thanks:

To Jesus, Our Lady, St Joseph, Mother Meera, St Anthony, St Michael, and all my Angels, Saints and Guides, I thank you so much for the joy of my writing.

To my brilliant family including aunts, uncle and cousins, who are so caring and supportive. It means more than you'll ever know. We're very lucky to have each other.

To Mary and Yvonne . . . who *demanded* their own acknowledgement. Hope this is OK for you and I love you both very much.

To all my dear and much-loved friends, who are a great blessing in my life. I would especially like to thank Anne Barry and Anita Notaro, who were friends in deed when I was a friend in need. Thanks so much for the visits, the shopping and the freezer filling when I was encased in the cast. And to Deirdre Purcell for the perfect holiday.

To Alil O'Shaughnessy, ditto above and for offering to bring my car for the NCT, not to talk of proofing the ms.

To Tony Kavanagh, who also proofed diligently and sent me hilarious texts and emails. No one can beat you for brunch!

To Aidan Storey, who made Divine Timing real for me. It's a joy to know you.

To Sarah, Felicity and Susannah, dear friends as well as agents.

To Jean, Leanne and Nicola, who make it such a treat to go to the hairdresser's.

To Francesca Liversidge, who is such a supportive editor as well as being a much-loved friend.

To all at Transworld, who give 100 per cent and more. I really appreciate the effort and support you give my novels and me.

To Gill, Simon, Geoff, Eamonn, Gary and Jean, who went all out to make *Two for Joy* a biggie. It was great. Thanks so much.

To Declan Heeney . . . Dec, what can I say? You're the best. (You're in the book!)

To my colleagues in HHI, who also come under the heading of much-loved friends.

To Professor Ciaran Bolger, who has given me hope.

To Assistant Matron Betty O'Kane, John Byrne, Maria Meehan and all in the Bon Secours Hospital, Glasnevin, for their consistent kindness.

To Cathy Delmar of Bridal Corner, Prospect Avenue, who was so helpful in keeping me up to date on bridal wear.

Dear Reader, I hope you enjoy this book. Love, Light and Blessings shine on you.

All men should strive
To learn before they die
What they are running from, and to,
And why.

James Thurber

The Engagements

1

'Let's have a double wedding!' Carol Logan burst out impulsively, brown eyes sparkling with giddy anticipation.

Oh no! Jessica Kennedy's stomach lurched as she gazed at her friend with undisguised dismay. A double wedding with Carol and Gary was the *last* thing she wanted.

'Hey, that's not a bad idea,' Gary, her friend's fiancé, approved. 'What do you think, you guys?'

'I suppose it's an option.' Mike, Jessica's boyfriend, eyed her quizzically.

'I don't know,' Jessica demurred, privately raging with him. Surely Mike would know that she wouldn't want a double wedding.

'Oh come on, Jessie, it would be fun, we could invite all our friends and have a great bash and split the cost between us,' Carol urged enthusiastically. Jessica could see she had the bit between her teeth. She knew what lay behind her friend's proposal and she felt a surge of resentment that her friend could be so self-centred as to hijack her and Mike's wedding for her own purposes.

Nip it in the bud now! she told herself sternly, wishing she wasn't such a wimp. She wasn't good at drawing her boundaries, as her cousin, best friend and great adviser, Katie, was always telling her. Katie'd freak when she heard this. She and Carol didn't get on at all.

'Er . . . I don't know, Carol. It won't be for ages yet, and besides, Mum's really looking forward to organizing the wedding,' she fibbed. 'It's given her a whole new lease of life.'

'Well, that's fine, she can organize it. You know my parents won't be particularly interested, it's not as if they're going to be paying for mine. My mother probably won't even bother her ass to come. It might mean she'd have to stay sober,' Carol added with a hint of bitterness. 'Gary and I will be paying for our own, that's why it would be nice to split the costs.'

'Oh come on, Carol, it's not that bad. We're not *paupers*,' Gary interjected tersely.

'I'm not saying we *are*! I just said we'd be paying for the wedding ourselves,' Carol said huffily, her animated expression turning sulky.

'Look, let's sleep on it and not reject the idea out of hand. As I said before, it's an option. Nothing's set in stone,' Mike said easily, squeezing Jessica's hand. She didn't squeeze back. She was mad with him for even considering the idea in the first place.

'Oh well, if Jessica's not keen on the idea there's no point.' Carol sulked. 'Forget it.'

Jessica bit her lip. Now Carol was in a huff, which was a real bummer. She could keep up her huffs for ages. Jessica usually caved in after a day.

Gary glanced at Mike and threw his eyes up to heaven. 'Another pint, mate?'

'I don't think so, I really need to do some serious swotting this weekend. Exams are starting on Monday.'

'Poor bugger,' Gary sympathized. 'I'd hate to be you. You should have gone into IT like me.'

'Company car, great salary,' Carol interjected smugly, never able to resist a bit of one-upmanship.

'Well, Mike will have all that too *and* letters after his name. He'll probably have his own engineering company,' Jessica retorted childishly.

'Steady on.' Mike grimaced. 'I've to get my exams first.'

'You'll walk it, mate, walk it,' Gary said supportively.

'Well, I'd better go and get the head down anyway.' Mike stood up and held Jessica's jacket for her.

'I'm hungry. Can't we go to Temple Bar or Flanagan's for something to eat?' Carol grumbled.

Mike slanted a look at Jessica's grim expression.

'Not tonight. After next week, I'm all yours. See you, guys.' He moved out into the crowd milling around the upstairs bar of The Oval.

'Night, Gary, night, Carol.' Jessica edged her way around the table.

Carol kept her gaze averted and muttered a goodnight. Gary raised his almost empty beer glass in farewell. He didn't look very happy, Jessica noted. He probably knew he was in for a good whinge session. She sighed as she followed her beloved downstairs and out on to Abbey Street. It was a busy, buzzy Friday night. Dublin was alive and kicking.

It was balmy out. A warm breeze whispered on the air, refreshing after the stultifying heat of the bar. They turned left and walked towards O'Connell Street in silence.

'OK, get it over and done with. I know you're mad.' Mike dropped an arm around his girlfriend's shoulder.

'Oh Mike, I'd *hate* a double wedding. You know

I want it to be special for us. Why did you even say it was an option?' she burst out, stopping and looking up at him.

'Sorry, Jessie. I didn't know you felt so strongly about it. I wasn't thinking. It could be nice and a bit of fun.'

'*Fun!* With her weird family and all his brothers getting pissed! Are you mad, Mike? It would be a disaster. We wouldn't get a look in.'

'OK, OK.' He spread his hands placatingly.

'You'd like it. Wouldn't you?' she accused.

'Look, Jessie, it doesn't bother me one way or another. I just want what you want,' Mike growled, his patience beginning to wear thin.

'What do you mean, it doesn't matter to you one way or another? What kind of a thing is that to say? It's our wedding we're talking about. It's supposed to be the most important and special day of our lives. Doesn't it mean *anything* to you?'

'Would you calm down, Jessie. We're not getting married for ages. I've to get my exams first and get on with my new job. So stop making a mountain out of a molehill. You're like a briar. What's wrong with you?' He stood looking down at her, rubbing his hand wearily along his jaw, trying to suppress a yawn.

'It's Carol. She's driving me nuts. Muscling in

19

on everything we do.' Jessica exhaled a deep breath and snuggled in against Mike. 'I was really looking forward to going away for that weekend on our own and now they're coming and I won't have you to myself.' She and Mike had planned a weekend sailing on the Shannon to celebrate the end of his finals. As soon as Carol had heard their plans she'd immediately suggested a foursome, much to Jessica's dismay.

'And you know why she wants a double wedding?' She scowled as they resumed their walk towards the capital's main thoroughfare. 'She's afraid Gary's going to chicken out and not go through with it. And it would be much harder for him to do that if we were having a double wedding.'

'Ah, don't say that,' Mike chided.

'Why not, it's the truth,' Jessica said bluntly.

'You women! The ideas you get in your head. Come on, forget about them, let's go and have a bite to eat ourselves,' he suggested.

'Will we?' She brightened. 'But what about your swotting?'

'I'll get up early and go into the library to-morrow. Come on, it would be nice to have a meal on our own, wouldn't it?'

'Yeah.' She snuggled in close against him, her

bad humour evaporating. She loved being with Mike. He was so easy-going and good-humoured, and even her worst PMT moods didn't faze him and that was saying something. Come to think of it, PMT was why she'd been so ratty earlier, she really should take some V6 or evening primrose oil. She always meant to buy some when she was passing Nature's Way but somehow she never got round to it.

'Sorry about being so crotchety earlier.' She squeezed his hand. 'I think I've got PMT.'

'Aha, the old PMT. Just as well your hormones and I are old buddies at this stage.' Mike slanted an affectionate glance in her direction.

'Yeah, well, I'll make it up to you when you're going bald, and can't get it up and are having a midlife crisis,' she teased, loving the way he accepted her, PMT and all.

They held hands as they retraced their steps along Abbey Street and headed to Temple Bar. They were going to eat in Luigi Malones, one of their favourite haunts.

'I'm having the rack of baby ribs,' Jessica announced as they made themselves comfortable at their favourite table, at the window that looked out on to the bustling streets of the most trendy hot spot in the city.

'You have that every time we come here, you're such a creature of habit. Be adventurous. Try something different. The fajitas here are something else,' Mike urged.

'I know, but I love the sauce on the ribs and I can taste yours as well. Win win situation.' Jessica grinned at him, happy to have him all to herself. She leaned across the table and kissed him lightly on the mouth.

'I love you very much,' she said.

Mike's eyes crinkled in a smile as he took her hand in his. 'I love you too, my little tetchy crosspatch.'

Jessica giggled and felt immensely happy. She knew her wedding day, whenever it was, was going to be the happiest day of her life and, one thing was for sure, Carol could forget the idea of having a double wedding. When she walked up the aisle there'd be one man waiting at the altar. She and Mike were going to have a wedding they would never forget. Carol and Gary could do their own thing, and if Carol didn't like it, tough!

2

'Do you want another drink or do you want to go and have something to eat?' Gary drained his pint and looked questioningly at Carol.

'Suit yourself,' she muttered.

'Carol, don't take it out on me. It's not my fault Jessica's not on for a double wedding,' he retorted.

'She's so selfish sometimes,' Carol burst out indignantly. 'It's all right for her, she's got everything, lovely family, great flat, great job. Everything just falls into *her* lap. She should think about other people now and again.'

'Oh, come off it now, Carol!' Gary frowned. 'Jessie's a good friend to you.' He was starting to lose patience. Seeing his change of mood, Carol immediately became conciliatory.

'Don't mind me, I know she is. It's just it would have been nice to have a double wedding with them. You know what my family are like. A disaster. Who'd want to get married with a mother who'll probably go on the piss and a father who doesn't give a damn?'

She flashed a glimpse through her lashes at him and saw him frowning.

'You'll have a good wedding, Carol, don't worry,' he said flatly, and his tone caused a flicker of fear to race through her. She knew that tone of voice well. It was his Under-Pressure-And-Not-Wanting-To-Be-Bothered-With-This tone.

'Oh, let's forget the old wedding. What do you want to do?' she said gaily, rubbing her hand along his arm.

'Let's go back to my place,' he suggested.

'Only if you promise not to try and get me into bed,' she warned.

'Aw, come on, Carol. Mike and Jessica are at it like rabbits. Give me a break. We're engaged. I'll use condoms. Can't you go on the pill? Jessie's on the pill,' Gary urged.

'Well, go marry her, then,' she flared.

'For heaven's sake, Carol, if you go on the pill you won't get pregnant,' Gary said in exasperation.

'No way. I had a scare once, before I met you, and I'm not going through that again. And besides, I'm not going on the pill to get fat and have a stroke at forty.'

'Don't be ridiculous, you're only using that as an excuse.'

'Fine, if all you want is sex go get yourself a slapper. I'm off.' Carol grabbed her bag and stood up.

'Suit yourself.' Her boyfriend shrugged and she felt like thumping him. Furious, she made her way out of the crowded pub and trudged unhappily towards her bus stop. Gary wouldn't come after her, she knew that. He was too stubborn. She shouldn't have lost her cool. Now she'd have a fraught weekend waiting for him to ring her, worrying and fretting that he'd go off and meet someone else and that would be the end of them. The end of her dream of walking up the aisle.

It was all Jessica's fault, she thought irrationally, kicking a Coke can viciously and sending it skidding into the gutter. If Jessie hadn't turned up her nose at having a double wedding she wouldn't have been in a bad humour and she and Gary wouldn't have ended up having a row.

It was all right for Jessie; she was secure in Mike's love. They were an extremely united couple. They laughed a lot and were very relaxed in each other's company. She and Gary were a different kettle of fish. She wasn't at all sure of him. Her boyfriend had a roving eye that caused her sleepless nights. She'd see him looking at other women, flirting and winking at them. Why he even bothered with her she was never sure. She wasn't a looker like Jessie. She was tall and well built, unlike her curvy, sexy friend, her cropped, spiky black hair a million miles away from the other girl's silky, copper mane.

Sometimes, in her darkest moments, she wondered if Gary secretly fancied Jessie. A couple in front of her laughed, the man's chuckle deep and hearty, the girl's giggly and infectious. Carol glowered at them and quickened her pace to overtake them. A lovey-dovey couple was the last thing she needed right now. As she turned into O'Connell Street she saw an eleven bus in the distance. She'd make it if the traffic lights at the Henry Street junction turned red. She took a deep breath and began to run, weaving between the night-time revellers congregating outside Eason's and the GPO. She ran easily, her long legs loping along. She was fit and limber from hours of playing tennis, and as she glanced behind her and saw the bus gaining on her she put on an extra spurt and saw with satisfaction the traffic lights turn from green to amber and then red. She raced across Henry Street, swerving to avoid a drunken youth who was stumbling bleary-eyed into her path.

'Idiot!' she cursed as her bus stop came into sight and she slowed her pace. She didn't like the atmosphere on O'Connell Street, it could be quite menacing. It was amazing the difference a couple of minutes' walk could make.

It was only when she was sitting on the bus, gazing out at the queues for the late-night films at the Savoy, that she realized that she was hungry and in no hurry to go home to her shabby bedsit on the North Circular Road. The adrenaline rush from her sprint to catch the bus subsided, and she slumped dejectedly in her seat. The bus was almost empty – there was still an hour to go before last orders were called in the city pubs. An elderly man nodded off in a seat at the back of the bus and two young teenagers giggled at a shared joke, oblivious to her misery, their giddy exuberance in stark contrast to her woe. Her heart was in her boots. He didn't love her, if he did he would never have let her leave so easily. Gary had made no effort to come after her, the bastard. Right now she hated him.

Gary studied the pint of Guinness in front of him with pleasure: black velvet topped with a smooth, creamy head. He lifted the pint glass and drank slowly, savouring the taste. If Carol wanted to be childish he wasn't going to indulge her. He was heartily sick of her nonsense. She was starting to get on his nerves. Laying on the pressure with a trowel. Why couldn't she just calm down and get things in perspective? They were young, life was for living and having fun. There was plenty of time for weddings and mortgages and all that boring grown-up stuff that he just didn't want to be bothered with. It was bad enough being engaged, he thought grumpily. The minute Mike and Jessica had announced their engagement, he knew he was in for trouble. And boy, was he right. Gary gave a deep sigh that came from his toes. Carol had kept up the pressure until one night after a couple of pints too many and because he was feeling decidedly horny he'd asked her to marry him. They'd nearly gone the whole way but she'd chickened out at the last minute, and it was too late to back out of the engagement because she'd insisted on phoning Jessica and Mike practically the minute he'd proposed. He would have looked a right heel if he'd backed off.

Gary chewed his lip. Carol drove him mad sometimes but she intrigued him too. Sometimes she could be sweet and playful and she was a damn sexy woman. He'd first seen her playing mixed doubles with friends of his and watching her limber, long-legged stride across the court had been a stirring experience in more ways than one.

He took a long draught of his beer. He wasn't going to think about it now, it was too aggravating, and he was tired after a week's hard work fixing computers owned by idiots who didn't know how to use them. He stretched out his legs, took his paper out of his jacket pocket and turned to the sports pages. This was an unexpected treat; he should make the most of it. No wittering women giving out to him, no pressure about weddings and buying houses, just him, his pint and his paper. What more could a man want? Well, apart from a wild roll in the sack. And he certainly wasn't going to get that from Carol tonight. But she wasn't the only woman in the world, he reflected lazily, as he signalled the barman to pull another pint for him and began to read the sports results.

3

Jessica yawned as she let herself into the flat. She was tired, happy and longing for bed. 'Are you sure you won't stay the night? I'll get up and cook you a big fry-up in the morning. And I'll send you off with a smile on your face.' She wrapped her arms around Mike and kissed him soundly.

'Stop it, you shameless hussy.' He raised his head and drew breath, grinning down at her. 'I was supposed to be studying tonight, my finals are starting Monday, Jessie. I have to have my wits about me and I need to get some last-minute swotting done, please, Jessie, have mercy. You know I can't resist you.'

She burst out laughing. 'What a spoofer you are! All right then, swottie, go home to your precious books. I love you. 'Night.'

'I love you too, talk to you tomorrow. Sleep well.' He gave her a bear hug and she waved him off regretfully. She loved sleeping with Mike, loved waking up in his arms, and especially loved their drowsy, contented intimacy. She closed the door behind her and gave a start when Katie, her cousin, popped her head out of her bedroom and dramatically put her finger to her lips.

'Drama Queen is here!' she whispered dramatically, pointing to the sitting-room.

'*Carol!* What's she doing here?'

'The Usual! Row with Gary. Romance all off! Suicide imminent! Good luck.' Katie threw her eyes up to heaven.

'Oh no!' Jessica groaned. Not tonight. She wasn't in the humour for high drama. She was knackered. All she wanted to do was go to bed. Frustration welled up. Why couldn't Carol deal with her rows herself? It was always the same. Every time she had a row with Gary . . . and that was every bloody second day . . . Jessica had to bear the brunt of it and she was heartily sick of it. This was the last time, definitely! She was going to tell her friend once and for all that she'd had enough. Carol could cop on to herself and get real. Jessica took a deep breath and marched into the sitting-room, determination written all over her face.

Carol was curled up on the sofa fast asleep, the

31

magazine she'd been reading slipping through her fingers. Jessica came to a full stop. 'Drat,' she muttered crossly, switching off the TV and putting the magazine on to the table. She stood staring down at the other girl and her heart softened in spite of herself. Poor old Carol, she looked so miserable even in sleep, a frown creasing her brow, her fingers curled tense and tight across her chest.

Jessica sighed as she went off in search of a quilt. Carol and Gary had such a tempestuous relationship. There was no peace for them, no harmony. They lurched along from drama to drama, she being needy, Gary withholding. How could it be worth it? It would drive her berserk, Jessica reflected as she removed the spare quilt from the bottom of the wardrobe. When she'd heard of their engagement she'd been more than a little shocked. She knew that Carol felt much more strongly about Gary than he did about her. She knew how much it bothered her friend and often wondered how she could endure a relationship that seemed so unequal.

'Let them at it and don't interfere,' Mike cautioned when she'd bring up the subject. But it was difficult to restrain herself sometimes, especially when Carol would pour out her fears and uncertainties about her relationship.

'Do you think he loves me?' she'd ask. 'What do you think he sees in me? I love him, I really, really love him. I wish he loved me as much as I love him. Do you think he loves me but just can't say it?'

If Jessica had got a euro for every time she was asked those questions she would have been a millionairess. It got extremely wearing after a while, but worst of all was when Carol would say accusingly, 'You're so lucky, Jessica, Mike is crazy about you,' almost as though she begrudged Jessica her happiness and wanted her to feel guilty about being loved and happy.

Sometimes she felt like telling Carol to stop annoying her and stop trying to spoil things, but the other girl had a way of making her feel sorry for her and she'd back off and keep her irritation bottled up. Now, when she'd finally decided to have it out with her friend, Carol was flakers on the sofa, denying Jessica her chance. She yawned. Perhaps it was just as well; she was too tired for friction and besides, in her heart of hearts she had to admit that she wasn't the best at confrontation, her tendency being to pacify and smooth over troubled waters. She wished she could be more like Katie, who had no trouble at all saying what she felt, and tough if anybody's sensitivities were hurt.

Gently, as quietly as she could, for now she truly did not want to endure one of Carol's marathon ear-bashing sessions, she laid the soft quilt over her friend, switched off the lamp and slipped out of the sitting-room to the haven of her own bedroom. All she wanted to do was fall into bed and sleep her brains out. It was a stroke of luck that Carol had fallen asleep on the sofa. She might have calmed down after a night's sleep and Jessica wouldn't have to share her bedroom. Tomorrow could take care of itself, she thought tiredly as she gave her face a perfunctory cleanse, tone and moisturize.

'What's happening?' Katie knocked on her door and slipped into the bedroom. She perched on the side of the bed and nibbled on a bowl of hot, buttery popcorn.

'Want some?' she offered, holding out the dish.

'No, thanks, I'm stuffed. Mike and I went to Luigi Malones.'

'Ha ha! Mystery solved. Her Highness was extremely miffed that you weren't here and wanted to know where you'd got to because you'd refused to go for a meal with herself and Gary. I told her that you were probably riding each other ragged but that didn't go down too well either,' Katie said airily, licking her fingers.

'You're awful.' Jessica giggled.

'Yeah well, there I was having a perfectly lovely, slobby Friday night in, watching Graham Norton, when Miss Havisham arrives weeping and wailing and turning up her nose at my little pig-out. Honestly, I was raging. I hadn't had one for yonks, trust her to arrive when I was right in the middle of it. It really spoilt my pizza. Do you think we could make it a condition of tenancy that she's barred?' Katie suggested sourly as she wriggled her tongue between her teeth, trying to eject a particularly stubborn particle of popcorn.

'Ah, don't be like that, Katie. She doesn't have many friends.'

'I'm not surprised,' interjected her cousin tartly. 'Honestly, just because she plays tennis and is fanatical about keeping fit is no reason to look down her pointy little nose at me. At least I've curves, not angles,' Katie snorted indignantly.

'Of course you have,' Jessica soothed. Katie was a curvy, statuesque brunette who struggled with a fluctuating half-stone which was the bane of her life. It didn't help that Carol offered 'helpful' tips on keeping fit and dieting when she was being particularly bitchy.

'Why doesn't she just break it off once and for all if she's so unhappy? I bet Gary would be out of it so quick you wouldn't see him for dust if he got the chance. Honestly, thank God I'm not that desperate for a man.' Katie sniffed.

'Stop it, Katie, don't be such a wagon,' Jessica chided. 'Gary's no pushover. If he wanted out, I think he'd get out. Sometimes they get on very well and we all have great fun.'

'In the words of my dear old granny, it will all end in tears, mark my words,' Katie predicted, wagging a finger at Jessica.

'Yeah, well, do you want to know the best of it, little Miss Know All?' Jessica grimaced. 'Carol wants us to have a double wedding . . . so there!'

'What!' shrieked her cousin. 'You're joking!'

'Would I joke about that?' Jessica arched an eyebrow.

'Cripes. What did you say?'

'I sort of said I'd think about it. Mike, the idiot, was no help and Gary thought it was a good idea.'

'You know why she wants a double wedding? It's because if you agree it'll make it all the more difficult for Gary to back out . . . Lordy Moses, that Carol is one cute little hoor.'

'I know, I know,' Jessica said wearily. 'I don't care, I'll worry about it tomorrow. I'm whacked.'

'There, there, petal, you have a good night's sleep. You'll need it for the morrow when yon wench will no doubt twist your ear,' Katie teased.

'Goodnight, Shakespeare,' Jessica said drily, as she kicked off her sandals and slipped out of her white jeans. Ten minutes later she was curled up in bed, her eyes drooping tiredly as she tried to forget about her problems with Carol and endeavoured to dwell instead on Mike and how much she loved him. It worked, and she fell asleep having decided to surprise him the next day at lunchtime and whisk him off for a pint and a sandwich in Conway's, or, if he preferred, a fry-up in the Kingfisher.

Carol stretched and licked her dry lips. She felt hot, sticky and uncomfortable. Her shirt was all twisted up around her and her shoes felt too tight for her feet. She didn't know where she was. She sat up, bleary-eyed, peering into the dark. Moonlight spilled through a split in the curtains and she remembered that she was at Jessica's.

Memories came trickling back. The row with Gary. Being too disheartened to go home to her bedsit and walking past her front door to go to Phibsboro to get a nineteen bus to Jessica's place. It had been so annoying when she got there to find that her friend wasn't home. She'd decided to wait for half an hour even though it meant watching

Katie stuffing her face with popcorn and pizza, which she'd disdainfully refused a portion of, even though she was starving. She wouldn't give Katie Johnson the satisfaction of eating her pizza. Carol prided herself on eating properly and keeping fit. She must have fallen asleep and either Katie or Jessica had covered her with a quilt.

This night had been a complete disaster from start to finish. She hated sleeping on sofas. Usually when she stayed over with Jessica she slept on a fold-up bed kept in her friend's bedroom. It was probably a bit late to go rooting and rummaging and making up a bed. She hauled herself off the sofa, switched on the lamp and checked her watch. Two fifteen, definitely too late. Jessica wouldn't be impressed, she was always grouchy if her sleep was disturbed.

Carol sighed deeply, feeling very sorry for herself. Her stomach rumbled and she headed for the kitchen and opened the fridge door. There were three slices of cold pizza, some cottage cheese, a few withered tomatoes and a couple of slices of cooked ham curling up at the edges. She found a heel of a brown loaf in the bread bin, buttered it and spooned on some cottage cheese, and put a slice of pizza on a plate. She poured herself a glass of milk and took the unappetizing repast back to the sitting-room, where she ate it un-enthusiastically and was rewarded with galloping heartburn for her efforts. In a foul humour, she undressed to her underwear and covered herself up with the quilt, expecting not to sleep a wink. Her last conscious thought was to wonder had Gary gone home alone or was he with another woman, one who'd give him what she wouldn't. Gary with his dark good looks and inviting brown eyes would have no trouble getting off with any woman. That was his problem. Women were too easy for him. She knew one of the reasons he was drawn to her was because she hadn't succumbed to his lover-boy charms.

Neither would she, she vowed, because her resistance was her trump card and if that was played, she wasn't at all sure that he wouldn't move on to someone else. That was the crux of their relation-ship. She just wasn't one bit sure of him.

Gary stretched lazily and smiled down at the woman in his arms.

'That was good,' he said, caressing her cheek.

'Mmm,' she murmured drowsily. 'You always were good in bed.'

'What do you mean "were"?' he demanded indignantly. '*Are* good in bed, Jen. *Are!*'

'Well, you're getting on, you're heading for thirty.' She yawned.

'Twenty-six, I'm a baby,' he retorted.

'So what's brought you back to my door?' She leaned on her elbow and looked down at him, her long black hair tumbling over her shoulders.

'Missed you,' he said succinctly.

'Or missed riding me?' Jen said drily. 'What's wrong, won't your *fiancée* do the business?'

'Don't be like that,' he said uncomfortably.

'I'm right, aren't I?'

'Shhh, don't spoil the evening.'

'You're a shit, you know that, don't you?'

'But you still like me.' Gary flashed a sexy, confident smile.

'You're so arrogant, Gary, I wish I didn't.' Jen frowned. 'This is the last time. You ended it, don't forget, not me.'

'Big mistake,' he said smoothly and silenced her with a kiss.

4

Jessica stretched luxuriously and turned her head to glance at her alarm clock. Seven thirty a.m., she'd need to be getting a move on if she wanted to get to work in time. She was a broadcasting assistant in the Radio Centre in RTE and it was all go, go, go. She hoped the traffic wouldn't be heavy. She'd been late twice in the last month and her boss hadn't been too impressed. Then she remembered it was Saturday morning. Oh bliss, she thought happily. Lie-in day. What a treat.

She snuggled back under the duvet and lay contentedly watching the sun slant its early morning rays on to the end of the bed. She liked this cosy little room in the two-up two-down, small, redbrick house she shared with Katie – it reminded her of home and the small cottage she lived in with her mother in Arklow. The cosiness of the house had drawn her to it, a little jewel after some of the cramped, boxy, ugly flats she and Katie had viewed.

In a small side street off Prospect Avenue, it was a quiet little enclave at Hart's Corner, a stone's throw from the Botanic Gardens and the darkly gloomy Glasnevin Cemetery that somehow lent a gothic air to the surrounding streets.

She and Katie had been living in their little house for almost six months now and they loved it. The pretty mint-green floral curtains fluttered in the breeze and the sun beamed its dappled rays on to the buttery cream walls of the bedroom. She could do with dusting, she noted lazily as the sunbeams reflected on to the dust particles that covered the chest of drawers. The mirror on the front of the wardrobe badly needed a polishing; she'd do that later, she decided, as well as washing the contents of her bulging laundry basket. Her eyes drooped and she dozed off again. The next she knew, Carol was standing at the foot of the bed demanding to know if she was ever going to wake up.

'What time is it?' She sat up groggily, her heart sinking. She'd forgotten all about Carol.

'It's quarter to ten. Katie said to tell you she's decided to go home and she'll see you tomorrow night,' Carol informed her irritably. 'I'm going to the shop to get some fresh brown bread, have the kettle on when I get back.' She didn't even wait for Jessica to respond, but marched out of the bedroom and down the stairs. Jessica lay back against her pillows, fuming. This was her house, her Saturday morning lie-in, and Carol as usual had just taken over and done what she wanted. She was the queen of the *Me, Me, Me* planet. Jessica scowled. She yawned and rubbed her eyes. It looked like a peachy day outside. One of those unexpectedly warm, blue-skied days in early summer. No wonder Katie had gone home, she'd be on the beach for the day, knowing her. It was a pity Mike was studying, they could have had a nice day for themselves, up the mountains or at the beach.

She got out of bed and headed for the shower. Carol could stick on the kettle herself when she got in. She stood under the lukewarm spray, realizing that her uninvited guest had used all the hot water. She could see Carol's black hair clogging up the plughole and that infuriated her even more. Carol never cleaned up the bathroom after herself. The water got progressively colder and she washed quickly and towelled herself dry.

The doorbell shrilled and she wrapped the bathtowel around her and went to open the door.

'You used all the hot water and you didn't clean the shower out after you,' Jessica snapped as she stood back to let the other girl in.

'Don't blame me, Katie had a shower too,' Carol retorted. 'And it's not very nice to give out to me when I've gone to the trouble of getting a nice breakfast for us.'

'Yeah, well, I won't be eating too much, I'm going to surprise Mike in the library and take him to lunch,' Jessica said ungraciously and then felt a heel when she saw the flicker of hurt in her friend's eyes.

'Sorry,' she backtracked. 'That was rude.'

'I'm used to people being rude to me,' Carol said in a sulky tone as she headed towards the kitchen with her groceries.

Fraught, Jessica went back up the stairs to her bedroom and towelled her hair dry before styling it with the hairdrier.

Carol had the table laid and a bowl of fresh fruit and yoghurt set out for Jessica.

'There's muesli and brown bread as well. I know you like a fry-up on Saturday but this is much healthier for you,' she said in a subdued sort of voice.

'Thanks for going to all the trouble,' Jessica said brightly. 'Sorry I wasn't here when you arrived last night. I didn't know you were coming.' She didn't mention going for a meal with Mike; Carol was in enough of a martyr mode without getting into the huffs about imaginary slights.

'Well, I thought you were going straight home.'

'Ah, you know yourself,' Jessica bent her head over her fruit and took a mouthful. 'What's on your agenda today?' She changed the subject.

'Don't know,' Carol said mournfully. 'Do you know what that bastard said to me last night?'

Here it comes, thought Jessica stoically. 'Who?' She feigned surprise.

'Gary of course,' Carol snapped.

'What did he say?' She bit into a luscious strawberry, her thoughts drifting to Mike and the surprise he'd get when she arrived to take him to lunch.

Carol took a gulp of her milk. 'Well, he wanted me to go back to his flat, he wants to sleep with me, but you know I won't. He said you were on the pill and that you and Mike were at it like rabbits and he wanted me to go on the pill too, and I just told him I wasn't going to go on it because I didn't want to put on weight and have a stroke, and he said that was just an excuse and I said if he wanted sex go and get himself a slapper. It's so *insulting*, Jessica!' It all came out in a torrent of frustration and resentment.

'I just don't understand you, Carol. It's not as if you're a virgin. Why won't you sleep with Gary? How can you not? You're engaged after all, and I know it's nothing to do with your religious beliefs, 'cos you don't have any.' She grinned. 'I can't keep my hands off Mike. I love sleeping with him.'

'It's not that I don't want to, I do,' Carol snorted. 'It's just, Gary's such a ladies' man, he gets it all too easy. I know him. I know the way he thinks, Jessie. If he thinks that I'm a pushover he'll be off to pastures new.'

'You don't know that,' Jessica said gently. 'Why would he ask you to marry him if he didn't love you?'

'Because he thought he'd get me into bed,' Carol said despondently. 'Do you really think he loves me, Jessie? If I was sure of him I'd sleep with him in a flash, I really would.'

'Well, if you're not sure of him, do you honestly think you should be marrying him?' There, she'd finally asked the question she'd been biting back for so long.

'But Jessie, I *love* him. I *want* to marry him. Once we're married I'll be as happy as Larry, I just know I will. Won't you please consider a double wedding? It would be such a great day. You know I've a crap family – I don't even care if any of them are at it. But it would mean so much to be with you and Mike. It would give us an extra bond,' she pleaded.

'Aw, Carol, can't I be your bridesmaid?' Jessica suggested desperately. 'A double wedding could be an awful lot of trouble.'

'You can have your own way in everything, honestly,' Carol said earnestly, sensing weakness. 'Please. Please. Please. It would be the nicest thing that's ever happened to me in my whole life. Mike said he wouldn't mind and Gary would love it. I know that. We'd have such fun,' she wheedled.

'I'm not sure, I'd need to talk to Mam,' Jessica said weakly, hating herself for not having the guts to say an outright 'no'.

'I'm sure she won't mind. I'd say she'd be quite happy for the two of us to organize it.'

'Well, she was looking forward to getting involved. It's the first time since Dad died that she's got a bit of her old spark back.' This wasn't exactly true, but Carol wasn't to know that.

'Oh!' Carol bit her lip. 'Well, she can do as much as she wants to.'

'I'll talk to her. So what are your plans for the rest of the day?' Jessica changed the subject.

Carol bit into a slice of brown bread and shrugged. 'Go back to the kip, do a bit of washing and go and hit a few balls around the courts in the afternoon. I'm not going to sit by the phone waiting for Gary to ring me. You're so lucky, Jessie, you know exactly where you stand with Mike.'

There it was again, the faintly accusatory tone that drove Jessica nuts. She took a drink of tea and said nothing, but Carol didn't notice, she was getting into her stride. 'Why can't Gary make more of an effort? I mean, I had to remind him it was my birthday and he never does anything romantic, he'd never think of buying me flowers unless I suggest it. It takes all the good out of it when you have to suggest it yourself.'

'Some men don't think like that,' Jessica said wearily. 'He's good to you in other ways. He painted your bedsit for you and got draught-excluders for your door.'

'Yeah well, if he was really that concerned about where I live, why doesn't he suggest getting a flat together? Whenever I suggest looking at houses he switches off. We're getting married, for God's sake, we need to be making plans.' The other girl was not to be pacified.

Doesn't the fact that he doesn't want to know and isn't interested in making plans suggest something to you? Jessica wanted to say, but she refrained. There was no point. Carol only wanted to hear what she wanted to hear; she'd only resent Jessica even more for stating the obvious.

She tried to put herself in her friend's shoes. If it were she and Mike, would she be able to cope with his apparent disinterest? Would she hang on so desperately to a relationship that seemed so unfulfilling? Jessica shivered. If Mike ever broke it off with her, she'd want to lie down and die. She was crackers about him, but at least she had the comfort of knowing that he was crackers about her too and that meant an awful lot. A wave of pity for Carol swept over her. It was a horrible way to be. Unsure. Uncherished. Not knowing whether she was truly loved or not. Carol was right, she was very, very lucky.

'Let's have the double wedding if that's what you want,' she blurted, and then almost couldn't believe she'd said it.

Carol's stern unhappy features lightened as a melon-slice grin creased her face. She jumped up off the chair. 'Do you mean it? Do you really mean it? Oh Jessie, thanks so much,' she said fervently, hugging the daylights out of her. 'Oh Jessie, you're the best friend in the whole world. Thanks a million. It will be the best day of our lives. You'll see.'

'I'm sure it will,' Jessica murmured, trying hard

to believe it. She'd issued the invitation. There was no going back, she'd just have to get on with it.

'I think it's going to be really nice and special. We've been friends since we were little, living across the road from each other, going to school together, coming to Dublin to work. And now getting married together. Isn't it lovely, Jessie?' Carol was bubbling with excitement. Her eyes were alight with happiness. Jessica couldn't help but smile at her. She had to believe that Carol was right, that it was going to be a special day for them. She just wished she could ignore the niggle of unease that wouldn't go away.

5

'You're just an old softie.' Mike grinned at her as he forked some sausage and mushrooms into his mouth.

'Oh God, what have I done? I ended up feeling so sorry for her. I just heard myself saying it. She does that to me all the time. Makes me feel sorry for her. What is it about her that does that to me?' Jessica groaned.

'Look, don't lose any sleep over it. It doesn't matter who's there and who isn't. At the end of the day when you and I make our vows, it will just be the two of us looking into each other's eyes and that's all that's important. And at least Carol's going to have happy memories of her wedding day and all because the most beautiful, kindest-hearted girl in the world was generous enough to share her special day.' He leaned across the wooden table and kissed her on the cheek. 'Did I tell you how much

I love you today?' He smiled, his blue eyes warm and tender.

'I love you too.' Jessica felt heartened by his words. Mike might call her an old softie, but he had a very soft heart himself and would do anyone a good turn. She was so glad she had called into the library to bring him to lunch. Carol had been on a high as she'd done the washing-up, tutting about the state of the sink as she sprayed Flash around vigorously. Jessica had left her to it, relieved to be on her own as she drove towards the college in Bolton Street.

She'd parked in the staff car park, it being fairly empty as it was Saturday, and hurried past the porter's desk at the side entrance and up two flights of stairs. She smiled in anticipation as she clipped along the polished wooden parquet floors that led to the library, the noise of her footsteps echoing in the morgue-like stillness that permeated the college. The girl at the desk hadn't even lifted her head as she slipped through the turnstile that led into the library. It was penny-dropping silent, the only sound the rustling of a newspaper read by one of the students in the reading room opposite the librarian's desk. Jessica walked into the big mahogany-shelved library and turned right to the study area. Students sat in rows of desks; some engrossed in their studies, others daydreaming out through the large plate-glass windows as the sun streamed in, lending a somnolent, lethargic air to the room.

Mike was deep in his *Rogers & Mayhew's Thermodynamics*, a textbook Jessica had come to loathe almost as much as did her fiancé. She walked quietly to where he sat, surrounded by books and the clutter of study.

'Hi, sexy,' she whispered huskily into his ear. He gave a start and looked up, surprised. His face creased into a smile.

'What are you doing here?' he whispered.

'Taking you to lunch,' she whispered back.

'Shhh.' A crabby bespectacled girl with a pale face and lank, greasy hair, seated at the next desk, glared at them.

'Shhh yourself,' Jessica hissed back crossly.

Mike laughed and closed his books. 'Come on, I'm starving.'

They walked out into the corridor and once the heavy doors of the library creaked closed behind them, Mike took her in his arms and kissed her soundly. 'I missed you last night,' he murmured against her hair.

'I missed you too,' she said breathlessly, eyes shining with pleasure. 'Just think, this is the second last Saturday you'll have to study, and then I'll have you all to myself.'

'For a little while,' he said gently. 'I'll be starting work soon, don't forget.'

'Don't remind me,' she groaned as they emerged into the bright sunshine.

'The Kingfisher or Conway's?' She squinted up at him.

'Hmmm, soup and a sandwich versus a fry-up? Let's hit the Kingfisher,' he said, taking her hand and heading down the side street that led towards Parnell Street.

It was while they were eating that she told him about Carol's overnight stay and the blurting out of the offer to agree to the double wedding. When he called her an old softie and told her she had the kindest heart, Jessica wished she could marry him there and then.

They were having coffee and idly chatting about Mike's forthcoming job with Wicklow County Council when Jessica said out of the blue, 'Mike, why wait? I know we planned to save for a house before we married instead of renting a place together. Let's go to the Credit Union and get a loan and get married sooner rather than later. What's the point in hanging on? I don't want a big palaver. Do you?'

He looked at her, surprised. 'No, just the family will suit me, Jessie. It would be good being married, wouldn't it?' he said, smiling his wide, sexy smile at her. 'I wasn't really looking forward to being in digs in Wicklow during the week and coming up to see you at the weekends.'

'You know Mam said you could live with her,' Jessica reminded him.

'I know, but until I get a car it wouldn't be practical to live in Arklow if I was working in Wicklow. It would be a ten-mile journey on the bike at least,' Mike pointed out.

'The only problem is, you were going to get a loan from the Credit Union for your car. We can hardly get one for a car and a wedding.' Jessica chewed her lip.

'One of the lads over in mechanical engineering does car repairs in his spare time, he's looking out for a car for me. I can get an old banger for the first year until we're on our feet a bit. We can use yours to swan around in and impress the neighbours with.'

Jessica giggled. Her little Renault was not at the cutting edge of motoring, but it got her where she wanted to go and she was extremely proud of it. It was her first car and she lavished care and attention on it, even going so far as to attend a car maintenance course after Mike had slagged her about not knowing her spark plugs from her sink plugs.

'So will we go for it?' he asked with a glint in his blue eyes.

'Will we?' Her eyes reflected her excitement, dancing with expectation. She certainly hadn't expected when she got up this morning that she'd be making wedding plans. When she and Mike had got engaged on Valentine's Day earlier in the year, they'd anticipated it would be at least two years before they'd tie the knot, now here they were talking about getting married some time this very year.

'Right then. I'm going back to do a bit more swotting, we won't be doing anything if I don't get my exams. You go and phone priests, and hotels and whoever else you have to phone and sort things,' he said cheerfully.

Jessica's jaw dropped. 'We have to talk about it, Mike, and decide where we're getting married. And can we afford a hotel and stuff like that! And besides, everywhere would be booked up. You'd never get a venue at this short notice,' she protested, common sense beginning to kick in.

'I thought you wanted to get married in Kilbride church. And isn't The Four Winds Hotel right beside your mother's?'

'Yes, but—'

'Ring the priest. Get a date, then ring the hotel and see what their prices are. I bet you'll get a date no problem mid-week. The Four Winds is such a small hotel I wouldn't say they do a lot of weddings.' He shrugged and smiled at her as if to say, *What's the fuss?* 'Easy peasy! Honestly, you women make such mountains out of molehills. You're gas. See you later.' He planted a smacker on her lips, raised his hand in farewell and left her sitting staring after him half amused, half frustrated.

He made it all seem so easy. Typical man. She ordered fresh coffee; she needed another shot of caffeine. If the priest in the beautiful little church nestled in the Wicklow countryside that she loved agreed that she could be married there, and if they could afford a small reception in The Four Winds Hotel, everything else would fall into place. Mike was right to a degree. Two phone calls would sort out the most central things.

And then she thought of Carol. Would the other girl want to get married in a small country church? Would she want a more sophisticated, showy sort of wedding? Jessica frowned. It wasn't up to her to make the compromises. If Carol didn't want the small, simple wedding that she and Mike were proposing, that was tough, she thought with uncharacteristic firmness.

She finished her coffee, picked her bag off the floor and headed for the door. She'd told Mike that she was going to stroll around the shops in Henry Street and the ILAC Centre, but when she emerged on to the street the noise and fumes of the traffic oppressed her and impulsively she hurried back to where she'd parked the car. She needed fresh air. It would have been glorious to go home to her mother's and spend the rest of the afternoon on the beach, but she was working tomorrow and besides she wanted to have a meal cooked for Mike later. The great thing about living in Glasnevin was that she could be at the sea in twenty minutes.

The warm weather was so welcome after a long, wet winter and a mediocre spring. People everywhere were dressed in shorts and T-shirts and summery dresses. Moods were light-hearted; people smiled at each other and commented on the good weather and Jessica, a country girl at heart, wanted to be out enjoying it.

She drove north on to Dorset Street, on through Drumcondra until she came to the Griffith Avenue junction, where she turned right, heading for Clontarf and the sea. The sun was sparkling on Dublin Bay, glittering and glinting, silver on sapphire blue. The palm trees that fringed the parkland along the coastline swayed gently in the breeze. The car parks were full, and it seemed as though the world and his mother had come out to enjoy the sun. She edged into a tight space between a Volvo and a Peugeot, congratulating herself on her manoeuvring skills until she hit the kerb a whack and had to perform the whole manoeuvre again.

It was good to feel the salty, tangy air. People were lying on the grass, chatting, reading or simply enjoying the warm rays of the sun on their bodies. Children cycled on their bikes or skated between the pedestrians, who strolled along or marched briskly depending on their fitness levels. Gulls wheeled and circled, their raucous cries evoking memories of childhood and long days spent at the seaside. The rich smell of seaweed wafted on the breeze. Bees hummed indolently, a sure sign of summer. A sense of well-being enveloped her. This was a perfect day. Jessica inhaled deeply and set out at a smart lick. If she was going to be a sooner rather than later bride she'd want to get into shape. She didn't want to look like a tubby little dwarf alongside Carol.

She sighed, thinking of Carol. It was such a pity

she and Mike couldn't get married on their own. Perhaps when the other girl heard their plans she'd pull out and there'd be no hard feelings.

'God,' she prayed silently as she strode along enjoying the bracing fresh air, 'please don't let Carol and Gary want a quiet country wedding, please let it be just me and Mike.'

6

Carol let herself out of Jessica's house and strode briskly down Prospect Avenue. She was exhilarated. Her friend had agreed to a double wedding. Now Gary wouldn't be able to tell her to stop fussing when she suggested dates and mortgages. Hopefully he would enjoy the wedding much more than if they were getting married on their own. Jessica wouldn't regret her decision. It was definitely going to be the best day of their lives.

It was a pity she was having a row with Gary. He could be such a stinker sometimes. Just this once, she'd let bygones be bygones and forget their tiff, she decided magnanimously. She was dying to tell him the news. She'd tried phoning him from Jessica's but there was no answer. It wasn't totally unexpected. He could be playing squash or doing a workout at the gym. She wasn't going to get into a tizzy about it.

She wondered had he phoned her. She hoped he had. It was good for him to know that she wasn't sitting in moping and hanging on to the phone waiting for him to call. The best way to deal with Gary, she had learnt over the past two years, was to play it cool.

That was how she had enticed him in the first place. It seemed like an eternity, she thought ruefully, but she could still remember every second of those heady days when she'd fallen head over heels in love with him.

She'd been playing a doubles match in a tennis tournament and her regular partner and friend, Amanda, was not playing because of a hamstring injury. Lily, the girl she was partnered with, wasn't the best player in the world and had consistently double-faulted. She wasn't too fast on the court either and had lost them the first set. Carol was raging. She hated being beaten, and the pair on the other side of the net were targeting Lily's weak spots with gusto. As they changed sides after a disaster of a game she noticed one of her opponents blowing a kiss to a man on the sidelines. He too was in tennis whites and he was a hunk and a half, she thought enviously.

She had seen the girl, a tall, willowy blonde

called Jen, on the circuit. She drove a big Honda, and often arrived to matches in smart tailored business suits, carrying a briefcase. She was like someone out of *Vanity Fair* or *Hello!*, Carol's favourite magazines. Carol would love to swan into work in a sharp business suit carrying a briefcase. She worked as a senior staff officer in the City Council offices and had no need of a briefcase or even sharp suits, as she as often as not wore her uniform. Although she didn't like admitting it, Carol was jealous of her and her seemingly affluent lifestyle, and it was galling in their first match together that Jen and her partner were winning. She was a good tennis player, but Carol knew she was a better one and there and then she decided, Lily or no Lily, she was going to win. Jaunty Jen was not going to throw her tennis racket triumphantly in the air after this match.

Carol played like a demon and rang rings around poor Lily, who became even more nervous and intimidated as Carol whizzed around her. As they approached match point Carol had never felt so focused in her life. She sliced an ace down the line and felt a surge of triumph as, moments later, Jen mentally crumpled and played a return shot into the net. Another powerful ace and it was all over.

'Jeepers, Carol, that was some match. Well done, I know I didn't do much to help,' Lily apologized as they walked to the net to shake hands with their opponents. *You can say that again*, Carol thought irritably, but she merely shrugged and said nothing, her silence making poor Lily feel even more inadequate as a player.

'Good match,' Jen said tightly, proffering a limp hand.

'Any time,' Carol said airily. She hated limp handshakes. As she came off the court she saw the hunk studying her admiringly.

'Well played,' he said.

'Thank you,' she replied coolly, and continued in to the clubhouse, dying to have a shower, her legs aching from all the running.

The relief of standing under the reviving hot jets was indescribable, and Carol relaxed and lathered soap all over. There was nothing like winning at tennis. It gave her such a buzz, but today for some reason it felt a thousand times better. Jen had not liked being beaten. Carol knew *exactly* how she felt. There were players you could cope with losing against and there were ones that really got to you. Losing to Jen would have got to her. And for some perverse reason she was glad the other girl had lost in front of the hunk. As far as she knew they were an item. The circuit's golden couple.

Later, as she sipped a Club Orange at the bar, a voice behind her said, 'Let me buy you a drink, you deserve one after that marathon.' She turned to find the hunk smiling sexily and holding out his hand. 'Gary Davis.'

'Carol Logan,' she reciprocated, noting approvingly that his handshake was firm, unlike that of his girlfriend.

'Well, Carol Logan, you certainly played like a pro today.'

'No point in playing otherwise.' She withdrew her hand from his lingering handclasp.

'So what can I get you?'

'I'm fine, thanks,' she said casually.

'Aw, come on, how about champagne to celebrate?'

Carol laughed. *What an over-the-top show-off.* Did he think that she was easily impressed?

'Some other time, perhaps, but thanks for the offer. I think your girlfriend is looking for you.' She glanced over to the door to where Jen was staring over at them.

'She knows where I am,' he drawled.

'So she does. Excuse me.' She slid off her stool. 'I'm just going to join my friends.' She left him standing, staring after her as she crossed the bar to join Jessica and Mike.

Over the next couple of months she encountered Gary and Jen on the circuit. She kept him at arm's length, refusing his offer to buy her a drink, instinctively knowing that the way to hook Gary was to play hard to get. And hook him she wanted to, badly. He was a challenge, no doubt about it. Women flocked to him. He had an easy, sexy charm, and he knew it. His girlfriend had an ever watchful, possessive air about her, understandably. Being Gary Davis's girlfriend was not for the faint-hearted.

Things came to a head when she played opposite him in a game of mixed doubles. It was a hard-fought match and she didn't give an inch; as they squared up against each other, the glint in his eye was matched by the determination in hers and they battled over every point. His serve was powerful but she held her own against him, and even though they lost by a game, she was at least comforted by the fact that she had certainly been no pushover.

'You have to let me buy you a drink after this,' he informed her when they met later on at the bar.

'I don't have to let you do anything,' she said tartly.

'Are you afraid of me?' he demanded.

Carol chuckled, highly amused at his attitude and secretly delighted that she was getting to him.

'Don't be ridiculous, Gary.' She arched an eyebrow at him. 'Why on earth would you think that?'

'Well, I've being trying to buy you a drink for ages and you keep saying no and running off on me as if I had the plague,' he said plaintively.

'Gary, I'm just not pushed about drinking, but if it's such a big deal I'll have a Club Orange.' She was extremely pleased with her strategy; she'd certainly reinforced the impression that he was chasing her and that she wasn't the slightest bit interested.

'Oh, come on, have something stronger!' he urged.

'Nope! I'm playing matches all over the weekend. I don't need to be slowed down by alcohol,' she explained calmly.

'God, you're very dedicated. You don't give an inch on court.'

'Neither do you,' she pointed out. Their eyes met and held and some intangible bond ignited between them. Gary smiled at her.

'A kindred spirit,' he said softly and she knew there and then that he was the one she wanted.

'Do you think so?' she challenged.

'I know so,' he said huskily, turning on the charm. 'Have dinner with me and let's find out.'

'I don't two-time. You're Jen's boyfriend.' Her blunt response took him by surprise.

'Oh! How high-minded of you.' His tone was faintly jeering.

She shrugged. 'Say what you like, but that's my policy. It saves me a lot of trouble.'

'I suppose you have a point,' he allowed, as he ordered the orange drink for her and a beer for himself. 'So what drives you then?' He sat back on his stool and turned to look at her, his brown eyes staring unwaveringly into her own. His stare was disconcerting but she made a conscious effort to ignore it.

'I play to win,' she said simply.

'In everything?' His eyes never left her face.

'Why not?' she said lightly, breaking his stare to take a welcome drink of the ice-cold orange.

'And if you lose?'

'Tomorrow is another day.' She grinned, enjoying the banter and the sexual frisson that sparked between them.

'Are you seeing anyone yourself?' he queried offhandedly.

'Not any more.' Carol took another sip of her drink. 'He said I preferred tennis to him.'

'And did you?'

'Tennis is a very *satisfying* game.' She eyeballed him as she finished her drink and stood up. 'Thanks for the drink, I'll see you around.' Head up, back straight, she walked out of the bar without looking back. Two weeks later, she heard on the grapevine that it was all off with Jen.

The next time she saw him he said briskly, 'I'm footloose and fancy-free. It wasn't working with Jen and me. Care to have dinner with me?'

'Sure,' she said easily, and saw his mouth open in surprise. He'd been expecting a battle of wills. She laughed, delighted to have wrong-footed him.

'I'm going to have my hands full with you,' he murmured, his eyes warm as they surveyed her from head to toe.

'Me? I'm a pussy cat,' she teased, writing down her telephone number and passing it to him. 'Call me, I have to go. I'm due on court in ten minutes and I need to get changed.'

'Have a good game.' He smiled.

'Indeed I will,' she assured him, on cloud nine that she had him where she wanted him. It had been one of the most satisfying moments of her life.

* * *

Carol sighed as she marched across Binn's Bridge, shading her eyes from the prisms of sunlight that dazzled up from the Royal Canal. It had been fun then, almost a game, albeit a game that she intended to win, but as things got serious with them and she continued to fall even more in love with him, life became much more of a roller-coaster. Gary started putting pressure on her to sleep with him and she would have in a heartbeat if she'd felt secure about him. It became an unspoken struggle between them, and each was equally determined as to the outcome.

So far she was shading it, she conceded. She was holding out with great difficulty, it had to be said, about sleeping with him, much to the frustration of both of them, but so far it had paid off. They were engaged. Nevertheless she now understood Jen's watchfulness, as she had become watchful herself in the face of his constant flirting with other women.

It was difficult. She often wanted to rage at him and tell him not to be such an obnoxious bastard, but that would be playing the game his way and she wouldn't give him the satisfaction. Only to Jessica did she pour out her fears and doubts. Jessica was her touchstone, her comforter, and her shoulder to cry on.

They had known each other since childhood, living across the road from each other in Arklow, a small seaside town on the east coast. They'd gone to school together, survived the teenage years, and Carol had followed the other girl to Dublin. Jessica knew all about Carol's difficulties at home. She never put on a façade with her like she did with everyone else. When her mother's nerves went and she hit the bottle, it was Jessica she confided in. While her parents fought like cat and dog for years before her father left, it was Jessica who comforted Carol. If it wasn't for her friend, sometimes Carol didn't know what she'd do.

Katie was the big thorn in Carol's side. She too had grown up in Arklow with them, and because she and Jessica were cousins, the bond was close. Carol had always been jealous of it, and of her. No doubt she would be Jessica's bridesmaid at the wedding. That wouldn't be so bad, she thought smugly. How nice it would be to swan up the aisle as a bride knowing that Katie was probably pea-green with envy behind her.

She let herself into the gloomy, red-brick terraced house where she had a bedsit on the first floor. When Jessica and Katie had moved into their house just over a mile away, she had been full sure that they would have invited her to share, but the

71

invite hadn't been forthcoming and she'd been devastated. She'd blamed Katie, but she'd been hurt that Jessica hadn't insisted. After all, she was living in a grotty little bedsit that her friend was always giving out about.

Carol could well have afforded to rent a nice flat or apartment but she was paranoid about saving. Money had been tight when her father left, even though he sent money every week and paid the bills. Nancy had scrimped to buy drink. Carol had vowed to save as much of her salary as she could so that she could have a safety net of cash for the future. Paying rent was money down the drain, she reasoned, so she got a place that didn't make a big hole in her purse.

Carol sighed as she turned the key in the lock and put her shoulder to the dirty beige wooden door with the flaking paint. She pushed hard. It really was a kip, she acknowledged, as she studied her abode. A single divan bed faced the door. She had covered it with a lilac candlewick bedspread and cushions lay dotted along the wall so it doubled as a sofa. One window facing on to the street gave the only natural light and an ancient chipped Belfast sink stood beneath it. At right angles to the window and sink lay a small counter top, with a tiny two-ringed cooker and a bockety fridge that wheezed and rattled like an eighty-year-old. A small black fireplace that accommodated about two briquettes in its diminutive grate was her only source of heating, and she had one rickety armchair that sagged in the middle and had cigarette burns all along the arms.

A woodworm-infested wardrobe, crammed to the brim, completed the furnishings and black sacks of clothes and other bits and pieces tumbled untidily in the corner. She hated it so much she never brought anyone up to it, and she'd only stayed in it because she'd hoped that Gary or Jessica would take pity on her and ask her to move in.

Gary had been horrified when he'd seen it the first time. 'What the hell are you doing living in a gaff like this? My God, woman, it's the pits.'

'Well, we're not all loaded like you,' she retorted, playing the poor mouth. 'I'm saving for a car.'

'Go for promotion at work,' he suggested.

'Yeah, yeah,' she said wearily. 'Me and a thousand others.'

'I thought you'd be a piranha in the work pool.'

'Excuse me, I'm a Senior Staff Officer. I have a staff working under me,' she boasted.

'Well done,' he said admiringly. 'But this place is a dump, Miss Senior Staff Officer. I'll paint it for you if you like,' he offered. 'You've got to get rid of those cabbages on the walls.'

'They're roses,' she pointed out.

'They're not like any roses I've ever seen,' he retorted, gazing around at the uninspiring décor. 'I can see why you wear yourself out on the court, so you'd be too knackered to stay awake. I'd get nightmares in this place. What colour do you want me to paint it?'

'Are you serious?' Carol was utterly touched by this unexpectedly kind offer.

'Sure,' he grinned. 'It will only take a couple of hours.'

'I'd better OK it with the landlord,' she murmured.

'You do that, and get back to me,' he said matter-of-factly. She was ecstatic.

'He wouldn't do that unless he had strong feelings for me, sure he wouldn't?' she asked Jessica, who'd assured her that men did not go around painting girls' bedsits if they didn't feel something for the girl involved. True to his word, once the landlord had given his permission, Gary had painted the room a bright, warm, buttermilk yellow that lightened the gloom of the previous dark green.

Yellow walls notwithstanding, she'd be delighted to shake the dust of the cramped little room off her heels, she reflected, as she filled a kettle of water to make herself a pot of tea.

Ten minutes later she was scowling as Gary's phone rang and rang unanswered. Here she had momentous news to tell him and he wasn't at home. Nor were there any messages for her. Frances, the bank official who lived on the ground floor, would always leave a note for her if anyone called when she wasn't there.

It wouldn't have killed him to ring her, the skunk, she thought crossly, all her previous joie de vivre evaporating.

Gary held the car door open for Jen and watched admiringly as she slid elegantly out of the car. He had taken her out to Dun Laoghaire and they were going to walk along the pier before having a bite to eat, in Roly's. It was nice being with his ex for the day, and she was clearly enjoying being with him.

He wasn't being very fair to her, he acknowledged a little guiltily. He knew she was hoping he would come back to her, but much and all as he liked her, she was a bit too career-minded for his tastes. She was a sales rep for ASCO, a big American pharmaceutical company. She'd worked her way up to being a regional manager, and that had been one of the final nails in the coffin for him. He didn't want to be dating a woman who was doing better than he was. And besides, there was no mystery to her any more. No challenge; not like Carol, who could drive him mad as easily as she could charm him.

Jen might pretend that she wasn't going to see him any more but he knew her better than that. She was a pushover for him and he might as well enjoy her while he could. She'd called him a serial heartbreaker once and he'd been secretly pleased at the label, even though she'd obviously meant it as a gratuitous insult. He liked women, he liked flirting with them, but if they were foolish enough to fall in love with him, he couldn't be blamed for it. People had to take responsibility for their own emotions.

Carol was cool. Sure she wanted to get married, but sometimes he felt it was more the idea of being married that appealed to her, and not his over-whelming allure. Carol could be extremely offhand with him; her walking out on him in The Oval was a case in point. No other chick he'd ever dated had walked away from him, no matter how intense the row. He glanced at his watch. Two fifteen: he'd let her cool her heels, he wouldn't phone. He'd see her at the club tomorrow. He'd never been one to make the first move in a row. She'd better get used to it.

Carol lifted the phone and heard the familiar dial tone. It seemed to be working. Her fingers hovered. She desperately wanted to phone Gary. She'd spent the whole afternoon in the bedsit hoping he'd ring, but not a peep. She'd nearly gone mad looking out at the sun splitting the trees. He was such a swine sometimes. Well, to hell with him, she was damned if she was going to make the first move.

She trudged back up the creaking stairs and flung herself on her divan. Nine-thirty, too late to make arrangements with any of her friends to go out drinking. She didn't want to stay in feeling sorry for herself – the night would drag.

She could go for a jog. That's what she'd do, she decided. She'd go for a jog up to Glasnevin. Jessica and Mike might be in The Gravediggers, their cosy local, having a drink, and she could join them. Better than sitting moping on her own.

She changed into her Adidas tracksuit and slipped some money into her pocket. She liked jogging, liked the feeling of pushing herself hard and liked knowing that she was as fit as she could possibly be. She was a huge admirer of Pilates but the workout video was difficult to do in the small confines of her bedsit; nevertheless Carol did her best to do the routine at least three times a week. Some day she was going to have a room in her house that she could convert into a gym area, all wooden floors and floor-to-ceiling mirrors, and she'd work out to her heart's content. If only Gary would get his act together and start looking at houses with her. Thinking of him intensified her bad humour, and she headed out into the twilight fuelled with anger and fear as she pounded the streets, wondering just exactly where her fiancé was.

7

'Feeling better?' Gary said drily as he detached himself from a group at the bar and gave Carol a kiss on the cheek.

'Nothing wrong with me, never better,' she replied snootily. The bloody nerve of him to be so casual about it all. It was eleven thirty on Sunday morning and she hadn't heard a toss from him since Friday night.

'I didn't think there was much point in phoning you, you being in such a bad mood and all.' He grinned at her.

'Yeah, well, why would I not be in a bad mood when I'm engaged to an ignorant bastard?'

'Ooohhh, nasty!'

'Not nasty, merely truthful. I'll have a Club Orange, please.'

'Wild woman, aren't you?' he teased.

In spite of herself, Carol relaxed and smiled at

him. He was here now, she was glad to see him, there was no point in having aggro between them for the rest of the day.

'So will we have a knock-up before you take me to lunch?' she inquired.

'OK, go change when you've finished your drink. Where do you want to go for lunch?'

He was extremely laid back and agreeable, she thought suspiciously, wishing she knew what he'd been up to and whom he'd been with. But she wouldn't give him the satisfaction of asking, so she shrugged and said, 'I'm easy.'

She changed into her whites and they played a couple of games, neither of them giving an inch. Later, as they sat eating lunch in the Royal Dublin, Carol said casually, 'Jessica and I were talking and she thinks a double wedding would be a good idea after all.'

Gary lowered the forkful of food he was about to eat and looked at her, puzzled, to say the least.

'I didn't think she was that gone on the idea. She certainly didn't give that impression,' he said slowly.

'Well, obviously when she had a think about it she changed her mind,' Carol replied non-chalantly, but she'd noted the flicker of dismay in his eyes and felt that old familiar niggle of fear that

Gary was less than committed to the idea of marriage.

'And when are they thinking of getting married?' he asked warily.

'Don't know. Another year or so at least, I'd say.' She kept her gaze firmly on her plate.

'Maybe we'd be better off on our own?' He toyed with his roast beef.

'You liked the idea on Friday night.' Carol struggled to keep the irritation out of her tone.

'I suppose I hadn't given it much thought. Just say they want to get married somewhere we don't want.'

'Is there anywhere you don't want to get married? I thought you didn't give a toss.' She looked at him sternly.

'Well . . . I . . . I . . .' he blustered.

'Yes?' Her stare never wavered.

'I think I'd like a registry office marriage,' he said feebly.

'Don't talk nonsense, Gary, we'd never get away with that,' Carol said briskly, doing a magnificent job of hiding her disquiet. 'I think a double wedding is the perfect option and I told Jessica so,' she added emphatically.

'Oh! Oh . . . right so.' Gary took a gulp of his wine, looking far from happy.

Carol felt like thumping him. Talk about making a woman feel cherished and wanted when it really mattered. Well, at least she'd broached the topic. That was the first hurdle cleared. The next thing was to set a date. She was going to pin Jessica down and get things sorted. Jury's or the Burlington were nice hotels, she mused. Or they could get married in the airport church and have their reception at the Airport Hotel and be ready to fly out on their respective honeymoons. It was a pity she hadn't seen Jessica and Mike on Saturday night. They weren't in the pub when she popped in, neither were they at home.

She hoped they'd be at the tennis club later in the afternoon. The four of them usually met up in the club on Sunday afternoon and had a couple of drinks. Jessica was working this Sunday but it was only until one-thirty. That would give her plenty of time to get home, have lunch and get to the club by mid to late afternoon. She was definitely going to bring up the subject.

At least things were moving in the right direction. After a constructive chat with Jessica, decisions could be made and firm plans could be put in place. Carol rubbed the band of her engagement ring with her thumb. Sooner rather than later if she had anything to say about it, she'd also be wearing a gold band on that selfsame finger. And Gary'd be wearing a matching one on his ring finger too. Carol smiled to herself. Their exchange of wedding rings would be the most fulfilling moment of her life, she had no doubt about it.

Jessica sipped a cup of coffee as she sat in the control room waiting for the guests to emerge from studio. Five minutes to go and she'd be escorting them to reception and her morning's work would be finished. The producer yawned and rubbed a hand over a stubbly jaw. 'That's it, I'm going on the dry, definitely,' he vowed, as he did every Sunday. Jessica grinned.

'I'll get you another cup of coffee,' she soothed. She slipped out of studio to get the required coffee, thinking how much more relaxed it was working in the Radio Centre on Sunday, compared to a weekday. The corridors, usually humming with the constant flow of people, were graveyard quiet. Studios were empty, and the huge open-plan offices upstairs were almost deserted. In comparison to the frenetic activity on the daily programme she worked on, the Sunday magazine show was a doddle, and Jim Collins, the producer, was so laid back he was almost horizontal.

'It's a good show. Lots of phone calls on the lack

of sportsmanlike behaviour in football and rugby. Eddie is giving it socks,' Jim said with satisfaction when she came back with the coffee.

Eddie Doorley was a sports commentator with an unpredictable temper, and his inclusion on a programme panel always promised a lively, sparky show. She could see him through the glass panel gesticulating wildly, his face fire-engine red as he made a point.

'Go, Eddie, go,' Jim chortled as he gave Ronan Dillon, the presenter, the signal to wind it down. Half a minute later, the mic went green and the four guests began to emerge, Eddie still in full flow. Jessica presented them with their fee forms to sign, congratulated them on their performances, and before they knew it was leading them up the stairs at the end of the corridor, to reception and the exit.

'Well done, Jessica, thanks,' Ronan said wearily. 'I didn't want to have to sit listening to Eddie jawing for another half-hour.'

'Me neither, Ro,' Jim agreed. 'Are you on for a pint up in Kileys?'

'Too right I am. Jessica?' He cocked an eyebrow at her.

'Not today, thanks, Ronan, Mike's starting his finals tomorrow. We're going to hit a few balls around on the tennis court so he'll loosen up a bit.'

'Good thinking,' Jim approved. 'Are you on next weekend?'

'Nope, you'll have to cope without me.'

'Aw, Jessie, that means we'll probably have Viv Reid and you know what a fusspot she is. How can you do this to me?' Her producer groaned.

'Ah, don't fret, you'll survive, just have an extra couple of scoops on Saturday night.' She patted him on the arm. The three of them walked up the stairs together, joking and laughing, and as Jessica walked across the foyer to the automatic doors she thought how fortunate she was to be in a job that she thoroughly enjoyed. Carol worked in the Civic Offices and she was forever moaning and groaning about how stressful her job was. She was constantly telling Jessica how lucky she was.

She felt a little guilty thinking of Carol. She and Mike had been in bed enjoying a welcome, sexy interlude when there'd been a knock on the front door. 'Oh no!' she groaned, lifting her head from Mike's shoulder. 'Who on earth is that?' She slipped out of bed and peered out of the window. 'Oh heck! It's Carol. Why can't she give me a break?' she muttered, drawing back hastily, afraid she'd be seen.

'You'd better let her in.' Mike threw her dressing-gown at her.

'I don't want to.' She scowled. 'I just want to spend a bit of time with you, Mike. I had her all this morning. Every time they have a row I have to endure an earbashing. I don't care if you think I'm a wagon, I'm not answering the door. She knew that I was going to be with you tonight, she's just being a selfish cow,' she exploded, feeling frustratingly guilty as the doorbell shrilled again. She looked at Mike.

'It's up to you,' he said.

'Aw, Mike, now you're making me feel bad.' She grabbed her dressing-gown and pulled it on, her heart sinking as she prepared to go downstairs. She glanced out of the window and saw Carol's retreating form in the deepening dusk and didn't know whether to be sorry or glad.

'She's gone.'

Mike held out his arms to her. 'That's settled then, and don't feel bad – you were going downstairs to let her in so you're not a wagon. Now come here and destress me.'

'It's me that needs destressing,' she said grumpily as she got back into bed. 'Just when I was feeling nice and relaxed.'

'I'll relax you,' he said lazily, his blue eyes

smiling into hers as he drew her close against him and cupped her breast in his hand. He stroked her lightly, teasing her as his hands slid down to the silky skin between her thighs, and soon Carol's unwelcome visit was the last thing on her mind.

It had been a lovely, sensual night, made all the more so because they had the house to themselves. If Carol hadn't called it would have been perfect.

Jessica hurried down the steps of the Radio Centre, inhaling the warm summer air appreciatively. They'd been blessed with the weather for the past week and there was no sign of it breaking. Maybe it was going to be one of those scorchers of a summer that she and Mike would be really able to enjoy once his exams were over.

She waved at the security guard as she drove out of the sprawling complex with its attractive landscaped grounds. The traffic was light along the Stillorgan dual carriageway and she was home in twenty minutes. The smell of roasting chicken wafted into the hall as she let herself into the house and her mouth started to water. She was starving. Mike must be cooking. He was a great cook, far better than she was, and he often made them Sunday dinner. She hadn't expected him to cook today, she thought he'd be stuck into his books.

'Hiya.' She poked her head around the kitchen door. Mike was stirring a pot of gravy and the aroma wafting up under her nostrils reminded her of Sunday dinners at home in Arklow. 'Mushy peas as well!'

'The whole enchilada. Roasties, stuffing, and baked parsnips,' her fiancé informed her smugly as he whipped the crispy, succulent golden chicken out of the oven and whacked her with the tea towel when she pilfered a spoonful of stuffing. 'Stop it! You'll ruin your appetite.'

'Just as well we're not playing a match later. I won't be able to run around the court after this feed.' She licked the spoon appreciatively, savouring every crumb. 'What made you decide to cook a dinner? I thought we were having salad and cold meats.'

'Ah, when I went to do the shopping I saw these plump little organic chickens and I got the longing for a few roast potatoes.' He took out his tray of crisp, sizzling roasties and Jessica groaned, knowing a pig-out was imminent.

'Just go and sit down,' Mike ordered. 'You're getting under my feet, I'll have it dished up in a minute.'

'Yes, sir,' she said meekly, plonking on to a chair at the round dining-table in the small, extended kitchen.

'This is scrumptious, Mike,' she enthused appreciatively a few minutes later as she bit into a crispy roast potato. 'How come you always get yours so crispy? Mine are always soft and soggy.'

'Have your oil and tray really hot and give the potatoes a shake in a colander after you've par-boiled them before you oil them,' Mike instructed authoritatively.

'Yes, Delia,' she jeered affectionately, and he laughed.

'You may mock, but it's just as well I can cook or we'd starve. The least you could do is go on a cookery course before you marry me. I mean, who else could make a cup of coffee with gravy granules?'

'Swine. I was pissed, I thought it was the coffee jar I was using. They're practically the same. How totally ungallant of you to even mention it.'

'And what about the time you got your paprika and your nutmeg confus—'

'Stop, just stop it right now or I'll call off the engagement,' Jessica warned.

'Promises, promises,' Mike scoffed, and got his hair pulled for his impudence.

They strolled hand in hand into the club later that afternoon and saw Carol waving gaily at them. 'Hi, you guys, I thought you were never going to come.'

'Well, we did actually, twice.' Mike's eyes glinted.

'Lucky bastard,' Gary said enviously.

'Tsk,' tutted Carol. 'All you pair ever think about is sex.'

'Well, at least he's getting it – all I'm doing is thinking about it,' Gary retorted.

'Oh, shut up and go and buy a round,' his fiancée snapped, not at all amused.

'Better do what I'm told,' Gary said drily as he got up to go to the bar.

'Girls, excuse me, I just need to have a word with Ronnie Condon for a minute.' Mike excused himself. Ronnie, the affable rotund club administrator, was very popular and great fun.

'That Gary is an insensitive bollix,' Carol fumed as Jessica sat down beside her.

'Ah, lighten up, Carol, it was a joke.'

'No it wasn't,' she said sulkily.

'Look, if you pair are going to have a row and be in a snit, Mike and I will just go and start whacking a few balls around,' Jessica said irritably, wishing she was over with Mike and Ronnie. The two were guffawing heartily at the bar.

'Oh, don't be like that, please, Jessie. Let's talk about the wedding and cheer ourselves up,' Carol wheedled.

'*I was perfectly cheered up until I met you two,*' she felt like saying, but she refrained from comment with difficulty. Sometimes two minutes in Carol's company was enough to put her in a bad humour. She'd once worked on a programme about self-help books and read in one of them that people could be divided into categories called 'Drains' or 'Radiators' in terms of the energy they put out. Right now, Carol was being her drainy self and Jessica didn't feel like spending the afternoon trying to cheer her up. There were times when she would make a huge effort and finally manage to get the other girl in good form, and by then she'd be totally drained herself and fit for nothing. When she'd seen the drains and radiators comparison, she'd understood it completely.

'Have you any ideas? When are you thinking of doing it?' Carol asked anxiously. 'I told Gary that you'd changed your mind. So at least he's getting used to the idea that there *is* actually going to be a wedding. So this is as good a time as any to start making plans. Have you any?'

'Well, yes, actually. Mike and I discussed it,' Jessica said slowly. 'Er . . . we want to get married this year in Kilbride church and we want to have the reception in The Four Winds Hotel.'

Carol stared at her, stunned, and Jessica felt her

insides tighten. This was it, for once in her life she was sticking to her guns. If Carol wasn't happy she could nix the idea of a double wedding, and Jessica wouldn't mind one little bit because right now she was heartily regretting her ill-judged, impulsive offer.

8

'This year! Kilbride! The Four Winds!' Carol rattled out each exclamation like bullets from a machine-gun. 'You want to get married in Wicklow!' She couldn't have been more shocked if Jessica had said she wanted to get married on the moon.

'Why? Where did you think I'd want to get married?' Jessica looked at the other girl in astonishment. How could this be such a surprise to her?

'I thought you'd like a Dublin wedding. I mean, I thought you'd go for a fairly up-market hotel like Jury's or the Burlington or even Clontarf Castle or the Regency.' Carol was clearly dismayed. 'Most of our friends are in Dublin.'

'Most of our families are in Arklow,' Jessica pointed out.

'But sure they'd love a day out. Going to a hotel at home is no treat,' she retorted heatedly. 'And

The Four Winds. Sure that's not much bigger than a blinking guesthouse,' she said derisively. 'It's not a proper hotel at all.'

'Look, Carol, even if we wanted to, we couldn't afford the hotels you're talking about. Certainly not if we're getting married this year. And we'd have never got a date. They'd be completely booked out. And The Four Winds is lovely. We like it,' Jessica retorted.

'I thought you wouldn't be getting married for another year at least,' Carol glowered.

'When we talked about it, Mike said he didn't want to be in Wicklow all week and then travelling up to Dublin at weekends. Once he starts working we're going to rent a place even though it's money down the drain, especially when we're trying to save for a house too.' Jessica took a deep breath. 'So, Carol, we're not going to be spending a fortune because we just don't have it. We just want a simple, homely wedding and we'll quite understand if you want to do your own thing. So feel free to say no to what we're planning. Much better to say no to things now than to have misunderstandings later on.'

'Oh!' Carol murmured, deflated by Jessica's uncharacteristically firm tone and by the stark choices presented.

'Why did you decide on Kilbride rather than Templerainey church? Templerainey is far bigger. It's got a much longer aisle,' she said sulkily.

'I just really like Kilbride. It's such a lovely, small country church. And if we're not having that big a wedding we won't all be rattling around in it. Anyway, Dad's funeral was from Templerainey, it's got sad memories. Both Mike and I like Kilbride.' Jessica defended her choice spiritedly.

'Well, it looks like you've decided everything,' Carol said tartly.

'As I say, you don't have to do what we're doing. Do your own thing by all means.' Jessica was beginning to feel uncomfortable. She glanced around looking for Mike, wishing he would come back and rescue her.

'But surely if we're having a double wedding I get some say?' Carol said plaintively. Jessica felt her irritation levels surge. She didn't want a double wedding; it was Carol who had suggested it and Carol who'd said that Jessica could plan it as she wanted. Now she was backtracking and moving the goalposts. If it was as awkward as this, so early in the proceedings, it could end up a total nightmare.

'Carol,' she said gently, managing to conceal her irritation, 'you wanted the double wedding. I wasn't sure if it was a good idea. And I'm still not sure. You obviously don't like what Mike and I are planning so perhaps we'd be better off going our own separate ways.'

There, she'd said it, hard as it was. Jessica hated having to be forceful, she didn't like hurting people's feelings and she thoroughly resented having her Sunday afternoon ruined with this extremely unwelcome conversation.

'Oh! Oh, no, no!' Carol said hastily as she spied Gary weaving between the tables with the drinks. 'Look, say nothing, I'll have a chat with Gary and see what he thinks and we can talk things over then.'

Bloody hell, Jessica thought in dismay. *I thought I'd done it.*

'Fine,' she managed. 'But we're hoping to finalize a date very soon, so I'll need to know.'

'Sure, sure,' Carol agreed.

'So, Jessie, what's the score?' Gary handed her a white wine spritzer.

'Same old thing,' she said lightly, wondering whether she should make any comment at all about the wedding. Carol had said to say nothing, but surely Gary was as much involved as anyone and had a right to an opinion. She glanced at Carol but the other girl was rooting in her bag, avoiding eye contact. Fortunately Mike arrived and he and

Gary began an animated discussion about the football results.

Jessica sipped her drink. Typical men. How come Mike and Gary *weren't* discussing the wedding? Let them thrash out the bloody thing, she thought darkly, her previous good humour completely evaporated.

'Mike, if you want to get a few games in before you start studying, you'd want to get a move on,' she reminded her fiancé grumpily.

Mike looked taken aback at her tone. He glanced from her to Carol and intuited that all was not rosy in the garden.

'Ah, give the guy a break,' Gary chastised. 'You can't rush a pint.'

'No, Jessie's right.' Mike drained his glass. 'I want to smack a few balls around the place to relax the old brain and bod and then just cast an eye over my notes. Tomorrow's D-day.'

'Good luck, Mike, hope they go well for you,' Carol interjected.

'Ta.' He smiled down at her.

'Yeah, buddy, break a leg or whatever you do in exams.' Gary lifted his glass to him. 'We'll go on the piss to celebrate when you're finished. You ladies can have one of your girlie nights,' he decreed.

'Why can't we go on the piss with you?' Carol demanded.

'There's going on the piss and going on the piss – you wouldn't want to be there.'

'You're dead right, Gary,' Jessica drawled.

'Sarky! Sarky!' Gary teased. 'You're in a bit of a mood today.'

'No I'm not.'

'PMT?'

'Smart bastard. Come on, Mike.' Jessica wasn't in the humour to banter with Gary, she just wanted to get out on court and vent her frustration.

'What's up?' Mike asked as they walked towards the changing-rooms.

'Nothing.'

'Fibber.'

'It's Carol!' she growled. 'She doesn't like what we're planning, can't believe we're having the wedding at home. So I told her that we should go our separate ways and thought that was the end of the double wedding crap. But she's still talking about going ahead and the thought of having to put up with her sulks and arguments for the next few months is doing my head in. Why on earth does she want to keep on with it if she doesn't like what we want?'

'But Jessie, you *did* say to her that we could have a double wedding. Fair is fair,' he said reasonably. 'She should have some say.' Not what she wanted to hear.

'Well, I'm sorry I did,' she snapped irrationally as she came to the ladies' changing-room.

'Oh, for crying out loud, Jessie, you did. Accept responsibility for opening your big mouth and deal with it. You pair get yourselves sorted.' Mike strode into the men's changing-rooms, leaving her standing with her mouth open. It was most unusual for him to bite her head off. Tears smarted her eyes. Her lovely day was turning into a disaster. She struggled for composure as she changed into her tennis gear. Mike didn't have to rub her nose in it. She knew very well that she'd agreed to the double wedding. But that had been in a moment of weakness when she'd felt sorry for Carol. Now she was bitterly regretting that weakness and feeling totally inadequate. He didn't have to be quite so rude and accusatory about it. She felt like telling him to get lost. She felt like going home. If he wasn't starting his finals in the morning she bloody well would have.

There you go, putting someone else's feelings before your own again. What a wimpy doormat. Jessica groaned as she tied her laces. She hated feeling like a doormat. She had to start being a bit more assertive. Katie was always telling her to stand up for herself. Unfortunately this wasn't the weekend for it.

Mike was sitting on a bench when she walked outside. She sat beside him and fiddled with the strings of her racket, unwilling to be the first to speak. They sat silently watching the end of a game, waiting for the court to become free, the thwack of tennis balls and trilling birdsong the only sounds to break the stillness of the after-noon. The sun was warm on Jessica's shoulders. It should have been blissful and relaxing sitting here with Mike; instead she felt as taut and tightly strung as her tennis racket.

'Do you want to toss for side or serve?' he asked as the other couple finished their match.

'I'm not fussed,' she said snootily.

'Suit yourself.' Mike marched on to the right-hand side of the court and bounced the ball with his racket as he waited for her to position herself. She'd hardly turned to face him before he let fly a ball at her. She managed to return it but he lobbed it back over her head and she couldn't get to it. She was raging. How unsporting of him to wrong-foot her like that. The game started with Jessica serving. She calmed herself and breathed deeply.

Even though he was the stronger, faster player, she was technically more proficient and she narrowed her gaze against the glinting sun and threw the ball in the air. She was aiming for an ace, but he read her intention and returned it with ease. She managed a backhand, dropping it lightly over the net, and he just missed the return.

'Ha!' she derided, childishly, she had to admit.

'Ha, yourself!' he riposted, and they looked at each other and burst out laughing.

'Sorry,' he apologized.

'Me too.' She leaned across the net and kissed him.

'Well, one thing about it all, we won't be bored,' he grinned. 'Now come on until I beat the socks off you.'

'You can try,' she taunted, but she was smiling as she walked to the base line and waited for him to serve.

One of the things she loved most about Mike was that he never held a grudge and he never held a row. He was under a lot of pressure, he didn't need her whinging about Carol, she acknowledged, feeling thoroughly ashamed of her outburst. He was right, she had got herself into the double wedding mess. She could have said no outright but she just didn't have the bottle for it.

She'd dithered like the wimp she was and then caved in. She had to accept responsibility for her actions. If the joint wedding was going to happen she was just going to have to get on with it and make the most of it.

9

'You're doing great.' Jessica bent down and kissed Mike. He was flopped on the sofa, flicking through a folder of notes. It was the third day of his exams and they were tough going.

'Come on, you guys, chow's up,' Katie called from the kitchen.

'Thank God, I'm starving!' Mike hauled himself up from the sofa and yawned tiredly. He put his arm around Jessica and they strolled into the kitchen, where Katie was stirring a creamy sauce that was to accompany her chicken and rice.

'Will you come and live with us when we're married?' Mike grinned as he took his seat at the table.

'I don't think you could afford me.' Katie winked at Jessica. 'Don't worry, I'll give her a few recipes that a seven-year-old could follow.'

'The cheek of the pair of you,' Jessica retorted. 'Have I ever poisoned either of you?'

'No, but you've come close,' Mike teased.

'Right, that's it. When your exams are over, I'm going to do a dinner party and you'll eat your words, smarty pants.'

'That's probably all I'll eat.' Mike couldn't resist it and Jessica had to laugh.

'You're a brat!'

'But you love me,' Mike said smugly.

'Urrggg! Stop it, you two,' Katie ordered as she put two steaming plates on the table.

'I was thinking of taking tomorrow afternoon off and going home to talk to Mam about the wedding. I should OK it with her before we make any final arrangements. Do you want to tell your parents?' Jessica asked as she sat down beside him.

'Yeah, I'll give them a call but they'll be easy enough, they've been through the ordeal three times already. The last two were my sisters' weddings, so Ma will be glad to take a back seat and not have the hassle of arranging, I'd imagine.' Mike wolfed down a forkful of chicken and rice.

'I know, and your parents are so laid back there'll be no problems, but it would be good manners to make sure that they're happy enough, so ring them,' Jessica warned. Mike was terrible for putting family stuff on the long finger.

'I will, I will,' he said a little testily. 'I am trying to do exams.'

'Stop using that as an excuse; you can ring them tonight from here. It won't take five minutes. And don't forget to sort out your letters of freedom, from your parish priest.'

'Nag, nag, nag.' Mike scowled.

'Listen, buster, I can't do *everything*. It's only a few phone calls,' Jessica said indignantly.

'Would the pair of you shut up arguing, I'm trying to enjoy my dinner,' Katie complained.

'Sorry,' Mike apologized.

'Me too,' Jessica added. 'Thanks for cooking dinner.'

'I suppose it's a bridesmaid's job to look after the so-called happy couple now and again,' her cousin said drily. 'What I want to know is, who's going to be the best man? Don't tell me you're going to pick Tony, 'cos he's married and no use to me in the slightest.'

'I have to pick Tony, he's my only brother.' Mike shrugged.

'But, Mike, I know Tony's a hunk, but he's a *married* hunk, couldn't you ask Lenny or Barry? They're gorgeous *and* eligible,' Katie wheedled.

'Barry's seeing someone—'

'Since when?' Katie was disgusted.

'She's doing architecture. He spilt a glass of milk over her in the canteen and they hit it off.'

'Ah, shag it. Well, Lenny then?'

'Katie, Lenny might be good-looking and all that, but I wouldn't ask him to be my best man in a million years. He's the type that would go on the piss and not turn up, or else turn up pickled. And he's not the type of guy I'd like to see you going out with. He's not good enough for you. You can have a great laugh with him, he's good company but he's very unreliable,' Mike explained earnestly.

'Yes, Daddy,' Katie said drily.

'Think of me as the brother you never had,' Mike teased.

'Come on, Mike, help a girl out here. I need a man for your wedding.'

'Right. There's going to be a hell of a party when the exams are over, so why don't you come and see what's on offer? I really didn't think studenty types would be your choice. You being a nurse and surrounded by all those surgeons and doctors.'

'You must be joking,' Katie scoffed. 'I wouldn't go out with a doctor if I were paid to. God, no!'

'Stay calm, Katie, we'll find you a man, won't we, Jessie?'

'Indeed we will,' her cousin assured her. 'Never fear.'

'Well, it's imperative I have one for the wedding. I don't want Carol looking down her smug nose at me through her wedding veil,' Katie confessed. 'Sad, isn't it?'

'Very. I'm surprised at you.' Jessica frowned.

'I know. It's just that she has a knack for making you feel inferior.'

'Will you give the girl a break, you're always giving out about her,' Mike admonished.

'You wouldn't understand,' Jessica assured him.

'It's a woman thing,' Katie declared.

'The more I see of you women in action the less I understand you.' Mike shook his head.

'Oh, be quiet and eat your dinner,' Jessica retorted.

'You don't need to understand, just do as you're told,' Katie said, straight-faced, and he laughed.

Jessica smiled as she remembered their messing the following day, as she ran down the steps of the Radio Centre and got into her car. It was such a bonus that Mike and Katie got on so well, there were no stresses and strains between them.

When she and Carol were teenagers she'd had to put up with Carol being terribly jealous if she'd been seeing a fella and her friend wasn't. Carol had given some of Jessica's boyfriends a terrible time. Until she'd started going with Gary, she hadn't been too friendly to Mike either. Jealousy was a terrible affliction, it could really make your life a misery, Jessica mused as she turned right, out of RTE, and headed for the Stillorgan dual carriageway.

The lunchtime traffic was light, and as she cruised through Foxrock towards Cornelscourt her heart lifted. She loved the journey home. Five minutes later, with green lights all the way, the scenery came into view and, as the suburbs disappeared after Loughlinstown, and the green and gold of the countryside became predominant, and the Sugar Loaf was etched against the horizon, Jessica felt a mixture of joy and apprehension. Though she was dying to tell her mother about the wedding, she knew there'd be sadness. Even now, three years after her father's death of a heart attack, the emptiness hadn't gone away.

One minute Ray Kennedy had been vibrant, healthy, full of life, the next he'd been collapsed over the side of his boat, his fishing companions trying frantically to revive him as they waited for the ambulance to arrive.

It had been a crisp, autumn Saturday morning,

the intense heat of summer a distant memory, the sun a creamy benign orb that no longer had the power to warm as the nippy breezes of autumn made their presence felt. Her father had been looking forward to a good day's fishing and had promised Jessica and her mother a feed of mackerel for tea. There was nothing like the taste of a freshly caught succulent mackerel cooked under the grill with a scattering of salt and a lick of butter, the perfect supper. Jessica always enjoyed the booty from her father's fishing trips.

She and Mike had been repainting her bedroom when a neighbour had come rushing in and told them to get down to the beach fast as her father had collapsed. Heart beating in terror, she and Mike had run as fast as they could in time to see her father being lifted into the ambulance.

'Let me go with him,' she'd pleaded, but the ambulance man had said gently, 'It's too late, love. You should be there to tell your mother and bring her to the hospital.'

'Is he dead? Is Dad dead?' Jessica grabbed him by the arm. 'Do something. Give him oxygen. You're not even trying,' she screamed hysterically.

'Stop, Jessie.' Mike took her arm, his voice firm and calm. 'Is Ray dead?' he asked steadily.

'Yes. I'm sorry,' the ambulance man said. 'Take her home to be with her mother.'

Shaking with fear and shock, she stood watching the ambulance drive off out of sight. Marty and Conor, Ray's two friends, were ashen-faced as they came over to her.

'He just collapsed. It must have been the strain of pushing the boat on the rollers. If only we'd known, we'd never have let him do it,' Conor said gruffly, trying not to break down.

'Do you want me to tell Liz?' Marty asked gently. For a moment Jessica was tempted. How could she tell her mother that her father was dead? Liz loved Ray as much as the day she'd married him. They were devoted to each other. Her mother's life would be destroyed.

'I . . . I'd better tell her myself,' she managed, before breaking into great body-shaking sobs that brought tears to Mike's eyes as he hugged her to him and tried to comfort her. Out of the corner of her eye she could see the group of strangers and neighbours that had gathered to see the drama.

'Let's get out of here,' she whispered, holding Mike's hand as tight as she could. Even though she knew he was there, being as kind as he could, she had never felt so alone in her life.

The walk back to the house was a complete blur

whenever she tried to remember it. Her only memory was of Mike making her hot, sweet tea and the stomach-clenching wait for her mother to return home from her shopping trip down the town. She thought she was going to be sick as she heard the car swing into the drive.

'Mike, Mike, what will I say?' she asked frantically.

'I'll tell her,' Mike said quietly, his face as white as her own as he stood up and squared his shoulders.

'Are you pair skiving?' Liz Kennedy asked merrily as she walked into the sitting-room, laden down with shopping bags.

'Mam!' The words came out as a croak.

'Mrs Kennedy.' Mike went over to her. Liz looked from one to the other and alarm darkened her bright blue eyes.

'What is it? What's wrong? It's not Ray, is it? Has something happened to the boat? I didn't hear the lifeboat flares.'

'Mr Kennedy collapsed. I'm sorry, Mrs Kennedy. He's dead.' Mike managed to get the words out in a very calm way, and even in her shock and grief Jessica gave thanks for the quiet strength of her boyfriend.

The light went out of her mother's eyes. She

seemed to crumple as Mike led her to the sofa beside Jessica.

'Oh, Jessica.' Liz gave a low keening sound and buried her face in her daughter's neck. 'Oh, Jessica, I want to die too. How will I live without him?'

'Don't say that, Mam, he'd hate you to say that.' Jessica wept as she held her mother close, and Mike went out to make more tea.

Liz had insisted on waking Ray in the house.

'I don't want him in a funeral parlour. It's too cold and lonely. I'm bringing him home.'

'Whatever you want, Mam, whatever,' Jessica agreed, wondering if she was in the middle of a very long, weird nightmare.

Seeing her father dressed in his favourite fishing jersey, lying in a coffin, had been surreal. He looked like he always looked, with a half-smile on his face as if he was asleep. She half expected him to sit up with a huge grin and say, 'Ha ha! Fooled ya!' He was such a practical joker, Jessica and Liz never knew what he was going to do next.

It was hard to believe that he'd never barrel through the door and envelope the pair of them in one of his rib-crushing bear hugs, saying happily, 'How are my women?' He'd been such a fun dad. He'd taught her to fish, and she could still remember the excitement of the tug on her line when she'd hooked her first mackerel. They'd made a fire on the beach, and he'd wrapped it in tinfoil with a lump of butter and salt and cooked it and a couple of flowery potatoes on the heated stones. They'd drunk hot, sweet smoky tea out of a billycan and watched the sun set and a thousand twinkling stars emerge in a dark navy sky.

'This is the life.' He'd smiled down at her, wrapping her in his thick Aran sweater and she'd yawned and smiled back, nestling into the warm jumper, inhaling the sea and musk scent that always meant her dad to her. She'd fallen asleep in his arms as he'd carried her home as full as an egg after their open-air supper, and she could vaguely remember Liz taking her from him and undressing her before putting her into her snug bed. She'd opened one bleary eye and seen the two of them smiling down at her and she'd felt completely safe and happy.

She remembered the giddy, carefree evenings when he'd come home from his work as a car mechanic and go off to the beach, where he taught her to find periwinkles on the rocks. Every trip to the beach with her dad was an adventure. When he took her out in his boat, she felt she was queen of the seas as they rocked gently on the waves and the sun warmed her through and through, the little puddles of water sloshing around the bottom of the boat and the smell of damp sand and salty seaweed nicer than any perfume.

It was only when she had kissed his forehead and felt the clammy, marble coldness of him that she knew there was no life in him and she'd never sit in the stern of his boat, fishing with him again.

Liz was helpless with grief. It was Mike and Jessica who had made all the arrangements and dealt with the undertaker. Carol had been a tower of strength. She had taken charge of the kitchen and fed a steady stream of tea and sandwiches to the many callers who had come to pay their condolences. Katie had arrived home the following day from London, where she'd been working, and she had stood with Jessica at the removal and the funeral like the rock that she was.

Her father's funeral had been the one time in their lives that Katie and Carol had put aside their differences and for that Jessica would always be grateful.

Her mother had been like a zombie for the year following Ray's death. Her eyes dazed and dull in her head, every day an effort to get through. Sometimes when she was at home for the weekend Jessica would hear her sobbing into her pillow, calling Ray's name. Asking why had he left them. She felt so helpless in the face of her mother's grief, even as she struggled with her own.

She was angry with God and her father, even though at one level she knew that it was unreasonable. Why had he left them and plunged their lives into misery? Why had God punished them with this heartless, incomprehensible act? Ray Kennedy was a good man, kind to family and friends, yet he had been taken and murderers and terrorists walked the earth unpunished.

Jessica had stopped going to Mass in her anger and cursed God, and his cruelty.

'Your anger will pass, it's only natural,' a priest had told her, but she hadn't believed him and told him she didn't want to talk about it. One spring day, two years later, she had been out practising her driving in her mother's car. She'd driven on the N11 towards Dublin and was planning to visit a friend in Redcross when a sudden impulse had her turning right at Lil Doyle's pub instead of left.

She drove up the winding country road where her grandparents had lived and passed their little cottage, now lived in by a young couple with a growing family. Jessica remembered visiting her grandparents as a child and when her grandmother had died she'd remembered asking where she'd gone.

'Back up to Holy God,' her father had told her matter-of-factly.

'Did he put his hand down and did Granny step on to it?' she'd asked.

'Yes, love,' Ray had said, smiling at her innocence. Standing beside him at the grave she'd remembered Ray saying to a neighbour, 'It comes to us all without exception. It's my turn now to deal with it.'

The memories came flooding back as she drove along through the yellow gorse-edged road, the forsythia bursting out in glorious abundance, the gift of spring to the countryside.

'It's my turn now to deal with it,' she murmured, and felt a flood of grief envelop her. She pulled into the gateway of the small country church that nestled atop a hill. Crying, she walked into the church and sat on a hard, shiny, well-worn pew. The church was cool and peaceful; prisms of light shining through the stained-glass windows, dancing on the white linen altarcloth. Spring flowers dressed the altar, daffodils, tulips and bluebells, and the peace and serenity of the place brought a balm to her.

'I miss you, Dad,' she cried, tears pouring down

her cheeks. 'Help me, God, help me accept that it was my turn.'

'I will.'

Startled, she turned around. Had she heard a voice? Was someone in the church with her? But no one was, and yet Jessica could have sworn that she had heard a voice say, 'I will.' A voice so calm and full of love that her soul felt peaceful and for a moment she had felt a serenity and sense of well-being that was indescribable.

How long she sat in the little church she could not tell, but for the first time since her father had died she no longer felt alone. His spirit was still there, and whether it was her imagination or the voice of God, the great knot of grief that had held her in bondage was loosened and she felt a sense of tranquillity that life was as it should be.

'Dad, help Mam,' she prayed. 'Jesus, bring peace to my mother.'

As she genuflected and blessed herself to leave, she knew that this was the church she wanted to marry Mike in, and for the first time in a long, long while she felt a flicker of happiness.

Remembering that life-changing moment as she drove along the N11 towards home, Jessica sighed. That was the day her anger had gone, and when she told Mike about it, shyly, afraid he might think she was for the birds, hearing voices, he had hugged her tightly to him and said, 'You handled your turn very bravely. I was so proud of you the way you looked after your mother. I think you're great.'

'Do you?'

'You know I do, I wouldn't be marrying you otherwise.'

'I suppose not, but it's nice to hear that you think I'm great, now and again,' she murmured against his chest, feeling immensely happy.

As she passed Lil Doyle's she glanced up to her left, knowing her little church was there and that later in the year she would be walking up its aisle as a bride. She hoped her mother liked the idea.

'Hi, Mam, I'm starving, have you something nice to eat?' she called cheerily as she let herself into the house fifteen minutes later, a big bunch of irises and tulips in one hand, a box of cream cakes in the other.

Liz Kennedy's eyes lit up at the sight of her daughter. At least she was looking like her old self, Jessica approved, noting her mother's recently highlighted hair and the smart black jeans and lilac fleece.

'Hello, love,' she greeted her. 'They're gorgeous, you shouldn't have gone to such trouble,' she reproved, holding out her arms to Jessica, who dropped her load on to the counter and hugged her mother tightly. 'I've a steak and mushroom pie in the oven—'

'Oh, Mam, my favourite. Can I have loads of pastry?' Jessica begged, her mouth beginning to water.

'Of course you can,' laughed Liz. 'Now tell me what brings you home midweek?'

'Mike and I are going to get married as soon as we can—'

'Lord above, Jessica, you're not pregnant—'

'*Mam!!*' Jessica exclaimed indignantly.

'Sorry, sorry,' her mother apologized hastily. 'I wouldn't mind, it's just I think you're a bit young and you've all your life ahead of you.'

'Well, I'm not. I'm on the pill, you know.'

'Sorry.' Liz slipped on her oven gloves and took the steaming, golden pie out of the oven. 'What's the rush then?' she asked as she set about serving their meal.

Jessica settled herself at the ready laid table. 'You know Mike's got the job with Wicklow County Council—'

'Yes, and he can live with me if he wants.' Liz spooned steak chunks and mushrooms on to a plate.

'Well, he'd need a car to drive to Wicklow and we were just talking about it and neither of us want for me to be in Dublin during the week and him down here as we'd originally planned, so we decided to hell with it, get married sooner rather than later. Neither of us is after a huge big wedding anyway. What do you think?'

'If it's what you both wish, it's fine by me,' Liz assured her as she placed her meal in front of her.

'We were thinking of getting married in Kilbride and having the reception in The Four Winds.'

'Well, that would be handy,' Liz approved. 'And I'm glad you've picked Kilbride church. Ray was buried from Templerainey; I'd feel terribly sad walking up that aisle with you. Kilbride is a much better choice.'

'I know. There's no sad memories in Kilbride,' Jessica said gently.

'Do you want me to make your dress?' Liz arched an eyebrow.

Jessica burst out laughing. 'Your sewing is as good as my cooking. Better not,' she spluttered.

'Just thought I'd offer,' Liz grinned. 'Will you ask Tara to make it?'

'I guess so, I'd say she'd be disappointed if I didn't.'

'Well, she is your godmother and she's great on the sewing machine.'

'I know. Katie always has fabulous clothes,' Jessica murmured as she devoured a piece of feather-light pastry.

'I'd better do a guest list,' Liz said as she sat down opposite her daughter. 'I'll do the flowers myself. I might not be able to sew but I can do a nice job with flowers even if I say so myself.'

'Er, there's just one other thing . . .' Jessica swallowed and took a drink of milk. 'We're thinking of having a double wedding with Carol and Gary.'

'What!' Liz's jaw dropped.

'Carol and Gary,' Jessica said weakly.

'You're not serious?' Liz said in dismay.

'Why?' Jessica's heart sank at her mother's response.

'That lot. You know what they're like. Nancy Logan lives on her nerves. Between trancs and drink she's nearly comatose most of the time. That young Nadine is wild. The two aunts don't speak to each other. Is the father alive or dead? Oh, Jessica, do you have to?' she groaned.

'Sorry, Mam.' Jessica bit her lip.

'Whose idea was it or need I ask?'

'It was Carol's,' Jessica admitted.

'And why didn't you just say no?' Liz demanded.

'Oohh, you know Carol, it's very hard to say no. I just felt sorry for her.'

'But it's your wedding. What does Mike say?'

'He doesn't mind. You know men?'

'Is there any way you can get out of it?'

Jessica brightened. 'I could say you wouldn't have it,' she exclaimed, seeing the perfect excuse.

'You can't do that, Jessica,' Liz exclaimed indignantly. 'Nancy would get in a huff and you know how unstable she is, and anyway I wouldn't do that to Carol. She's had enough rejections in her life, I'm not going to be the cause of another one. You're not going to blame me for it if you can't put your foot down yourself.'

'Oh!' Jessica couldn't hide her disappointment.

'Isn't she an awful little rip, butting in on your big day like that?' Liz said crossly. 'She's always the same. She'd better not start dictating to me though, that's all I'm saying.' Liz stared at her daughter, her lips a thin line of disapproval.

Oh no, it's going to be an absolute shambles. Jessica was enveloped in a cloud of gloom at the thoughts of her impending wedding.

* * *

Liz sat at her dressing-table smoothing cleanser on to her face. She felt more lonely and disheartened than usual. Jessica's up-coming wedding was going to be even more difficult than she had anticipated. It would be bad enough walking up the aisle with her daughter, trying not to think of Ray, trying to ignore the aching sense of loss that was her constant companion, without having to worry about the potential mayhem that the Logans could cause. Absentmindedly she licked her lips and grimaced at the taste of the lotion. 'Urrggh!' she tutted crossly. She took a sip of wine from the glass that reposed on the dressing-table. They had opened a second bottle after dinner and Liz had enjoyed the rich, fruity Australian Merlot. She didn't care to drink on her own. It was a habit she could get too used to, she felt, so it was a treat when Jessica came home to skull a couple of glasses of wine and feel pleasantly giddy and tipsy.

She wasn't in the slightest bit tipsy or giddy tonight though. Jessica's unwelcome news about the proposed double wedding had upset her. Liz sighed and poured some toner on to a pad. If she were completely honest with herself, she'd have to admit that once Jessica had got engaged to Mike, Liz had dreaded the idea of the wedding. She could hear her darling daughter pottering around in the bedroom next door. It was lovely to have her at home. Jessica's light-hearted presence filled the house, temporarily dispelling the sense of solitude that living alone engendered. She was full of plans about the wedding, full of optimism and looking forward to finding a house with Mike.

She and Ray had been like that once. Buoyed up with the confidence of youth, they had taken so much for granted, she reflected. She stared at her reflection in the mirror. An oval face framed by short, feathery, copper tresses whose few strands of grey were camouflaged by golden highlights. A small snub nose with a dusting of freckles that she hated. A nice enough mouth, neither too full nor too thin, she supposed. She had a slender build that gave her a youthful enough appearance and she'd kept herself fit, dreading the idea of ageing. Liz frowned, annoyed at her vanity. She wasn't pushed now; she could age all she liked. What difference did it make? She wasn't out on the hunt for a man. She didn't look her age, she acknowledged, but her hazel eyes with their flecks of gold were turbulent and unhappy and the lines around her mouth were grooved deeper than she liked. It was a horrible thing to have to admit, but she envied her daughter and couldn't help comparing Jessica's joyful future with her own empty one.

How shallow was that, she thought, disgusted with herself.

She was being thoroughly selfish. Jessica's wedding wasn't about her, and it was up to her to make sure her daughter had as good a day as she possibly could. Ray's absence would be keenly felt by both of them. They were in the same boat in that respect.

But at least Jessica would have Mike to put his arms around her. She'd come home to an empty house, Liz compared unhappily, as in spite of herself tears spilled down her cheeks and she buried her face in her arms to try and stifle the sound of her sobs.

When would the ache go? When would the loneliness and misery ease? It was three years since Ray's death. It might as well have been yesterday, she thought in despair. It was so difficult to accept that their lives together had been so brutally and swiftly ended. It was still almost impossible to believe that she would never snuggle in to him at night or spend hours talking and teasing each other, hearts filled with love and affection.

With Ray she had felt completely and contentedly at ease. He knew her and understood her as no one else ever had. With him she had been totally herself. Now he was gone and she was bereft.

'You're relatively young, Lizzie, you might find someone else,' a well-meaning friend had said, having invited her to a party the previous Christmas.

'Maybe.' Liz had given a non-committal shrug. In her heart of hearts she knew there was little likelihood that she would want to get involved with another man. Ray had been her soulmate. Anyone else would be a poor second best. She couldn't help feeling bitter. If they'd been in their sixties or seventies she might have coped with her loss more easily. But she still felt young; she still had emotional and sexual needs. She was a normal, healthy woman and life stretched ahead of her. It wasn't that she didn't have friends and a good social life. She had, but being surrounded by people was no protection against her abiding feelings of aloneness.

She got up from the dressing-table and went over to the large pine wardrobe that lay along one wall of the bedroom. She opened it and took out a maroon Lacoste pullover that she had bought Ray one year when they were on holiday in Spain. She slipped it on over her nightdress and buried into its softness, still getting the faint musky scent of her husband. Liz stood staring out through the Velux window of the dormer. In the distance she could see the lights of a fishing boat shimmering on the sea. Ray had loved the sea.

'But he's gone now and you have to get on with it. You have to let him go,' Liz muttered angrily. 'You can't keep going around wearing his clothes, you're only doing your head in.' She wasn't the only person in the world to be bereaved – why was she so slow in coming to terms with it? Why was she constantly wallowing in her grief? She was pathetic.

Being a relatively young widow was difficult at the best of times, she thought glumly, as she took another gulp of wine. Several men of her acquaintance had made lecherous, unwelcome approaches that she'd spurned in no uncertain terms. She'd been shocked at their assumption that because she hadn't been with a man for the last few years, she was gagging for it. Their arrogant vulgarity affronted and disgusted her. Had she sent out any signals, albeit unwittingly, she wondered in dismay? Or was it just that they were insensitive, uncouth gobshites? Did other women who'd lost their husbands have these problems, or was it just her?

'Don't mind those scabby fuckers,' her sister, Tara, fumed when Liz broached the subject with her. 'As if any woman would look twice at them.

Don't even take it personally, Liz, they'd try it on with anyone. Sad, pathetic gits. Is it any surprise their wives have probably stopped shagging them? A nympho wouldn't give that pair of losers a look-in.'

Liz had laughed at her sister's outrage. It made her feel marginally better. But then Tara was her champion and always had been. Her sister had got her through the darkest times and was always supportive on this new, rocky unwelcome road of widowhood.

The wives of two of the couples she and Ray had loosely associated with had become quite watchful if she was talking to their husbands. Liz couldn't believe it. What did they think? That she was going to jump on them? Maybe she was naïve. But why did they think that her behaviour was going to be any different now? Hadn't they known her for years? Why did they feel safe with her when she was part of a couple but now that she was on her own view her as a threat? Why did they think that she had suddenly turned into this predator, where no man was safe? Had they no conception of how empty her life without Ray was? Had they no clue as to how much thoughts of her husband still consumed her? There was no room to think about other men. Ray was all she'd wanted in a man. No one else could fill his shoes.

How he would laugh if he were here with her. Liz smiled, her sense of humour coming to the rescue. If her darling Ray were alive, he'd jolly her along about the wedding and it wouldn't seem at all a hassle. But Ray wasn't here and there was nothing she could do about it. She was just going to have to put on a brave face and get on with it. With her sister's help she'd get through it and try to make the wedding the happiest occasion she possibly could for Jessica and Mike.

10

'Come on, you guys, let's hit the road.' Mike rinsed his coffee cup under the tap and turned to look at the others, sprawled around the kitchen table in Gary's apartment.

'Fine by me.' Carol drained her cup and grabbed Gary's mug from him. 'Come on, you, we'll be here all day.'

'Oi! I wasn't finished with that,' he retorted indignantly.

'You can have plenty of coffee when we get to Banagher,' Carol said briskly.

'For crying out loud, it's seven a.m. I need a bloody cup of coffee,' Gary growled.

'Come on, Gary, don't mind those two sad Capricorns that don't know how to enjoy life. Let them at it, we'll have a lovely lie-in tomorrow, and they can get up at the crack of dawn and make breakfast and do the boat checks and set sail and wear themselves out, the poor sad sods.' Jessica yawned so widely she nearly gave herself lockjaw.

'No problem to us,' Mike said smugly, winking at Carol.

'You're my type of woman, Jessie. What am I doing engaged to a lark? Us owls should stick together,' Gary said.

'Umm.' Jessica yawned again.

'Are we safe with you driving, you won't fall asleep at the wheel?' Carol asked worriedly.

'The cheek of you,' Jessica retorted. 'I'll be fine when we get going. Come on, the sooner we get there, the sooner we'll be out on the river.'

Carol picked up her shoulder bag. 'I'm ready.'

Grumbling, Gary hauled himself up from the kitchen table and gave a perfunctory look around. 'Is everything off?'

Carol checked his cooker switch. 'Yep. Come on, give me a hand to clear the table.'

'Leave it, it's fine,' he instructed, unfazed by the marmalade-smeared knife, the toast crumbs and the bottle of milk lying untidily on the melamine table.

'You're a lazy git,' Carol tutted, but she left the dirty table as it was. She wasn't Gary's house-keeper, she'd told him once, and was very put out when he'd told her, 'No one's asking you to be.'

Jessica noted her friend's tight-lipped expression and hoped the pair of them weren't going to bicker for the three-day cruising break on the Shannon.

She'd been so looking forward to a tranquil few days with Mike, lazing along the meandering, majestic river, and then Carol had muscled in and suggested a foursome.

Still, they were all here now, and once people had got over their early morning moods it could be a bit of fun. She was driving. Gary had said he wanted to be able to drink and he didn't want to be tied, driving. Mike had no car and wasn't insured on hers, Carol didn't feel confident enough even though she had taken lessons, so that left Jessica. She didn't mind, she reflected as she slid in behind the wheel. She really wanted Mike to enjoy himself. The exams had been tough but he felt he'd done OK. Now he needed to wind down.

'Can I sit in the front? I don't want to be queasy.' Carol didn't even wait for an answer but just plonked herself in the front seat.

'Aw, Carol, I wanted Mike to map-read for me, I'm not too sure of the route,' Jessica protested. She wanted to be with Mike in the front.

'I'll read it for you,' she said jauntily.

'That will make you sick,' Jessica retorted. 'Why didn't you take a Sea Legs?'

'I forgot.' Carol scowled.

'I'll direct you from the back,' Mike said easily, folding his long lean body into the seat behind her.

'Are you all right there? Are your knees up to your chin?' Jessica fretted.

'I'm fine,' Mike assured her.

'What about my knees and my chin?' Gary demanded petulantly from the other side.

'Ah, bugger you, if you wanted comfort you should have driven your big company car.' Jessica grinned.

'Well, if we'd left at a reasonable hour of the morning instead of the crack of dawn I might have,' he grunted.

'Crack of dawn, my ass,' jeered Carol, settling herself comfortably and stretching out her legs in front of her. She really could be a selfish cow, Jessica fumed as she checked her mirror and started the engine. As long as she got her own way, everything was fine.

The traffic was light as they crossed the city and headed west, and the atmosphere lightened as Jessica endured an unmerciful slagging from the pair of male chauvinists in the back.

'Hold tight, I think we're on a chicane,' Gary

remarked as she took a bend dotted with red and white roadwork cones, fairly sharply.

'Clench your buttocks, there's another one ahead,' Mike teased. 'Hope you're wearing black underpants.'

'Shag off, the pair of you,' Jessica giggled, her sense of humour getting the better of her. It was a soft pastel morning, the sun lightening to buttercup yellow behind them, chiffon wisps of early morning mist hugging the treetops.

'I'm hungry. Can we stop in Mother Hubbard's for a proper breakfast?' Gary asked plaintively.

'You've just demolished two Weetabix and four slices of toast,' Carol remonstrated.

'It's the country air,' her boyfriend declared indignantly.

'What do you mean the country air? We haven't got past Lucan yet,' Jessica scoffed.

'I'm a bit peckish too, come to think of it,' Mike remarked. 'I think a stop in Mother Hubbard's sounds like an excellent idea. Good thinking, buddy.'

'Jessica's the driver. She's in charge. It's her decision,' Carol interjected.

'That's right, it's my decision, so depending on the behaviour from the back, and by that I mean no smart comments, we'll see,' Jessica said smugly, glancing in her rear-view mirror to see Mike grinning at her.

'I wouldn't stand for that, Mike.' Gary shook his head. 'Nip it in the bud now. Don't start letting her dictate at this stage or you won't have a leg to stand on when you're married.'

'Maybe you're right, Gary. In fact that's sound advice, my son. We're stopping at Mother Hubbard's, woman,' he informed Jessica, poking her through the back of the seat. 'The Master has spoken and be careful driving over those pot-holes while you're at it. My ass hasn't as much padding as yours and the suspension in this car leaves plenty to be desired.'

'Mike Keating! The *nerve* of you!' Jessica expostulated, turning to glare at him after she had swerved to avoid a dead bird mashed on the road.

'I surrender! I surrender! Just look where you're going. Please keep your eyes on the road. You're in complete charge,' Mike babbled cravenly, his hands over his eyes.

'I want my mammy,' wailed Gary.

'That's the way to treat 'em,' approved Carol, tittering in the front.

The banter was flying as Jessica pulled into the car park of Mother Hubbard's restaurant little over an hour later. They were all in great form and she felt peckish herself after driving.

'A full Irish for me.' Mike rubbed his hands in anticipation of the fry-up that awaited them as he uncoiled himself from the back of the car and stretched his cramped limbs.

'Me too.' Gary yawned. 'Just what I need to wake me up.'

'Jessie?' Mike inquired.

'Yeah, I could go a couple of rashers and sausages.'

'You lot, you'll have clogged arteries before you're forty.' Carol wrinkled her nose and frowned.

'What are you having, Miss Goodie Goodie?' Gary pinched her ass.

'Stop it, you,' she squealed. 'I'll have fruit and yoghurt.'

'You're a wild, wild woman,' he grinned, throwing an arm affectionately around her shoulder. Carol's face glowed with happiness and Jessica felt glad for her. It was nice to see herself and Gary having a laugh and relaxing in each other's company. Maybe she was wrong to think that they weren't right for each other. Every couple was different. All relationships weren't as easy-going and companionable as hers and Mike's.

She slipped an arm around her fiancé's waist.

136

'Smashing day, isn't it? It will be gorgeous on the river.'

'Just as well, if your woman gets queasy in the back of the car, she'd probably spend the trip barfing every time we hit a wave,' Mike whispered.

'That was a new one on me,' Jessica said drily, snuggling in as Mike's arm tightened around her.

Twenty minutes later the three of them were up to their ears in a steaming, tasty fry-up. Carol sipped orange juice and ate her fruit and yoghurt.

'So what's the plan when we get there?' Gary asked lazily as he pronged a mushroom with his fork.

'Well, we have to shop for a few provisions—'

'Offie won't be open that early,' Mike pointed out.

'We can stock up before we leave. Banagher is full of pubs,' Jessica explained patiently. 'I suggest we get our basics—'

'I hope we don't have to cook – can't we eat out?' Carol remarked.

'Mike and I aren't made of money, Carol, we're saving for a wedding, don't forget—'

'Oh, let's not talk about that,' she said hastily, her face going a deep shade of puce.

'Listen, if we're getting married the last week in September—'

'This September?' Gary put his fork down and looked at Carol and then at Jessica.

'Yeah, I told you during the week that we'd set the date, didn't you say it to Ga—' Comprehension dawned. Carol hadn't discussed it with her boyfriend, obviously. 'Oh!' Jessica said, flustered.

'And when were you going to tell me this?' Gary studied his fiancée stonily.

'Sometime during the weekend when we were all together,' Carol muttered irritably, annoyed at being wrong-footed.

'Now's as good a time as any,' Mike observed cheerily. 'Last Wednesday in September. Kilbride church. Four Winds. Is that OK for you?'

'You want to get married in Arklow in September?' Gary said slowly.

'Kilbride church is in Wicklow, technically speaking,' Mike said lightly. 'But that's the gist of it. If it doesn't suit you, Gary, that's no problem. Do your own thing by all means.'

The colour drained from Carol's face as she watched her fiancé through lowered lashes. Jessica saw her friend's fingers roll tight into fists under the table and felt sorry for her.

'Maybe we should wait, Carol. We'll be broke too if we take the plunge in September, and I was hoping to go to the Munich beer festival in

October with Kenny McCarthy. We'd sort of made arrangements,' Gary said slowly.

'Look, Gary, if you've made arrangements to go to the beer festival with Kenny McCarthy, that's fine. I don't think it should interfere with our wedding plans,' Carol said coolly. 'And once we're married you'll be able to claim tax for me, you might even get a rebate, you can spend it on beer in Germany,' she added tartly. 'Now make up your mind. It's not fair on Mike and Jessie. Are we having a double wedding with them or not?'

Jessica felt her own nails bite into her palms as three pairs of eyes turned to look at Gary.

'We need a simple yes or no, mate,' Mike said firmly.

Gary shifted in his chair and looked at Carol. 'We'll be broke. I was going to take you away for a couple of days to France.'

'We can go to France on our honeymoon if you want, just make up your mind one way or another, Gary!' she snapped.

'Let's leave it,' he said lightly. 'It's a bit soon.'

'Fine,' Carol said tightly.

Jessica couldn't believe her luck. It was just going to be her and Mike after all. God had answered her prayer. She couldn't even bring herself to look at Carol. She knew her friend was gutted. But that wasn't her fault, she argued silently. She'd been prepared to go through with the double wedding. It was Gary who had chickened out.

'More coffee, anyone?' Mike lifted the coffee pot and broke the uneasy silence that had settled on them.

'Not for me, thanks, Mike. I'm just going to pop to the loo.' Carol picked up her bag and pushed back her chair.

'I'll have another,' Gary declared, looking anywhere but at Carol.

'I'm fine, thanks,' Jessica murmured. She'd got what she wanted. Her and Mike on their own for the wedding. Why wasn't she happy? Why did she feel so guilty, knowing that Carol was in the loo probably breaking her heart crying? Why was her happiness always tinged with guilt because Carol's life was such a mess? She wasn't responsible for her friend, why did it always seem as though she was? She never felt like that with Katie. Her and Katie's friendship was one of equals. Why, oh why couldn't it be the same with Carol?

11

Carol just managed to lock herself in a toilet cubicle before the hot tears spurted down her cheeks. Why had Jessica opened her big mouth about the wedding? She'd been going to broach it at some stage over the weekend when Gary was relaxed after a few pints. Now it looked as if she'd never walk up the aisle with him.

Her frustration knew no bounds. How could he be so casual about it all? Didn't he love her? Didn't he want to marry her? He gave every appearance of not wanting to and it was extremely hurtful, not to talk about embarrassing.

Why did he stay with her if he didn't want to marry her? Even worse, why did *she* stay with him? Why didn't she just tell him to get lost? Why didn't she simply do herself a favour and end it? He was a selfish, arrogant, thoughtless bastard who never, ever put her first and she hated herself for being such a doormat.

She was an attractive woman, Carol assured herself. She'd find someone else. But it was Gary she wanted. Her head drooped on her chest as she flipped down the lid of the toilet and sat down. She wanted Gary because she needed to know she could keep a man she had set her sights on. She'd been rejected by a man once . . . her father. No man was ever going to walk away from her again. If anyone did the walking it would be her, and she wasn't ready to walk away yet. Not by a long shot. Carol set her shoulders and lifted her chin.

'Play it cool,' she muttered as she scrabbled in her handbag for a tissue. Gary Davis wasn't ever going to know how much he had just hurt her. She'd never give him the satisfaction, she vowed, as she marched out of the toilet and prepared to do a swift repair job to her ravaged make-up.

Swiftly she dusted Egyptian Wonder over her cheeks and applied fresh lipstick and mascara. She ran a comb through her hair and studied herself in the mirror. Her brown eyes had lost their sparkle and looked dull and lifeless. 'Snap out of it,' she ordered, tweaking a black, silky feather of hair over her forehead. She looked fine, she assured herself. She looked just fine. That bastard would never know just how much his casual indifference had wounded her. Her heart contracted as the sharp new laceration joined the others that festered painfully. It was too much to bear. Her poor heart was in flitters; she should cut her losses and run. Tears threatened to well up again but she bit her lip hard and struggled to regain her composure. 'You can do it, come on. He's not worth it,' she whispered, just before the door was pushed open and a woman and child entered. She had to go. She couldn't stay skulking in the ladies' for much longer.

Taking a deep breath, Carol straightened her shoulders and, head held high, she strode out of the ladies' back to their table.

'That's better,' she said, falsely cheery. 'Have you lot nearly finished your breakfasts yet? Time's moving on, we should be too.'

She saw Gary eye her warily. 'Come on, Gary, eat up,' she chivvied. 'Wow, Jessie, look, there's a fine thing coming in.'

'Oohh yeah, he's a bit of all right,' agreed Jessie as they ogled a denim-clad trucker who had just entered the restaurant. Tall, tanned and rangy, he looked like a young Clint Eastwood.

'Do you mind! If we did that to a woman, you pair would be up in arms,' Mike objected.

'Not at all,' Carol declared. 'We're all for equality, aren't we, Jessie?'

'Sure,' grinned her friend, and Carol could see the relief on her face that she hadn't caused a scene. Bitterness surged. It was all right for Jessie sitting there smug and contented, she was sure of her place in Mike's affections. She had the joy of planning a wedding to someone that loved her.

Still standing, she drained her glass of fresh orange juice. 'Are we going?' she demanded, trying not to sound truculent. It was vital to behave normally and not let on that she was wounded to the core.

'Yeah, let's go,' Jessie agreed, mopping up the last bit of egg yolk with a piece of bread.

'There's no rest on you women.' Gary took a last draught of his coffee as Mike went up to pay. He didn't see the look of vitriol that Carol flashed his way before she turned away and started for the door.

Jessica watched Gary, waiting for him to offer to pay half the bill. Gary and Carol were mean with money unless they were buying something for themselves. Mike and she often ended up paying for the other couple unless they were specifically asked for their share. It infuriated Jessica. Mike only had a part-time job and was putting himself through college; Gary was working full-time.

'I'm off to the jacks, see you at the car,' he said casually, and sloped away from the table without a bother.

She could feel her previous good humour evaporating. Although Carol had behaved as if Gary's postponement of the wedding made not the slightest difference, and done it very well, Jessica thought admiringly, she had seen the tell-tale weepy red in her friend's eyes and known she was in turmoil. And when Carol was in turmoil she never kept it to herself. Some time over the next few days Jessica knew she was in for a session, and in the small confines of a boat there was no escape.

She should have put her foot down and said she and Mike were having a weekend for themselves. And Mike should have objected too, she thought crossly, as she saw her beloved paying the cashier.

'You make sure that they pay half,' she insisted when Mike rejoined her at the table.

'Ah, forget it,' he said easily.

'I will not forget it, Mike, we're not a bloody charity,' she hissed. 'They're always sponging and I'm sick of it. We're saving to get married. There's going to be a kitty on that boat and you're getting what you're owed for the breakfast.'

Mike threw his eyes up to heaven. 'OK, OK, suit yourself,' he sighed and then she felt mean for getting at him. This was supposed to be his break after the exams.

'Mike, it's not that I'm mean,' she explained earnestly as she linked his arm, 'but they do take stuff like that for granted and it's not fair.'

'I know you're not mean, I know what you're saying. I hate asking for the money.'

'We shouldn't have to be asking. They're too bloody casual.'

'OK, we'll organize a kitty like you say. Now don't get grumpy on me,' Mike coaxed. 'Come on, let's go and try and cheer poor old Carol up, even though she's putting a brave front on it. But there's no point in them getting married if his heart isn't in it.'

'I know,' sighed Jessica. 'I've told her that until I'm blue in the face but it doesn't make any difference.'

'He's a queer hawk, sometimes,' Mike mused. 'I just don't think he wants to tie himself up.'

'Do you?' Jessica looked up at him, wondering did he ever have any doubts about them as a couple.

'Do I want to tie myself up?' He smiled down at her, the smile reaching his eyes and crinkling them up the way she loved. 'In knots, Jessie, in knots, as long as it's with you.'

She felt a lump come into her throat and swallowed hard. How could she not love Mike? She was so lucky. Her dad must really be looking after her, she thought gratefully as they reached the car.

'You OK, Carol?' she asked kindly as she opened the door for her friend.

'What do you think?' the other girl said disconsolately.

Jessie gave her a quick hug, conscious that Gary would be out any minute. 'Everything will work out for the best,' she whispered.

'Oh don't talk nonsense. That's easy for you to say,' muttered her friend. 'Come on, let's get going.'

'Sure, as soon as Gary gets in,' Jessica said coolly, stung by her friend's ungraciousness. There was no need for Carol to take it out on her; she'd only been trying to help.

Gary washed his hands and ran a comb through his curly black hair, whistling as he did so. The pressure was off, he wasn't getting married this year, life was good, and he was going to get well and truly bombed tonight, he decided. And, surprisingly, Carol hadn't got into a mega huff and made a scene. She'd seemed quite cool about the whole thing. They'd have their own wedding in a few years' time. They were young; they should enjoy life without tying themselves up in debt. The beer festival would be a blast – he intended getting drunk and getting laid as often as he could while he was in Germany.

Now that this whole wedding issue was settled, he was going to have a ball for the weekend. He could even get lucky. Carol might give in and sleep with him and that would be the icing on the cake.

As happy as a lark, Gary headed towards the car all prepared for an untroubled, boozy weekend on the river.

Mike sat in the back of the car, arms folded across his chest. The tension between Jessica and Carol was palpable. He'd heard how sharply Carol had cut Jessie off and it annoyed him. Jessie had been trying to help. It wasn't her fault that Carol was having difficulties. Carol was such a strange girl. She was so jealous of Jessica and never lost an opportunity to put her down. No matter how hard Jessie tried, it was never enough for Carol. He'd have given up on her long ago if they'd been friends. Women were funny creatures, he mused. He couldn't make head nor tail of them. Still, one good thing about it all, Jessie was going to have the wedding she wanted and he was glad of that. She deserved it. Although he hadn't minded when Carol had first mooted the idea, looking at the hassle it was causing between the girls it wasn't such a good idea, he conceded. A double wedding would have been full of stresses and tensions. They were better off on their own.

He watched Gary strolling over to the car, looking laid back and carefree. He had no idea how strongly Carol felt about him. He couldn't see it at all. He was a bit of an eejit really, Mike reflected, although cute enough when it came to money. You wouldn't get too many pints out of Gary, he thought wryly. Jessie was right. They weren't a charity; the pair of them could pay their way this weekend and, what's more, the petrol money was coming out of the kitty as well. Mike stretched his legs out as much as the cramped space would allow, wishing he were on his own with Jessie.

'Which one is ours?' Carol asked, perking up somewhat an hour later as Jessica drove into the Silver Line Marina.

'One of those.' She pointed out a shapely six-berth cruiser, white with red trim, bobbing up and down against a jetty.

'It's nice.' Carol sounded impressed, and Jessica relaxed a little. There hadn't been much talk for the latter part of the journey but now that they were here humours were rapidly improving. Gary and Mike were craning their necks trying to get a good look, eager to be up on deck and on the move.

'We'd better check in at reception and then go and do a shop for the basics.' Jessica eased into a parking space, relieved that they had finally arrived.

'OK, you go and check in and Gary and I will bring the gear down to the jetty.' Mike uncoiled himself out of the back seat.

'Aye, aye, Captain,' Jessie grinned. 'Come on, bo'sun.' She linked her arm in Carol's, deciding to ignore her friend's earlier petulance. She wanted them all to enjoy their weekend, and she could feel her anticipation rising as she watched the cruisers floating in the sun-dappled water.

Three-quarters of an hour later the four of them were sitting at the small table in the compact lounge waiting for the kettle to boil. They'd been given their maps, binoculars, and the fuel and water tanks had been filled. The boat swayed gently at its moorings, the water lapping against the sides. They were looking forward to setting sail.

'Right, as soon as we have our cuppa, we'll get our supplies and get going,' Carol declared. The excitement of being on the boat had kicked in and they were all starting to relax and have fun.

Mike cleared his throat. 'We need to organize our kitty. Bills divided by four, all agreed?'

'Sure,' Gary assented. Carol nodded.

Mike stepped down into the tiny galley and took a bowl out of the press. 'Kitty bowl, and so far we've to divide out the petrol money and the brekkie bill.'

'Don't forget I didn't have a full breakfast like you gluttons,' Carol remarked tartly. 'And don't include me in the alcohol bill either.' Jessica gave Mike a discreet nudge and he returned the pressure with his elbow. Tight as Carol was with money, this was a new low. Not paying for drink was fair enough, but quibbling about the breakfast bill was a bit over the top. Jessica couldn't help but feel if Carol was being so parsimonious about a breakfast bill, what would she be like about an entire wedding bill.

'You girls should go and do the shopping. Mike and I will do the manly things like checking the engines and the oil—'

'Get lost.'

'You must be joking, you male chauvinist pig.'

The two women turned on Gary, who guffawed at their outrage.

'It was worth a try,' he grinned.

'Good try, mate,' laughed Mike. 'Pity it didn't work. We'd better go and get it over and done with and carry the bags or our lives won't be worth living.'

'Too right.' Jessica gave him an affectionate poke.

They trooped up to the supermarket joshing and laughing, arguing over the contents of their various shopping baskets. Fortunately the off-licence was open, so they stocked up on beer and wine and headed back to their cruiser eager to be off. Mike and Jessica had gone cruising before and knew their route; they were heading for Clonmacnoise, an ancient monastic settlement with a round tower, bathed in history.

When Mike started the engines and Jessica slipped their mooring ropes, they yelled and cheered as they chugged out into the grey meandering river, the sun glinting and glittering on the water, the breeze invigorating against their faces. Mike steered confidently between the red and black perches that marked their route along the river and Jessica came and stood with her arm around his waist, happy for him that his exams were over and he was finished studying.

'Right, I'm going to sunbathe,' Carol announced.

'Do you want to have a go steering?' Mike offered. 'Just let me know if you do.'

'Ta, but I want to lie on deck and feel the sun warming me up. You get a great tan on the river.'

'You're absolutely right.' Jessica raised her face to the sun. 'I think I'll join you.'

'Oi, you pair! This isn't a luxury cruise. You're crew!' Mike remonstrated.

'Aye, aye, skipper, you're doing such a good job we couldn't interfere,' Jessica teased, as she followed Carol below deck to change into their bikinis. Carol and Gary were sharing the forward cabin with the two bunks, on Carol's insistence. Jessica and Mike had the cabin with the double bed in the stern. When they had been booking the cruiser, Carol had asked Jessica if she would share the two-berth cabin with her and let Mike and Gary have their choice of the double beds in the lounge and stern, but Jessica had been adamant. She was sleeping with Mike, and Carol could make her own arrangements with Gary.

'Aw come on, Jessie, pleezzee. If I have to share a bed with him I'll—'

'No, Carol. Just don't start, OK. Mike and I are sleeping together; put Gary up on deck in a hammock if you want to,' Jessica had retorted firmly.

Her friend had not been best pleased, but seeing that Jessica was unyielding, didn't argue any further. Nor, to Jessica's surprise, had she made any comment when Jessica and Mike had dumped their bags into the double cabin. But then the goalposts had moved and the double wedding was off. Was Carol and Gary's relationship off? At this stage nothing would surprise her.

'Sorry I was a cow earlier, I didn't mean to be churlish,' Carol murmured as her friend reached the bottom of the ladder that led from the upper deck. 'I couldn't believe when Gary decided to postpone our wedding. I was so looking forward to the double wedding.'

'That's OK,' Jessica said warily. A penitent Carol was always something to be cautious of. Carol in penitent mode had a way of extracting favours, as Jessica knew to her cost.

'What's his problem, do you think?' Carol fretted, ready for an in-depth analysis of her boyfriend's troublesome psyche.

'Look, let's not waste a second of that sun in

case the weather isn't so good tomorrow,' Jessica urged. 'We'll talk up on deck.'

'Oh! Oh, OK.' The other girl clearly wanted to have a big moaning session, but this time, Jessica was determined. The sun beckoned and she wanted to be out in the fresh air enjoying it, not standing below decks listening to Carol going on and on like a broken record.

They went to their respective cabins and changed rapidly into their bikinis. Jessica gazed in admiration at her friend's long-limbed, toned figure that hadn't an ounce of fat. Perhaps she was right not indulging in cholesterol-laden fry-ups. Her athletic, healthy body was the result of a disciplined lifestyle that Jessica envied, especially when it was time to bare all at bikini time. She held her tummy in as she clambered up the ladder after her, wishing that she wasn't quite so curvaceous and at least two inches taller. She emerged up behind her on to the deck and laughed as the two men whistled in admiration. Carol grinned and sashayed along the side of the boat, aware that Gary was scrutinizing every inch of her.

'Hey, gorgeous!' he called. She blew him a kiss. *Look and dream and wish*, she thought viciously, knowing that she was looking her very best. By the time this mini cruise was finished Gary Davis's tongue would be hanging out.

Conscious that her fiancé was staring at her, she gracefully spread her towel on the deck and began to smooth sun cream on to her legs. Slowly, sensuously, she massaged the cream into her body, stretching this way and that, arching her neck and thrusting out her firm breasts. Beside her, Jessica slathered on her oil any old way, completely unaware of the sexual pantomime Carol was indulging in.

Not looking in Gary's direction but conscious of his gaze upon her, Carol slowly unhooked her bikini top and stretched, lissom as a ballerina, along her towel, massaging the milky sun cream on to her breasts.

'Hey, you're not going topless, are you?' Gary demanded. 'People will see – look, there's a boat coming.'

'So. Let it come, who cares?' Carol drawled lazily.

'I care,' Gary said heatedly. 'I don't want men looking at you – you're my fiancée.'

'Tough. I'm not having strap marks just because you're being prissy.' Carol closed her eyes and sighed with satisfaction. Gary could be quite the jealous type when other men looked at her, and she played on it. 'This is the life,' she declared.

Beside her, Jessica had no problems agreeing. A swan and five little cygnets glided serenely along the far bank. The trees swayed gently in the breeze, the reeds along the riverbank rippling lightly in unison. The sun caressed their limbs and the soothing, rocking motion of the boat was so relaxing Jessica felt herself drift into lethargy. It had been an early start and a long drive and she was tired. The steady thrum of the engine and the slap of water against the side of the boat was rhythmically soothing and her eyelids closed as the heat of the sun infused her body. Drowsiness overcame her and she drifted into contented sleep.

12

Liz Kennedy strolled along Arklow's main street, enjoying the feel of the sun on her face. She had just finished her shift in the small bakery where she worked part-time. Friday, being one of their busiest days, was the day she liked most. Before she left work she had agreed with Nell, her boss, that the bakery would give her a generous discount on Jessie's wedding cake.

She wasn't sure whether each of the couples were planning on having their own wedding cake, or sharing one between them. She hadn't thought to ask her daughter. It was something she'd need to clarify, but she wouldn't be able to do it this weekend, as Mike and Jessica were cruising on the Shannon.

She was walking past the card shop when she noticed Nancy Logan, Carol's mother, coming out of the post office across the street. Maybe Nancy might know what Carol's plans were for her wedding cake. She supposed she really should go and speak to the woman. After all, she too would be involved in this wedding. It was only good manners, Liz thought reluctantly, wondering what sort of humour the other woman was in. You never knew what way you were going to find Nancy. If she was drinking, she'd be aggressive and surly. If she wasn't she'd be feeling sorry for herself and would spend ages listing her complaints. Or else indulging in a tirade against her hapless husband, who had walked out on her ten years previously and made a new life for himself in Dublin with a new woman and a new family.

Liz wondered would Bill Logan be walking up the aisle with his daughter? Nancy would hardly stand for that. It was all going to be very fraught, to say the least. There were so many things to be organized and co-ordinated with Nancy and Carol and also Gary's family. It was all very well arranging to have a double wedding but it certainly meant twice the hassle, Liz thought crossly, as she dithered as to whether to speak with Nancy or not.

'Get it over and done with,' she urged herself, as Nancy fumbled with her handbag and dropped some loose change on the pavement. Taking advantage of a lull in the fast-moving traffic, Liz nipped across the road and bent down to help the other woman pick up her change. 'There you are, Nancy.' She handed the coins to her. 'How are you?'

'Thanks, Liz, I'm fit to be tied to tell you the truth,' the other woman responded crossly, taking a cigarette out of her bag and lighting it. She inhaled great deep puffs from it, and squinted at Liz through the smoke.

'What has you fit to be tied?' Liz asked kindly, thinking how careworn the other woman looked. Her brown hair was lank and unkempt and liberally streaked with grey. Her teeth were stained yellow from smoking; her face lined and grey-looking. It was hard to believe that they were around the same age.

'That Nadine was skipping school, and the headmistress called me in. Talk about making me feel small, she's a right rip, that one. Wouldn't let me smoke or anything. I felt about six years old,' Nancy grumbled. 'It's all Bill's fault. Nadine's never got over him leaving and of course he's got no time for us now that he's ensconced in the lap of luxury up in Dublin with that floozy of his.'

Liz gave a resigned sigh as Nancy launched into a tirade that lasted as far as the pharmacy. 'I have to nip in here for a prescription,' she fibbed. 'I was just wondering if you knew whether Carol wanted a wedding cake of her own or are they going to share the one cake between them? I've got a discount for Jessie's and Mike's. If Carol would like I can get a discount for her if she wants a cake of her own. And I suppose we should exchange guest lists. I know Mike and Jessica want to keep their list small and intimate. They don't have a fortune to be spending,' Liz rattled on airily.

Nancy took another deep drag on her cigarette and looked at Liz, puzzled.

'Guest lists! Wedding cakes! What on earth are you talking about, Liz?' She gave a wheezy cough that came from her toes.

'Er . . . the wedding,' Liz said patiently. She didn't get an overpowering whiff of alcohol as one so often did with Nancy, so why was she being so obtuse? She must be preoccupied with Nadine's misbehaviour.

'Are Jessica and Mike getting married? That's nice,' Nancy said dully.

'Yes, they're having a double wedding with Carol and—' Comprehension dawned. Oh heck! Liz thought in dismay. It looked like Nancy knew nothing about the wedding. Hadn't Carol spoken to her mother about it? What sort of a weird shower were they? Liz wondered as Nancy stared uncomprehendingly at her.

'A double wedding,' she said slowly. 'Carol and Jessica? Well, the little bitch, she never said a word to me about it. And is she expecting me to pay for it while that two-faced creep of a father of hers spends a fortune on that new brat of his and his *mistress*!' The last was uttered with slit-eyed contempt.

'Jessica only mentioned it to me last week,' Liz backtracked hastily. 'I'm sure Carol will talk to you about it soon. They're all on the Shannon this weekend. Isn't it great to be young?' she added with false gaiety, wishing heartily that she hadn't given in to her impulse to talk to Nancy.

'Is that right?' Nancy said sniffily. 'You seem to know far more about my daughter than I do. But then I'm always the last to know anything around this place. Nobody tells me anything. But they're quick enough to come telling me things when it concerns my kids,' Nancy complained bitterly, lighting a fresh cigarette from the butt of the other one. She flicked it on to the road angrily. 'I know nothing about any wedding, Liz, so I can't be of any help to you. Bye.' She marched on down the road, anger and frustration emanating from every pore of her thin, waif-like body.

'Oh bloody hell,' muttered Liz, as she slipped into the pharmacy and bought herself a packet of Nurofen that she didn't need at all.

The minute Jessie had told her about this double wedding notion she knew there was going to be trouble. It hadn't taken long, she thought grimly as she paid for her tablets and set off for home.

Nancy Logan hurried across the bridge that spanned the Avoca river, oblivious to the ducks that gabbled gregariously at the riverbank or to the small pleasure craft bobbing on the white-capped waves. A neighbour saluted her but she never noticed her as she hurried along angrily, her shoulders hunched, her face drawn and tight-lipped.

Humiliation seared through her. Twice this day she had suffered mortification and indignity. This was the third time she had been called to the school over her youngest daughter Nadine's behaviour and she was at her wits' end with her.

Miss Mackenzie, the headmistress, had been scathing. 'It's not good enough, Mrs Logan. We will not have the reputation of the school affected by your daughter's totally unacceptable behaviour. She has had two previous warnings. This is her last. I won't tolerate it, Mrs Logan. I suggest you deal with her in an appropriate manner,' the headmistress upbraided. 'For example, curtail her social activities. I've heard reports of her drinking in pubs in the town. Put a stop to it. I know she's not the only one, nevertheless she seems to be the one who causes the most trouble,' lectured the other woman bossily. 'No wonder she's missing school if she's hungover.'

Nancy felt like slapping her smug fat face. Unthinking, she took her cigarettes out of her bag and prepared to light up. '*Mrs Logan*, this is a non-smoking school!' Miss Mackenzie's beady black eyes reminded Nancy of two wizened little prunes as she glared at her.

'Sorry,' she muttered, shoving her fags back into her bag, mortified and raging at being made to feel like a six-year-old.

'I sincerely hope this is the last time I have to speak to you about Nadine, because she is very definitely on her last chance in the school. I hope I make myself clear, Mrs Logan.' The principal picked up a sheaf of papers and swept out of the office, leaving Nancy trembling with fury.

'Bloody, snooty cow, who the hell do you think you are? No wonder a man wouldn't have ye,' she muttered, as she opened her bag and took a hasty slug of the small bottle of vodka she'd brought for comfort. Tears smarting in her eyes, she left the parlour where the interview had taken place and walked as fast as she could down the beeswaxed polished corridor, the sound of her heels clacking noisily breaking the inexorable silence. Had that arrogant, self-important woman no idea of the hardships Nancy had endured? Her husband deserting her, leaving her with two strong-willed daughters to rear alone. Nadine was wild and unruly purely because she had no father's firm, guiding influence, Nancy thought sorrowfully as she let herself out of the convent and breathed the salty tangy breeze that whispered through the foliage of the tree-lined driveway.

It was an enormous relief to be out of the oppressive atmosphere that brought back bad memories of her own school days. Nancy took a surreptitious slug of her vodka and hurried through the wrought-iron gates, deeply relieved that the ordeal was over. She felt beleaguered and oppressed. She didn't know how to deal with Nadine. Her daughter took no notice of her. Grounding her didn't work; she'd sneak out anyway and just tell Nancy to shut up when she tried to remonstrate with her. How did you deal with a teenager who ignored you?

Nancy had tried stopping her allowance, but Nadine had just stolen money from her purse. Carol was no help, she hardly ever came home, and when Nancy tried to talk to her husband he just muttered excuses on the phone and hung up. It made her feel helpless and hopeless, and there were times when she hated her youngest daughter for being an affliction that she could no longer bear.

The final straw had been meeting Liz Kennedy and finding out that Carol was getting married and she hadn't even mentioned it. Carol might as well have slapped her across the face. She was a selfish, ungrateful daughter who had forgotten very quickly the sacrifices her mother had made for her. If it weren't for Nancy pushing her, she wouldn't be in that well-paid, safe, secure job in Dublin. As soon as Carol had got her job, she'd shaken the dust of Arklow from her shoes and left her mother and sister to manage as best they could with no help from her. She needn't come running to her looking for money to pay for her goddammed wedding.

Tears slid down Nancy's cheeks as she hastened across the bridge. She couldn't wait to get home and close the door on the world. There was no one she could turn to, no one who understood her misery. She was beleaguered and alone, and it was no wonder she was often tempted to swallow a handful of pills and drink herself into oblivion and end her miserable existence.

'Come on, Carol, have a drink,' Gary urged. He was busy barbecuing steaks and salmon, and having drunk several cans of beer he was cheery and feeling no pain.

'No, Gary, I'm fine,' Carol said edgily. She hated it when her fiancé tried to force drink on her. Drink meant loss of control, and if she lost control, God knows what she would end up doing. She'd sleep with him at the very least, she knew that. And that would be the end of them.

'Party pooper,' Gary taunted, but she ignored him and busied herself buttering thick chunks of Vienna roll to accompany their barbecue.

'Sure you wouldn't have a glass of wine?' Mike urged. 'We have plenty.'

'OK, then, just a glass of red, Mike. Thanks,' Carol agreed. One glass wouldn't kill her. Red wine in moderation was supposed to be good for you, but one was her limit. What Mike or Gary didn't realize was that she had a deep fear of alcohol. She had seen the effects drink had on her mother. She reckoned Nancy was an alcoholic, although her mother would deny it vehemently. Alcoholism ran in families. She was afraid to go too far down the road of drink in case she was inexorably sucked into it.

She knew the others thought she was a goody-goody, keeping off alcohol as some part of a healthy living option. They didn't understand. None of them understood. People at work thought she was stand-offish for not going to booze-ups any more. She'd gone to enough of them to dread the invitation to one. They always ended up the same, with people legless drunk by the end of the night, the more flaky ones hurling abuse at colleagues or bosses they disliked.

Once at a leaving do she'd seen a girl from a firm of solicitors throwing a glass of beer over her boss because he told her to calm down. When another colleague had intervened she'd abused her with a tirade of invective ending in the C word. Everyone in the pub thought it was hilarious, but it made Carol feel tense and sick. She hated it when Gary got drunk. Drunks enraged and frightened her, made her feel helpless and out of control.

She took the proffered glass and sipped gingerly. 'Good girl,' approved Gary. 'We'll have you squiffy in no time.'

Carol said nothing. She sat on a rock looking out

over the river, watching the sun begin to dip in the sky. It was a glorious evening. Birdsong and the cry of sheep intermingled with the slap of water against the boats and jetty and the sound of laughter and conversation as the various boat crews prepared their evening meals. Some chose to eat on their boats, others, like themselves, choosing to barbecue. The aroma from Gary's smoking barbecue was tantalizing, and Carol's stomach rumbled in anticipation. She was starving. It had to be the result of having spent most of the day on the river.

If Gary hadn't ruined it for her with his postponement of the wedding, it would have been a perfect day, she thought sadly as she sipped the rich, fruity red wine and ate a spare rib that her fiancé had cooked for starters.

She looked at Jessie and Mike, arms around each other's waists as they watched the sunset companionably from the river's edge. There were no uncertainties in their relationship. They always seemed so united. So rock solid. Perhaps Jessie was right. Perhaps it was time to face the fact that she and Gary were far from perfect together. In fact, comparing them to the other couple, Carol sometimes felt they were an unmitigated disaster. If Gary truly wanted to marry her, he wouldn't have humiliated and rejected her by postponing the wedding.

Maybe it was time to cut her losses and end it once and for all.

13

'Come on, woman, take me to bed.' Mike yawned and stretched. 'It must be the fresh air, I can't keep my eyes open.'

'Don't forget we were up at the crack of dawn,' Gary reminded him as he opened another can of beer.

'True, and we had a hair-raising drive—'

'Watch it,' Jessica giggled. She was pleasantly tipsy. It was close on midnight and it had been a long day.

'How 'bout you, sexy?' Gary raised his glass to Carol.

'I'm whacked too and cold,' she said tiredly. 'I'm going to bed.'

'The double bed?' Gary inquired hopefully. 'I'll warm you up.'

'No, thanks,' Carol said shortly. 'Night, all.'

Mike and Jessica exchanged glances. 'Let's make ourselves scarce,' he murmured.

They clambered on to their lightly swaying boat and climbed down the stairs to their cabin. Carol followed and made her way to the two-berth cabin at the front of the boat. She grabbed the extra quilt and sheets for the double bed out in the lounge, added the pillows to her load and dumped them on to the leatherette couch that turned into a bed.

'There, see if I care any more,' she muttered. She had spent the day trying to pretend that everything was normal between herself and Gary, and at times, as they'd enjoyed the first leg of their jaunt, it had seemed like it was. But then she'd see her fiancé joking, laughing, having fun with the others, seemingly without a care in the world, and resentment would flare and her good spirits would dip and it would be a struggle to maintain her equilibrium.

The cumulative disappointments of her relationship coalesced into a heaviness of heart that was almost physical. Today had been the toughest day she'd had in a long time, she reflected, as she walked slowly back into her cabin and began to undress. That's what her relationship with Gary was lately, disappointment after disappointment. Was that what her life with him would be like? Was that what she wanted? She couldn't keep running away from it any longer. It was time to face facts.

With grim determination Carol took off her engagement ring. There was no point in wearing it any longer. The charade was over. She placed it on the little shelf at the side of her bunk. Her finger felt naked without it. So many hopes had been invested in that ring, now all dashed. Well, at least she wasn't a total doormat and that could only be a good thing. It was a very small consolation.

Ten minutes later she was lying in one of the narrow bunks, listening to the steady, rhythmic swish of the water against the bow. She felt strangely calm. Even making the decision to end her engagement was a relief. Waiting for Gary to end it was doing her head in. At least she was the one to do the dumping. Better than being dumped for sure, she comforted herself.

Carol lay curled up and wide-eyed in the dark. They were sailing to Athlone tomorrow, and she was going to get off the boat and take a train or bus to Dublin. Now that she had made up her mind she wanted out. And she didn't want to spend another minute in Gary's company. He'd hurt her for the last time, she thought forlornly, as

173

hot, salty tears ran down her cheeks on to her pillow.

The boat creaked and dipped as he stepped on to the deck, and she hastily wiped away the tears, determined that he wouldn't find her less than composed. He'd had a good bit to drink, so there was no point in giving him his ring back tonight. It wouldn't have the impact on him that it would if he was sober. Come to think of it, she didn't even want to talk to him now. She switched out her light and heard him curse as he stumbled on the stairs.

'Hey, hey, Carol, you could have made up the bed for me,' he whispered loudly, sticking his head around her door. 'Come on out and make the bed with me and sleep in it with me. Having a ride with the boat rocking up and down will be brilliant. Come on, Hon, let's give it a lash.'

Carol's lips tightened. Gary was incredible. He never let up. He was such a self-centred bastard. It was always about him ... always. Never, ever about her. Fury suffused her and put iron in her soul. She was glad he was drunk, otherwise she would have rounded on him and all the hurt and anger she had swallowed down this past year would have erupted into a volcano of fury. And that wasn't how she wanted to walk away. She was going to walk calmly, coolly, just as she always was with him when the stakes were high. He was never going to know how deeply she felt. She wouldn't give him the satisfaction, she thought bitterly, as she heard him curse under his breath and close her door none too gently.

To her surprise, she slept well. Anger and heartbreak had turned to exhaustion and the gentle swaying motion of the boat had a womblike quality that rocked her to dreamless sleep. She woke just as the dawn was breaking through the pearly mists on the river. Quietly she climbed out of her bunk, wrapped a fleece around her and made her way up on deck. Mike and Jessica were already there, watching the sunrise with delight.

'Isn't it beautiful?' Jessie enthused, motioning to the majestic grey stone tower rising out of the pink-tipped wisps of misty dawn with a white-gold sun rising behind it. The beauty of the scene before her was so mystical, so ethereal, that her breath caught in her throat. Loneliness smote her. A scene like this was for sharing just the way Mike and Jessica were experiencing it. Would she ever be able to share beauty like this with anyone? Not with Gary, that was for sure. He'd never see such magnificence. He'd be too busy whingeing and moaning about being up so early.

With a resigned sigh, she left Mike and Jessica to their magic moment and climbed below deck to put the kettle on for a pot of tea. She clattered around the small galley hoping that she would wake Gary up and annoy him, but he snored on oblivious. She brought her friends up two mugs of hot steaming tea and a plate of buttered toast and marmalade. They fell on it gratefully and Carol envied them their simple enjoyment of life. When they asked her was she not joining them she made the excuse that it was too chilly. She didn't want to be a gooseberry and besides, horrible though it was to admit, she was jealous of their closeness and happiness when her own relationship was falling disastrously apart.

She put her orange juice, yoghurt, muesli and tea on a tray and took it into her cabin, where she ate, looking out of the small porthole at the mists caressing the river and the tips of the trees.

Now that she had made up her mind that it was over she was anxious to leave, and she wished that they would get under way and head to Athlone.

It was another two hours before they finally started up the engines. Gary had dawdled over his breakfast and then they'd decided to have another mug of tea on deck after the engine and oil checks.

'Sure what hurry are we in anyway?' Gary said cheerfully, quite unaware of Carol's intentions. She couldn't decide whether to tell him she was going back to Dublin before they set sail or wait until they got to Athlone. She looked at him standing on deck, hair damp from his shower, his forearms tanned and muscular as he coiled a rope, and felt a wave of sadness for what they could have had if he hadn't been such a jerk. She turned away and slipped below to her cabin to pack her bag.

'Carol's very subdued, isn't she?' Jessica remarked to Mike as she steered their boat away from their berth and out into the river.

'Don't get involved, let them at it,' Mike advised. 'And steer out a bit into the middle, you don't want us to run aground.'

'Did I tell you how to steer, bossy boots? Zip it!'

'OK, but don't come screaming to me if you land up in the bank—'

'Oh, go and make me a cup of coffee and stop talking rubbish,' Jessica ordered crisply, throttling forward to full steam ahead once she was clear of the jetty and the other cruisers.

'Go easy,' Mike exclaimed.

'Coffee.'

Her beloved disappeared below decks, eyes rolling dramatically, and Jessica settled back into her seat to enjoy steering the boat. She was thoroughly enjoying herself. It was a pity that Carol wasn't; it took the good out of things. She smiled over at her friend, who had just come up with her book. She sat down on the wooden deck, face raised to the sun.

'Are you OK there, Carol? Will I ask Mike to get you a cup of coffee?' she asked, slowing down as river etiquette required when passing another cruiser coming in the opposite direction.

'Naw, I'm fine.' Carol yawned and patted some suntan cream on to her face.

'Do you want a go?'

'No, you keep on driving.'

'Steering,' Jessica corrected her with a grin. 'How are things? Everything sorted?' she inquired delicately. Gary was stretched out, preparing to snooze, in the bow. He was obviously still recovering from his hangover. He couldn't hear their conversation.

'I've made up my mind about something,' Carol said slowly, coming to stand beside Jessica.

'And what's that?' Jessica throttled up again and their speed increased.

'I'm breaking it off with Gary,' she confided, shoving her hands into her jeans pockets.

'What!' Jessica turned to look at her, astonished. Never in a million years did she think Carol would have the guts to end it.

'Look where you're going or we'll be aground. You're very near that perch,' Carol said drily.

'Yikes!' Jessica hastily adjusted the wheel, and concentrated for a moment or two on getting back into the middle of the river. 'Have you said it to him?'

'Nope, I'm saying it to him when we get to Athlone. I'm giving him his ring back and I'm going back to Dublin.'

'Oh, Carol, I'm sorry.' Jessica put an arm around her friend's shoulder and hugged her.

'Well, you were always telling me I should end it if I wasn't happy. I guess I'm taking your advice.' Carol stared unhappily into the distance, face taut.

Jessica couldn't be sure, but was there an accusatory barb in the last sentence? 'Only end it if it's what you want to do, not because of anything I've said,' she said carefully.

'Well, you never thought we were right for each other,' Carol retorted, and Jessica suddenly had the feeling that she was being blamed, that the break-up was all *her* fault.

'At the end of the day, what I think doesn't matter. It's what you think that counts,' she countered defensively.

'Yeah, I know.' Carol gave a wry smile. 'I never thought I'd have the guts to do it. I'm kinda glad I'm not a total wimp.'

'I think you're doing the right thing and I think you're really brave. The right one is out there for you, you'll see.' Jessica offered the old cliché as sincerely as she could.

Carol's face crumpled and tears filled her eyes. 'I thought he was the right one. I'm not very good at judging men. I really love him but he doesn't love me,' she whimpered.

'Carol, don't cry, please don't cry. It will be all right. Honest,' Jessica comforted earnestly, hating to see her friend so miserable

'I know, I know.' Carol wiped her eyes with the back of her sleeve. 'Listen, will you do me a favour?'

'Sure, anything.'

'When we get to Athlone, will you and Mike make yourselves scarce for a few minutes until I get it over and done with?'

'Of course, Carol,' Jessica agreed unhesitatingly.

'And don't tell Mike until I'm gone. He's so nice, that if he gives me any sympathy at all I'll start bawling and I really don't want to do that. I want to be totally composed. I'm not making a holy show of myself in front of Gary Davis.'

'Dead right you're not. Don't give him the satisfaction,' Jessica said grimly, as Mike's head appeared through the hatchway and then the rest of him, with her coffee.

'Want a cup?' he asked Carol.

'What, me poison my body with coffee? I think not.' She arched an eyebrow at him and he laughed.

'Some peppermint tea then?'

Carol smiled and reached up and kissed him on the cheek. 'You're a nice guy, Mike, pity there aren't more like you.'

'Well, that's nice. Did you hear that, Jessie?' He winked at Carol and jerked his thumb in Jessica's direction. 'She thinks I'm a bossy boots.' He grinned.

'Well, maybe you are just a bit, in the nicest possible way,' Carol teased. 'Couldn't cope with it myself, but horses for courses.'

'Thanks, so now I'm a horse,' Jessica interjected drily.

'A stubborn mule would be more like it,' Mike suggested.

Jessica stuck her tongue out at him. 'Get down

181

to the galley, boy, where you belong, and bring me up a cheese sandwich – I'm starving.'

'You've only just had breakfast,' he protested.

'That was ages ago, all this fresh air is making me ravenous.'

'*She's* the bossy one,' Mike declared as he went below to do as he was bid.

'That's the difference between Mike and Gary,' Carol mused. 'If I asked Gary to go and make me a cheese sandwich he'd be just as likely to tell me to get lost. He's a selfish pig.' She couldn't contain her anger.

Jessica didn't know what to say. She couldn't really jump to Gary's defence without seeming disloyal to Carol, and she didn't want to agree with her either, in case, at some future date, they got back together and Gary would once again be the big cheese.

'Umm,' she murmured, pretending to concentrate on a narrow stretch of water ahead.

By the time the lock at Athlone came into sight she could feel a tension headache coming on, knowing what was ahead. Would Gary go back to Dublin too? Jessica hoped he would. It would be very awkward otherwise. Carol was below in her cabin; Gary was stretched out on deck reading a big chunky thriller at the front of the boat, happily unaware of what lay ahead for him.

'Mike, when we dock in Athlone, you and I have to make ourselves scarce. Carol wants to have a few words with Gary,' she murmured, as her fiancé peered through the binoculars to see if there were many cruisers queuing to get into the lock.

'They're not going to have a row, are they?' he groaned. 'I thought she was taking the postponement very calmly. Too calmly in fact.'

'Hmm, well, she's not, so we'll leg it for an hour or so, OK?'

'OK, whatever you say,' he said easily. 'Do you want me to take over now?'

'I'm fine,' Jessica said firmly, determined to stay in command of her vessel, annoyed that he felt he was the only one who could steer them into a lock.

'Locks can be tricky, you should slow down a bit,' he warned. 'I think I should do it. You can do one of the smaller ones.'

'Just get Gary and Carol to stand by the ropes,' Jessica said tightly, beginning to feel a bit nervous as the lock began to loom large and the weir to the right of them suddenly seemed very threatening. Pride, however, would not let her hand over. Mike's attitude was now thoroughly annoying her.

'Hey, you guys, look to your ropes, lock coming up!' Mike yelled.

Gary scrambled to his feet and Carol hurried up the ladder.

'Hey, are you not taking over, mate?' Gary called in surprise as he uncoiled his rope.

'Jessica wants to take her in.' Mike hooked his thumbs into his jeans and shrugged.

'And why not?' Carol said tartly. 'You go, girl. You're well able for it.'

Oh crumbs! Jessica thought anxiously as her palms began to sweat. She couldn't back down and lose face now, but as she steered nearer the lock and the current seemed to get stronger she was half petrified. There were four other cruisers ahead of them, but to her relief the huge lock gates swung open, disgorging the cruisers coming back down river. At least she'd be able to steer straight in without having to tie up at the quay first. She eased back on the throttle, feeling the pull of the current as it tugged the boat to the right.

'Don't slow down too much or you'll swing out towards the weir,' Mike warned.

'You're a bit near the wall there,' Carol warned moments later as they closed in on the lock, close on the tail of another cruiser. She grabbed a mop and pushed them away from the wall.

'Mind the gates, mind the gates! For crying out loud, Jessie, watch where you're going! Will you slow the bloody thing down!' Mike was nearly dancing a jig with agitation.

'Shut up,' she hissed. 'I can't concentrate with you yelling in my ear. You just told me not to slow down too much.'

'I'm not yelling in your ear!' he roared. 'Look what you're doing. For God's sake, mind your stern.'

The warning came too late as she whacked the stern off the gate.

'For crying out loud, Gary, use your boathook and push us away and stop standing there doing nothing,' she yelled over at him.

'Ah, calm down, woman,' Gary called back lazily, enjoying the drama. 'Let Mike do it. You're making a bags of it.'

'You shut up,' Carol ordered furiously.

'Let me do it,' Mike barked. 'You're making a show of us.'

To her absolute disgust, he pushed her aside and took the wheel.

Incensed, Jessica rounded on him. 'How *dare* you, Mike,' she stormed. 'You've no business—'

'Be quiet, Jessie.' Mike manoeuvred the cruiser into place skilfully. 'Throw up the ropes,' he instructed his crew. Gary was breaking his heart laughing as he joined them a minute later.

'There's women drivers for you,' he jeered. 'They should leave it to the experts.'

Carol was stony-faced.

'There, that's how you do it,' Mike growled as he switched off the engine.

'Is that right, Mister Know-All. Well, if you ever, *ever* manhandle me again and treat me like that, you'll be getting your ring back just like that laughing hyena is getting his.' She glowered at Gary. 'You think you're so funny, don't you? Well, Carol's going to wipe the smirk off your face and not before time, Mister Smart Guy.'

'What?' Gary chortled. 'What are you talking about?'

'Jessie!' exclaimed Carol. 'That's not the way I wanted to do it!'

'Sorry,' muttered Jessica, almost in tears of temper.

'Hey, what does she mean by that crack?' Gary demanded, staring at Carol. 'What do you mean, that's not the way you wanted to do it? Do what?'

Carol took her ring out of the back pocket of her jeans.

'You didn't even notice I wasn't wearing it. Take your ring back, Gary, I don't want it. I'm ending it,' she said coolly.

'You're *what*?' His voice rose.

'Don't yell at me, Gary. I'm ending it. It's not what I want. You're not what I want—'

'Is this because I postponed the wedding? I thought you were being a bit cool,' he demanded.

'It's just an accumulation of stuff, Gary. Postponing the wedding's only a small part of it. The tip of the iceberg.' Her voice was admirably steely and she was totally composed.

'What else is there?' he said aggressively.

'This is neither the time nor the place. I've no intention of discussing our relationship and *your* deficiencies in the middle of the Shannon, if you don't mind. As soon as we tie up, I'm out of here. I'm going back to Dublin.'

'You can't do that,' he protested, stunned.

'Watch me,' she snarled.

'Now look what you've done,' Mike exclaimed in dismay as he watched Carol stalk below deck.

'I haven't done anything. She was going to break it off anyway, she told me earlier,' Jessica exploded wrathfully, enraged at his attitude and lack of loyalty. 'And you know something else? I'm going home too, I've had enough of you and this bloody cruise. Go and piss off.' She disappeared down the hatch, leaving Mike and Gary staring at each other.

'Have they got double dose PMT or something?' Gary muttered, shaking his head in disbelief.

'Don't ask me! They're women, aren't they? You don't need any more explanation than that,' Mike snapped, browned off at the turn of events.

'Do you think we should call them up to do the ropes?' Gary asked, as the lock gates creaked slowly open what seemed like an eternity later.

'You can risk it if you want. I'm keeping the head down,' Mike muttered as he started up the engine.

'Yeah, maybe they'll have cooled down by the time we've tied up over there.'

'You're being a bit optimistic, aren't you, mate?' Mike replied as he steered slowly out of the lock and headed across the river to tie up at the quays opposite.

'We could always just carry on going, and not tie up at all? Lough Ree takes a couple of hours to cross. They might have come to their senses by then,' Gary said slowly.

'Are you crazy? Jessie'd go berserk. She's really mad with me as it is. I should have been a bit more diplomatic about taking over, I suppose. She's got a fierce temper when she's riled. Which isn't that often, thank God.'

'I've never seen her as mad as that. Her eyes were spitting fire. I thought she was going to clatter you. Carol was completely the opposite, all cool and snooty. You can't fight with her properly – she just goes all cold and icy. She's some nerve giving me my ring back. I might keep it if she's not careful,' he said sulkily. 'That would really call her bluff.'

'I wouldn't say anything about bluffing if I were you, not unless you want to end up in the drink,' Mike advised drily.

'I *need* a drink.' Gary scowled as he picked up the rope and prepared to jump quayside.

Down in the double cabin, Jessica stuffed her clothes into her bag. She was damned if she was staying on the boat with that pair of male chauvinists. Mike had treated her like a child, an imbecile, and she wasn't having it. He'd want to learn a bit of respect.

She wondered if Carol was annoyed with her. She shouldn't have said what she'd said. She was so mad at Mike, and Gary had seriously got to her with his smart-arsed comments, that it had just come blurting out of her. Now she wished she'd kept her mouth shut. Carol had a right to be irked with her, she thought gloomily as she slipped out of her cabin and made her way through the lounge. They were still chugging along the river, although she could see the quayside looming closer.

'Carol,' she said hesitantly, knocking on the other girl's door. 'Carol?'

The door opened and her friend stood there, bag packed, make-up on, jacket over her shoulder.

'Carol, I'm really sorry, I was just so angry—'

'Forget it, Jessie, I would have probably done the same myself. Just who do that pair think they are, treating us like idiots? We soon wiped the smirks of their faces, didn't we?' she said viciously. 'Are you really coming home?'

'You bet I am.' Jessica was grim-faced.

'What about the car?'

'Bloody hell, I forgot about that.'

'We could rob the kitty and get a taxi back to Banagher,' Carol said slowly.

Jessica gazed at her friend in admiration. 'Good thinking. Anyway, they'd only spend it on getting pissed otherwise, so we're helping them as well as helping ourselves.' She stepped up into the galley and took out the kitty bowl. 'How much?'

'All of it!' Carol said firmly. 'Let's treat ourselves to a nice nosh-up on the way home.'

A bump and a throttling back of the engine noise told them they were at the quayside. They bumped against the wall again, the boat rocking unsteadily. 'Not a perfect mooring by any manner or means. Captain Bligh is losing his touch,' Jessica said acerbically.

Carol laughed in spite of herself. 'You should have seen his face when you let fly. He was flabbergasted.'

'I should think so,' Jessica retorted. 'How dare he treat me like that? He'd better cop on to himself.' The engine stopped.

'Ready?' Carol looked her straight in the eye.

Jessica took a deep breath. 'Yep. I'll just get my bag.'

A minute later they were up on deck.

'Aw, come on, girls,' Mike groaned. 'Don't be like that.'

'Don't be childish,' Gary remonstrated. 'That's taking things too far, grow up.'

'No, *you* grow up, Gary Davis.' Carol threw her bag on to the quay and stepped off the boat.

'Don't do this, Jessie,' Mike warned.

'Why, what will you do? Spank me for being naughty?' she said sarcastically. 'You're not my father, Mike, stop acting like you are. You showed a complete lack of respect for me over in that lock.'

'Ah, stop talking nonsense, Jessie, you were making a dog's dinner of it. I had to step in and take over or you'd have damaged the boat—'

'I would *not* have damaged the boat. I'd have been fine if you hadn't been yelling in my ear making me lose concentration,' Jessica fumed, following Carol on to dry land.

'If you go that's the end of us.' Mike's face suffused a deep puce with temper.

'Fine!' Jessica retorted. 'Fine! Fine! Fine!'

14

'Let them go.' Mike was hopping mad as he watched Jessica walk along the quays, head in the air. He couldn't believe that she was leaving him stuck on the Shannon, ending the couple of days they had so looked forward to. He couldn't believe that she would flip over something as silly as a tiff about who steered the cruiser into a lock. And he couldn't believe that she'd been so crass as to interfere in Carol and Gary's business just because she couldn't keep her temper. But most of all he couldn't believe that she'd walked away when he'd said that if she did it would be the end of them.

That cut to the quick.

He watched them disappear up a side road that led to the town.

'Goodbye and good riddance,' he muttered.

'They'll come running back,' Gary scoffed. 'They'll probably go up the town, indulge in a bit of retail therapy, have a coffee and come back full of the joys.'

'Aren't you concerned that Carol's given you your ring back?' Mike asked, puzzled at the other bloke's lack of disquiet.

'Nah! It will all blow over. She's mad about me. She probably thinks it will make me change my mind about postponing the wedding, but she's barking up the wrong tree there. She won't be getting the ring back for a while though, and by then you guys will have made all the arrangements for your wedding and it will be too late. So really, she's played right into my hands. It's win, win, mate,' Gary maintained confidently.

Mike frowned. Gary was very casual about his relationship; *he* might just be the one barking up the wrong tree, he thought cynically, as he sat behind the steering-wheel wondering what to do next.

'Let's go for a pint,' Gary suggested. 'It's lunchtime, we could get a chippie or something seeing as our women aren't going to cook for us.'

'Ah, I'm not really hungry.'

'Let me give you a word of advice as regards women,' Gary said firmly. 'Never, ever let a woman come between you and your pint, or you and your grub, or you'll spend your life parched and starving. Now come on. I've had plenty of experience with temperamental women and the best thing you can do is ignore their little tantrums and get on with normal life.' He punched Mike in the arm. 'Come on, Mike, chin up and be very cool with her when she comes crawling back and she'll think twice about pulling a stunt like that again. Believe me.'

It hadn't knocked a feather out of the other man, Mike reflected as he went below deck to get his wallet. Maybe Gary was right. He was taking this all too seriously. But he and Jessica rarely fought and it was distressing when they did.

Gary poured some Hugo Boss between his palms and slapped it on to his cheeks. There were a few nice birds on some of the boats moored along the quays; he might bump into some of them in the pub and indulge in a bit of light flirting just to pass the time. He couldn't very well bring one back to the boat and shag her. It might upset Mister Goody-Goody too much. He'd probably rat on him to Carol. But if the opportunity arose and he was invited back to one of their boats he was going to jump at it like a shot, Gary decided, as he dragged a comb through his curly black hair.

Just who did Carol think she was, throwing his

ring back at him in front of Jessie and Mike? She'd a bloody nerve, he thought indignantly. She was very close to being kicked out of his life for good. There were times he'd regretted getting pissed and asking her to marry him. Now was his chance to get out of it for good if he wanted and the sweet thing was he wouldn't emerge from the débâcle looking like a shit. Oh no siree, he thought as he studied his reflection in the mirror. Carol had done the walking and now he was in total control of his own destiny. He grinned, noting his even white teeth and how good the light tan he'd got on the river made him look. He felt as free as a bird and he was going to damn well enjoy that freedom for a while. Although she didn't realize it, Carol had done him the greatest favour ever and he was going to make the most of it.

'You know, I bet we won't be gone twenty minutes before Gary suggests going to the pub and he'll be chatting up every blonde bimbo he gets the chance to,' Carol said glumly as they sat in a small café, she drinking hot water and lemon, Jessica drinking strong coffee.

'I can't believe Mike issued an ultimatum like that. That's very serious,' Jessica grumbled. 'He shouldn't play games with our relationship.'

'Maybe he *was* serious,' Carol remarked unhelpfully. Jessica's eyes widened.

'Well, if he was, I'll never speak to him again,' she said irrationally, biting into a large, gooey chocolate éclair, the most comforting thing she could lay her hands on to help sustain her through her emotional turmoil.

She was very, very hurt that Mike had issued such a harsh ultimatum. Did that mean that every time they had a row he was going to use emotional blackmail on her? Well, he'd picked the wrong woman to try that little ploy on, she thought angrily, as she demolished the éclair without having tasted any of it.

'Here's our taxi, let's go,' she said crisply, seeing the taxi pull up outside. They'd asked one of the waitresses to call it for them when they'd ordered their snack.

'Yeah, let's shake the dust of Athlone off our feet. It won't hold happy memories for me,' Carol said darkly as she hefted her bag off the floor.

They sat in silence in the taxi, lost in their own thoughts, and despite the taxi man's best efforts to engage them in conversation, he eventually had to give up when their monosyllabic rejoinders made it quite clear he was getting nowhere fast.

It was a relief to get behind the wheel of her

own car eventually, and without further ado Jessica started the engine. She reversed out of her parking space in the marina, unable to believe that she was driving home to Dublin without Mike and that their relationship was in serious trouble.

Carol sat beside Jessica, glad that she didn't have to drive the long trip to Dublin. It was a real bonus that she wasn't stuck on her own on a bus or train after the trauma she'd endured. It was an even bigger bonus that Jessie and Mike were having a spat. It didn't make her feel so totally alone. Selfish, she knew, but she couldn't help it.

Gary hadn't made much of an effort to get her to stay, she thought bitterly. In fact he'd palmed her ring quicker than a pickpocket would. Carol was under no illusions that Gary would come begging on his knees for her to come back to him, and that was the most hurtful thing of all. Tears stung her eyes. There was only one thing to do to get over this and that was to cut him out of her life completely. There was to be no looking back. If she saw him at the tennis club it was vital to remain cool and frosty. She would have to put on the act of her life. No question. But would she be able to carry it off? Had she the courage? Her lip trembled and she bit hard, not wanting Jessie to see her crying. As they drove out of Banagher and headed for Dublin, Carol wondered had she made the biggest mistake of her life.

15

Jessica sat at her desk, sick to her stomach. It was the Tuesday after the Bank Holiday, three days after 'The Row', and she didn't know if Mike and Gary were home or not. Mike hadn't phoned to apologize and she was damned if she was going to apologize to him. She'd talked to Carol earlier and she hadn't heard a dickie-bird from Gary. It was soul-destroying.

Jessica couldn't believe that Mike hadn't called. Surely he must have realized that he'd stepped way over the line with his behaviour on the boat? Surely he'd see how macho and disrespectful he'd been? She'd never figured him for one to hold a grudge. It disappointed her hugely.

Her stomach clenched and tightened, and tendrils of fear fluttered against her heart. Mike was her rock. Her sustenance. He was the one person in the world she could truly be herself with. He was the one that made her not only feel loved and cherished but very contented. Why wasn't he ringing her? Surely it couldn't be over. It was only a silly row.

Jessica sighed deeply.

But it was more than a silly row, it was about his perception of you, she argued silently as she typed up a potential guest's biog for her boss.

It was your ego.

It was about standing up for yourself and demanding respect.

It was about pride and not losing face.

'Oh shut up,' she muttered angrily.

'What did you say?' Mona, the girl at the desk opposite, lifted her head and looked at her questioningly.

'Nothing, sorry, made a mistake, just talking to myself,' Jessica fibbed.

'First sign of madness,' Mona said smugly.

'You'd know,' Jessica retorted. Mona was a nosy wagon who never had a good word to say about anyone, not to talk about whinging and moaning about her aches and pains. She was a martyr to her back. Mona by name and moany by nature, Jessica thought nastily, as she clattered the keys of her computer to discourage further conversation.

'How did the cruise go?' Mona asked chattily,

coming over to perch on Jessica's side of the desk.

'Fine,' Jessica said crisply. 'Mona, I don't mean to be rude but I'm way behind and I don't have time to talk right now.'

'Oh, suit yourself,' Mona said huffily, flouncing back to her chair, where she comforted herself with a double dose of Nurofen to ward off an impending headache and disc twinge.

The phone rang on Jessica's desk and she almost leapt off the chair with fright and nerves. Was it Mike?

Oh God, please let it be Mike, she prayed. If he only made the first phone call she'd forgive him everything, she decided, picking up the receiver.

'The Adrian Jordan programme, Jessica speaking, can I help you?' she said calmly, although her heart was thudding against her ribcage so frantically she was sure the caller could hear it.

'I'm looking for the Pat Kenny show,' a voice said plaintively.

'Sorry, you're at the wrong extension. I'll put you back to the switch,' Jessica said flatly, as her heart sank like a lead brick. She felt like crying. How could Mike do this to her?

The day dragged even though she was up to her eyes, and every time the phone rang and it wasn't him it was like a nail to her heart. At one stage,

Katie rang for an update and even she was shocked that Mike hadn't got in touch.

'I hope he's OK,' Jessica fretted. 'I hope nothing happened to him; maybe I should ring.'

'Stop panicking, nothing's happened to him. You'd have heard if it had. Bad news travels fast. Besides I haven't heard anything on the news about a cruiser sinking on the Shannon,' she added gaily.

'Oh my God, I never thought of that,' Jessica said in an utter panic.

'Jessie, I was joking,' Katie said exasperatedly.

'Well, that's not funny.' Jessica's voice rose an octave.

'Sorry. Look, give it another day and then ring him, how about that?' Katie suggested.

'OK,' Jessica said heavily. 'I'd better go.'

'It will be OK,' Katie comforted.

Jessica chewed the top of her pen frantically to stop herself crying. She'd never felt so miserable in a long, long time. Could she wait another day? Maybe she'd call him tonight when she got home.

'Call for you, Carol,' Denise Kelly called to Carol, who was standing at the photocopier, frustratedly trying to get it to work.

'Coming,' she replied, pressing the start key one

last time. The machine wheezed into life and spat out three copies of the document she was photo-copying. She grabbed them from the tray and raced back to her desk. Maybe it was a miracle. Maybe Gary had had second thoughts and was missing her like crazy.

'Hello,' she said airily, determined not to let on that she was in turmoil.

'And when were you going to have the manners to tell me about your wedding, Miss?' her mother's voice came querulously down the line.

Carol's heart sank. She knew that tone of old. Alcohol-fuelled, and it was just eleven thirty in the morning.

'Can I call you back at lunchtime, Ma, I'm at work,' she murmured, unwilling for her colleagues to hear her conversation.

'I know you're bloody well at work. I rang you there, didn't I? Do you think I'm stupid?' her mother slurred faintly.

'So can I ring you at lunchtime then?' Carol struggled to keep the impatience out of her voice.

'Oh sure I'm only your mother, the last to hear anything unless it's bad news like with that Nadine one. I'm only the one who was left on her own to rear two ungrateful daughters. You probably ring Liz Kennedy more than you ring me. She was able to tell me about your wedding and that you were off gallivanting on the Shannon – she knows everything.'

Carol closed her eyes in dismay as her mother launched into a tirade about how hard done by she was.

'Ma,' she interrupted in desperation, 'I'll phone you later. Bye.'

Without waiting for an answer she hung up. Her palms were sweaty and her stomach was tied up in knots. You'd think I'd be used to it by now, she thought unhappily. Her mother had been on the booze for years, but it still made Carol sick to her stomach with tension when she was on a bender.

No wonder Nadine was a handful, growing up with that, she thought guiltily. As soon as she'd finished school she'd upped sticks and left home, leaving her younger sister to face the music on her own. It was something she wasn't very proud of. She must invite her sister up for a weekend and try and talk sense into her. It would be easier now that she wasn't engaged any more. She'd tended to keep her family very much at a distance from Gary, not wanting to scare him off.

Jessica's mother must have mentioned the double wedding. Pity she'd opened her big mouth, because there wasn't going to be one and her mother was getting into a tizzy over nothing.

Bill Logan cursed as the phone rang. His secretary was out sick and his day was turning into a right shambles.

'Hello, yes,' he clipped.

'I just want you to know that our daughter's getting married, and I'm damned if I'm paying for it out of the meagre pittance you give me. So you'd better stop bringing your little tart on her fancy foreign holidays and start saving your money,' his estranged wife ranted down the phone.

Bill's neck muscles tensed. A call from a clearly drunken Nancy, just what he didn't need this morning.

'Call me when you're sober,' he barked and hung up. The phone rang again a minute later, shrilling, demanding to be answered. His hands clenched into fists. Fuck her, he wasn't bloody answering that phone again today. It rang and rang and rang, making him feeling like a prisoner in his own office.

Eventually it stopped and he felt the tension begin to seep out of his body. Even after all this time of distance and separation, Nancy could still get to him. She could still make him mad and apprehensive when she was pissed.

So Carol was getting married! His little girl. Bill felt a fierce sadness and a guilt that was so intense he could almost taste it. His daughter hated him, blamed him for deserting her and her sister. She wouldn't want him at her wedding, that was for sure. He'd forfeited the right to walk her up the aisle. He couldn't believe how much it hurt.

With a sadness that he'd thought he'd overcome a long time ago he picked up the phone and dialled his partner, Brona, the only woman who would understand how lonely and distressed he felt right now.

'Hi, Jen, Gary here, give me a call when you get a chance. Thought you might like to know . . . I'm footloose and fancy-free.' Gary spoke cheerily into his ex-girlfriend's answering machine before picking up his list of calls and heading out of the office.

There was no point in hanging around, now that his engagement was off. There were women to be laid and pints to be drunk and he intended to enjoy the next few weeks. No woman had ever walked out on him before. Carol could get lost.

Why had she ended it with him? he wondered disgruntledly. It was so out of the blue. He certainly hadn't seen it coming. He'd never figure her out as long as he lived, he thought crossly, as he threw his briefcase and some computer parts into the back of his car. What did she mean when she'd said that she wasn't going to discuss his inadequacies in front of the others? What did she *mean* by his inadequacies? She was hardly referring to his sexual prowess, since she'd never really experienced it, much to his frustration. If she'd had sex with him he was damn sure she'd never have given him his engagement ring back.

Maybe it was frustration that had made her illogical. Whatever it was, he didn't like being ditched. No, he didn't like it one little bit, Gary thought crankily, his previous good humour beginning to evaporate as he realized that he was going to have to let on to Jen that he had ditched Carol and not the other way around.

Mike glanced at his watch and pulled the hood of his windcheater over his head as the rain began to pelt down and in the distance, towards the sea, a crack of thunder rolled across the heavens and flashes of lightning rent the glowering skies. Back to normal, he thought wryly, the sunny balmy weather they'd enjoyed on the river a distant memory. He quickened his pace. He didn't want to be late. It was almost five. He broke into a quick jog, turning into the well-tended landscaped grounds of his destination. A couple of minutes later he was at the car park and he waited patiently, sheltering under a nearby tree until he saw her running lightly down the steps, trying to get her umbrella up as she ran.

Mike stepped out from his place of shelter.

'Jessie, Jessie,' he called, his heart lifting at the sight of her. She stopped, stunned, and then her face broke into the biggest smile ever and she ran to him and flung herself into his arms.

'Oh, Mike, I'm sorry. I'm so sorry. I really missed you. I love you. I'm really, really sorry.' She was nearly crying and he hugged her tightly to him, never wanting to let her go.

'I'm sorry too, I was a shit. I love you, Jessie. Let's never do that again,' he said fiercely, before bending his face to hers and kissing her with a passion that left them both breathless.

16

'He was waiting for you in the car park,' Carol said faintly. 'Did you let him have it?'

'No.' Jessica sighed. 'I was just so glad to see him we fell into each other's arms. It was a silly tiff, that's all.'

'I don't believe it.' Carol couldn't hide her exasperation or her disappointment. 'You're too soft with him, Jessica. You let Mike walk all over you,' she remonstrated. Honestly, there were times she could murder her friend. Didn't she have any backbone? She wouldn't have given in so easily.

'He made the first move, he came to meet me,' Jessica pointed out sharply.

'Don't take the nose off me!' Carol said tartly. 'Did he say anything about Gary?' She tried her best to keep her tone casual.

'Not really,' Jessica hedged.

'I suppose he spent the rest of his time on the Shannon getting pissed.'

'Something like that,' Jessica agreed. 'Are you going to contact him?'

'What for? I gave him his ring back. He didn't exactly bend over backwards to give it back to me, did he?'

'I suppose not.' Jessie had to agree.

'Look, I'll let you go, I'll see you at the club during the week,' Carol said briskly. 'Glad everything's OK for you. Bye.' She hung up the receiver, ran upstairs to the flat and threw herself on her bed. So Jessie and Mike were back together. That row hadn't lasted very long, she thought contemptuously. Jessie was a doormat.

At least she wasn't. Bitterness engulfed her. Gary hadn't contacted her. Or wasn't likely to either. Well, she was damned if she was going to give him the satisfaction of getting in touch with him. She looked at the silver-framed photo she had of him on her mantelpiece. Curly black hair, in need of a cut, heavy-lidded, sexy chestnut-brown smiling eyes with the longest, blackest lashes she'd ever seen. A lopsided grin that could lift her heart more than anything else in the world. Heartache smote her. Could she live with not seeing him any more? The last few days had been pure misery. Waiting for him to ring to say he missed her, yet knowing in her heart of hearts that it wasn't going to happen.

Some of her clothes and make-up were in his flat, and a couple of Elvis tapes that she really liked. She had a perfectly legitimate excuse for calling him, she argued with herself. But Gary would like it if she did that. He'd see it as a weakness in her. He'd take it as a sign that she was missing him and regretting what she did. She had a better idea. Carol jumped up off the bed and went to a box on the top of her wardrobe. Pulling out a notepad and paper, she sat down again and wrote swiftly:

Hi Gary,
Could you do me a favour, please? I've left some clothes and my Elvis tapes in your flat, could you bung them into a bag for me and leave them at reception in the club?
Cheers,
Carol.

She wrote his address on the envelope, folded the letter and sealed the envelope. Cool and casual, perfect, she thought with satisfaction. He wouldn't be expecting a letter from her. It was much more formal and distant than an email. That would give him something to think about. She rooted in her wallet. She had a stamp somewhere. Finding it, she stuck it viciously on the envelope. Two minutes later she had changed into her jogging gear. There was a sub post office in Phibsboro; the bastard might even get the letter first thing if she posted it before last post.

With grim purpose she let herself out of the flat and began to jog up the NCR. The downpours of earlier had lessened and a sultry, thundery, oppressive heat hung like a dank, dirty grey dish-cloth over the city. She hated running in this type of weather, it made her feel hot and sticky, but she had a purpose and she quickened her speed as she ran past Mountjoy. She swerved to avoid a puddle and bumped into a Garda who had just emerged through the prison gates. 'Ooops! Sorry,' she apologized, coming to a stumbling halt.

'Hey, what's the hurry? You dropped your letter.' He bent down and picked it up for her.

'Oh, oh, thanks,' she said, flustered. He grinned at her.

'I could arrest you for deliberate assault, but I'll just give you a caution this once.' He had smiling hazel eyes and spoke with an attractive West of Ireland accent.

'That's very kind of you. I wouldn't fancy a night in there.' She indicated the prison behind her.

'I've seen you jogging before. Do you live near here?' he asked conversationally.

'Yes, just down the road,' she said in surprise.

'Do you ever jog into the pub?' he asked, hazel eyes twinkling.

'Depends who's in there,' she flirted, enjoying herself.

'If I was there in an hour might you jog your way in and buy me a drink for saving you from prison?' He arched a black eyebrow at her.

'Well, I don't think there's any reason that I couldn't. Anything has to be better than prison,' Carol found herself saying.

'The name's Sean. Sean Ryan.' He held out his hand.

'Carol Logan,' she reciprocated, enjoying the feel of his firm handclasp. He wasn't bad-looking at all, she thought approvingly. It would be good for her to go for a drink with him. Especially today when she was so down. Something might come of it, and she could make sure Gary got to hear she was dating a Garda. That would give him something to think about. Her eyes sparkled in anticipation. The day or rather the evening was

214

turning out a whole lot better than anticipated.

'OK so, Sean Ryan, see you in Arthur's in an hour.'

'If not I might have to come and arrest you for fleeing the jurisdiction. What number did you say you lived in?' he teased.

'I didn't.' She grinned. 'See ya.'

She jogged off beaming. 'Eat your bloody heart out, Gary Davis, I've just found myself another man. Ha!' she murmured, excitement lending a spring to her strides.

Jen Coughlan flung her briefcase on to the sofa, poured herself a glass of chilled Chardonnay and switched on her answering machine. Hearing Gary's breezy tones ring out into her lounge gave her a start, and she took a long sip of her wine before replaying the message. So he was footloose and fancy-free. She couldn't help the way her heart leapt at the news. The engagement must be over and he wanted to see her again. What went wrong there? Could she go through that roller-coaster with him again? Agony and ecstasy, she thought wryly, opening the doors to her French windows to stand on the small wrought-iron balcony of her apartment overlooking the Grand Canal.

Gary Davis was a womanizing shit, she knew that better than anyone, and when he had dumped her and started going out with that iceberg Carol Logan she'd been gutted. When she'd heard they were engaged, she couldn't believe it. And then he'd come back to her for a couple of one-night stands, sort of hinting that he wanted them to get back together but never actually doing it. Finally she'd put her foot down and told him to get lost.

And now this. Typical Gary behaviour. She could tell him to get lost time and again for all the notice he took of her. Jen gazed across the rippling gunmetal water of the canal to where the traffic crawled along bumper to bumper in the evening rush. She didn't even notice, she was in such a state of turmoil. Why on earth would she even consider going back to him? He was out of her life, let him stay out of it. What was it about him? Jen sighed deeply. She was an intelligent woman in a high-powered position, climbing up the ladder of success. She was attractive, desirable and could have anyone she wanted within reason. Why did she want him?

Because he was damn sexy and great fun and she'd never felt as alive and living on the edge as she had when she'd been with him. The challenge of keeping him at her side had been all-consuming and her life with him had been an emotional see-saw. When it was good it was very, very good, and when it was bad it was the pits. She grimaced at some of the hurtful memories, remembering what it was like waiting for him to ring. Remembering what it was like watching him flirt with other women.

Who had ended the engagement? It had to be him. She couldn't see Carol doing it. When she'd got engaged she'd been insufferable, flashing the ring around. Why had he ended it? Was it because Gary had finally realized that *she* and not Carol was the woman for him? His phone call seemed to substantiate that train of thought. Jen felt a rising sense of excitement.

Perhaps at long, long last Gary Davis had come to his senses. She walked back into her apartment and kicked off her high heels. Pouring herself another glass of wine, she switched on the News and drew her long legs up under her on the sofa. She wasn't going to call him tonight. She didn't want to seem too eager. But now that there was a chance of getting together with him again she was dying to call him. She picked up the phone, tempted, but reluctantly replaced the receiver. Over-eagerness would be a fatal mistake. She'd give it a day or two and contrive to bump into him in the club. That would be the best way to do it, Jen decided as she stretched like a cat and picked up the phone to tell Lindsay Richards, her best friend, the latest.

Gary checked his messages before leaving the office, miffed beyond measure that neither Carol nor Jen had been in contact. He must be losing his touch, he thought wryly as he shrugged into his jacket. It had been a boring, boring day. Women shouldn't be allowed to have computers. One dope, convinced she'd had a crash, hadn't checked her connections and it had taken him two seconds to plug in her adapter properly. A needless call that had taken a half-hour's bumper-to-bumper driving. Another old idiot, who was writing a play, had called to say a virus had deleted his magnum opus. He wanted an expert who knew what he was about, immediately. Needless to say 'back up' did not figure in his vocabulary. The old coot had managed to file away his 'masterpiece' in his Excel file and then had the cheek to blame the error on the computer rather than his own ineptitude.

The only vaguely meaty challenge Gary had had was trying to get to the root of a systems failure in a local newspaper office. He'd spent four hours grappling with the problem, finally getting the system up and running to his satisfaction. Back in the office to finish his paperwork, he'd been a little taken aback that there were no personal messages for him.

He drove home, confidently expecting a message to be waiting for him on his home machine, and was very put out when he saw that there was no flashing light indicating a message of any sort. The least Carol could do was give him a reason for ending their engagement. It was a bit much throwing his ring back at him without having the manners to explain her reasons. And Jen could have called. She was the first woman he'd contacted since becoming single and free.

Feeling extremely disgruntled, Gary poured himself a beer and changed into his gym gear. A workout was definitely called for. Women! Who needed them?

Carol popped her letter in the post-box and hurried along to a phone-box further up the street. She dropped a couple of coins into the box and dialled her mother's number. Might as well get it over and done with. She'd been putting it off all day.

''Lo?' Nancy muttered, still obviously the worse for wear.

'Hi, Ma, it's me. Sorry I couldn't ring until now but we were very busy at work,' she lied.

'What do you want?'

'Well, you rang me earlier about the wedding,' Carol said patiently, the old familiar tightness in her stomach.

'Did I? I don't reme . . . don't remember,' her mother slurred.

'I rang just to let you know that I won't be getting married. I broke off my engagement to Gary.'

'Good. Thash very good. No man's worth it. I should never have married your fath—'

The beeps went and Carol went to put another few coins into the phone. Then she thought wearily, what's the point? She hung up agitatedly. She stepped out of the phone-box unsure what to do. If she was going to call in at the pub she'd never have time to go for a jog in The Phoenix Park, so she decided to head for The Broadstone, and up by the Black Church on to Dorset Street. She could then stroll back up the NCR to ACD's. She wasn't going to change clothes. That might give the wrong impression, she decided, as she got into her rhythm, her feet pounding the pavements, exhilarating her as she pushed her body to the limit.

An hour later she pushed open the heavy door of Sir Arthur Conan Doyle's. Dark and smoky, noisy and companionable, the pub was busy. She peered around looking for the Garda. He was standing in civvies – jeans and a dark-green Polo shirt - at the bar. He raised his glass at her and waved. She edged her way through the throng and smiled at him. 'Hi.'

'Hi, yourself. Did you have a good run?'

'Good enough.'

'What can I get you?'

'A Club Orange would be fine,' Carol said gratefully, looking forward to a nice cold drink.

'Sure you wouldn't like anything stronger?'

'No, thanks. I play tennis and I'm in training,' she said firmly, and rather liked him when he didn't press the issue.

'There's a table over there.' He pointed to the corner, where a couple were getting up to leave.

'Well spotted,' she approved, following him to the table.

'It pays to keep your eyes open.' Sean eased himself into the seat beside her and smiled at her.

She smiled back. 'I guess it does.'

She took a sip of her drink, feeling quite relaxed. It was strange; she didn't feel the need to be cool and sophisticated with Sean like she had with Gary. There was no pressure on her to make an impression. She'd obviously done that or he wouldn't have asked her out for a drink. It was a refreshing experience, she thought, surprised, as she sat chatting easily to him, sipping her ice-cool drink.

'I think you should ring her, Bill. At least offer to walk her up the aisle, it's your right as a father. Don't let Nancy dictate to you,' Brona Wallace exclaimed indignantly. Bill smiled down at his partner, nestled against his shoulder.

'Carol's very hostile. I don't blame her.' He sighed.

'Look, it's time she grew up. You're her father. You sent your hard-earned money home every week for years and still do, she shouldn't forget that. The least she could do is meet you for a cup of coffee if she's expecting you to fork out for the wedding.'

'We'll see. I'll think about it. Needless to say, Nancy was pissed and extremely aggressive.'

'My poor darling,' Brona said sympathetically, hugging him tightly. 'I don't know how you stuck it for as long as you did.'

'I don't know either.' Bill shook his head at the awful memories of his disastrous marriage.

'Call her. I'm sure she'll be glad to hear from you at a time like this, any daughter would,' Brona said confidently.

'OK, OK, I will,' Bill declared, kissing her tenderly.

Nadine Logan tottered up the path to her front door, her impossibly high heels killing her. She felt more than a little queasy. She'd drunk a skinful with her friends Martina and Colette, and then they'd stuffed themselves with chips. She hoped her mother was in bed. She'd been drunk when Nadine had come home from school to change out of her uniform. She'd started going on about Carol's wedding. She hadn't shut up about it since Liz Kennedy had said it to her the previous week. Nadine was heartily sick of it. One thing was for sure, she thought woozily, she was damned if she was getting tarted up in a long silly dress to be a bridesmaid. No way was she going to look like a prize prat trotting up the aisle of a church after Carol.

She opened the door with some difficulty; the key was giving her trouble. Her heart sank when she saw the light on in the sitting-room. She waited for her mother to launch into a diatribe, demanding to know where she'd been until this hour of the night. Not a peep. Slowly Nadine exhaled the breath she'd been holding and peered around the door. Her mother was draped across the sofa, head back, mouth open, snoring loudly. The vodka bottle was at her feet. Beside her on the sofa, Nadine could see her parents' wedding album.

'Why do you do that to yourself?' she muttered angrily. 'Forget him, he's gone.' She stood looking at her mother and felt a terrible helpless sadness sweep over her.

'Don't think about it, don't think about it,' she ordered, horrified at the lump in her throat and the damp prickling her eyes. Furiously she wiped her eyes. Crying was a weakness she would never give in to. She looked at the open album and saw a photo of her parents smiling into each other's eyes, happy, carefree. Viciously she tore the page out of the album and shredded it with difficulty. An anger so deep and intense washed over her she could hardly breathe. She grabbed the album and the torn photo and raced out to the kitchen. With hands that shook, Nadine opened the back door and shoved her parents' wedding album into the rubbish bag, burying it deep into the detritus of potato peelings and milk cartons and mouldy bread and cheese.

'There, that's where you belong,' she raged, taking deep breaths to ease the pounding of her heart. Her rage had sobered her up somewhat and, resolutely, she locked the door behind her and with deep resignation went to try and put her mother to bed as she had done countless times in the past.

Jessica wrapped her legs around Mike and groaned with pleasure as he entered her. 'Oh Mike, Mike, I wanted you,' she murmured against his ear, holding him tightly to her.

'I love you, Jessie,' Mike muttered, touching her and caressing her until she moaned with pleasure, whispering endearments to him, joyful at their union.

'Oh, Jessie, that was good,' Mike said huskily when both of them were spent and sated and she was snuggled up against his shoulder.

'At least I'm good in the sack, if I'm no good steering into a lock,' she teased.

'Shush.' He smiled down at her, placing a finger against her lips. 'Let's not go there. Humble pie's not the nicest-tasting pie in the world.'

'Sorry, I didn't meant to harp on. I'll never refer to it again,' she said solemnly.

'I take it we won't be going cruising on our honeymoon?' Mike said drily.

Jessica giggled. 'Too right, Buster. We'd be divorced by the time we got to Lough Ree.'

'One good thing, I suppose,' Mike said sleepily as he put his arm around her and cuddled up to go asleep.

'What's that?' she yawned, snuggling right in to him.

'We won't be having a double wedding.'

'Thank God for that,' said Jessica and closed her eyes.

They were asleep in minutes.

17

'Hi, Jessie, where's Mike?' Carol greeted her friend, surprisingly cheerful, as she joined her in the bar of the tennis club.

'He's out on court. He'd arranged a match with Kevin Delaney. We've a court booked for seven-thirty. What are you doing?'

'I'm playing mixed doubles with Larry Allen, but I'm not sure who we're playing against. I hope it's Gary,' she added maliciously, 'because we'll beat the socks off them.'

'You haven't heard from him, I take it then,' Jessica said drily.

'What do you think?' Carol retorted, eyes busy scanning the bar for her ex. 'Have you seen him?'

'Nope. I'm not long here.'

'Wait until I tell you, Jessie,' Carol said excitedly, lowering her voice. 'I met a gorgeous bloke on Tuesday night. He's a Guard. I had a drink with him and we're having a drink later tonight and going to the pictures on Friday.'

'You're joking!' Jessie was gobsmacked.

'No. I'm serious. I was jogging down to Phibsboro and I literally bumped into him coming out of Mountjoy. He told me he'd arrest me for assault if I didn't go for a drink with him.' She giggled.

'Hey, that's great. Is he nice?' Jessica was delighted at her friend's news.

'He's lovely. Taller than Gary, Sean's his name, he's six foot two, hazel eyes, brown hair, cut tight, very sexy. He's from Sligo.'

'A country boy! I thought you only went out with city slickers,' teased Jessie.

'I know. But he's really nice and good fun. We get on like a house on fire. He's into keeping fit and sport. We're going to go swimming in Vincent's early in the mornings,' Carol informed her.

'Quick work, Logan,' Jessica approved, privately astonished at how quickly Carol had rebounded from Gary.

'I know,' Carol said smugly. 'Gary, eat your heart out.'

'That's no reason to go out with someone,' Jessica warned.

'Oh, don't be so smug,' Carol sniffed. 'Of course it is. I did the dumping and I'm going out with someone new. That's exactly the kind of thing Gary would do. I'm just pipping him at the post. It's easy knowing you've always had it easy with men, Jessie,' she said in exasperation. 'You might be a bit more understanding if you hadn't.'

'Don't be like that, Carol,' Jessica said indignantly. 'You sound as if you begrudge me my happiness.'

'No, I don't,' Carol shot back defensively. 'That's not fair!'

'All I'm saying is don't hurt your nice Guard in the process of getting your own back on Gary,' Jessica retorted drily, knowing she'd been right about the other girl's begrudgery.

'I won't.' Carol couldn't hide her irritation. 'God, I've only met him. We're not planning to walk down the aisle, for crying out loud.' She threw her eyes up to heaven. Trust Jessica to try to put a damper on things. It was obvious she'd never had her heart broken and had to keep up appearances.

'Come on, let's go and change,' Jessica said, and Carol followed, annoyed that the other girl had seen through her strategy so easily. She liked Sean, of course she did. But she liked the idea of making Gary jealous a whole lot more.

Gary threw the plastic Roches Stores bag containing Carol's clothes and precious Elvis tapes into the back seat of his car. She had some nerve, he thought angrily, remembering the short, impersonal little note that had arrived through his letterbox the previous morning. When he'd read it, he couldn't believe it. She couldn't even be arsed to lift up the phone to him. She'd sent him a crappy little note. What kind of an ignorant cow was she? By God, he was really going to let her have it the next time he met her at the club.

It was time someone put Miss High and Mighty Logan in her place and he was just the man to do it. And as for Jen Coughlan . . . Gary's scowl deepened. She could get lost. She was out of the frame. Definitely. She hadn't even had the manners to get in touch with him either. It was the last time he'd be phoning her. There were plenty more fish in the sea.

Thoroughly annoyed, Gary gunned the engine and sped down the road, with a face on him that would stop a clock.

* * *

Jen took extra special care with her make-up, brushing more mascara on to her lashes than she normally would, and adding an extra dusting of blusher. It was very possible that she'd see Gary at the club tonight. The tennis season was in full swing; the odds were that he'd be rostered to play a doubles or singles match. She couldn't help the flutter of nervous anticipation at the thought of seeing him. She was very proud that she'd played it so cool, but there was no point in overdoing it. If he wanted to get back with her she should go for it. Knowing Gary, he wouldn't be on his own for long. She checked the strings on her racket and slipped it into its cover. She'd had a couple of sunbeds to bring up her tan and her tennis whites would show it off to perfection. She looked terrific, she thought confidently, as she took one last look at herself in the full-length cheval mirror in the corner of her bedroom.

She'd changed the sheets on the bed and tidied up the apartment just in case he came back with her tonight. She sprayed some Chanel No. 5 on her neck and wrists and pressed the spray lightly around the bed so that the scent would linger. Tonight she might be back in Gary's arms, making wild passionate love in her double bed. It gave her quivers just to think about it.

It was almost worth the split for the reunion they were going to have.

He saw her before she saw him. She was standing, in her whites, laughing at something her tennis partner was saying, and Gary had to admit she looked good. Carol was a sexy woman. She didn't look too perturbed at their broken engagement and that annoyed him. It annoyed him even more that she'd been the one to end it. It wasn't in the natural order of things, he thought grimly, as he strode into the men's locker room to change. When he emerged from the changing-rooms ten minutes later there was no sign of her. He was scheduled to play in ten minutes' time; he could go for a drink or watch the action out on the courts.

He'd been stuck indoors all day and he could do with a bit of fresh air, he decided, and headed outside. Carol was at one of the far courts waiting to play. She saw him, gave a casual wave and turned away.

Rage ignited. How dare she treat him so contemptuously? This was the woman he'd asked to marry him, Gary fumed, forgetting entirely that he'd been in no rush to walk down the aisle with her and that it had been his suggestion to postpone the wedding. He marched over to where she stood, engrossed in the final set of the match on court.

'A word,' he growled.

'Oh, hi, Gary,' Carol said coolly. 'Sure. What can I do for you?'

'You can tell me why you ended our engagement for one,' he said curtly. 'You owe me that much at least. I really don't think much of your behaviour, to be honest.'

Carol stared at him. 'And I don't think much of yours,' she drawled. 'You know why I ended our engagement? One, I got fed up being with someone who thinks he's the centre of the universe. It's all Me Me Me with you, Gary. Our relationship was all about you and what you wanted. I rarely got a look in.'

'It's because I postponed the wedding, isn't it?' he taunted. 'That's the real truth.'

Carol was furious. How typical of him to turn it back to her. 'Actually,' she heard herself say, 'I've met someone else.' It popped out unbidden, but her ex-fiancé's reaction was satisfying in the extreme.

'You met someone else?' he echoed, astonishment and disbelief written all over his face. 'You met someone while you were with me?' His voice rose an octave.

'Yep,' she fibbed, delighted at his reaction.

What a perfect excuse for breaking it off with him. Sean had given her the perfect out, even if she did have to stretch the truth a little. This would drive Gary nuts. He had an extremely jealous and possessive streak to him, which she'd always exploited to her advantage.

'Who is he? What does he do? Where did you meet him?' Gary was hopping mad.

'He's a Guard. His name is Sean, he's from Sligo, he's six foot two, and—'

'A Guard! You're dating a culchie clodhopper!' Gary couldn't believe his ears. How long had this been going on? He was puce with temper.

'Look, one of the reasons I broke off the engagement, and I emphasize *one*,' she drawled, 'was to pursue a relationship with Sean. Nothing's happened that I'm ashamed of. I haven't slept with him. I wouldn't do that to you. I don't two-time,' she added pointedly, as she saw Jen Coughlan emerge into the evening sun from the clubhouse.

'Sleep with him? What do you mean sleep with him? You wouldn't bloody sleep with me,' Gary spluttered.

'I know,' Carol sighed. 'But he's a very, very sexy guy. When he wears his leathers on the bike, he's sex on legs,' she exaggerated, really putting the boot in. 'I'm meeting him tonight for a drink in

The Gravediggers after the match, so I should get my skates on. Don't be cross, Gary, we just weren't meant to be. I didn't mean enough to you or we would be getting married in September. And you didn't mean enough to me, or I wouldn't be seeing another guy tonight. Let's just put the past behind us and stay friends,' she invited kindly.

She thought Gary was going to burst a blood vessel, he was so angry.

'Friends! I don't think you know the meaning of the word, Carol Logan,' he snapped.

'Calm down, Gary. Think of the great time you'll have at the beer festival. No ties. You can spend all around you. You won't have me nagging at you,' she said lightly, thrilled at the way their encounter was going. That would teach Gary bloody Davis to take her for granted. 'Look, I have to go, our court's free. I'll see you around. I didn't meant to hurt your feelings, I'm very fond of you,' she announced, adding insult to injury. She walked over to the baseline and hit a practice shot to one of the players at the opposite end.

Gary was dumbfounded. No woman had ever treated him the way Carol just had. She'd met someone else. He was a sexy guy. The words tumbled around his head. His brain felt like a wash cycle on spin. She was *fond* of him! He'd never been so insulted in his life. And all the time he'd felt he was the one in control in the relationship. He'd been so confident of her feelings for him it hadn't cost him a thought to postpone the wedding. Just as well he had. She could have continued seeing this bloke she was clearly smitten with, through their marriage, he thought self-righteously. All the time she was seeing a culchie Garda behind his back. It was unbelievable. And she expected him to stay friends. She had two chances of that, he thought furiously, as he turned on his heel and strode towards the clubhouse.

'Well, hi, stranger, got your message, things were mad busy so I couldn't get back to you, but I kind of guessed I might see you here tonight.' Jen Coughlan stood in front of him, glowing and tanned.

'Hi,' he muttered, unable to hide his annoyance, both at her and Carol.

'What's wrong?' she asked, concerned. 'Carol giving you a hard time?'

'Other way around, I think,' he retorted, unwilling to admit that any woman would ever get the better of him by giving him a hard time.

'So you said you were single and free – what's up? Is the engagement off?' Jen probed, madly curious. She'd watched the couple embroiled in what seemed a heated exchange.

'You're damn right it is,' Gary growled.

'Did she give you back your ring?' Jen said sympathetically, putting her hand lightly on his arm in a gesture of solidarity.

'I broke it off,' Gary declared. 'I found out in time that she wasn't the woman for me.' He glowered in the direction of Court Five.

'Oh dear,' Jen murmured. 'Well, better to find out now than after the wedding,' she added diplomatically.

'So what are you up to?' Gary focused his heavy-lidded stare on her.

'Busy as ever,' she said lightly.

'Seeing anyone?'

'Oh, you know yourself. A couple of dates here, a couple of dates there, nothing serious.'

Gary caught sight of Carol slicing an ace down the line. He certainly didn't want to give her the impression that he was pining for her, he decided. He was going to make sure to have a woman on his arm every time he saw her. Jen would do fine for starters. He knew he'd decided to freeze her out for not answering his call, but the whole scenario had changed after Carol's unbelievable revelations and he didn't want to be wrong-footed for a second more than was necessary. Besides, Jen had genuine feelings for him, she'd taken him back even after his engagement to Carol, he thought self-pityingly, truly stung at Carol's betrayal of him.

'Come and have a drink with me later?' he invited, his mind racing. If Two-Face Logan could go drinking with her so-called sexy man in The Gravediggers, he could stride in with Jen on his arm. That would show his ex that he wasn't wasting any time getting over her.

'Love to, we'll catch up on all the news,' Jen agreed. 'Better go, I think my court is free.' She waved at him and he watched her go. He had her where he wanted her, but for some unfathomable reason the knowledge gave him no satisfaction.

18

Carol fought hard to concentrate. She was so exhilarated at the way her encounter with Gary had worked out she was finding it hard to focus on the game.

He'd really been mad, his eyes spitting fury, she thought gleefully as she lobbed a ball over the net. Telling him that she'd met Sean and letting him believe that it had been during their time together had been a brainwave. It had really knocked the wind out of his sails. The last thing he'd expected. She'd got out of the relationship with her head held high and given him something to think about. That's what he got for taking her for granted.

His reaction to her news had been most gratifying, she reflected, as she smashed a shot into the net and lost a point which could lose them the set if she didn't cop on and get her game together.

'Concentrate,' she muttered, shooting an apologetic look at her partner.

She was glad when the match was over; she wanted to be alone for a while to replay every second of her confrontation with Gary. Barely waiting to shake hands with her partner and opponents after finally losing the match after a tightly fought last set, she hurried into the privacy of the showers. Carol breathed a deep sigh of relief as she stood under the steaming hot jets, enjoying the heat on her aching muscles.

He must really care if he was so irate about her seeing someone else. It had to mean something, she assured herself. And her slipping in the bit about her being tempted to sleep with Sean because he was so sexy had been a masterful stroke. He'd been really shook up by that little nugget. That in itself was a triumph, she thought joyfully, as she lathered peach and almond shower gel on to her taut limbs. Maybe it wasn't all as hopeless as it seemed.

Another thought struck her. She could invite Sean to the Mid-Summer's Ball in a couple of weeks. Gary would definitely be at it; he was the club treasurer this year and the committee always attended. That would certainly rub his nose in it. And if it really got to him, who knew, he might ask her to get back with him. But this time it would be on her terms and they'd be up the aisle so fast he wouldn't know what had hit him. Happier than she'd been since the disastrous Shannon cruise, Carol let the water wash away all her aches and pains and felt renewed and invigorated at the prospect of driving her ex-fiancé mad with jealousy at the Mid-Summer's Ball.

Yes! Yes! Yes! Jen mentally raised her fists as she walked away from Gary and headed for her court. She'd played it so cool, pretending sympathy for his plight. It was good to know too that it had been he who had ended it. If he'd told her that Carol had given him the ring back she'd be a tad perturbed to say the least. It would mean he hadn't come back to her by choice. She straightened her short white skirt. She knew she looked good in it. She was glad too that she'd worn her new cream linen trousers and black halter neck to the club. It was an elegantly casual outfit as well as being sexy. Hopefully Gary'd take her somewhere cool and sophisticated for a drink afterwards.

Resolutely putting the events of the past few days out of her head, Jen strode out on court and prepared to play her best.

* * *

'This is my good friend Jessie and her fiancé, Mike, and this is Katie, Jessie's cousin. Everyone, this is Sean Ryan,' Carol said gaily, making introductions. They were all in The Gravediggers, where they'd arranged to meet after their matches. Katie had popped over from the house to join them.

'Anyone for a drink?' Sean asked politely after he'd shaken hands with them all.

'We're fine, thanks.' Jessica smiled. 'You go ahead.'

'Let me guess, a double vodka on the rocks,' he teased Carol, 'or just your usual boring old Club?'

'You know me so well,' Carol laughed.

'Won't be a minute,' he said before making his way to the bar.

'He's gorgeous,' breathed Katie. 'Has he got any friends?'

'Of course. He's very sociable,' Carol drawled, gratified to see Miss Smart-Ass-Katie drooling at the mouth as she watched Sean lope up to the bar.

'He's nice,' Jessica said politely. 'I hope it goes well for you.' She was still smarting from Carol's barbs earlier.

'Don't see why it shouldn't,' the other girl said offhandedly. 'How did your matches go?'

Jessica relaxed a little now that they were on neutral territory, so to speak, and they all analysed their matches until Sean came back with his and Carol's drinks.

'Katie thinks you're absolutely gorgeous and she was wondering if you've any friends,' Carol announced blithely. 'We're always trying to find a man for her.'

Katie blushed to the roots of her hair. *Bitch!* she swore silently. Mortified.

'I bet she's got no problems finding a man,' Sean said gallantly, ignoring her blush. 'But any time you feel like coming to the Garda Club, let me know and we can make a night of it.'

'Sounds fun,' Jessica said hastily, knowing how embarrassed Katie was and furious with Carol for being such a smug wagon. Who did she think she was, rubbing Katie's nose in it for being temporarily manless?

'Oh, look,' Katie said airily, indicating the door. 'There's your ex-fiancé, Carol, it didn't take him long to get over you.'

It was Carol's turn to blush as Sean looked over to the door and back at her in a very quizzical manner. She could see Gary and Jen Coughlan making their way to the bar. Gary had his arm protectively around the other woman.

For a moment their eyes held and then he looked away disinterestedly.

'You were engaged?' Sean said conversationally. 'You never mentioned it.'

'Yes, until last week, believe it or not. Carol's some woman to go.' Katie beamed across the table at her arch-enemy.

'Just as well I'd broken it off, or I wouldn't be able to be here with you,' Carol responded coyly, slanting a sideways glance at Sean to see how he was reacting.

Privately she was fuming. Wait until she got her hands on that malicious cow, she'd have her guts for garters. How *dare* she discuss her private business in front of Sean?

'He seems to have got over it quick enough then,' Sean observed. 'Tasty dame he's with. Great chassis.'

Mike laughed. 'You're not wrong there, for sure.'

Jessica elbowed him in the ribs. 'Stop drooling, you.'

'He used to date her before he met me,' Carol said flatly. She didn't like Sean's obvious appreciation of Jen. She was shocked at how deflated she felt seeing Gary with the other woman. Suddenly the game was no fun any more. For two pins she'd leave, but she wouldn't give Gary the satisfaction of knowing he'd got to her. Drawing on all her inner resources, Carol did her best to sit with a smile on her face pretending that she hadn't a care in the world.

Gary took advantage of the fact that Jen had gone to the loo to sneak a quick look over to where Carol and the gang were sitting. It felt strange to be apart from the group. They'd gone out together as a bunch for so long that he'd almost automatically turned to head in their direction until he'd seen Carol and the tall, rangy, brown-haired man and felt his stomach lurch.

He studied them discreetly. They all seemed to be having fun. There were lots of laughs coming from the table, although Katie looked a little uncomfortable. She and Carol had always sparked off each other. They couldn't under any circumstances be called bosom buddies.

Carol was sort of nestled in against the man, laughing up into his face, which was bent attentively towards her. Gary felt like smashing his fist into the other bloke's perfect white teeth. He took a long gulp of his pint. As soon as he was finished his drink he and Jen were out of here. She'd hinted earlier about going back to her place.

That was before he'd pulled up outside The Gravediggers. She hadn't been impressed. He'd probably blown his chance of a shag, he thought glumly, wishing he was anywhere but where he was.

Jen touched up her lipstick and stared at her reflection in the mirror. She looked a million dollars, even if she said so herself. Fat lot of good it was doing her here, she thought angrily, as she gazed at her gleaming blonde tresses flowing down against the flimsy black lace of her top.

She'd thought Gary was taking her somewhere classy. He'd soon put paid to that idea when he'd pulled up outside The Gravediggers pub in Glasnevin.

'Dying for a decent pint,' he'd explained when she'd looked at him in surprise. When she'd seen Carol Logan and her group over in the far corner she'd copped on. Carol was with another man and Gary obviously wanted his ex to know he was with someone too. She was only a pawn in his game and it infuriated her.

Was it that he wanted Carol back and wanted to make her jealous? Or was it that he wanted his ex to see that she had no chance and that he was back with Jen? She couldn't quite figure it out and it was doing her head in.

He could get lost tonight, she decided. She wasn't bringing him back to the apartment. She'd see how things were going before she let Gary Davis into her bed again.

'Were you using me to make your ex jealous?' Sean looked Carol straight in the eye as they sat in his car outside her flat.

'No, I wasn't!' she said heatedly, but couldn't hide the blush that came to her cheeks. 'I didn't know he was going to come to The Gravediggers. I think he was trying to make *me* jealous by bringing her to the pub. Don't forget we were there first. So *he* followed *me*, not the other way around,' she added triumphantly.

'True,' he agreed easily. 'Are you still in love with him?'

'I ended it,' she pointed out.

'That wasn't what I asked.'

'I don't know. I don't think so,' Carol said agitatedly.

'Maybe you should take some time,' he said diplomatically. Tension gripped her. Don't say he was giving her the brush-off already.

'I like being with you,' she said frankly and couldn't believe she'd said it. 'I was looking forward to going swimming with you in the mornings.'

'Fair enough, so, we'll give it a shot and see how it goes.' He leaned across and kissed her lightly on the lips. He had a nice firm mouth, she noted approvingly, and a good strong jawline. Sean was very clean-cut. Gary had a tendency to jowls, or would have by the time he was forty.

'Off to bed with you, woman,' Sean said firmly, clipping his seat belt on.

'Would you like coffee?' she asked, hoping he'd refuse the offer. It was a bit soon for him to see the kip upstairs. It might put him off.

'I think you've had enough excitement for one night,' he said drily, and she had the grace to laugh. 'See you Friday. I'll stay here until you're inside.'

'Sir Galahad,' she joked. She let herself into the flat and blew him a kiss before closing the door. She was wrecked. She yawned exhaustedly. It sure as hell had been a roller-coaster of an evening. She'd been gutted when she'd seen Gary with Jen Coughlan. It hadn't taken long for them to get together again. Anyone but her, she thought bitterly. Everyone would say he'd gone running back to her. It was galling.

And then that . . . that spiteful little *spinster*

Katie with her big mouth. She'd nearly died of embarrassment in front of Sean when the little bitch had deliberately told him about her broken engagement. She'd been planning on telling him that she'd been engaged further down the line. She was quite unprepared for little blabbermouth's bombshell to Sean, who was clearly not impressed, she recalled. Although he'd handled it very well. And at least he wasn't dropping her like a hot potato.

Some day she was going to let Katie Johnson have it right between the eyes, Carol vowed, as she undressed in the moonlight and dived into bed without even bothering to put on the light. She lay tossing and turning, trying not to imagine what Jen and Gary were doing together in his bed or hers. Heartache swamped her, raking her heart with pain. If she'd had any sense she'd forget about Gary and concentrate on the lovely man who'd been sent to her. But where did sense come into it? Love and sense were diametrically opposed, certainly as far as she and Gary were concerned.

'You certainly got your own back on Carol tonight,' Jessica grinned, as she sat with her flatmate drinking hot chocolate and dunking gingernut biscuits.

'Oh, she's such a cow!' Katie scowled. 'Did you hear her in front of that guy making a holy show of me? I was mortified. "*We're always trying to find a man for her*,"' she mimicked. 'I hate her guts. Smug wagon! How does she do it? She's engaged on Friday, ditches him on Saturday and is going out with a hunk by Tuesday. And he *is* a hunk.' Katie sighed longingly. 'And he's a gentleman too. Far too nice for the likes of her. I just couldn't believe it when she told him that I thought he was gorgeous. I wanted to crawl under the table. He was very nice about it. He knew I was mortified.'

'I know.' Jessica stretched and yawned. 'I wonder will they still be together for the wedding? He'd be a guest then.' She smiled ruefully. 'At least it won't be a doubler.'

'It will be interesting to see if they last, but I'll tell you one thing, I was watching her when Gary walked in with that other one. She was far from happy and she's far from over him. That's definitely not finished yet, you mark my words,' she added darkly.

'I think it is,' Jessica disagreed.

'You mean you're hoping it is at least until your wedding is over,' her cousin observed perceptively.

'Let's not even go there,' Jessica groaned, dipping another gingernut into her hot chocolate. She wished Katie hadn't said what she'd said. There was still a long time to go until September.

19

'Phone call, Carol.' Imelda Kelly waved the receiver at Carol as she strolled back to her desk after her tea break.

'Ta, Mel.' Carol took the phone from the other girl and perched on the side of her desk. 'Hello?'

'Carol, hi, it's Dad,' said a disembodied male voice at the other end of the phone.

'What do *you* want?' Carol's voice turned surly.

'Please don't be like that, Carol. I heard you were getting married. Your mother phoned me. I wanted to talk to you about it. I want to help pay for it. I want to be with you on the day.' Her father spoke quickly, anxious that she heard what he had to say.

'I don't need your help now or ever, thank you very much, and don't ever ring me at work again. Goodbye,' she said curtly, her heart hammering in her chest. She hung up the phone, raging with herself. Why did she still react the way she did when her father spoke to her? Why did her throat tighten and her stomach clench? It was more than ten years since he'd left, she was an adult now and she certainly didn't need him. Why was she still so affected by even a phone call, unwanted though it was?

Ire took over. He had such a cheek, she fumed, doodling so viciously on her pad that she broke the top of her pen. Did he think that all he had to do was say he'd contribute to her wedding and she'd fall into his arms and say, 'Thanks very much, Daddy, let's forget the past, it's all wiped clean because you've pulled out your chequebook.' Anybody could write a cheque, it only took a minute. If he thought that'd impress her, he was sadly mistaken. And how dare he think he had any rights at all to be with her on her wedding day. He'd forfeited those rights ten long years ago. He had some nerve though. *And* he was totally selfish. He wanted to be part of her wedding day – what about Nancy's feelings? Had he considered them? Hardly. He must know her mother would freak if she thought he was going to waltz into their lives for a day, do his so-called caring father bit, and waltz off again. The more she thought about it the more enraged she got.

What was it about men? Often when she'd been with Gary she'd been convinced that he had his life divided into various compartments in his head. She'd been in one of them, the smallest one, she thought wryly. As soon as he was gone from her, the drawer was closed and she didn't figure until he saw her again. Was that what it was like with her father? she wondered unhappily. Now and again he opened the drawer filed 'Daughters', but closed it pretty quickly and eased his conscience by increasing his direct debit to the bank for their upkeep. Did he think that money made everything all right? Was he that much of an idiot? He was no better than Judas was, she thought bitterly as she bent her head and applied herself to her work.

'She hung up on me,' Bill said sorrowfully to Brona that evening as he sat dangling his three-year-old son on his knee. 'She was so cold, it was like talking to a stranger. My child detests me so much she can't even bear to talk to me.' Tears trickled down his cheeks.

Brona was horrified. 'Oh darling, don't cry.' She took the toddler from him and sat him in front of a video before sitting down beside Bill and putting her arms around him.

'I've made sure they never wanted financially. I

worked morning, noon and night to provide for them and I've never had a word of thanks.'

'I know you have, love. Who knows that better than I?' Brona soothed. 'She's being thoroughly ungrateful. I mean, let's face it, Ben is their half-brother, it's not his fault the way things turned out. You'd think they would have made a bit of an effort to get to know him.' She couldn't hide her disdain.

'It's all such a mess.' Bill rubbed his eyes. 'Was I so wrong to try and make a new life for myself? Am I to be punished because I walked away from hell?' He turned to Brona. 'It was a nightmare, you know. She was drunk so often. Or else hysterical, wanting to know did I love her. She accused me of having affairs and I swear to God, Brona, I wasn't. You were the first woman I got to know and I'd made the decision to leave by then.'

'I know, I know. Look, forget it. You did your best, but it's her loss.' Brona kissed the top of his head, noting how grey he'd gone. That Carol Logan was a hard-hearted bitch; had she no feelings at all for her father? They weren't so particular about taking his money, though. They'd no qualms at all there, she thought bitterly. Perhaps it was time that Miss Carol Logan was told a few home truths about her treatment of her father.

* * *

'So it's just Mike and me and family and friends,' Jessica informed her mother, as they walked along the beach enjoying the sunset. It was Friday evening and she and Mike had travelled down to Wicklow to sort out his accommodation. He was starting work the following Monday.

'Well, thank God for that.' Liz couldn't hide her relief. 'You know I met Nancy on the street a week ago and she was in a sad way. It was obvious that she knew nothing about the wedding and she was very angry that I seemed to know more about Carol's goings-on than she did. You should have seen the face of her when I told her that you were all on the Shannon. Do they talk at all or have they any sort of a relationship? They're a very peculiar family. That Nadine one spends half her time in the pub at night from what I've heard, and she's only fifteen.' Liz shook her head at the idea.

'I know, it's terrible,' Jessica sighed. 'If I had a younger sister going wild like that, I'd be dead worried about her. It doesn't seem to bother Carol at all. She never comes home.'

'I suppose it's understandable the way Nancy carries on. It's a terrible shame, though. She was a gorgeous-looking girl, and full of life when we were younger. I think she got postnatal depression after Nadine was born and she wasn't treated for it. It was after that that everything went downhill and she started drinking. Bill had an awful life with her, I can't say otherwise, but I did feel very sorry for those two girls when he left.'

'Some of that probably explains why Carol stuck with Gary for so long. She probably didn't want to admit to herself that the relationship was a disaster. He's a very selfish bloke. I wouldn't have put up with him for as long as she did, but I'm glad she's not going to marry him,' Jessica confessed.

'So what happened? Why is it all off?' Liz tucked her arm companionably into her daughter's as they strolled at the water's edge.

Jessica shrugged. 'Basically I don't think he wants to get married. Certainly not in September. Mike said we needed to know so we could start making plans, and Gary said he thought they should postpone. I did feel very sorry for her because she thought it was going to happen. It's all she wants, to be married to him. Anyway she decided enough was enough and gave him back his ring.'

'Good girl, Carol,' Liz commended. 'I'm delighted she didn't let him walk all over her.'

'And she met this gorgeous Guard two days after she broke it off with Gary, you wouldn't believe it,' laughed Jessica.

'I'd believe anything of Carol,' her mother said drily. 'So it's just family and friends, now. That's fine. I've organized the wedding cake and Lily Doherty is going to get me the greenery for the flowers – you did say you wanted my gladioli for the altar, didn't you, and freesias for your bouquet?'

'Yeah,' Jessica said happily, feeling a tingle of excitement. For the first time in weeks she was finally beginning to look forward to her wedding. 'It can't come quick enough. I'm really going to miss not having Mike around. It's going to be weird.'

'You'll manage. At least he's got good digs,' her mother comforted.

'I know. It's just I'm so used to seeing him and being with him. I'm going to miss him in the club too.'

'He'll be there at weekends. And he's got a good job, Jessie, that's a great start in life.'

'I know,' Jessica murmured, but her stomach felt like there was a great big lump of lead in it at the thought of driving back to Dublin on Sunday night, knowing that Mike was miles away from her in Wicklow.

'Hi, gorgeous, where are you?' Gary called as he let himself into Jen's flat with the key she'd given him half an hour earlier. They'd decided to have a night in and he'd gone down to the offie to get a couple of bottles of wine. They planned to order in a Chinese. Gary was looking forward to it. It had been a tough week, workwise. Two other guys were out sick and he'd been run off his feet. And for some reason he was having trouble sleeping. He kept seeing Carol smiling up into that Guard's face and it bugged him. What did he have that Gary didn't have? He couldn't hack it that Carol had been seeing someone else while she'd been with him. It was unbelievable. Usually it was the other way around, he had to admit.

He couldn't help wondering if she had slept with him. Had she wrapped those strong toned legs around him and made him groan with pleasure? It was a thought that tormented him.

Jen had been cool enough too. Another novel experience. He was really losing his touch, he thought heavily. She hadn't invited him back to the apartment until tonight. Unheard of in all the time he'd known her.

He went into the kitchen and uncorked the wine to let it breathe. She must be in the loo.

'Hi.' He heard her voice behind him, and turned to see Jen standing in the doorway in a pair of black satiny French knickers and a lacy camisole that emphasized each glorious rounded curve of her breasts. Her nipples were hard and the sight of them made him hard.

'Oh, Jen,' he groaned, pulling her to him, 'it's about time.' Fleetingly, as he led her to the bedroom, he wondered what Carol would look like in French knickers and a tight black camisole.

20

Brona Wallace waited tensely in the reception area of the Civic Offices for Carol to arrive down in the lifts. She'd given the whole idea of confronting Bill's daughter a lot of thought over the past week. She hadn't said anything to Bill. He wouldn't want her to do it, but she felt strongly that if she discussed the matter with Carol, woman to woman, she could make the younger girl understand just how much her father was hurting by her cruel rejection of him. If she could get her to understand that Bill loved her very much, Brona was certain Carol would have a change of heart.

She saw a young woman stride out of the lift to reception and then saw the receptionist point in her direction. Brona stood up and arranged her face in a pleasant smile. Carol wasn't what she expected. She'd expected someone less ... less confident, perhaps. This woman walking towards her had a no-nonsense air about her that caused Brona momentarily to wonder if she'd made a mistake in coming.

'Yes, can I help you?' Carol was asking politely, a look of puzzlement in her brown eyes.

'Hi, you must be Carol.' Brona held out her hand. 'I'm Brona Wallace—'

Carol looked at her in astonishment and pulled her hand away as if she'd been stung.

'What do *you* want?' she demanded, and her tone was none too friendly.

Brona began to bristle. Didn't Carol realize that this wasn't easy for her? She was coming to endeavour to make peace between father and daughter; the least she could do was try and meet her half-way.

'Look, I think it's important that we talk. Your father's very upset by your refusal to even talk to him—'

'So he sent you around here to do his dirty work,' Carol sneered.

'Excuse me.' Brona drew herself up to her full height, wishing that the other girl wasn't tall enough to be looking down her sneery nose at her. 'Let's get one thing straight, Bill doesn't know I'm here. I came to attempt to persuade you to put aside your differences and ask you to try and see

262

how much he loves you,' she exclaimed indignantly. 'You know, your father works his fingers to the bone still and has done all these years to send your mother money. He's always provided very well for you and you haven't even the decency to acknowledge that.'

Carol's face darkened in fury and Brona felt a tingle of apprehension.

'Now you listen here to me, you interfering busybody,' she hissed. 'My father walked out on me, my sister and my mother ten years ago and he left us to our fate—'

'Your mother drove him to leave. She's an alcoholic and she wouldn't go for treatment no matter how much he tried to get her to.'

'*Exactly*,' spat Carol. 'My father left me and my little sister in the care of an alcoholic and no amount of money will ever camouflage that. He could have taken us with him. He didn't. He abandoned us physically, morally, emotionally and spiritually. Who did our homework with us when our mother was pissed? Who looked after her when she couldn't even make it to the loo? Who cooked and cleaned for us and got us out to school when she was plastered drunk? Not him. He signed cheques and did direct debits. Certainly he fulfilled his financial responsibilities; no one's disputing that. But that's easy. You don't have to be physically present when you're dishing out cash to salve your conscience. You know something?' She pointed a finger aggressively in Brona's face. 'We had a life of misery while he swanned off to Dublin and met the likes of you. So you get the fuck out of here and don't you dare ever, ever come near me again, you smug little know-all. Let me tell you, you know nothing about the way my father treated us. The nerve of you coming here lecturing *me*. I don't want that bastard near me, do you hear me?'

Brona shrank back at the ferocious anger in the younger woman's face. She was shaken to the core.

'Get out of here and don't dare ever come to my place of work again. Get your self-satisfied little mush out of mine and go and play happy families with my father, because happy families is something I know nothing about, thanks to him.' She turned on her heel and strode back to the lifts.

Brona was trembling. What a huge mistake this had been, she thought shakily, as she tried to ignore the curious stares of the people in the foyer and hurried out of the building and down the steps on to the quays. Tears of fright and shock ran down her cheeks. This wasn't a scenario she'd imagined at all. She'd imagined going home to Bill with the wonderful news that she'd talked Carol around and a reconciliation was very much on the cards. Instead she now had to confront the fact that the man she adored and looked up to and felt sorry for because of his disastrous marriage might not have behaved as honourably as she'd thought.

Brona hurried along the quays as the rush-hour traffic trundled past and cars, buses and lorries belched fumes into the hot, sultry air. The Liffey stank to high heaven and she wanted to get away from here as fast as she could.

She tried to banish Carol's words but they kept coming back in sickening clarity. Abandoned, physically, emotionally, morally and spiritually. That's what Carol had accused her father of. There was no arguing with it. No nice way of putting it. Bill Logan had abandoned his children and in her heart of hearts she couldn't dispute that, much as she wanted to. Brona sobbed into her tissue as her beloved partner came crashing down off his pedestal right in the middle of Wood Quay.

Carol just made it to the loo, where she puked uncontrollably as rage, grief, despair, sadness and hatred swept through her. She couldn't believe she'd said all those things. It had come pouring out of her like a torrent. She'd felt that her feelings

about her father were well under control –
obviously not, she thought agitatedly as she lifted
her head, wiped her mouth with a tissue and
flushed the loo. She pulled down the toilet seat
and sat on it, her hands trembling as she ran her
fingers through her hair.

How dare that self-important, sanctimonious
woman come to where she worked and deign to
lecture her about her treatment of her father? How
dare she? Carol was so incensed she thought she
was going to be sick again. She swallowed hard and
managed to quell her queasiness.

She couldn't believe how shaken she was, how
angry. She thought she'd managed to put her
father's betrayal of them behind her a long time
ago. The ferocity of her feelings frightened her.
She wanted to get out of here. She needed to be
alone.

Oh no, not alone, she screamed silently, but there
was no one to run to, no one who understood.
Jessie was the only one she could tell, the only one
who might understand, but she'd gone to Wicklow
for the weekend to help Mike settle into his digs.
She had to pull herself together and pretend that
nothing was wrong, otherwise it would be all over
the office that there'd been a drama in reception.
Drawing on every ounce of strength she had,

Carol wiped her eyes, straightened her uniform and walked back to her office.

Sean dried himself off after his shower and splashed some aftershave on to his face. He dressed quickly, conscious that he was running late and he wasn't taking the car. He didn't want to keep Carol waiting. He sighed as he towelled his hair dry. She was a strange girl in some ways. Hard to get close to. He never knew what was really going on in her head. There was always this reserve. She had this tough outer façade, but behind it, he felt, there was a great deal of softness that she didn't want seen.

He was enjoying being with her. The swimming was going great. She was fit and competitive and he enjoyed that. He wanted to take her hill-walking, which he thought she might like; he'd suggest it to her tonight.

She liked him, he felt, but there was sadness in her eyes sometimes and he knew she was thinking about that Gary bloke that she'd been engaged to. She didn't talk much about him and Sean didn't pry. He liked her friends. They seemed a solid crew. He'd had drinks with them midweek to celebrate Mike's new job and his leaving Dublin. That had been a good night, and he'd felt that

Carol had relaxed a bit more with him and enjoyed herself.

He was her rebound, Sean acknowledged with a grimace as he pulled a short-sleeved shirt over his head. It didn't make him feel great, he had to admit, but he'd persevere for a while and see how they went.

She was waiting for him on the steps of Eason's and she looked so woebegone and peaky he was dismayed.

'What's up with you, my good woman?' he teased as he put his arm around her and gave her a hug. She rested her head against his chest.

'Nothing,' she murmured, her reply muffled.

'You look a bit shattered. Is something wrong?' he persisted.

To his horror she started to cry. Frantically she dried her eyes.

'Sorry, sorry, it's nothing. Look, I think I'll go home if you don't mind, I don't feel a hundred per cent,' she managed to say before bursting into tears again.

'What's wrong, Carol? Is it the bloke?' he asked sympathetically.

'Let's get out of here,' she pleaded, wiping her eyes on her sleeve. It was such a childlike gesture his heart went out to her.

'Will you tell me what's wrong?' he asked gently, shielding her from the gaze of curious passers-by.

'Not here,' she said, composing herself a little.

'Will we go and have a cup of tea somewhere? Or a drink?'

'No . . . I might start crying again. I'm sorry, Sean.'

'That's OK, I know where we'll go,' he said quietly, taking her hand and jay-walking across O'Connell Street towards North Earl Street.

She followed him unquestioningly, and looked at him in astonishment five minutes later when they stood at the steps of the Pro Cathedral.

'Come on, we'll find a quiet little spot and you can tell me what ails you and then we'll decide what to do with ourselves,' Sean said firmly, determined to get to the bottom of her problem.

It was comforting in the dusky twilight of the cavernous cathedral and the lights of the candles gave a sense of ease. A few people, mostly elderly, were scattered around the church, rosary beads slipping silently through their fingers. An old wino snoozed in one of the pews. The scent of beeswax polish reminded him of school. He led her to an empty seat away from the nave.

'What's up, Carol?' he asked as he sat down beside her and turned to face her. Head bent, unable to look at him, she shook her head.

'Come on, tell me. I might be able to help.'

'No one can help me,' she said brokenly, and her torment was so raw he felt for her.

'Try me,' he urged.

'Oh, it's family stuff,' she muttered.

'Yes . . . and what's wrong with your family?'

And then it all came out . . . the alcoholic mother, the father that had walked. The fear and anger and grief and hatred all bubbling just below the surface having been unleashed by the visit of that misguided woman who was now her father's partner.

Sean wasn't shocked. He'd seen enough of dysfunctional families in his job not to be. But he was dismayed for Carol. She was obviously struggling with a lot of issues and it needed someone with more expertise than he had to help her sort them out.

He held her tightly as she cried against his shoulder. 'Would you have done that? Would you have walked away? You're a man, can you explain his thinking to me?' she wept angrily.

'I don't know,' he said truthfully. 'Until you walk in someone else's shoes you can't know how you would act in their position.'

'It was wrong, though, wasn't it? He shouldn't

have left us to deal with it. We were only kids,' she cried.

His heart went out to her. 'I know,' he soothed, stroking her hair. 'I know.'

Carol raised a tear-streaked face to him. 'I'm really sorry, Sean,' she apologized. 'I've never spoken of this to anyone, except Jessie. I'm sorry for burdening you with it.'

'It's no burden,' he said kindly. Surely she'd spoken to her ex about it, he thought in surprise.

'Did you ever talk to Gary about it?' he asked casually.

'No.' Carol shook her head. 'What was the point? It's something I have to deal with myself. He wouldn't want to know about that kind of stuff.'

That bloke seemed to be some sort of tulip all right, Sean thought in amazement. Imagine being engaged to a woman and not even copping on that she was damaged and hurting. It was a blessing she'd come to her senses and handed him back his ring.

'Would you ever consider counselling or see someone from Al Anon?'

'Ah no!' Carol sat up and wiped her eyes. 'I don't need it. I'm over it all really. It's just that Brona one coming into work unexpectedly brought it all back, I suppose. She'd an awful cheek, hadn't she?'

'Yes, she did, Carol, forget her,' he said firmly, wishing he could get his hands on the silly fool.

'Look, why don't you head off to Slattery's and I'll get a bus home? I'm a bit whacked to say the least.' She sat up straight and ran her fingers through her hair.

'You know, I'm not really in the humour for Slattery's. I'd like to spend the night with you,' he said honestly. 'But as your place is a bit small and there's no privacy in my place, I have a suggestion – and please don't think I'm being forward,' he said earnestly, anxious that she wouldn't take his suggestion the wrong way.

'What's that?' she responded warily.

'My sister's away in France at the moment and I'm keeping an eye on her house and feeding her blasted cats,' he grimaced, and Carol giggled in spite of herself. 'We could spend the night in her house. It's got two bedrooms,' he said hurriedly. 'It's a nice house. It's a little bungalow out in Clontarf. I could cook us something to eat.'

'Wouldn't she mind?'

Sean shook his head. 'Not in the slightest. We look out for each other.'

'OK,' she agreed, to his surprise. 'I'd like that. I don't feel like going back to that kip.'

'It's time you got a better flat than that place,' Sean said briskly as he stood up. 'I'll help you look for one.'

'You're very kind.' Carol looked at him as if she was seeing him for the first time.

'Do you think so?' He grinned down at her. 'The criminal fraternity of the city might not agree with you. Come on.' He took her hand and headed over to the statue of the Sacred Heart. 'Let's light a candle for you, my mother swears by them.'

'Oh!' she said, astonishment flickering in her eyes. 'I didn't think you'd go for that sort of thing.'

'I surprise myself sometimes,' he said, half-embarrassed. It had been an impulsive suggestion but she smiled at him and he was glad he'd suggested it. He slipped a few coins into the box and lit a half-dozen candles for her. What harm could they do? he thought ruefully as he put his arm around her shoulder and walked out into the sultry summer's evening.

21

'He's such a nice bloke, Jessie, he was so kind to me. I was mortified, bawling all over him. You know me, I never cry in front of people.'

'I know,' Jessica said faintly, amazed at what she was hearing. She and Carol were in the bar at the club. It was Monday night and she was missing Mike madly, even though it was less than twenty-four hours since she'd said goodbye to him.

'That woman had an awful cheek, didn't she?' Carol declared. 'Honestly, Jessie, I nearly gave her one in the chops.'

'That's understandable,' Jessica murmured. She'd listened to Carol pouring out her heart to her about her horrible encounter with her father's new partner for the last hour, and while she felt very sorry for her friend, she was feeling a little bit sorry for herself too. OK, Mike going to live in Wicklow might not have the magnitude of Carol's drama but it was her little drama, and just for once she'd have liked to have the focus on her. Carol paused for breath and continued.

'But Sean was so understanding about it all. He didn't want me to be alone and we stayed the night in his sister's house.' She rattled on.

'Did you?' Jessica sat up and stared at her friend. This *was* news. 'Did you sleep with him?'

Carol shook her head. 'No, and that's what I like about him. He could see I was shattered, so we just talked and he cooked a lovely pasta dish and then I went to bed. He's a real pet. Could you imagine Gary if we were in a free house?' She scowled.

'So are you going to start dating him seriously?' Jessica probed.

'I like being with him. He's fun, and he's very fit and sporty and I like that. We'll see.' She smiled at her friend. 'And guess what? I'm moving flat.'

'You're what?' Jessica couldn't believe her ears. 'At last. How did this come about?'

'Sean's friend, he's a Guard too, owns a house in Phibsboro that's let in flats. One of them is vacant. It's self-contained and I wouldn't have to share a bathroom, and I'd have a separate sitting-room. Sean took me to see it on Saturday and I gave the landlord a week's notice. We're moving my stuff in on Wednesday and Friday evenings. That's when he's off. What do you think?'

'I say definitely go for it,' Jessica urged, delighted at the idea of Carol getting out of that hen coop on the NCR.

'The rent is a bit higher, though—'

'Oh, for God's sake, Carol, you can well afford it. You're on a good salary. Spend some of it on decent accommodation, at least.'

'I know. You're right. And the great thing is, it's still in the area. I'm actually nearer to you and the club, and still on my bus route.'

'Look, it's great, a whole new start. Enjoy it,' Jessica said warmly. 'Come on, let's go out and knock a few balls around.'

'I wonder will Gary be here with Jen?' Carol surveyed the bar and beyond.

'What difference does it make if he is? You're with someone new. Your life's on track, you're moving flat. I'd hang on to that Sean guy, he seems like a very decent chap,' Jessica said firmly as she followed her friend out to the courts. 'And I'll move a car load of stuff if you need it. It's just I'll have to do it earlier rather than later because Mike will be coming up on Friday night and I want to spend as much time as possible with him.'

'You make it sound as if he's gone half-way

around the world – he's only in Wicklow, for God's sake,' Carol said dismissively, and Jessica felt like smacking her. Wicklow might just as well be half-way around the world at the moment. Mike was there and she was here and she missed him. She was dying to know how the first day in the job had gone. He was ringing her at half nine and she was aching to talk to him.

It had been horrible saying goodbye to him the previous night. She'd seen his digs. He was staying with a widow and her son in a neat little house down near Bridge Street right in Wicklow Town. His room was tidy, if on the small side, and Mrs Meehan, his landlady, would cook a dinner for him in the evenings.

He'd decided to go into digs temporarily; in the meantime, he was keeping an eye out for a place for them to live, somewhere between Bray and Wicklow, so Jessica wouldn't have to commute too far.

He'd got an old banger of a car that would get him from A to B. That was something, although her mother felt he should come and live with her in Arklow now that he was mobile. But if he did that, he'd be spending as much money on petrol as he would be on rent, they'd explained patiently. Jessica knew Liz wasn't entirely convinced.

Jessica was going to commute from Dublin one night a week, most likely Wednesday, to be with Mike. She wouldn't be able to stay in his digs though, unfortunately. Mrs Meehan didn't seem the type who would approve of unmarrieds sharing a single bed. Their sex life would be gone to the dogs, Jessica thought gloomily, as she threw a ball in the air and prepared to serve. Weekends only. Even though her mother was very liberal in her approach and took it for granted that they shared a room whenever Mike stayed over, Jessica could never manage to have sex under Liz's roof. She invariably became tense, aware of every sound, and sure that the bed was creaking even more loudly than normal. Her mother's bedroom was next door and she just couldn't relax enough to do it. Mike understood and never made an issue of it. Jessica felt he was as uncomfortable as she was with it, so kisses and cuddles were as far as they went at home. It would have to be the back of the car on Wednesday nights for a bit of nookie. Roll on September, she thought fervently, as Carol ran her ragged around the court.

Mike lay on his bed and yawned his head off. He was knackered: he'd been on site at seven a.m., and even though he'd enjoyed his first working day, it had been a bit of a strain trying to remember all the names and take in all the information that he'd been given about the job. He was steeped in luck to get this job, he reflected. The N11 was being upgraded. Ashford and Rathnew were to be bypassed in the years to come. There were plenty of meaty challenges to keep him on his toes and he was looking forward to it. He just wished Jessica was with him so he could share all the events of the day with her. He'd had a good dinner, lamb chops and plenty of gravy and mashed potatoes and veg, but he wasn't in the humour for going down to the sitting-room to make polite conversation with his landlady and her son.

It would be great having a place of their own. He'd noticed a nice little cottage in Ashford for sale, but that might still be a bit of a trek for Jessica commuting out to RTE. Besides, they didn't have enough money for a deposit, he thought ruefully. Not with the wedding coming up.

Mike glanced at his watch. Ten past nine. He'd told Jessica he'd phone her at half. He was out of credit on his mobile and he'd forgotten to get some. He didn't want to use the payphone in the hall. He wanted a bit of privacy. He'd go to the call-box up near the bank and call her. It would be good to go out and get some fresh air before going to bed. Hauling himself to his feet, he ran a comb through his hair, made sure he had enough coins for the phone, and headed off to talk to his beloved.

The following Wednesday Carol made sure to take extra care with her make-up. She'd been half-tempted not to go to the club tonight when she'd heard that Jessica was driving down to Wicklow to meet Mike. But she was rostered for a game of mixed doubles and she didn't want to let her partner down. She had a feeling that Gary and Jen would be there, and she had no desire to watch the other woman swanning around the club with a smug smirk on her puss. To that end, she'd asked Sean to collect her there later, and she'd make sure he had at least one drink so she could show him off. She wanted to ask him to come to the Mid-Summer's Ball the following week, and she hoped against hope that he wouldn't be working and that he'd say yes.

She sighed, looking at her reflection in the mirror. There was no sign of the roller-coaster of emotions she was feeling. One minute she was exhilarated, on top of the world, the next she was in the pits of depression unable to stop thinking about Gary and Jen. Imagining them making passionate love, and feeling gutted that he had let her go so easily.

They were at the bar when she strolled in, and out of the corner of her eye she caught Gary looking at her. She pretended not to see them and responded gaily to a greeting from one of the other members.

She stayed chatting with the other girl for a while before making her excuses to go to the changing-room. She was just pulling her white skirt up over her thighs when Jen glided in.

'Oh, oh, hello,' she said coolly.

'Hi,' Carol was equally cool.

'Look, this is awkward, I know, and I hope you weren't too upset about Gary breaking off your engagement, but—'

'Sorry?' Carol arched an eyebrow.

'I hope you're not too upset because Gary er . . . umm . . . broke it off.' Jen faltered under Carol's supercilious stare.

'I think you're under a misapprehension here, Jen. Gary didn't break it off with me, I broke it off with him—'

'He told me otherwise,' Jen snapped.

'He's lying. I broke it off with him in public in the lock at Athlone in front of Jessie and Mike. But it's no skin off my nose who you believe.

You're welcome to him,' she said coldly, before stalking out of the locker room, head held high.

Gary was such a creep saying it was him that broke it off. He had no integrity whatsoever. *Sean wouldn't do that*, she thought, and banished the thought. She didn't want to get into comparisons; deep down she knew Gary wouldn't even rate a comparison with Sean.

Gary was standing at the clubhouse door, tying a lace on his runner.

'Jen's not too happy – she was offering condolences on you breaking off with me. I set the record straight. You shouldn't tell fibs, Gary, it's much easier if you tell the truth in the long run,' she said disdainfully as she walked by him.

It would be interesting to see the repercussions of *that*, she thought with satisfaction, suddenly looking forward to her match.

Jen Coughlan sat on the bench tying up her runners. Humiliation seared her soul. Carol Logan had not been lying, she knew by her whole superior attitude. Gary Davis had left her wide open as a result of his lies. Now she'd be the laughing stock, and the one people pitied when it got out that Gary had been dumped and not the other way around. She'd be seen as the fool that took him back. Why was she such an idiot? She cursed herself. Why did she believe his lies? Why did she always take him back? There was only so much shit a woman could take, and she'd taken her quota. Tonight Gary Davis would be going home on his own. She'd had it with him. He was history.

Gary's heart sank. He'd seen the look of disdain Jen had thrown him as she passed his court and knew he was in trouble. He should have known better. It was bound to get out that Carol had ended the engagement and not him. Women couldn't keep these things to themselves. They always had to be getting one over on each other. He was better off without the species, he thought irritably as he played a crap shot and lost his serve game.

His humour was not improved when he went looking for Jen after his match to discover she'd already left. He was definitely blown out now. Pissed off, he went into the bar to have a quiet drink only to see Carol, looking fabulous in a pair of tight-fitting jeans and a black spaghetti-string top that clung to every toned curve. She was laughing at something a man was saying to her, and Gary realized with a sense of shock that it was that bloody Guard she was going out with. They moved to the bar and ordered drinks, and rather than retreat and lose face he stepped up to the bar beside her.

'Hello, Carol,' he said casually. 'How did the match go?'

'Fine,' she said airily. 'This is a friend of mine, Sean Ryan. Sean, this is Gary Davis, my ex.'

'Hello.' Gary nodded but made no move to shake hands. The copper nodded politely.

'We're just having a quickie. Sean's helping move my stuff to my new flat,' Carol informed him briskly. 'See you around.' She picked up her glass of orange and headed for a table, followed by her new boyfriend.

She was moving flat. This was a new departure. It probably had a bedroom with a double bed rather than her virginal single-bed bedsit. She definitely must be sleeping with him, Gary thought jealously. The thought infuriated him.

Another thought struck him. If Jen wasn't speaking to him he had just over a week to find another woman to go to the bloody Mid-Summer's Ball with him. That was all he needed, he thought morosely as he took a slug out of his pint and tried not to look over at Carol and her fella.

'I don't think your ex was too happy to see you with someone else,' Sean remarked as he lugged two black sacks down the stairs of Carol's bedsit a little while later.

'Tough,' Carol said crisply as she followed him down with a half-dozen assorted bags.

'You enjoyed letting him know that you were moving flat,' he said, straight to the point as usual.

'I'm a woman, Sean,' she retorted.

'True, that says it all,' he grinned.

She pulled the front door closed and stowed her bags in the boot of his car.

'Are you working Saturday night week?' she asked nonchalantly as she sat into the car beside him.

'Ah . . . let's see.' He looked into the distance and did a quick mental calculation. 'Nope, I'm working the Saturday after that. Why?'

'How would you like to come to our Mid-Summer's Ball? It's usually good crack. It's in The Marine in Sutton. Jessica and Mike will be at it.'

'Will his nibs?'

'Don't know. I put Jen, his girlfriend, straight about the fact that I'd ended it and not him – she had the nerve to hope I wasn't too upset because he'd ended it, according to her. So I don't know if they'll get over that little hiccup. Who cares anyway?'

'I think you do,' he said perceptively.

'Look, you don't have to come if you don't want

to,' she said testily. 'I'm not fussed whether I go or not.'

'Don't get huffy,' he grinned. 'I'll go if you'd like me to.'

'Don't be too enthusiastic,' she retorted.

'Ah, stop, do I have to dress up in a monkey suit?'

'Yeah.'

'Right.'

'Do you not like dinner dances?'

'No,' he said bluntly, and she laughed at his honesty.

'If you don't want to go I won't hold it against you,' she assured him.

'Ah sure we'll give it a try.'

'How come a lovely fella like you is single?' She was curious.

Sean laughed as he started the engine. 'I was going with a girl in Sligo and she wasn't too happy at me coming to Dublin. She did an "It's Dublin or me" ultimatum.' He glanced across at her. 'I don't like ultimatums.'

'I must remember that,' Carol murmured. 'Doesn't like dinner dances and doesn't like ultimatums.'

'But likes swimming, hill-walking and sexy women joggers,' he teased, and she laughed and felt a most unexpected flicker of happiness.

22

'Wow, that's a gorgeous dress,' Jessica said almost enviously as Carol stepped into a black jersey silk halter-neck dress that moulded itself to every curve of her body.

'Yours is gorgeous as well,' Carol reciprocated, pleased at her friend's reaction.

'It's not drop-dead sexy like yours is!' Jessica made a face. Her dress was a peach spaghetti-strapped floaty chiffon-type dress that hinted at the ethereal more than the sexy. It was the kind of dress Carol would never have got away with.

'Look, the two of us are drop-dead gorgeous. Wait until the guys see us. They won't be able to walk, they'll be so horny.' Carol giggled.

Jessica laughed. It was great to see Carol in such good form. The break from Gary had been the best thing that had ever happened to her. 'How's the flat going?'

'Oh, I don't know myself having so much space, you'll have to see it,' Carol enthused. 'You're right, I should have done it years ago. I suppose I thought seeing as I was engaged to Gary I'd be moving in with him and there wasn't much point.'

'Oh,' Jessica murmured. 'I hear it's all off with Jen. I wonder will he come to the do tonight?'

'I bet he will. He wouldn't have it said that he couldn't get a date. He'll be with some blonde bimbo, wait until you see,' Carol predicted confidently.

'Won't you mind?' Curiosity got the better of Jessica.

'I don't know,' the other girl confessed. 'Sometimes I'm fine, usually when I'm with Sean, other times I'm miserable.'

'I think you've done very, very well under the circumstances. Much better than I thought you would,' Jessica said admiringly as she dusted some blusher on to her cheeks.

'I think that's because I met Sean. He kinda took the sting out of it. It was nice to show Gary that I could get another man and very quickly too. I know you don't approve and don't think it a reason to go out with anyone. You'd understand if it happened to you.'

Prudently Jessica refrained from comment,

pretending to be too busy concentrating on applying her mascara. A ring at the doorbell caused them both to grab their bags and wraps. It was Sean and the taxi. They'd decided to go as a foursome. Carol had come over to Jessica's to get dolled up and Mike was downstairs in his tux.

Two wolf whistles greeted their appearance as Sean and Mike stood waiting for them in the sitting-room, drinking a beer.

'Who are these women?' Mike asked, handing each of them a glass of champagne.

'I've no idea, never met them before,' deadpanned Sean, who looked rakishly sexy in his dress suit.

'And we could say the same of you pair,' Carol retorted. 'They do scrub up well when they want to, don't they?' She turned to Jessica, who was beaming at Mike as if she hadn't seen him for a year.

Carol threw her eyes to heaven. 'Would you look at that pair, can't take their eyes off each other. It's sad.' She smiled at Sean, who leaned down and gave her a kiss on the cheek.

'You look fantastic,' he said admiringly.

The front door opened and Katie poked her head around the sitting-room door. 'Very glam,' she complimented. 'Nice dress, Carol,' she said magnanimously.

'Thanks,' Carol said curtly.

'Have a glass of champers,' Mike offered.

'Oh, lovely. Where did that come from?' Katie asked, giving Sean a shy smile. He smiled back at her and winked.

'I bought it. I'm a working man now, not a penniless student. It's great,' Mike declared, pouring her a glass.

'Well, cheers, and have a great night.' Katie raised her glass to them.

'Pity you're not coming,' Carol said, straight-faced. But there was no mistaking the barb. Sean shot her a glance but said nothing.

'Been to one, you've been to them all,' Katie drawled. 'I'm not really the dinner dance type.'

'No, you'd prefer a barn dance or a harvest hooly, you little culchie, you,' Mike slagged.

'Oh yeah, under a harvest moon and a starry sky if possible,' Katie sighed.

'Are you a country girl at heart?' Sean asked, surprised.

'I sure am.' Katie nodded, draining her glass. 'And this country girl's been on her feet all day in A & E and the only place she's going is her bath and bed. Night, all.'

'Goodnight,' they chorused, with the exception of Carol, who took another sip of her champagne.

'We should head off,' Jessica suggested, and obediently the others drained their glasses and trooped out to the waiting taxi.

It was a giddy group that piled out of the car at the hotel, and they entered the function room laughing and joshing. Carol studied the table plan and found their table, and the men went off to the bar to get the drinks.

'Is he here? You look,' Carol urged as she sat down at their assigned table, which had two other couples.

Jessica looked around, waving at people she knew. And then she saw Gary sitting with a petite redhead at the committee's table.

'Yep, he's here all right. He's sitting at the top table with a redhead,' she murmured discreetly.

'Knew it,' Carol snapped and her lips tightened. 'Wasn't I right? Didn't I tell you?'

'So what?' soothed Jessica, her heart sinking at the other girl's change of form.

'Bastard,' Carol muttered.

'Don't let him see that you're annoyed. That would be playing right into his hands,' Jessica advised.

'Don't worry, I won't,' Carol said exasperatedly, and Jessica felt like telling her to get lost. Back to normal, she thought wryly, wishing the other girl's good humour had lasted for the night.

Mike and Sean returned with the drinks and Carol put on her best act for them. She laughed and joked and was the heart and soul of the party and all the while kept her gaze studiously averted from Gary's table.

Sean looked at her intently a few times, noting the heightened colour in her cheeks and the determined gaiety she was projecting.

They ate the tasty meal that was served and laughed and banged the table when the spot prizes were drawn, and when the music started all of them got up, eager to get on the dance floor.

'Enjoying yourself?' Sean asked as he spun Carol around the floor.

'What? Oh, sure,' she said distractedly, trying to get a glimpse of Gary and his new woman.

'Over to the left, near the band,' Sean said drily.

'What?' Carol looked at him, perplexed.

'Your ex is over near the band on the left-hand side and he's dancing with a redhead. That's who you were looking for, isn't it?'

Carol had the grace to blush. 'Sorry,' she murmured, embarrassed at being so transparent.

Sean sighed. 'Forget it, Carol. And my advice to you is to forget him too. Give yourself a break and start afresh.'

'Easier said than done.' Carol shook her head.

'She isn't a patch on you,' he murmured.

'Who?'

'The redhead.'

Carol laughed, genuinely amused. 'You're lovely,' she said, and planted a big kiss on his cheek.

Sean smiled down at her. 'You're one complicated woman,' he informed her. And she laughed again and nuzzled in against him for the slow set that had just started.

Gary chewed his lip and tried to ignore the carry-on of Carol and her culchie copper out on the dance floor. She was smiling up at him, laughing and kissing him, and he wanted to rampage through the couples on the dance floor and tear her out of his arms and drag her out of the hotel and ask her what the hell she was playing at. He was consumed with jealousy at the sight of her, as sexy as hell in that black number, wrapping herself all around that man, who was doing nothing to discourage her.

'What's wrong? You look like a demon!' Sandie, his date, asked. She was a rep with a software company and she'd always flirted with him when she was in the office. She'd been thrilled when he'd asked her to the dinner dance. Sandie didn't, of course, realize that Carol was there. Gary hadn't got into the nitty-gritties of his relationships with her.

'Sorry, touch of indigestion. All the stress of organizing this damn thing,' he lied.

'Oh, you should try a brandy and port or something. Very good for the tum,' the redhead assured him.

'Right, maybe I'll go to the bar and get one. Can I get you anything?' he asked, leading her off the dance floor. She was an awful chatterbox and he was finding it irritating.

'I'll have a brandy Alexander,' she announced giddily.

Expensive date, Gary thought crossly as he made his way to the bar. He saw Sean and Carol leaving the floor and craned his neck to see where they were going. Damn! They were going outside. He couldn't very well follow them. It would look too obvious. That fucker was probably taking her outside to give her a good grope, if not more. The thought made him almost spit. He stood at the bar and took a slug of his brandy. Sandie could bloody well wait for hers; he was going to get smashed, he decided. What else could a man do?

What a bummer the last few weeks had been.

Carol giving him back his ring. Jen screeching down the phone at him like a fishwife and calling him all the names under the sun when he'd phoned a few days after the incident at the club, to see if she was still coming to the dinner dance as his guest. He'd never get the chance to warm his slippers under her bed again, he reflected, still shocked at the dockers' language she'd used.

And it was all Carol's fault, and he was bloody well going to tell her before the night was out, he decided recklessly, draining his brandy goblet in double quick time.

He made his way outside, where couples sat at tables enjoying the balmy breeze and twinkling lights across the bay. Carol and the copper were standing on their own and he was pointing out something in the sky to her.

Gary marched over to them and tapped Carol aggressively on the arm. 'You! I want a word with you. What the hell are you playing at? What are you doing with this clodhopper? You should be with me. You were engaged to me. We were supposed to be getting married,' he ranted.

'Calm down,' the copper said quietly.

'You butt out of it. What will you do . . . arrest me?' Gary sneered, squaring up to the other man.

'Stop it, Gary, and grow up,' Carol snapped,

furious. 'How dare you make an exhibition of yourself and drag me into it? Go and sober up.'

'I miss you,' he muttered. 'What's he got that I haven't?'

'Ah, stop it, Gary, and don't annoy me – you're pissed and I don't appreciate it,' Carol said coldly. 'Come on, we're going home, Sean.'

'What's wrong – are you afraid I might flatten him?' Gary jeered.

'No, you idiot. I'm afraid he might flatten *you*.' She looked at Sean. He was perfectly composed. 'Let's go, will we?'

'Sure, whatever you want,' he said calmly.

Gary watched them walk back into the function room. 'That told them,' he muttered. 'The coward was afraid to fight me.'

'There you are!' said Sandie crossly. 'Where's my brandy Alexander?'

'Sorry, had to deal with a problem. It's on its way,' he mumbled, wishing heartily that she were on hers. What had he seen in her? No class, not like Carol had, and he'd lost her to a culchie. Feeling desperately sorry for himself, Gary made his way to the bar and ordered himself another double brandy.

* * *

'Sorry about that,' Carol apologized.

'Not your fault. He was pissed.'

'How did you keep your cool? I was afraid you were going to clock him!' she marvelled.

Sean laughed. 'Never lose your cool with a drunk, it's one thing you learn on the job. Do you want to go home?'

'I think so. I don't want him annoying me for the rest of the night. Do you mind?'

'Not really. Katie's right, once you've been to one you've been to 'em all.'

'Oh, she only said that because she couldn't get a man,' Carol said dismissively. 'I just need to go to the ladies'. Will you go and organize a taxi at reception?'

'Sure,' he said politely.

'I'll just tell the others we're going,' Carol said, disappearing off to look for Jessica and Mike.

Sean stood on the steps of the hotel, hands in his pockets, looking up at the stars. In the bright city lights he could just make out the Plough and Orion's Belt. In Sligo on a starry night, the sky seemed so near you could almost reach up and touch the velvety blackness. He knew exactly what Katie meant when she'd said she was a country girl at heart.

He frowned, remembering Carol's treatment of the other girl. It was a side of her that wasn't very attractive. She'd been downright rude. He sighed. He hadn't been exaggerating when he'd said that Carol was a complicated woman. Too complicated for the likes of his country boy's heart, he thought ruefully as he saw her coming through the doors.

'Here's the taxi. That was good timing.' He took her arm and they walked to the taxi. She was quiet on the journey home and he was glad. He wasn't in the humour for idle chit-chat.

'You're coming in, aren't you?' Carol asked, surprised when he made no move to get out of the taxi when it pulled up outside her door.

'I think I'll call it a night, Carol. I'll phone you tomorrow,' he said evenly.

'Oh. Oh, OK.' She was crestfallen, he could tell, but he just wanted to go home to bed and have a think about things. He gave the taxi driver his own address and sat back in the seat and gazed un-seeingly through the window.

Carol liked him, but mostly she liked using him to make Gary jealous, he acknowledged grimly, and that wasn't on. She'd spent the evening trying to watch her ex surreptitiously. He wasn't a fool, and it annoyed him. He should cut his losses, he decided. If Carol wanted to engage with Gary she could do it on her own time. He'd had enough.

Carol slid the black dress over her shoulders and slipped out of her underwear. She smelt of stale smoke and perfume, so a quick shower was on the cards. She was a little dismayed that Sean hadn't come in with her. He'd been a little subdued on the ride home. It must have been the scene with Gary. Drunken prat. She frowned as she stood under the spray and soaped herself. He'd made a real exhibition of himself tonight. She lifted her face to the spray. What bliss it was to have her own bathroom. She'd hated using the shared bathroom in her old flat with its dirty, chipped bath and yellowing plastic shower tray.

So Gary missed her, did he? Or was that just drink talking? If he missed her so much why didn't he phone her and ask her to get back with him? Of course he didn't have her new address, now, she thought forlornly. That would put paid to that little idea. But he could always call her at work if he wanted to.

She'd accidently dropped her mobile phone down the loo months ago and had not yet replaced it. It had annoyed him that she hadn't got a new one. She'd kept meaning to and she wished she had one now.

Carol lathered shampoo into her hair and rubbed it in hard. She didn't know what to make of this evening really, but she had the feeling that she'd annoyed Sean. Carol sighed. He was a man, wasn't he? And no man liked playing second fiddle. But she couldn't help that she still had feelings for Gary. Sean would simply have to make allowances, she thought crossly, as she stepped out of the shower and began to towel herself dry.

'Who the bloody hell's on the phone at this hour of the morning?' Mike groaned as he leapt out of bed and went downstairs to answer the phone. He had a fine hangover and he'd been woken from a deep sleep.

'Who was it?' Jessica asked groggily, emerging from under the duvet when he came back a few minutes later.

'It was bloody Gary looking for Carol's new phone number.' Mike yawned volcanically and dived back into bed.

'You didn't give it to him, did you?' Jessica demanded.

'Of course I did. It must be something urgent for him to be ringing at half eight on a Sunday morning.'

'For God's sake, Mike, you should have checked with her. Maybe she didn't want him to have her number,' Jessica spluttered, hardly able to believe her ears.

'Don't be daft, Jessie. Of course she wants him to have her number. She spent most of last night looking over Sean's shoulder for him.'

'Oh no! What does he want with her?' Jessica groaned. 'Just when she was getting over him. Sean's perfect for her.'

'No, he's not, even I can see that,' Mike retorted. 'He's far too calm and stable to give her the drama she needs. Carol's a drama queen, Jessie. She thrives on it. You know that. What difference does it make anyway whether Gary has her number or not?' Mike grabbed her and threw his leg over her.

'Ah, stop.' Jessica pushed him away. 'I know exactly what's going to happen. She's made him so jealous he's going to ask her to come back to him and she'll only agree if they get married in September with us. You wait,' she wailed.

'Did you ever think of writing a novel?' Mike scoffed. 'Because you have a vivid imagination.'

'No, I haven't,' Jessica said unhappily. 'I just know Carol!'

* * *

'It's half eight on a Sunday morning, and where did you get my number from?' Carol snapped when she recognized the voice at the other end of the line.

'It doesn't matter. And I know you're awake. You never sleep in. Look, Carol, I need to see you. We need to talk. Seriously,' Gary declared emphatically. Her eyes began to sparkle. 'Is that bloke with you?'

'That's none of your business,' Carol said coolly.

'Well, get rid of him and give me your address. I want to see you.'

'Did it ever cross your mind that I might not want to see you?' Carol retorted.

'Don't play games with me, Carol, you want to see me as much as I want to see you.' Gary was in no humour to be trifled with. Carol was silent, trying to judge how far she could push it.

'I'll meet you at the big glasshouse in the Botanics at twelve o'clock.'

'Why can't I come to your new flat?'

'Because you can't,' she said crisply. 'Yes or no?'

'OK,' he said grumpily.

'See you then,' she said airily and put down the phone. Her heart was racing. He was crawling back to her. She had him where she wanted him. Did she want him back, was the big question. She padded into her small but spotless kitchenette and poured herself a glass of orange juice.

She knew that whatever decisions she made today were going to have a lasting impact on her life. Dating Sean had been a revelation to her. His niceness left her unsure. Sean was no challenge. Gary was. She'd never be bored with Gary or he with her. Life with him would be a roller-coaster, but better a roller-coaster than a boring flat road with no hills. That would suit Mike and Jessica but not her, never her, unfortunately, she thought with a sigh.

She and Gary had some deep invisible bond and even if she were with another man he'd always be in her head, she reflected. Jessica would call her a fool for giving up someone as nice and as good to her as Sean, but she didn't understand that, deep down, Carol couldn't cope with a nice man and that was the be-all and end of it.

She ate a leisurely breakfast, had a shower and slipped into a pair of skin-tight jeans and trainers. She pulled a black sleeveless lycra top over her head and tucked it into her waistband. She looked fit and sexy, she approved, studying her reflection in the full-length mirror in her wardrobe. She smoothed some tinted moisturiser on to her face, dusted some brown and gold eyeshadow on to her eyelids, mascara'd them and applied some lipstick and a spray of perfume. She pulled on a lilac peaked cap, tucked her sunglasses into her waistband and glanced at her watch. Eleven forty-five. A nice leisurely jog up to the Botanics should keep him cooling his heels for a while, she thought calmly, stepping out of her flat and closing the door behind her.

It was a glorious day. A fresh southerly breeze had replaced the sultry weather and the skies were clear blue with just the tiniest cotton buds of clouds drifting by. Carol got into her rhythm and began to enjoy her run. She always felt so in control when she was running, and today she felt even more in control. Today was the day when she took charge of her life for good. If Gary didn't marry her in September he was out of her life. At least she'd have Sean to fall back on, she comforted herself.

Fifteen minutes later she jogged through the big green wrought-iron gates that led into the Botanic Gardens. She kept running straight towards the enormous sprawling glasshouse and saw Gary pacing up and down. She slowed to a trot, grinning. 'Gotcha!' she muttered.

He saw her and walked towards her. 'You jogged!'

'Of course I did,' she replied coolly, but she was glad to see him.

Gary shook his head. She was a cool cookie for sure. Any other woman would have been dolling herself up to the nines trying to make an impression, he thought.

'So?' she said crisply. 'What do you want?'

'You,' he said bluntly, offering her the engagement ring.

They stared at each other. Carol knew it was crunch time. She was at the fork in the road and she had to decide which way she was going. What she was going to say would affect her whole life to come. She took a deep breath. All she had ever wanted was within her grasp. Or was it? Sean had showed her a different way. A nicer way. She banished the thought.

'September. Kilbride church. The Four Winds Hotel with Jessica and Mike,' she said succinctly.

'Or else?'

'That's it, Gary. That's the deal.' For Carol it was as if time stood still as she waited for his answer.

'Ah, to hell with it. Why not? I've missed you,' he said, pulling her into his arms and kissing her hungrily.

She kissed him back. It was good to be in his arms again, but in a detached sort of way, as if she

305

were outside her body, she felt surprised that she didn't feel happier. Now that she'd got what she wanted it felt a little bit hollow. What was wrong with her? she thought irritably. She remembered the unexpected moments of happiness she'd felt with Sean. He'd treat her far better than Gary ever would, she conceded sadly. She was throwing away a different sort of life, a good sort of life. *Stop it*, she ordered, and returned Gary's kisses before suggesting they call on Jessie and Mike to break the news.

'Good idea,' he agreed, slipping the engagement ring back on to her finger and putting his arm around her waist. 'They might cook us a fry-up – I'm starving.'

Jessica's stomach lurched as she opened her front door and saw Carol and Gary standing beaming on her doorstep.

'Who is it?' Mike called from the kitchen, where he was cooking breakfast with Katie.

'It's us,' called Carol cheerily, waving her left hand under Jessica's nose to show off her now restored engagement ring. 'Put our names in the pot, we've great news for you.'

'And what's that?' Mike asked warily, coming out into the hall, followed by Katie.

'Great news, you guys, Gary and I've just got engaged again.' She beamed radiantly.

Mike shot a worried glance at Jessica, who stood as still as a statue, waiting for the dreaded words she knew were coming.

'We sure did,' grinned Gary, punching Mike on the arm. 'Order an extra wide red carpet, we're going to need it.'

'Yep,' said Carol gaily, 'we just couldn't let you two go down the aisle on your own. It would be too, too lonely. The double wedding's back on after all. Isn't it brilliant?'

23

'When did this happen?' Jessica asked weakly.

'Ten minutes ago in the Botts,' Carol said triumphantly.

'Well, mate, you won't be on your own at the altar.' Gary patted Mike on the back. 'I'll be with you all the way.'

'Well, yeah,' Mike said slowly. 'It's just, we've booked the church and hotel now but only for a single wedding. It might be difficult to change.'

'Nonsense,' Carol said briskly. 'Give me the numbers and I'll ring the hotel and the priest and sort it. We've loads of time still.'

'It's not the parish priest. A friend of Dad's is performing the ceremony,' Jessica retorted, unable to believe the way her wedding was once again being hijacked.

'Ah, great,' Carol said confidently, deliberately

308

ignoring Jessica's glower. 'He'll be no problem if he's a friend of the family.'

'What about Sean?' Katie interjected curtly.

'What about him?' growled Gary.

'Gary's the one for me,' Carol said coldly. 'And not that it's any of your business,' she glared at the other girl, 'but I'll tell him later that I'm getting married in September.'

'A lucky escape for him,' Katie drawled rudely, and disappeared into the kitchen.

'She's such a bitch.' Carol scowled.

'So what's cooking? I could eat a horse.' Gary rubbed his hands together and followed Mike into the kitchen. 'I got pretty smashed last night.'

'Tell me about it,' Mike said glumly as he opened another packet of bacon and placed the strips on the grill.

'Might as well do it in September and get it over and done with. Anything for a quiet life. I can't be doing with all this high drama,' Gary confided, pouring himself a glass of orange juice and drinking it thirstily.

'I suppose.' Mike was completely unenthusiastic, but Gary never even noticed.

'They can't see beyond themselves,' Jessica complained bitterly an hour and a half later, after the other couple had left, having eaten all around them. Even Carol had tucked into the fry-up, which was most unusual for her.

'They never even offered to help with the washing-up. You're right, Jessica, they're totally self-centred,' Katie grumbled, scrubbing the greasy wire tray of the grill.

'I *knew* it was going to happen. I *knew* we'd never get away with it. You'd think they would have copped on when you said about everything being booked, Mike. Can they not see we don't want them? Can't they take a hint?' Jessica was totally pissed off.

'What have you just said? "They can't see beyond themselves."' Mike shrugged.

'*Won't* see beyond themselves,' Jessica snorted. 'Carol knows very well that I'm not happy about it and she's ignoring it. What are we going to do?'

'What can we do,' Mike sighed, 'short of telling them outright we don't want to have a double wedding with them?'

'And if we do that, and they end up not getting married, Carol will blame me and haunt me about it for the rest of my life.'

'You've hit the nail on the head there, Jessie,' Katie observed. 'So what you have to ask yourself is: do you want her friendship or don't you? Can you live without her? That's what it all boils down to. You're in a no-win situation.'

'Right now, no and emphatically yes, to answer both your questions,' Jessica retorted. 'But unfortunately, Katie, you're right, as usual, so it looks like we're stuck with the couple from hell!'

'I don't believe it. When did this happen?' Liz shrieked down the line.

'This morning,' Jessica said forlornly.

'Where does that one get off? She can't be mucking you around like this. Tell her it's not possible. Tell her the hotel's all booked.'

'Mike tried that tack, it didn't work.'

'Well, I'll tell her then,' Liz said crossly.

There was silence on the line and she knew her daughter was tempted by the offer. 'I will. It won't cost me a thought. She had her chance. I'll ring her right now if you give me her number. Who does she think she is, dictating your wedding?'

'Ah, you'd better not, Mam, it would cause an awful row and you'd have Nancy on your back for the rest of your life, just as I'd have Carol.'

'That's no reason to let them commandeer your wedding.'

'I know, I know. It's a very awkward situation and it's all my own fault because I didn't say no outright in the first place. And Carol won't let me out of it without a row.'

'So what,' Liz challenged. 'Let them bloody well go to hell with their arsing around, one minute getting married, the next they're not. What happens if they have another row and break it off again?'

'That's not going to happen, I don't think,' Jessica said wearily. The last thing she wanted was for her mother to get on her high horse. When Liz got going all hell could break loose.

'I'm going to ring Madam Logan and give her a piece of my mind. It really is too much, Jessica.' Liz was not to be pacified.

Jessica winced at the other end of the phone.

'Mam, I don't think that's a good idea. I don't want unpleasantness between the two families. You know Nancy. If she got a bee in her bonnet about it she'd give you an awful time.' If Liz and Carol had a ding-dong on the phone there'd be skin and hair flying and God knows what might happen, especially if Nancy got involved further down the line.

'It's a pity about her,' Liz snorted. 'Well, if you change your mind let me know. I'm not happy about this. Not happy at all,' she declared emphatically. If she could get her hands on Carol Logan she'd murder her and that selfish bugger she was engaged to.

'Sean, hi,' Carol said awkwardly. 'Look, I just wanted to let you know, something unexpected happened this morning. Gary called me and asked to meet with me. Er . . . we're back together again. We're getting married in September,' she blurted.

'You're what!' He sounded shocked.

'Getting married in September,' she repeated briskly. 'Look, I can't thank you enough for all your kindness to me. I'll never forget you, but I love Gary—'

'I don't think you should go back to him,' Sean said sternly.

'It's not for you to say, Sean,' Carol said tartly. 'Look, I have to go, I've to call my mother. Thanks again for everything. Have a good life,' she said flatly and hung up. She ignored the darts of sadness that she cared not to acknowledge and picked up the phone again and dialled her mother's number. There was no answer, unfortunately. This was one phone call she definitely wasn't looking forward to. The sooner it was made the better.

Sean looked at the receiver in his hand and started to laugh at the irony of it all. He'd tossed and turned for ages the previous night, wondering how he could tell Carol that he didn't think they should keep dating. He didn't want to hurt her. That was his main priority. She had enough hurt in her life without him adding to it.

He replaced the receiver, then took a carton of milk out of the fridge and poured himself a glass. He couldn't believe that Carol would even consider getting back with that idiot she'd been engaged to. Let alone marry him.

It was going to be an absolute disaster. When she'd told him that she'd never spoken to Gary about her father and his desertion of them, he'd been shocked. She'd been engaged to the bloke, for God's sake. He was the very one she should be confiding her troubles in.

Well, apart from his male pride being hurt at her dropping him like a hot potato the minute the boyfriend looked sideways, it was a good way to end it, he reflected. He hadn't caused her any hurt, and perhaps he might have if he'd ended it. Carol might have felt rejected, having just come out of a broken engagement. She might think that all men did was reject her. He was glad he hadn't added to that pattern. Carol had got what she wanted, he hoped it all worked out for her.

'Just to let you know, Jen, Carol and I are back together,' Gary said into the answering machine. 'I

314

prefer to tell you myself rather than for you to hear it on the grapevine. That would be tacky and insensitive. Sorry I missed you. Take care of yourself.' That felt good, he thought with satisfaction, remembering the way she had cursed down the phone at him. He hadn't been a bit impressed with her childish behaviour. What difference did it make who broke the engagement off, him or Carol? Why had it been such a big deal to Jen? He'd only told a little white lie, for God's sake. Women were the oddest creatures. Sometimes he couldn't make head nor tail of them.

He stretched out on the sofa, opened a can of beer and switched on the football. Surprisingly, now that the decision to get married in September was finally made, he was quite cool about it. He was glad Carol was back where she belonged. With him, and the copper was nowhere in the running.

Carol picked up the receiver and dialled her mother's number again. She was hoping against hope that Nancy was there – she didn't particularly want to phone her from work. To her huge relief, Nancy answered after a couple of rings. She seemed coherent enough today, Carol thought gratefully, fiddling with her engagement ring. 'Ma, remember I phoned you the other day and told you the wedding was off?' Carol wriggled uncomfortably in the chair, not sure what way her mother would take her news.

'Did you? You phoned me. I don't remember,' Nancy said coldly.

'Oh!' Made sense, Carol thought wryly. 'Ma, I'm taking a few days off work next week, I'm going to come home to make plans for my wedding. We'll talk then.'

'You're coming home. I suppose I'd better tidy the place up,' her mother said tiredly.

'Get Nadine to do it,' Carol instructed.

'That one, she never lifts a finger,' Nancy moaned. 'Are you sure you want to marry this fellow? I think you'd be better off staying single. No man's worth the hassle. Look what happened to me!'

'It doesn't happen to everyone, Ma,' Carol said tightly.

'We'll see then, won't we?' her mother said ungraciously. 'I won't be wearing a hat at this wedding and if you invite your father I'm not coming.'

'Don't worry, Ma, I won't be inviting him,' Carol retorted.

'Who are you going to get to give you away? Your Uncle Larry is dead. That just leaves your Uncle Packie.'

'Ma, I don't want anyone to give me away. I'm not a piece of merchandise. No one owns me,' she said fiercely.

'You can't walk up the aisle on your own.' Her mother was aghast.

'Watch me,' said Carol.

24

'Champagne is definitely nicer against your skin.' Tara held up a piece of brocade against Jessica's cheek and studied her niece intently. 'What do you think, Liz?' She turned to her sister.

'I think you're right. The white makes you a bit washed-out-looking,' Liz agreed. 'Or did you want to go for white?' she asked her daughter, hoping that she hadn't put her foot in it.

'I'd prefer the champagne too. It's richer. I think it's better against my hair,' Jessica said briskly. She'd taken a half-day off work to shop for her wedding dress material and she was anxious to get it, and her shoes, in the one afternoon. 'So let's concentrate on champagne.'

'Fine.' Tara grinned. 'Let's get going. What's the other one wearing?'

'It's going to be a surprise,' Jessica said drily.

'Who's making it?' her godmother asked,

wondering if it was anyone from Arklow that she knew.

'Oh, she's not getting it *made*. She's going on about a creation that she saw in Marian Gale's, a very posh boutique.'

'That will probably cost a fortune.' Tara raised an eyebrow.

'I know. So that's what you're up against. Think you can rise to the challenge?' Jessica said straight-faced.

'Cheeky wagon.' Tara laughed. 'Do you hear that one, Liz? If she's not careful I'll send her up the aisle with her hem hanging and her darts crooked.'

'Do you know what I was thinking?' Jessica said slowly. 'If I could get a nice beaded bustier and you could make a fairly straight skirt with a train at the back instead of having to make a whole dress, it could be very nice, couldn't it? And I'd get great wear out of the bustier. It would go lovely with a pair of elegant black trousers and high-heeled sandals. So it's not something that would be worn once and left hanging in the wardrobe.'

'Good thinking, niece. A bustier would suit your figure very nicely. You've got the boobs for it and the small waist,' Tara approved. 'In that case I suggest we get the bustier first so that we can come back here to Hickey's and match the material.'

'I know they do wedding dresses here, but there's a gorgeous bridal boutique just down the road from us and they had some lovely bustiers. That's where I got the idea from. It's in Hart's Corner. Could we nip back over to have a look? It wouldn't take long,' Jessica suggested.

'Sure. Whatever you want. You're the bride and I'm having a ball,' Tara declared.

An exhilarating two and a half hours later, Jessica was the proud owner of her wedding regalia. The saleswoman in Bridal Corner had been extremely helpful and knowledgeable. It was a relief to place herself in the hands of someone who knew the bridal business inside out and was able to make very pertinent suggestions.

With her help, Jessica selected a beaded champagne bustier encrusted with diamanté. The bodice criss-crossed at the back to come to just below the hip, accentuating her neat waist. At the saleswoman's suggestion, upon hearing that it was a September wedding, she selected a soft creamy pashmina to accessorize the outfit. Tara had completely agreed with the suggestion of edging the hem of Jessica's skirt with diamanté to co-ordinate with the bustier and finish off the look.

She decided against a veil, having tried a few on, preferring to wear a single yellow rose, with her hair swept up to the side.

Instead of paying two hundred euro for a pair of bridal shoes, the saleswoman had diplomatically suggested that they have a look in some of the large shoe shops for diamanté sandals.

In a state of high excitement they had driven back to the ILAC, parked, and hurried over to Hickey's to select the material for the skirt. Organza was very 'this season', the saleswoman in Bridal Corner had offered helpfully, and when Jessica had seen the richness of the material she knew it was precisely what she wanted.

Having selected her material, they legged it over to the ILAC and finally, having tried three shoe shops, had found the perfect pair of dainty sandals for forty euro in Barretts.

Jessica was thrilled with herself. Her selections were beautiful and classy but she hadn't spent a fortune and she hadn't tormented herself by dithering over this and that.

'You're some woman to go,' Tara said admiringly as she tucked into a spring roll in a Chinese restaurant on Abbey Street.

'I hate shopping. I made up my mind that I was getting my stuff today and that was it. You could drive yourself mad going to this place and that,' confessed Jessica. 'Thanks a million for coming, Tara.'

'You're welcome. I'm enjoying myself immensely,' Tara said warmly.

'You're going to look lovely.' Liz smiled at her daughter. 'Very classy and elegant.'

'Well, I didn't want a meringue. I'm not tall enough for it. And the veils looked a bit OTT on me, didn't they?'

'Cathedral length isn't you. And a short one would cut the outfit in half. I think you're right to go with something simple in the hair. The bustier is so decorative, it's all you need,' Tara agreed.

'Is Nadine doing bridesmaid for Carol?' Liz sipped her wine appreciatively.

'Nope. Flatly refused. A friend of hers is going to be her bridesmaid. I think she's better off, to be honest. Nadine's a loose cannon. You wouldn't know what she'd do on the day.'

Liz's lips tightened. 'She'd better behave herself at the wedding.'

'I'm sure she'll be fine,' Jessica backtracked hastily.

'Is her father coming to the wedding?' Liz inquired.

'Er . . . I don't think so.'

'Well, of course, there's been bad feelings between them for years, I can't say I'm surprised. Who's going to walk her up the aisle? I hope it won't be Nancy, because having seen the state of her lately she'll be staggering up it,' Liz sniffed.

Oh Lord! Jessica groaned inwardly. The day had turned out very well; she didn't want to have any bad vibes now.

'You know, Liz, I think we should pop into Michael H on our way back to the car. I just happened to notice a lovely dress and coat ensemble in the window when we were passing. It might suit you very well for the wedding,' Tara interjected diplomatically, aware of the rising tension.

'Good idea. Wouldn't it be great if we got your outfit as well? Would it be too much to hope for?' Jessica said eagerly. She could have kissed her aunt for changing the subject. Liz was still very annoyed at the double wedding plan and never lost a chance to let Jessica know that she wasn't impressed.

'I suppose so,' Liz said unenthusiastically. 'I haven't given much thought to what I'm going to wear.' Jessica felt a surge of irritation. Her mother was making no effort. She'd been very subdued all day, allowing Tara to take the lead. She could give the appearance of being interested, she thought resentfully. She knew what was wrong with her mother. Niggling at the back of her own mind lurked guilt. Guilt because she'd enjoyed herself buying her wedding outfit even while being aware that her mother's heart wasn't in it because she was missing Ray.

A dart of sadness pierced her. If her father were alive, she would be deliriously happy. Longing to walk down the aisle on his arm. But he wasn't and no amount of guilt or grief would bring him back. And besides, she knew that Ray would hate to think that they couldn't enjoy the wedding because he wasn't there. She understood where her mother was coming from and she felt terribly sorry for her. But part of her felt resentful, which made her feel guilty, which in turn made her feel resentful again and she felt like calling the whole thing off.

'It was just a suggestion,' she said, trying to keep the edge out of her voice.

'No time like the present, Liz,' Tara said briskly, demolishing a prawn cracker. 'We'll have a look. Might get some ideas. If you prefer I can make you an outfit.'

'Will you stop rushing me?' Liz said testily.

'Dear, if I was rushing you, you'd know about

it,' Tara drawled. 'Now eat up your greens and do what you're told.'

'You always were a bossy boots,' Liz said crossly.

'Prerogative of the older sister,' Tara said equably. 'If you're a good girl tonight you can have a whole bottle of wine. It might put a smile on your face. Great for your facial tone . . . smiles,' she said pointedly.

'Ah, give over,' Liz retorted, but it was said fondly, and Jessica gave a sigh of relief.

'Mam! It's gorgeous. It's really, really elegant,' Jessica raved an hour later as her mother stepped out through the wooden swing doors of the fitting cubicle in Michael H.

'Is it a bit Mother of the Bridey?' Liz demurred as she stood in front of a full-length mirror and studied her appearance with a critical eye.

'Well, that's what you are, you idiot.' Tara threw her eyes up to heaven. 'But I know what you mean,' she conceded. 'And no. It's an outfit that could take you anywhere. You can mix it and match it. Dress it up or down. I think it's smashing.'

'It is nice, isn't it?' Liz agreed, turning around to have a look at the back. It was a simple cerise linen shift dress, superbly cut, with a grey, full-length lightweight coat. The coat had cerise buttons and cerise edging at the collar and cuffs. As Tara had said, it could be worn anywhere.

'What do you think?' Liz asked Jessica, still unsure.

'I love it, but you're the one that will be wearing it, Mam, so it's up to you.'

'Hmm, I'm not sure. Maybe I'll leave it. I might take a trip to Gorey, there's a few good boutiques there,' Liz decided, retracing her steps back to the cubicle.

'I thought it was gorgeous on her,' Jessica whispered, disappointed as she and Tara flicked through the rails while Liz got dressed.

'So did I,' Tara murmured.

'She's in a dodgy sort of humour these days. It's really getting me down,' Jessica confessed.

'Try not to take it personally. I know it's hard for her. But damn, it's hard for you too. Do you want me to have a talk with her?' Tara offered.

'Oh, no, I don't think so, thanks all the same,' Jessica said hastily. 'That might really get her back up. And anyway, I don't want her to think that we're ganging up on her either. Both of us will just have to get on with it and make the best of it.'

'Well, you did good today, girl, and you're going to look beautiful. Mike's eyes will be out on stalks or my name's not Tara Johnston! In fact he might even *have* a stalk on him when he sees you in that bustier,' Tara declared.

Jessica giggled. Her aunt was incorrigible.

'What are you two laughing at?' Liz demanded suspiciously, coming up behind them.

'Aunt–niece confidentiality, I'm afraid. Rest assured it wasn't about you. You're not the sole topic of conversation, despite what you might think,' Tara said airily, holding a blouse up against herself. 'I think I'll try this on. Might as well treat myself to something, seeing as I'm up in the big smoke.'

'What was she saying to you?' Liz couldn't contain her curiosity as Tara headed for the changing cubicles. 'Was she giving out because I didn't buy the outfit?'

'No, Mother, she wasn't,' Jessica said tartly. 'She made a very vulgar joke, if you want to know.'

'Oh . . . oh,' Liz said, deflated. 'Are you going to share it with me?'

'I don't know if you're in the humour for vulgar jokes.' Jessica made a face.

'What does that mean?' Liz bristled. 'I'm no prude. How could you be a prude related to that one?' She indicated the changing-room where Tara was.

Jessica sighed. 'It's nothing to do with you being

a prude, Mam, it's just . . .' She hesitated. 'It's just . . .'

'What? Just what?' demanded Liz.

'There you go, that sort of thing,' Jessica said hotly. 'Always on the defensive, tetchy. I can't do anything right lately.'

They stared at each other over a clothes rail. Liz's face crumpled.

'I'm sorry, Jessie. I'm really sorry. I know I'm being a wagon, I can't seem to contain it. I think I must be starting the change or something. I am fierce tetchy these days, aren't I?'

'You're *not* starting the change, you're only forty-six, Mam!' Jessica couldn't hide her exasperation.

'Well, I could be,' Liz said defensively.

'No, you're not, you only had a blood test six months ago when you went for a cholesterol check. I remember you telling me about it, that the doctor did a range of tests, and you weren't menopausal. Don't be wishing that on yourself.'

'I'm not.' Liz scowled.

'Look, I know what's wrong with you. And I *do* understand,' she said earnestly. 'I know you're missing Dad like mad, so am I. But we've got to get on with things. That's why I wanted to keep the wedding as low-key as possible.'

Liz bit her lip and shook her head. 'I know, Jessie. I know. I'm being very self-centred. I'm sorry. Take no notice of me.'

'Don't be daft.' Jessica walked around to the other side of the rail and hugged her mother. 'We'll get through it together and try and have as good a day as we can.'

'You're right, love. And you're going to look stunning.'

'I hope so.' Jessica smiled, glad that they had cleared the air.

'Go on, tell me what that Tara one said to you,' Liz urged, tucking her arm into Jessica's.

Grinning, Jessica repeated Tara's assertions and was rewarded by her mother's loud guffaw, which brought a smile of relief to her aunt's face as she pranced out of the cubicle to show off her new blouse.

25

'Hi, Liz. Hi, Tara.' Carol greeted the sisters affably, following Jessica into the sitting-room. She'd jogged up from Phibsboro to see them. 'Did you have a good day shopping?'

'Very productive,' Tara informed her. She was sprawled on Jessica's couch with her shoes off, drinking red wine. She looked very fit and healthy for a woman in her late forties, Carol thought sourly. Tara did a lot of hill-walking and her shapely tanned legs would be the envy of many a twenty-year-old.

'What did you buy?' Carol perched on the side of an armchair and smiled down at Liz.

'I bought nothing. Tara bought a blouse and a new set of pinking shears and Jessie bought her wedding outfit.'

'What! Already?' Carol couldn't believe it. 'What did she buy? Let's see it. Did she bring it home?'

Tara held up her hand authoritatively. 'Sorry! No viewing until the day of the wedding. It's my baby until the wedding day.'

'Aw, Tara, come on, don't be a meanie,' Carol protested. 'Jessie, let's see what you bought. Have you bought everything?' she asked her friend, who had just walked back into the sitting-room.

'I sure did. I've no intentions of traipsing around day in day out trying to decide what to wear. I knew what I wanted; I went for it, and I've got the material and my shoes—'

'Your shoes as well? Were they an awful price? I was shocked when I went looking,' Carol said ruefully.

'Forty euro in Barratts,' Jessica informed her cheerfully. 'Glass of wine?'

'Forty euro in Barratts. You bought your wedding shoes in *Barratts*?' Carol couldn't believe her ears as she shook her head at the offer of wine.

'I certainly did, and they're gorgeous, and if you've any sense you'll do the same and not be spending a small fortune on a pair of shoes that you'll get precious little wear out of.'

'But it's your wedding day!' protested Carol.

'So?' Jessica said coolly.

'But don't you want everything to be special?'

'Of course I do. I'm not going to walk down the

aisle looking like Secondhand Rose, Carol, but I'm not spending a fortune either. We don't have a fortune to spend.'

'Did you get Katie's dress yet?' Carol changed the subject.

'No. We're going to have to shop for it one of these days.'

'Have you bought yours yet or are you having it made?' Tara said silkily.

'Actually I'm buying mine.' Carol fiddled with her engagement ring. She liked Tara about as much as she liked Katie. Mother and daughter were too alike for her tastes.

'Some of them are fairly pricey, if the ones we were looking at today were anything to go by. Do you remember that satin sheath we saw? It was outrageous. One thousand, five hundred euro. I'd make it for the price of the material,' Tara remarked.

'Not everyone is as talented as you, Tara,' Carol said drily, not sure whether she was being got at or not.

'We're heading out for dinner. I've booked a table in Kelly and Ping's at eight-thirty if you'd like to come,' Jessica interjected swiftly.

'Thanks, but no, I'll continue my run, Gary's meeting me in the club later. I just popped in to say hello,' Carol said hastily. Having dinner with Tara and Katie was an ordeal she could do without.

'By the way, I assume the men will be wearing morning suits?' She looked at Jessica for confirmation.

'Umm . . . well, actually Mike was thinking of wearing the new grey suit he bought for his interview.'

'You're joking, Jessie! He can't go up the aisle in a business suit.' She was clearly horrified.

'Well, he can and he will, Carol. Hiring suits costs a fortune. And you never know who's been in them. I'd hate to have to wear a rented suit, wouldn't you?'

'Men don't care. They don't think of things like that. Aw, come on, Jessica, I really want Gary to look his best. Top hat and tails is de rigueur. Isn't it?' She appealed to Liz.

'I'm not getting involved, Carol. Sort it out yourselves,' Liz said firmly.

'Well, Gary can wear top hat and tails if he wants to,' Jessica said matter-of-factly.

'Don't be ridiculous,' scoffed Carol. 'It would look stupid in the photos if Gary was in top hat and tails and Mike was in a suit.'

'We can do separate photos,' Jessica pointed out reasonably.

'I suppose,' Carol said sulkily, seeing that she was getting nowhere.

'I was wondering if it would be a good idea for you and Nancy and myself and Jessie to meet up and have a chat. We need to discuss the menu and so on and so forth,' Liz suggested. 'Why don't you both come over Sunday afternoon? We need to meet sooner rather than later and it would be good to have the arrangements agreed upon and finalized, don't you think?'

'If you say so,' Carol said curtly, standing up. 'I'll get Gary to bring me down on Sunday. See you then.'

'Bye, Carol,' Tara said cheerfully, ignoring the tension in the air.

'I can give you a lift down tomorrow if you want. We're leaving after breakfast,' Jessica offered. She knew Carol was in a huff over the suit business and as usual felt it was up to her to smooth ruffled feathers.

'No, thanks, I've a match tomorrow afternoon.' Carol didn't even look at her as she marched out into the hall.

'Right, I'll see you Sunday.' Jessica smiled brightly, determined not to be riled. She didn't want her mother getting on her high horse about tensions between herself and Carol. She had enough on her plate as it was, she thought resentfully, tired of having to constantly mollify the pair of them. It was her bloody wedding, for crying out loud – people should be mollifying *her*!

Carol picked up her rhythm as she jogged on to Botanic Road and headed northwards. She was pissed off big time. She might as well be a spectator at this bloody wedding for all the input she was having. Jessica had picked the date, the church, the venue, without reference to what she or Gary wanted. Now she was dictating the dress code. It just wasn't fair, she thought bitterly. For two pins she'd tell her so-called best friend to shove her fucking wedding up her arse. If only she wasn't so constrained. So desperate. If she pulled out now, she'd never get Gary up the aisle. When she'd suggested the double wedding, she'd never dreamed that Mike and Jessie would be such cheapskates about the biggest day of their lives.

The nicest thing in the world would have been to plan the wedding of her dreams, she thought wistfully. A wedding that wouldn't take place in the bloody sticks. She was damn sure she wouldn't be having her wedding reception in a parochial little hotel in a parochial little town where everybody knew everybody's business. It was galling to think that half the parish would know what was on the menu and approximately how much the wedding had cost.

She'd felt like telling Liz to stuff her meeting. What was the point in having a meeting to 'discuss' the menu and so on, when anything she suggested would be steamrolled by that pair of bossy wagons, Carol thought sourly as she pounded purposefully along the pavement.

If it were left to her she would have a wedding in Dublin in as posh an hotel as they could afford. She'd travel to the church in a white limo, and step out on to a red carpet, the queen of all she surveyed. After a poetic, artistic service she'd be photographed in the Botanic Gardens, before joining her guests to drink champagne while a stylish, sophisticated quartet played classical music in the background. They would dine like kings on lobster and quail, she thought wistfully, as she turned left and ran parallel to the Tolka River before turning right to tackle the Washerwoman's Hill.

Her wedding list would reflect her refined tastes, not for her chunky glassware and china from Woodies and Dunnes and Roches. She'd have the finest linen, the most elegant tableware, the most delicate crystal, she fantasized as she kept up the pace, ignoring her aching knees and lungs.

But what was the point, she thought mournfully as she crested the hill and jogged past the Bon Secours Hospital, bathed in the late evening sun. What was the point in spending a fortune on her wedding dress? No one except the nosy neighbours would see it and be impressed. She didn't give a hoot about impressing the neighbours at home, she thought disdainfully. They all looked down their noses at the Logans; they could go to hell. Maybe she wouldn't buy the fabulous brocade dress that had cost a fortune but had made her look like a vision in white. It would be wasted on the hicks down home. She could be parsimonious like Jessica and save herself a couple of thousand euro and buy a dress in a mediocre little bridal boutique, or even worse, get it made by Tara, she though disdainfully. How small-town tacky was that?

'No!' she muttered grimly. She wasn't going to sink to those levels. She was going to have a decent wedding dress, even if she didn't buy it in Marian Gale's, and damn it, she thought mulishly, she was going to have a wedding list, even though Liz had snootily said when she had mentioned the subject at one stage that 'it was far from wedding lists she was reared'.

Liz could huff and puff and think what she

wanted. She wasn't in control of everything, much as she might think she was. This was one show she wasn't running. Carol would have her wedding list, and what was more, she'd have the most sophisticated, glamorous wedding list those cheapskate hicks had ever seen, she thought determinedly as she sprinted with renewed vigour up the Ballymun Road.

'You know, Jessie, they *are* sharing the wedding and the expenses with us, you should let Carol have some leeway and input,' Mike said thoughtfully as they walked hand in hand along Brittas Bay the following afternoon.

'Oh, for God's sake, Mike, top hat and tails. It's so pretentious. *And* expensive,' Jessica said irritably, annoyed with him because his words had a ring of truth. She *had* made all the major decisions, it was true, but she had given Carol the choice to back out on several occasions if she wanted to.

'Jessica, we're not impoverished – we can afford to hire a dress suit,' Mike said firmly. 'I'm the one that will be wearing it and I don't mind, and if Carol wants us to dress up in monkey suits I think we should let her have some say.'

'Fine,' she said tightly.

'Don't get into a huff,' he warned. 'After all, fair is fair.'

'OK, don't lecture me,' she snapped.

'Don't forget you were the one who agreed to it, so don't get cranky with me.' Mike nudged her in the ribs and pinched her waist.

'Stop, I'm not in the humour.'

'How about a ride in the dunes? I know what's wrong with you, you're frustrated,' he teased.

'You can say that again, but not the way you mean,' Jessica said grumpily.

'What else has to be sorted?' he asked, drawing her close.

'Well, we're having a meeting on Sunday to discuss the menu. I have a selection from the hotel. We've to sort out the invites. The photographer, the church music and the band.'

'Has Carol expressed any preferences?' He eyed her quizzically.

'No, she's in a huff with me over the suits.'

'Well, now that we've agreed to go with her suggestion, she might get out of her huff. Why don't you give her a ring?' Mike suggested.

'OK, OK, I'll do it this evening. She's playing a match today allegedly. That was her excuse for not taking a lift.'

'Come on, now, Jessie, be fair. She probably is

playing a match. You know how involved she is. Ring her tonight so that when she comes down tomorrow she'll be in a better frame of mind. Let's try and not make this a battleground.'

'OK,' she murmured, subdued. Mike was such a decent bloke. Unwittingly he'd just made her feel a complete and selfish heel and childish to boot.

'I've a surprise for you.' Her fiancé changed the subject.

'What's that?' She made an effort to lighten up.

'I've made an appointment for us to view two houses for rent later on.'

Jessica brightened up. 'Where are they?'

'One's in Newcastle, the other's in Bray,' Mike said cheerfully.

'Bray wouldn't be so bad for commuting,' Jessica mused.

'Newcastle's not too bad if you come the back road,' Mike observed.

'I know, but the N11's a real nightmare, isn't it? The absolute pits,' Jessica grumbled. It had taken her over two hours to drive the fifty miles home, a few hours earlier. It hadn't helped that the sun was splitting the trees and the day-trippers from Dublin were heading to Brittas.

'Tell me about it. I'm working on it,' grinned Mike ruefully.

'I can't wait to have a place of our own,' Jessica said longingly, as she kicked off her sandals and allowed the white foamy waves to flow between her toes.

'It'll be great, won't it? I really miss you, Jessie. It's awful lonely without you.'

'I know, and besides, I'm spending a fortune on phone credit so we might as well put that money towards rent—'

'And petrol,' Mike interjected. 'Are you sure you won't mind the commute?'

'Not if it means being with you, and besides, the roadworks can't go on for ever and it will be a great road when it's finished. And to be honest, I'm not mad about the idea of buying a house in Dublin eventually. The prices are way over the top. It's crazy.'

'So where do you want to live?' Mike skimmed a stone across the top of the waves.

'Let's get married first and then we can see what's out there, will we? Sorry I was so grumpy,' she apologized.

'You grumpy? Never!' Mike grinned, and yelled when she splashed him with water.

That evening they drove up to a modern town-house on the outskirts of Bray. Two other couples were there before them and Jessica felt her tension levels ratchet up another notch. Just say she and Mike loved the house and so did the other couples. Would there be a bidding war based on offers of rental costs?

It was a house that had been furnished with letting in mind. Minimalist, not quite cheap but not high quality either. The two-bedroom house was small and cramped and she couldn't help comparing it with the well-appointed house she was sharing with Katie. It certainly didn't merit the fifteen hundred euro a month rent the landlord was looking for, she thought glumly, as she stood in the master bedroom with an ensuite so cramped you could hardly turn around in it. The double bed took up most of the room. Badly fitted melamine wardrobes and two cheap white lockers completed the furnishings. Mike made a face.

'Not mad about it,' he whispered. 'Did you see the back garden, it's a postage stamp.'

'I know. I just got the shivers when I went out into it. It was overlooked from every angle. There wasn't an inch of privacy.'

'Not us,' Mike murmured as another couple squeezed into the room.

'Yeah, but we have to be realistic. If we're trying to save as well as pay rent we're hardly going to get a palace,' Jessica said pragmatically as they walked down the stairs to the modest hall.

'I know, but it's the first place we've looked at. Let's try the Newcastle property. It sounds good. A detached three-bedroom bungalow on a quarter of an acre.'

'It does sound nice, doesn't it?' Jessica tucked her arm into his as they walked out of the tiny front garden to where the car was parked.

'What a nerve! To look for a thousand euro for this dump,' Jessie hissed an hour later as she wrinkled up her nose at the smell of musty damp that pervaded every room of the bungalow. Despite the fact that someone had gone to the trouble of spraying at least a can of room freshener around the place, the smell of must and damp was impossible to hide.

'The property hasn't been lived in for some time,' the estate agent said smoothly as she led them into a lino-floored kitchen that had seen better days.

'Not even if they gave it to us rent-free would I live in that kip,' Jessica declared as they got back into the car. 'What a waste of time. Are they all going to be like this? What if we don't find anything decent and affordable?' she fretted.

'Calm down. We will.'

'I don't want to live with Mam, do you?'

'I like your mother,' Mike said diplomatically.

'I love her,' Jessica said irritably. 'It's just I'd like us to be on our own. Am I awful?'

'No, you're not. It will be fine, Jessie.'

'I'd like to be able to jump on you when I'm horny. Like I am right now.' Jessica leaned across and kissed him passionately on the mouth. She'd missed him like crazy and even though they'd be sleeping together at her mother's tonight, she couldn't see them having a wild night. Her inhibitions always got the better of her.

'Come on, ya wild woman, I noticed a lane half a mile down the road, we could pull in and I'll sort you out.' Mike grinned at her when she drew back breathless. 'Variety is the spice of life.'

'Oh God, I needed that,' Jessica breathed half an hour later as she leaned against Mike, inhaling the male musky scent of him. She was straddling him in the back seat of the car, which was parked down a dry dusty lane, sheltered and shaded by two huge oak trees.

'What am I letting myself in for? A rampant woman. I'm wrecked,' he groaned.

'Ah, don't be such a wussie,' giggled Jessica, happy to be in his arms.

'Will I be able for you? Am I safe?' Mike asked

in mock alarm as she launched herself on him again and kissed him soundly.

'You've had it, boy. Do you want to have a rethink?' she teased.

'Well, now that you mention it, there's a tasty babe with very low mileage on he—' That was as far as he got before Jessica clamped one hand over his mouth and pulled his hair with the other.

They wrestled and laughed and kissed joyfully, happy to be in each other's company, temporarily laying aside the stresses and strains of looking for accommodation and preparing for a wedding.

'Maybe we should have stuck to our original plan,' Jessica reflected as they drove back towards Arklow late that evening. 'It was a bit impetuous deciding to get married so soon. We didn't think it out properly, sure we didn't. Would we have been better off getting ourselves settled in a house first?'

'The right house will come, stop panicking,' Mike said easily. 'And it couldn't be too soon for me to marry you.'

'Same here,' Jessica agreed, suddenly as happy as could be.

'Hey, why don't you give Carol a ring and tell her I'll get the monkey suit and then we'll stop in Il Cacciatore for one of their scrumptious Hawaiians.'

'Hmm, that sounds good. Now that you mention it, I'm ravenous.'

'I'm not surprised,' Mike said wryly and she giggled.

'It's not my fault if you're too sexy for your own good and I can't keep my hands off you,' she retorted as she rooted her mobile out of her bag and punched in Carol's number.

'Hello,' the other girl said snootily. Jessica's number had obviously come up on her caller ID.

Jessica ignored her sulky tone. 'Carol, hiya. Look, it's about the conversation we had about what the guys are wearing. Just thinking about it, you're probably right, it would look a bit odd in the photos if Gary was in formal wear and Mike was in a suit, so if you still want to we'll go for the posh gear,' she said magnanimously.

There was a momentary silence. 'So I finally get my way on something at last,' she responded coolly.

'If that's the way you want to look at it, Carol. You can always pull out. Don't let me stop you,' Jessica snapped, ending the call.

Grim-faced, she stared straight ahead. If this carry-on went on for much longer, she'd be a basket case.

Prudently, Mike said nothing but just kept on driving.

26

'I don't think you should do it. I think she's made her wishes quite clear,' Brona Wallace said angrily as she shrugged out of her dressing-gown and got into bed.

'I don't understand you, Brona.' Bill turned around and glared at her. 'You were all for me making my peace with Carol and walking down the aisle with her. And now you've done a complete about-turn. Why?' He sat on the end of the bed in his underpants, one sock on, one sock off, his skinny shoulders sagging.

Not a very inspiring sight, Brona thought apathetically.

'You tried to heal the rift, it didn't work, I'd leave it if I were you.'

Brona burrowed down under the duvet. Ever since she'd had the disastrous conversation with Carol she'd felt like a cat on a hot tin roof.

Bill had left his young daughters in the lurch. There was nothing to say that he wouldn't do the same to her and Ben if things got rocky. Imagine if she developed some horrible disease like MS or ME and she was left dependent on him, she fantasized gloomily, ever the pessimist. He could do a runner on her and their child if things got bad and the going got tough, just as he had on Nancy and his girls. She couldn't help thinking like this. She didn't want to. These horrible thoughts had just invaded her mind as the weeks passed and she couldn't ignore them.

'Look, she's my daughter. I owe it to her to try,' Bill said earnestly, getting into bed beside her.

A bit late now. Brona bit back the obvious retort.

'If you go down there tomorrow it will only make things worse,' Brona warned. 'How do you know Nancy will be there anyway? Did you call her?'

'And give her the chance to hang up? No,' Bill retorted. 'I'll take my chances and hope that she's not too sozzled at that hour of the day.'

'You're going to get your wedding gift thrown back in your face. You know that. I think you were mad buying it.'

'That's a risk I'll have to take.' Bill snapped off the light.

'I hope you kept your receipt,' Brona muttered caustically, turning on her side away from him.

Bill lay beside his partner, troubled and angry. What was her problem? Why had she changed her attitude about his attempted rapprochement with his daughter and become so cool and bad-tempered towards him?

He sighed the deep frustrated sigh of the beleaguered. Didn't Brona understand how important it was for him to be part of Carol's big day? It was hard to believe that his daughter was getting married. He remembered so well the day she was born and the surprisingly strong grip of her tiny, perfect hand on his finger. She'd always been such an independent little thing, he remembered fondly. 'I'll do it mine own self,' her favourite phrase. She had loved to play football with him in the back garden, and later when she was older he had taught her to play tennis. Their happiest times as father and daughter had been on the tennis court. Bill smiled in the dark, remembering her tenacity and how she fought for every point, determined always to win.

He and Nancy had been happy enough during Carol's early childhood, although his wife had always been insecure, watching him like a hawk when they were out socializing. He'd dared not spend too long chatting to a woman, or the grand inquisition would ensue and there'd be tears and tantrums.

It was after Nadine's birth that the nightmare had really begun. Nancy had become more and more irrational and had started drinking heavily. He'd stuck it for five years before he'd cracked and left the family home, feeling it was the best for all of them. He'd been exemplary in his financial care of them, he assured himself, as he lay, rigid and unhappy, beside Brona. He'd lived in a soul-destroying grotty little bedsit in Ranelagh for that first horrible year in Dublin as he tried to come to terms with the fact that his wife had turned into a looper, his marriage was over and he was practically homeless and penniless.

He lodged the major part of his pay cheque into Nancy's account, although over the years he'd opened another account to pay the household bills by direct debit when he'd realized that Nancy was spending a fortune on drink and the bills had been piling up unpaid. There had been such a screaming match when that had come to light. His biggest regret was that his children had witnessed that. He could still remember the two girls yelling at him and Nancy to stop shouting at each other. It still bothered him, but he was only human, and he'd been pushed to his limit. He'd been working his fingers to the bone, even doing a part-time telephonist's job at night to boost his income. Most of it went on Nancy and the girls and then to discover that she wasn't even paying the bills, that she owed money! That had been the lowest point of his life.

Tears prickled his eyes at the remembrance of that desperately lonely year. Was he to be given no credit for the contributions he made to the family home so that they could have a comfortable lifestyle? Carol was so cold towards him. She seemed to have no appreciation for the sacrifices he had made. He was the one who had been left without a roof over his head. He'd had to rent a grotty little room while they slept in their comfortable beds in their well-appointed house.

Bitterness seeped through Bill. Nadine had no respect for him, and had actually told him to fuck off on more than one occasion when at his wife's behest he'd spoken to her about her truancy from school and general behaviour. Nancy never lost a chance to badmouth him. Nothing he did was right. It was most unfair. She had poisoned his daughters' minds against him. It wasn't really their fault, he thought sorrowfully.

Brona had been his solace. He'd been able to pour out his despair and distress to her and she had comforted and consoled him and made him feel that he was a good, kind human being. When their baby son had been born he'd felt he was given a second chance. Now Brona was being very moody indeed and he didn't know what her problem was. He'd never known her to be like this and he was at a complete loss.

He plumped his pillows into a more comfortable position. He had made up his mind, and once Bill Logan made up his mind that was it, he thought grimly. He was going to Arklow tomorrow to see his wife and offer to pay for the wedding. He was going to make it clear that he very much wanted to be part of Carol's most special day. He wanted very much to walk her down the aisle. And he was bringing the expensive state-of-the-art hi-fi system that he had selected as his wedding present to his eldest daughter.

Surely, when she saw how sincere he was in his desire to be part of her wedding, she would soften and relent. He would remind her of how he had, and still did, support them financially. He would assure her that he would be happy to pay for her wedding out of love for her.

Brona could be as cynical as she liked, he

scowled, remembering her unkind barb about keeping the receipt, but he was very optimistic. This might be a fresh start for them all as a family, and eventually in time they'd be able to accept his relationship with Brona and have a loving sibling relationship with their little brother Ben.

'What time do you want to leave for Arklow?' Gary took a slug out of his bottle of Miller and eyed his fiancée warily. She hadn't been in the best of humours all day but she wouldn't tell him why.

'There's no point going before lunch, because Mam won't have got food in for us, so I suppose around two. Liz said to come over to her house between half three and four.' Carol ran the iron over the cream linen trousers she was planning to wear.

'Look, why don't we drive down and stop some-where en route for lunch? The Avoca Handweavers or Chester Beatty's in Ashford or wherever you want,' Gary suggested kindly.

'Hey, that's an idea. It would be nice to have a peaceful lunch together before we face the multitude. I'd like that.'

'Are you not looking forward to it? I thought you women loved planning things like weddings,' he asked in surprise, surfing the channels to see what was on.

'Oh, I am,' Carol fibbed. 'It's just that Mike and Jessie aren't anxious to spend a fortune, naturally. They're inclined to have quite a small wedding. Because Ray's dead, I suppose.'

'We can do our own thing if you want . . . I told you that before. I don't know what the rush is. I think we're fine as we are,' he retorted, eyes on a sports bulletin on the TV.

'No, no. Let's do it. It will be fine. You don't know any good bands, do you?' She changed the subject hastily, not wanting him to think she was giving him any excuse to wriggle out of the wedding.

'Yeah, I know a few. Remember that session we all went to in Swords, the Righteous Rockers?'

'They were great. We bopped all night,' Carol responded enthusiastically.

'One of my brothers knows them. I can get him to give them a shout and see what they charge.'

'Do they do weddings?'

'Wakes, funerals, christenings, bar mitzvahs, you name it.' Gary stretched and yawned. 'And by the way, one of the blokes at work gave me a few samples of invitations he does on the computer. They're good and they're half the price of the ones you have to buy in stationery shops.'

'Have you got the samples?' Carol couldn't believe that she was having this conversation with Gary. He was talking about wedding invitations. This surely was a step on the right path.

'I'll root them out and you can bring them with you if you want. Oh, bloody good shot,' he enthused as a footballer landed a goal into the back of the net.

It was all going to work out OK, she should stop worrying about it, she decided as she unplugged the iron. Jessica had come around to her way of thinking about the dress suits. If she could get her to agree to the Righteous Rockers for the reception, at least they'd have a lively night.

'Would you like anything for supper?' she asked.

'You,' Gary grinned, pulling her down beside him on the sofa. 'This is a much better flat than that last kip you were in. You should have got a place like this years ago. That copper did you a favour,' he murmured as he slid his hand up under her T-shirt.

'You think so?' she said softly, loving the feel of his fingers on her skin.

'And there's a grand double bed in the bedroom,' he said huskily, undoing her bra. 'Let's have our supper in there.'

If he hadn't mentioned the wedding invites, Carol most likely would have refused as she normally did. But she was tired of saying no. She was as human as the next person, and a sexy, loving interlude would be balm to her weary spirit. Her constant refusal to have full sex with Gary was a source of ongoing friction between them. She was well aware that he could, and possibly did, look elsewhere. Jen had been the living proof of that. She often wondered did he see the redheaded bimbo he took to the Mid-Summer's Ball.

'Have you got condoms?' She drew away from him, looking him straight in the eye.

'Do I what?' Gary looked at her, astonished. 'Are we going all the way?' he asked eagerly.

'You sound like a gauche sixteen-year-old,' Carol retorted, amused. 'Come on.'

'Oh yesss!' Gary jumped off the sofa and punched his fist in the air. 'You're so sexy you drive me nuts.'

'Do I?' Carol murmured seductively, stepping out of her jeans. His ardour was turning her on, and now that she'd finally made the decision to sleep with him she was looking forward to it. He grabbed her and kissed her passionately and she returned his kisses ardently, allowing herself to believe that he truly did love her. It was a raunchy, wild, swift coupling that left both of them bathed in sweat as they lay, limbs wrapped around each other, exhausted after their passion.

'It was worth the wait,' Gary murmured against her hair once his breathing had slowed down.

'Make the most of it, I don't want to worry about getting preggers,' Carol murmured, beginning to feel apprehensive now that they had finally done it. They still had three months to go to the wedding. Had she played her card too soon? True, it had been immensely satisfying. She'd enjoyed the power she had over him. Listening to his ragged breathing and excitement had been a powerful turn-on for her. But she didn't want the novelty of it to wear off for him until she had the wedding ring firmly on her finger.

'I wore a condom,' he said plaintively.

'I was at a good time in my cycle. The way you make love, I'd be petrified they'd burst. You're very, *very* vigorous,' she purred.

'You think so?' Gary was delighted at the compliment.

'Umm, let's do it again,' Carol urged. Let him taste the ecstasy again and keep him wanting, she decided, as she tightened her long legs around him and felt him groan as he grew hard inside her.

27

Mike turned over drowsily and flung his leg over Jessica.

'I love you. You're gorgeous,' he muttered, half asleep, the bed creaking under his weight.

'Stop it, Mike!' Jessica hissed, going rigid in his arms.

'Wha! What's wrong?' Mike opened bleary eyes. 'Oh! Oh! Sorry, I was half asleep. I forgot where I was,' he apologized, hastily removing his leg. They lay chastely apart and then got a fit of the giggles.

'This is ridiculous,' Jessica murmured, conscious that her mother was in the next room. 'Do you think it's just us, or do other couples feel a bit peculiar doing it in their parents' house?'

'We could swing from chandeliers and sing arias at the top of our voices and my ma and da wouldn't hear a thing.' Mike grinned.

'Well, your dad snores so loudly your ma has to wear ear plugs.' Jessica smiled over at him.

'Exactly!' Mike smiled back at her. 'It's nice waking up together again, isn't it?'

'Yeah, I wish we had our house.'

'We'll get one, don't worry,' he said reassuringly, stroking her cheek with his finger.

'I wonder how will we get on today?'

'Ah, it'll be fine, let's not get hyper about it. Let's make a pact to enjoy the lead-up to our wedding and our wedding as much as we can. Because we'll only be doing it once. OK?' he said firmly.

'OK,' Jessica agreed, leaning over to kiss him. The treacherous bed creaked again.

'I'm getting up.' Jessica laughed. 'My nerves are shot. I'm going to buy a new mattress for this bed. It came out of the ark.'

'It was kind of your mother to put the double bed in your room for us, lots of mothers wouldn't be that enlightened,' Mike said.

'I know, she's great. I still couldn't do it though,' Jessica said regretfully. 'Not even when we're married.'

'We could do it standing up,' Mike suggested.

'No!'

'I'm horny.'

'Me too, but I'm not doing it.'

'Will we do it in the shower?'

'No! I'm going to make the tea.'

'Spoilsport.' Mike threw a pillow at her.

'But ya love me,' Jessica said smugly. 'After breakfast will we scoot over to Lidl and get a couple of bottles of wine for this afternoon? Maybe Carol might lighten up and have one.'

'Yeah, but isn't her mother coming? And doesn't she have a bit of trouble with alcohol?' Mike reminded her.

'Jeepers, yeah. I forgot. Nix that idea.' Jessica hopped out of bed, relieved that thanks to Mike she hadn't made an appalling *faux pas*. 'I hope she won't be on the piss this afternoon.'

'We'll have a good strong pot of coffee brewing,' Mike suggested. 'And I'll make it! Mind, if she was under the weather, she mightn't notice if it was made with gravy granules,' he teased.

'Rotter!' Jessica giggled as she slipped into her dressing-gown and went down to the kitchen to put the kettle on for the tea.

Liz smiled as she heard the bed creaking and Jessica and Mike laughing and giggling in the room next to her. It was wonderful that they were so crazy about each other. She really ought to get a new bed for them to spare their blushes. There was nothing worse than a creaking bed when you weren't in your own house. She and Ray had been just like them once, she thought enviously. Madly in love and unable to keep their hands off each other. Sadness darkened her eyes as loneliness smote her.

Was it because of the forthcoming wedding that her loneliness felt so intense? she wondered dolefully. Would she ever get a handle on it? Would she ever be in control of it rather than it being in control of her? When did that point arrive in widowhood?

It was going to be hard walking up that aisle with Jessica. She was truly dreading it. In fact, she wasn't looking forward to this wedding one bit.

Nancy probably felt exactly the same, she thought with a pang of sympathy for Carol's mother. She too would be at the wedding un-accompanied. It was probably just as hard for her. What joy did she have in life? Very little, as far as Liz could see.

At least she and Jessica were very close. Nancy and Carol had a very fraught relationship, and Nadine was nothing but a source of worry to her. No wonder the poor woman had turned to the bottle.

She hoped that her neighbour wouldn't be hostile this afternoon. Hopefully she and Carol had discussed the forthcoming wedding. Surely they must have by now, Liz mused, pulling her quilt up under her chin.

She was reluctant to get up and face the day. Sunlight splashed on to her bed from her Velux window. It was another lovely bright morning. All the indications were that it was going to be another scorcher. She could set the patio table and serve afternoon tea outside. That might be more relaxing for Nancy and Carol, rather than sitting perched on the sofa trying to balance cups and plates on knees.

She'd made a lemon sponge, scones and a tea-brack, and she'd make some dainty ham and cucumber sandwiches. That should surely be enough. She heard Jessica going downstairs. Her daughter was on edge about this meeting, as she was herself. The Logans were so volatile. Planning a wedding was stressful enough without having to cope with that lot.

Her lips tightened. Carol was terribly manipulative and always had been since they were small children. She was the bossy boots. She was the one who had always played on Jessica's soft heart and got her own way. It had infuriated Liz.

She'd told her daughter to stand up for herself. Poor old Jessie had always done the running. Carol said jump and Jessie said, 'How high?'

She'd taken Carol to task often when they were children, but Carol listened to no one, not even to this day. Whatever Carol wanted, Carol got, even though the younger woman would deny that vehemently if it were put to her. Carol was completely centred on herself. And why wouldn't the poor unfortunate be? Liz thought ruefully. She'd had it tough as a child. Bossing Jessie around probably gave her the only feeling of control she had in her shattered life. But her childish bossiness had carried on into adulthood, and Jessie had tried to distance herself but could never quite succeed. Carol held on tightly, reluctant to let go. At least Jessie had not succumbed to the intense emotional pressure Carol had put on her to let her move into the house with herself and Katie. But she'd felt mean about it. She'd felt guilty as Carol did her usual 'poor me' carry-on. Carol did 'poor me' better than anyone. The chip she carried on her shoulder grew heavier and heavier. Her unhappy childhood had marked her and damaged her, but that wasn't Jessica's burden to carry and never had been.

Liz bit her lip. She should have put her foot

down about the wedding at the beginning when Jessica had asked her to intervene. But it was so hard to say no to Carol. You always felt you were being mean; she had that subtle way of making you feel guilty. Even as a child she'd been able to do it. What was it called? Liz racked her brain for a phrase she'd heard that described Carol's behaviour perfectly. Passive . . . something. Passive aggressive, that was it. If there was one person who typified that behaviour it was Carol Logan, and Liz was full sure there'd be plenty of passive aggressive behaviour this afternoon. Well, Carol was going to have to deal with it, Liz decided. Because today, she wasn't going to get her own way with everything and if Jessica wouldn't say no to plans that didn't suit, Liz damn well would, she thought grimly, throwing back her covers and padding downstairs to join her daughter.

It took Gary a moment or two to recognize that he was in a strange bed, in a strange bedroom and the sound of running water meant that someone was having a shower. He stretched, yawned, rubbed his hand over his stubbly jaw and glanced at his watch. Eight thirty on a Sunday morning, what an unearthly hour to be awake.

Then he remembered. He'd spent the night

with Carol. He wasn't dreaming, was he? he wondered for a moment, remembering wild, passionate lovemaking. No, he assured himself, he hadn't been dreaming. It had all happened. He and Carol had finally had proper sex and it had been great. He'd worn down her resistance, as he'd always known he would. It felt good.

She'd enjoyed it too. He'd turned her on. Gary liked giving his women pleasure. It made him feel good about himself. He still had it, he thought proudly. It would be a sad day when he couldn't get the woman he wanted.

Carol had dropped that copper like a hot potato and come running back to him. As it should be. He scowled. An unwelcome insidious thought seeped into his mind. Had the sex Carol had had with the clodhopper country boy been as good as the sex she'd had with him? Had she lain in Gary's arms last night and compared and contrasted technique and staying power? His feeling of well-being dissipated somewhat as jealousy flooded his veins. His jaw tightened. Maybe she'd had sex with him because the sex was so good with that Sean fella and she'd been hungry for it. It was a bit strange that after all this time putting him off she suddenly capitulated.

Another thought struck him. Maybe she was

bloody well pregnant and was going to pretend that he was the father. Women could be very, very devious. There was no doubt about it. He was no fool. And he was damned if he was going to rear another man's child.

Carol dried herself vigorously, eager to get on the road and start jogging. She liked running on Sunday mornings. Having the streets and foot-paths to herself enhanced the aura of well-being and sense of omnipotence that running gave her. When she was running she felt in total control of her life. The only time she did, she thought wryly as she slipped on her sports bra and pulled on her tracksuit bottoms.

The sun was glinting in through the bubble glass in the bathroom and through the open top window she could hear the sound of birdsong. It was another lovely day. If all went well at Liz's wedding summit, she and Gary might manage a walk along the Wildlife Reserve overlooking Arklow Bay. He'd been fast asleep when she slid out of bed; limbs sprawled to the four corners of the bed. Gary could sleep in until midday and later if she let him. They were completely different in that regard. She was a lark, he was an owl. She could never stay in bed once she woke up. She had

366

to be up and at it. She supposed she should have stayed in bed and enjoyed a kiss and a cuddle and breakfast on trays like Mike and Jessica did, but she'd been anxious to get a run in before she went home. She always felt her day had balance when she'd had her jog. She smoothed on some tinted moisturizer, traced some lipstick across her lips and padded into the bedroom to get her trainers.

'Oh, you're awake. I thought you'd be dead to the world still,' she said, surprised to see Gary yawning his head off.

'Where are you off to?' he asked grumpily.

'Going for a jog.' Carol sat on the side of the bed and pulled on her trainers.

'What about my brekkie?' Gary was wholly unimpressed.

'What about it? Help yourself to whatever's in the fridge.' She laughed at his disgruntled expression.

'Huh! Yoghurts and muesli. Are you not going to cook me a big fry-up?'

'No I'm not cooking you a big fry-up, my darling. I don't want you flattened by high cholesterol. I don't want to be a young widow.' She grinned. 'I'm only thinking of you. Come on for a jog with me?'

'At this hour of the morning? I'm going back to sleep,' Gary snorted.

'OK, sleep well, I won't be that long. It's such a cracker of a day we'd want to give ourselves a bit of leeway. Traffic could be heavy.'

'OK.' Gary burrowed down under the duvet. 'Enjoy your jog. By the way,' he sat up again, 'what did you mean you were at a good point in your cycle last night?'

'What?' Carol looked at him in amazement.

'That thing about your cycle. You couldn't get pregnant, could you?'

'No, I'm not ovulating,' she explained patiently.

'Oh!' he said. 'And when do you get a period?'

'In about twenty-five days' time, Gary. Can I go now? I need to get my skates on,' she said, bemused. Surely with all his experience of women he understood the ins and outs of a woman's cycle?

'See you,' he said, lying back down again, tanned and muscular against the white pillows.

She leaned over and kissed him on the mouth. 'Go to sleep, sexy, see you later.'

'OK,' he said, staring at her stomach.

'Toned, isn't it,' she said smugly, proud of her supple physique.

'What would you do if you ever got pregnant?'

'Keep as fit as possible,' she said firmly. 'Pregnancy isn't an illness or an excuse for letting yourself go to pot. It's a totally natural state of being.'

'Yeah, well, we won't be having kids for a while so you won't have to worry about it,' he said casually.

'No, we won't, at least until after the wedding,' Carol agreed, thinking how mature he was all of a sudden. Maybe he wasn't quite as laddish as he let on. It warmed her heart. 'See you later.' She kissed him again and waved light-heartedly as she left the room, happier than she had been in a long time.

Bill flipped Brona's egg, counted for five and scooped it out of the sizzling frying-pan on to her plate. She liked her fried egg just so, and he wanted her to be in a good humour today before he left for Wicklow. He'd already fed Ben, and hung out the washing, and once he gave his partner her breakfast in bed he'd prepare the potatoes and veg for the dinner.

He badly wanted her to be on side. He was feeling more than a little apprehensive about the trip to Arklow. Was Brona right? Should he butt out? She was so vehement about it.

No! he thought stubbornly. A daughter's wedding was an epoch in both her and her parents' lives that was generally a unique and singular experience, never to be forgotten. He wanted to share in that experience. It was his right as a father, no matter what Nancy felt or how much she objected. He hoped against hope that his wife would not be the worse for drink. If he could persuade her to let him play his part, he was sure Carol would soften her opposition and agree to let him fulfil his dearest wish. How proud he would be walking her up the aisle! Carol's wedding day would be the start of a process that would heal their wounded relationships, allowing them all to move forward with equanimity. Brona would have to admit that she was wrong to doubt him. She'd stand in awe at his maturity, resolve and compassion and their relationship would go from strength to strength.

Optimism surged through him at such positive thoughts. Whistling, Bill placed a crispy slice of fried bread – a special treat – on Brona's plate, and hurried upstairs with it, so that it wouldn't go cold.

'Here you are, Brona, love,' he said cheerfully, as he placed the tray carefully on his partner's knee and bent down to kiss the top of her head. Bill hardly noticed that she made no move to reciprocate. He was planning the menu for the first intimate dinner party he would give to introduce Carol and Nadine to their gorgeous little brother.

Nancy ran her tongue over her teeth and licked her dry lips. She felt ganky. Her head throbbed, her bones ached. She needed a drink and a cigarette and the sooner the better. Cautiously she opened one eye, and shut it pretty rapidly as the light that was glinting through a gap in the curtains pierced her eyeball like a laser.

'Oh my God,' she muttered, lying quite still, trying to gather herself together. She stretched out to her bedside locker, eyes still closed, and found her cigarettes and lighter. She raised herself gingerly into a sitting position and lit up. She drew the smoke deep into her lungs and coughed like a consumptive, wincing with pain. Eventually her coughing spasm abated and Nancy lay propped against the pillows, easing herself into the day.

Wearily, she wondered if Nadine had come home last night. She vaguely remembered staggering into the bedroom and passing out around one a.m. Her youngest daughter had not arrived home up to then.

And then Nancy remembered why she had gone on such a bender. Carol was coming home today with her boyfriend and they were all having a meeting over at Liz's to discuss the wedding.

Tendrils of fear fluttered deep in her tummy. She didn't like going to people's houses. It made her feel tense and anxious. Her hands shook as she lit another cigarette from the butt of the last one. She could say she was sick, she thought in desperation. Why did Carol want to get married? Imagine the hassle of a wedding. Couldn't she go to Rome and do it, or Mauritius or one of those exotic places? Nancy wasn't up to a wedding. She was hardly able to get through an ordinary day, she thought dispiritedly. She felt awkward in Gary's company. He was so posh and superior.

Carol had warned her to have the house tidy. And to make sure Nadine wasn't lounging around in her pyjamas. At least they weren't coming to lunch. Her stomach turned at the thought of food. She wouldn't be having lunch herself either. Nadine could cook herself a pizza out of the freezer or stick something in the microwave.

She leaned over to her bedside locker and scrabbled in the drawer. She found the half-litre bottle of vodka, unscrewed the top and placed it to her lips. She took a small sip, just to keep herself going. She had to have her wits about her today. Carol would go bananas if she thought she'd been drinking. Today was one day when she was just going to have to make the effort to stay sober.

'The traffic's crap,' Gary grumbled as they crawled bumper to bumper towards the Wyatville Road junction. Ahead of them towards Loughlinstown the traffic was hardly moving.

'Everyone's off to the beach, I suppose. I did say that, didn't I?' Carol pointed out. 'I suppose it's not surprising considering we're having one of the best summers in years.'

'Look at that bloody lunatic.' Gary jammed his thumb on the horn at a motorcyclist who had clipped his wing mirror as he zigzagged between two lanes of almost stationary traffic.

'I don't envy Jessie having to do this commute day in day out when she moves back to Wicklow,' Carol remarked, as they inched forward at a snail's pace.

'Me neither. I'd hate to live in the sticks.' Gary drummed his fingers against the steering-wheel.

'Speaking of which, where *are* we going to live?' She turned to look at him. She hadn't brought up the subject in a while, afraid the pressure would put him off and give him an excuse to postpone.

'Your flat or mine, I suppose,' he said casually.

'Gary! We can't live in a flat, it's money down the drain—'

'Well, we could save the money from one of our

rents and put it towards buying our own place,' Gary pointed out reasonably.

'Well, I think our two salaries combined would easily pay a mortgage,' she argued.

'Aw, Carol, what's the rush? We're young, what do we want to tie ourselves up with a mortgage for? Let's rent for a while, travel a bit, have fun,' Gary said irritably. He hated having to discuss things like mortgages. It made life seem so serious and intense.

'Umm,' Carol said non-committally. Gary was doing his usual head in the sand bit. She'd humour him for the time being, but once they were married he was in for a shock. She wanted a place of their own and the sooner the better.

'I was thinking,' she changed the subject, 'that we should have a wedding list.'

'A wedding list! What do you want one of them for?'

'Because it's a sensible way of getting presents that we need and want, rather than stuff we're never going to use and that doesn't suit our tastes,' Carol explained. 'Remember Rita and Ken got married last year and they got some hideous stuff. Rita gave a vile nest of tables to a charity shop and she was lucky they took them off her hands. We don't want sheets and duvet sets that won't match our colour schemes. We don't want duplicates of presents. Rita and Ken got three steam irons, for example. A wedding list cuts all that out.'

'I suppose you're right. It's a good idea actually,' Gary approved. 'We'll sit down and make a list of what we want. It will save us a fortune on pots and pans and toasters and stuff like that.' It always cheered up Gary's parsimonious little heart when he thought he was getting something for nothing.

Carol was delighted. At last things were beginning to fall into place and happening the way *she* wanted for a change. For the first time since Gary had put the ring on her finger she felt they were starting to row together as a couple. United . . . Just like Jessie and Mike. It felt comforting. She might even enjoy today's meeting after all.

'Let's eat in the Old Forge,' she suggested, relaxing as they drove on to the motorway after the Loughlinstown roundabout.

'Yeah, good idea. The grub's good there,' Gary agreed, pressing his foot on to the accelerator as the traffic ahead of them began to speed up and surge forward.

28

Carol felt her stomach tighten as they drove on to the sliproad off the N11 that led into Arklow. Gary eased down to thirty, and as they drove slowly along the familiar road Carol wished with all her might that she was going anywhere but home. To her right the stained-glass windows of Templerainey church glinted in the early afternoon sun. It was a much more imposing church than the little yellow country church they were getting married in.

She'd had no say in either the church or the hotel where they were celebrating their wedding. She scowled, resentment beginning to envelop her despite her best intentions. A young mother strolled along with a toddler and a baby in a buggy. How boring to spend a Sunday afternoon walking the streets. Couldn't she even go to the wildlife reserve? Carol thought irritably, remembering monotonous Sunday afternoons when Nancy had drunkenly insisted that Carol look after her sister and take her for a walk. Nadine's little legs couldn't walk as far as the reserve and she too had walked this very same street, Nadine in tow, hostile and unhappy.

Further along a group of teenagers joshed and chatted, the girls resplendent in the skimpiest of belly tops. Some toned and slender, others with bulges of puppy fat overflowing the hipsters that revealed swathes of pasty white flesh.

'Look at the state of that one, look at the size of her arse in those jeans. Does she never look in the mirror?' Gary pointed out a particularly plump little teenager who was the loudest of them all. Carol felt a stab of sympathy for her. She too had been on the plump and overweight side in her early teens. She'd comfort-eaten in those first horrible, scary years after their father had left them until once, in an argument with one of her schoolmates, the other girl had said, 'Shut up, fatso,' and walked away with her friends, laughing.

Those words were seared on to Carol's heart, and from that day she had cut down radically on her food consumption, saying the word 'fatso' over and over in her head when she was tempted.

'That other one's a nice little nubile,' Gary

remarked, eyeing a supple blonde bombshell who was flicking her hair over her shoulder. 'Give her ten years and she'll be a hot babe!'

'Oh, grow up, Gary. Listen to yourself,' Carol snapped.

'Hey, there's no need to bite my nose off,' he retorted heatedly. 'Don't take it out on me because you don't want to be here.'

'Sorry,' she muttered. 'Look, could you stop at the shop with the ice-cream cone outside, down towards the bridge? I suppose I'd better bring a box of chocolates or something.'

'Isn't there a garage down near you with a shop in it?' Gary growled.

'I don't want to meet any of the neighbours. They'd keep you yakkin' for hours,' she said crankily.

'OK, OK.' He indicated right with bad grace.

'Won't be a minute,' she said as he drew to a halt outside the shop.

'Don't be in any hurry,' he drawled sarcastically. 'I'm in as much of a rush as you to get to this little soirée.'

Carol could have kicked herself. Now she'd riled Gary, just when she needed him in her corner. They'd had a nice companionable lunch in the Old Forge, although her fiancé had moaned that if she drove he could have a few pints. One of the reasons she wasn't keen to let on that she had taken driving lessons and done her test was that she knew that if Gary knew that he'd insist on putting her on his insurance, so that he could drink as much as he liked and leave the driving to her. One of these days she'd have to get behind the wheel, she supposed.

She wondered what state Nancy was in. Her hand curled around her mobile phone. She'd finally got a new one. Should she ring, or just walk in home and face the music? There were a few people in the shop, so she dawdled by the magazine displays and keyed in Nancy's number.

It rang for ages and then Nadine answered.

'Hello,' her sister said crossly.

'Hi, it's me. We're in the shop. How's Ma?'

'How is she ever?' Nadine grumbled. 'She's been nagging me all morning to get up and get dressed and tidy up just because the great Carol and her posh git fiancé are coming to visit. Why should it interfere with me? That's what I want to know. I've a fuckin' hangover that would put Ma's to shame, all I wanted to do was stay in bed.'

'Is Ma pissed?' Carol asked anxiously.

'Naw, keep your knickers on. But she's got the shakes and she says she feels sick and she's not going to your silly meeting over at Liz's and she's got a hangover too. I don't see why I have to be involved, I didn't ask you to get married. I'm not a bridesmaid or anything,' Nadine whinged.

'Ah, get over it,' Carol snapped.

'Ah, fuck off.' Nadine swore and hung off.

Oh God Almighty, Carol groaned inwardly, staring at her mobile. She put down the larger box of Roses she'd selected and picked up the smaller box. Why should she spend a fortune on chocolates when that little cow would eat them all anyway? Gary had a very sweet tooth; perhaps if she bought him a bar of chocolate he might be appeased. She paid for the chocolates and a bar of Fruit and Nut and hurried out to the car.

'How are you, Carol? I hear congratulations are in order. It's fresh and well you're looking.' A friendly voice accosted her. Carol gritted her teeth and plastered a smile on her face. Nessie Sutton was the nosiest old gossip going. Just her luck to bump into her.

'Let's see the ring,' Mrs Sutton wittered excitedly. 'Ohhh, isn't it gorgeous? Is that your chap? Nice car – he must have a bob or two. How's your mother? She wasn't looking the best the last day that I saw her. Bit shaky on her legs, if you know what I mean,' she said slyly, her beady, malicious little eyes like two wrinkled black raisins in her pudding-bowl face.

Carol felt like giving her a kick in her ample fat arse.

'Can't stop to talk, Mrs S, we're running late—'

'Heard you're getting married down here – I thought you'd do it up in the big smoke. Will the Da be walking you up the aisle? It would be nice to see him again after all this time.' Nessie beamed sweetly.

You two-faced old hag. Carol was fit to be tied. This was exactly why she hadn't wanted to get married next or nigh where she'd grown up. It was clear the gossips were hard at it and speculation was rampant.

'Did you ever hear the old saying, Mrs Sutton, curiosity killed the cat, information made him fat?' She gave her neighbour a honeyed smile. 'I think you're carrying more than enough weight without me adding to it. See you,' she said brightly.

Nessie was affronted. 'Well . . . I . . . I . . . I never heard anything so rude in my life,' she stuttered, her podgy cheeks stained crimson.

'And I never heard anything so nosy,' Carol reciprocated. Now that she had gone this far she might as well push out the boat and go the whole hog.

381

Nessie waddled off in high dudgeon, wounded dignity emanating from every podgy pore.

Carol felt like crying. How dare that . . . that old crone stand in judgement over her mother? How dare she ask about their most personal business as if it were public property? It was obvious they were the talk of the town. But what was new about that? she thought bitterly. Some things never changed.

'Here's a bar of chocolate for you.' She handed Gary his chocolate. She didn't care any more whether he was appeased or not. Events could happen as they would, as far as she was concerned; after her encounter with Nessie Sutton she felt that so far this wedding was a total pain in the ass. Undoubtedly it was going to get much worse.

'Who was that?' Nancy asked apathetically. She was sitting at the kitchen table smoking. Her hands were shaking and her stomach was tied up in knots.

'Carol. She wanted to know if you were pissed,' Nadine said cruelly.

'You're an unkind little bitch, aren't you?' Nancy couldn't hide her hurt.

'Well, what do you want me to say? That she rang to see if we were all right and to tell us she's so looking forward to seeing us. Face facts, Ma, we're an embarrassment to Carol and her fella. I don't know why she's even bothering to invite us to this wedding.'

Nadine clattered her dinner plate into the sink.

'Wash that up,' Nancy ordered listlessly. 'Did you make your bed?'

'For what? They're not going to be going up to the bedroom,' Nadine scoffed.

'Don't be so cheeky, Nadine,' Nancy remonstrated.

'Why, what will you do? Slap me?' Nadine jeered.

Nancy swallowed, hard. It was so difficult trying to rear her youngest daughter. She had no respect for her mother. No fear of her. Hard as it was to admit, Nancy had lost control of Nadine and there was nothing she could do about it.

She stood up and went into the sitting-room. It looked presentable enough. After much nagging, Nadine had Hoovered it unenthusiastically. It had grown shabby over the years. The beige carpet had wine and tea stains and the brown velour sofa had grown threadbare in parts. The gold curtains were smoke-stained and badly needed dry-cleaning. The fireplace had traces of cinders, a legacy of the winter. Its old-fashioned red bricks were darkened with smoke and age. She really must do something with the place.

She lit a fresh cigarette and stubbed out the one she'd finished smoking. A silver car drew up outside and she saw Carol get out of the passenger side. Her daughter looked so groomed and affluent, she thought with a dart of pride. It was some comfort that one of them had done well for themselves in spite of all that had happened to them as a family. If only her two daughters were close, Carol might exert some influence on Nadine. But Carol had kept her distance once she'd gone to work in Dublin and was hardly likely to keep in touch much once she was married. She had her father's genes in her, Nancy thought bitterly.

She heard her daughter's key in the lock and saw her fiancé get out of the car. He was a good-looking chap, Nancy noted, as her hands curled into fists at her side and her heart seemed to do a double flip-flop of apprehension. Surely Carol and her boyfriend could go over to Liz's on their own? What did they want her there for? Couldn't they all make their own decisions? She'd just go along with whatever they decided. She didn't care one way or another who came to the wedding or what happened at it. She'd just tell Carol that she was sick and she couldn't go.

'Hello, Ma. How are you?' Carol thrust a box of chocolates awkwardly at her. She made no attempt to kiss her.

'Hello, Carol. Hello ... er—' For one nerve-racking moment her mind went blank. *What was it, Joey? Jerry?* Oh yes, Gary, that was it. Her alcohol-fogged brain had a moment of clarity. 'Gary,' she said with heartfelt relief.

'Hello, Mrs Logan,' he said politely, holding out his hand. She placed hers briefly in his, hoping he wouldn't notice how it shook, before withdrawing it swiftly.

'Sit down,' she urged, feeling that if she didn't sit down herself she'd collapse in a heap. She was longing for a drink. When would this nightmare be over so that they could all leave her alone?

'Would you like a cup of tea or coffee?' she asked politely, and then had a brainwave. It would be all right to offer a glass of wine, as it was well past noon.

'Gary, would you like a glass of wine?' she asked hopefully. If he said yes she'd be able to have one herself and it would keep her going for a while.

'He's driving,' Carol said sharply.

'Oh yes, sorry, of course. I forgot.' Nancy slumped into an armchair, defeated.

'We have half an hour or so before we go over to

Liz's. Why don't we decide who we're asking to the wedding so that we can have numbers for her?' Carol suggested. 'Where's Nadine?'

'She's out in the kitchen.' Nancy dragged deeply on her cigarette.

'Nadine,' Carol called. 'Nadine.'

'What?' Nadine appeared at the sitting-room door looking surly and uncomfortable.

'Come in and say hello,' Carol pressed.

'Hello.' Nadine threw a sulky glance in Gary's direction.

'Hi, Nadine, how's my sister-in-law to be?' Gary gave his best sexy grin.

'Oh, OK,' she grunted.

'Any chance of a cup of coffee? I'll help you make it,' he offered.

Oh God, I hope the kitchen's not a mess! Carol thought in panic.

'It's OK, I'll make it,' she said hastily. 'You sit down and talk to Mam.'

God, no! I'd prefer to try and get a smile out of the crotchety sister than talk to the dypso. She looks as if she's going to keel over. Gary tried to hide his dismay at the notion of trying to have a chat with the tense, nervy woman in front of him.

'No, you sit down with your mother and do the important bits. Nadine and I will rustle up a cup of tea, won't we, Nad?' He winked at the teenager. Under all the heavy pancake he noted a little blush. Good, he thought. There wasn't a woman on the planet that didn't succumb to the Davis charm.

'OK,' Nadine agreed a little less churlishly and led him out to the kitchen.

'I'd much prefer to let the women at it. I hate talking about wedding stuff,' Gary confided chummily, as he leaned against the kitchen counter and watched as Carol's sister filled the kettle. If she lightened up on the face muck she wouldn't be bad-looking, he observed, studying Nadine's skinny frame. She was tall, like Carol, and had the potential to be a stunner if she got rid of the tarty blonde highlights and the pierced belly button that made her look like a skanger.

'I hate weddings too,' Nadine confided. 'I think they're a load of crap. Why didn't you go and get married abroad or something?'

'I don't know. This thing came up about having a double wedding with Mike and Jessie and we're sort of stuck with it, I suppose,' he said glumly.

'I think you're mad getting married down here. All the nosy old bags will be around gawking,' Nadine informed him helpfully.

'Stop or I might do a runner!' He rolled his eyes up to heaven.

She giggled. 'Have you any good-looking friends?'

'I might have. Have you a boyfriend?'

'Yeah, I sort of go out with a guy called Mono. He's cool. He has a band.'

'That *is* cool,' Gary agreed. 'Are you bringing him to the wedding?'

'Am I allowed?' she asked hopefully, clattering mugs on to a tray.

'Sure. You're one of the most important people at the wedding. Sister of the bride. She has to be kept happy.'

'You see, I wanted to bring my best friend, Lynn, as well. If I ask Mono, Lynn'll get huffy, so I don't know what to do.'

'Ask the two of them, why don't you?' he said easily.

Her dull eyes lit up. 'Can I? Will Carol mind?'

'Of course not, and besides, I'm the boss.'

She looked at him doubtfully. 'Are you? Carol's kinda bossy.'

'I can handle her, don't you worry.'

'You're not bad, you know.' Nadine glanced at him as she spooned coffee into the mugs. 'I used to think you were posh and snooty.'

'And I used to think you were a grumpy little cow.'

She laughed. Heartily. And Gary caught a glimpse of the real Nadine and to his surprise . . . liked her.

29

'Is the kitchen clean?' Carol hissed.

'I beg your pardon.' Nancy sat up straight, annoyed at Carol's impertinence.

'Is the kitchen clean?' Carol repeated.

'Do you mind, Carol? I don't like your attitude. Don't come home here looking down your nose at us,' her mother said spiritedly. 'If you don't want to be here you don't have to, you know.'

'Ah, don't get cross, Ma,' Carol said, hastily backing down in the face of her mother's hostility.

'Look, I'm not feeling a hundred per cent.' Nancy wilted after her rally. 'Why don't you and Gary go over to Liz's yourselves? Whatever you want to do is all right with me.'

'No, Ma, you'd better come with us. Liz is expecting us,' Carol said firmly, taking a notepad out of her bag.

'Let her expect, she's not the queen,' Nancy muttered, lighting another fag.

'God, Ma, would you go easy on those things, you'll kill yourself and the rest of us too.' Carol waved her hands in front of her face in exasperation as a cloud of smoke drifted past.

'No harm if I was gone,' Nancy said self-pityingly.

Carol ignored her. She wasn't going to humour her mother's sympathy-seeking today.

'Right,' she said briskly, uncapping her pen. 'There'll be you, Nadine, Aunt Carmel and Aunt Freda and the uncles. Do you want cousins to come? And what neighbours do you want to invite?'

'I don't know,' Nancy said helplessly. 'What do you want?' Should we invite Aunt Vera – she always sends you birthday cards and lottery tickets? At least she never lost contact after your father left.' Vera was Bill's older sister. 'And what about your grandmother? She's still alive.'

'I'm not having them!' Carol snorted indignantly. 'If he's not coming they're not coming!'

'Right. Right, it's your wedding,' Nancy said crossly.

'Sorry. And by the way, Ma, I did ask Nadine if she wanted to be bridesmaid, you know, but she wasn't interested.'

'I know. Maybe you're better off to have your friend. That Nadine is gone to the dogs.'

'Well, she'd better behave herself at the wedding. And you—' Carol cast a stern eye in her mother's direction. 'Stay off the sauce for the wedding, Ma. I don't want you to make a holy show of me.'

'Excuse *me*! I don't drink that much,' Nancy protested with hurt dignity.

'Come off it, Ma.' Carol wasn't having that. 'Just tone it down.' The air bristled with tension. They sat in hostile silence, not looking at each other.

Finally Carol broke the silence. 'Who else do you want to invite?'

'I couldn't care less,' Nancy said huffily.

'Aw, Ma, come on. I need to get this sorted.'

'Who's paying for this anyway? Have you talked to your father?' Nancy demanded.

'Gary and I are paying for it ourselves.'

'Well, you should insist on some contribution from him.' Nancy's lips tightened into a thin line.

'I don't want one. I want nothing to do with him,' Carol said hotly. 'We can manage on our own.'

'Well, if that's the case, I wouldn't be inviting every Tom, Dick and Harry if you're going to have to pay for it,' her mother retorted.

'I know, but two aunts, two uncles and you and Nadine isn't much of a guest list,' Carol said miserably.

'What about Gary's family? How many are coming from there?'

'His ma; his dad is dead. His three brothers and their wives. Two cousins and a few friends.'

'That's plenty!' Nancy looked at her in surprise. 'What do you want to be feeding the world for?'

'I suppose you're right,' Carol said doubtfully. 'Is there anyone else you'd like to ask?'

'Ask your cousins if you want to,' Nancy told her.

'I don't really know them that well. They kept well away from us when we were kids.' Carol couldn't hide her bitterness.

'You're right. Don't bother with them. Why should we give them a day out? They never had any time for us.' For a moment mother and daughter were united in thought.

'Here's coffee,' Gary said cheerily, leading Nadine through the door carrying two steaming mugs, which he handed to his future mother-in-law and future wife.

Nadine carried a tray with a packet of chocolate biscuits and a sugar bowl and milk jug.

'You should have put the biscuits on a plate,'

Nancy scolded as she poured milk into her coffee.

'Only adds to the washing-up, doesn't it, Naddy?' Gary grinned at Nadine. She giggled.

'Your sister tells me she'd like to invite her best friend and her boyfriend to the wedding. That's fine with us, isn't it, Carol?'

'Oh! Oh, sure!' Carol couldn't believe her eyes or ears. *Naddy!* Gary had Nadine eating out of his hand.

'Right, that's settled,' Gary decreed, picking a mug off Nadine's tray. 'Have you sorted things with your mother?'

'I think so,' Carol said faintly.

'Great! Did you show them the invites you brought down? Let's see what the two most important wedding guests think.'

Carol rooted in her briefcase for the selection of invites and handed them over to Nancy. Gary had taken complete control, she thought in amazement. He had Nadine completely charmed. And Nancy was actually starting to relax.

She watched her fiancé studying the invite Nadine preferred as if he was completely engrossed. One thing about Gary Davis, she'd never be bored with him. Today she'd seen the best of him and she liked it. She liked it very much that he'd gone to the trouble of wooing her dysfunctional little family.

Maybe in his own peculiar way he loved her after all.

Gary glanced at his watch. 'Should we make a move? It's gone three thirty,' he said.

'I'll just give my hair a brush,' Nancy said slowly.

'I'll wash up,' Nadine offered.

Unheard of.

'I'll help.' Carol collected the mugs. She followed her sister out to the kitchen.

'Thanks for the coffee,' she said awkwardly.

'That's OK,' Nadine muttered.

'Ma's not too bad today,' Carol whispered conspiratorially.

'I know. But she's getting worse.' Nadine rinsed the mugs under the tap. 'I hate living here,' she burst out.

'Study hard and get out of it like I did,' Carol advised.

'And then who'll look after her?'

'We'll cross that bridge when we come to it. OK?'

'OK,' Nadine agreed, a lot less insolent than usual.

She is only a kid, Carol thought guiltily.

She was almost as bad as her father was. As soon

as she'd got a job in Dublin she'd hightailed it out of Arklow and left Nadine to take responsibility for their mother. No wonder her sister was resentful and ungracious. Carol stood in the kitchen beside her younger sister and was consumed with guilt. What a selfish cow she'd been for the last few years. It was a horrible feeling, and she didn't even want to think about it. Surreptitiously she glanced at her sister from under her lashes.

Nadine, head bent, was rubbing coffee stains off the inside of the mug. Her dyed blonde hair hung limply over her scrawny shoulders. She'd tried to put fake tan on and it was patchy and orangy and rather pathetic. Two spots bubbled like volcanoes under her makeup. She looked like a sad little tart.

What a miserable life she had, Carol thought, rigid with remorse. A lump the size of a melon threatened to choke her and she thought she was going to start crying. She knew exactly what Nadine had endured with their mother, anger, fear, anxiety, resentment, even a funny sort of love. She'd left her to shoulder the burden as she had once shouldered it, and blanked out all thoughts of guilt and responsibility. No wonder Nadine was hostile. As a sister, she had failed her completely, Carol acknowledged with gut-wrenching self-illumination.

She swallowed and swallowed until the lump

was more manageable. 'Listen, I've moved into a new flat. It's got a separate bedroom and sitting-room. Why don't you come up to Dublin some day, now that you're on holliers, and stay the night? We could go shopping for your wedding gear. The shops are always open late on Thursday nights,' she heard herself say.

Nadine looked gobsmacked. 'Me come up to Dublin to you?' she said flatly.

'Yeah, why not?' Carol said defensively. 'I've room now for you to stay. I didn't have before. The other place was such a kip you wouldn't ask a mouse to stay the night.' She made her lame excuses and felt like a heel.

'Yeah, I suppose I could take a trip up.' Nadine bent her head again, but Carol had seen the excitement in her eyes.

'Good,' Carol said crisply, regaining control.

'Would you bring me to Temple Bar?'

'Sure, Gary and you and I could have a night out.'

'Could we go clubbing?' Nadine pushed.

'We'll see,' Carol rowed back, hoping she wouldn't regret her impulsive invite. If Nadine got a taste of the good life in Dublin she might want to visit a lot and Carol wasn't quite ready for that.

'Will we bring those chocolates you brought over to Liz, Carol? I don't want to go empty-handed. Maybe I should bring a bottle of wine. I have one in the fridge.' Nancy came into the kitchen, wafting an overdose of Cerruti that had been a birthday present from Carol.

'The chocolates will be fine,' Carol said firmly. 'Come on, let's go.'

'I'll just put this out,' Nancy murmured, stubbing her butt into the overflowing ashtray that lay on the draining-board. She tipped the contents into the bin and followed Carol into the hall.

'Are you going out, Nadine, or will you be here when we get back?' Carol asked.

'I think I might go out the back and lie out and listen to my Walkman,' Nadine responded. She still wasn't feeling great after her night on the tiles.

'Lucky you – I've to go and listen to women wittering on about weddings.' Gary winked at her as he ushered Nancy and Carol out the door.

Nadine winked back.

'See you later.' She even smiled, a rare occurrence.

'You've really won her over,' Carol approved.

'The Davis charm. Irresistible!' Gary assured her as they walked down the road to Liz's house.

'Bighead,' Carol jibed, but she said it affectionately.

'Let's face the music and dance, Mrs Logan.' Gary smiled at Nancy, who smiled back uncertainly. She'd had a slug of vodka up in the bedroom when she was brushing her hair, so she wasn't quite as strung out as she'd been earlier. And she had to admit, Gary wasn't as posh as she seemed to remember. Anyone who could get a smile out of Nadine had to be nice. Still, she'd be glad when all this was over. The meeting was the first ordeal; there were a few others to get through before Carol was Mrs Gary Davis.

She took a deep breath as they walked up Liz's beautifully cobble-locked drive. She hoped Liz wouldn't shake hands. Nancy trembled like a leaf as Carol rang the doorbell.

Bill glanced at the clock on the dash. Three thirty. He was behind time. He'd planned to be in Arklow by this stage and he was only at the East Link.

Ben had picked this very afternoon to throw a tantrum, simply because Brona had told him that they weren't going for a walk along the beach as they usually did on Sunday afternoon.

Why Brona couldn't have taken him to Dollymount Strand herself was beyond him. She was being most unhelpful. She hadn't got up until all hours and then she'd decided she wanted to go to Superquinn to get their own-brand sausages for her mother because she'd promised her some. Now while Bill had to admit that Superquinn sausages were especially tasty and he understood Mrs Wallace's addiction to them, it wasn't a matter of life or death and she could just as well have got them the next day when she picked Ben up from the crèche.

She was just being awkward and obstructive. Behaviour that wasn't worthy of her, he thought self-righteously, as he wondered whether to risk double points and a fine by doing forty on the Sandymount road.

By his reckoning he should make Arklow by four-thirty. Still early enough. It wasn't dark these days until after ten, so he'd be home well before sunset.

He slid U2 into his CD player and settled back to enjoy the journey. The more relaxed he was the better. After all, he wasn't sure what kind of a reception he'd get from Nancy, and, if she was there, Nadine. But hopefully it would be the start of reconciliation for all of them. That would be worth any initial discomfort, he assured himself, as he stopped at the barriers to wait for a train to pass through the Merrion Gates.

30

'Here they are,' Jessica informed Liz, who was busy writing in a notebook.

'I've made out a list to include menus, flowers, photographer, cake or cakes as the case may be, church music, church fees, tea and coffee reception, finger food for supper. I think that about covers it. Doesn't it?' Liz put away her pen and went out to the hall to open the door for her guests.

'Finger food and tea and coffee reception, it's going to be really expensive, isn't it?' Jessica said worriedly. She was starting to panic about the price of things. She had savings, but because they were getting married sooner than planned she was worried that they wouldn't have enough and that they'd end up in debt. Both of them had agreed that they were paying for their own wedding. Liz was a widow and they wouldn't feel at all comfortable taking money from her.

'Stop panicking. We can keep our side of it as small as we want,' Mike said firmly.

'Hello, Nancy, come in. Hi, Carol. Hi, Gary,' Liz said warmly, ushering her guests into the sitting-room.

'Hi, Jessie. Hi, Mike,' Carol said airily. Gary nodded affably.

'Sit down, Nancy,' Liz said kindly. *She looks wretched*, she thought sympathetically, indicating an armchair by the fireplace.

'This is a lovely room, you did a great job on it,' Nancy managed, making a huge effort.

'The wooden floors make a huge difference and I got the builders to break through into the kitchen dining-room, so the glass doors here really lighten up the place. It was so dark before,' Liz explained. 'It's a long time since you've been here, I've had it done a few years now.'

'Ah, I don't go out much nowadays. You know, since Bill left me . . .' Nancy trailed away sadly.

'Gary's brought some sample invites that a friend of his does at half the price,' Carol interjected hastily, fearing her mother was going to go off into one of her self-pitying whinges.

'Oh, let's see,' Jessica said eagerly.

'Hold on a sec, would anyone like tea or coffee?

402

I thought we'd have a bite to eat on the patio later on. It's such a lovely day out,' Liz suggested.

'Nothing for us, thanks, Liz, we've all just had coffee at home,' Carol said politely.

'OK then, we'll get down to business.' Liz sat down on the chair opposite Nancy, and the two girls sat beside each other on the sofa with Gary and Mike sitting either side of them.

Carol took the invites out of her bag and passed them round.

'Would you mind if I smoked, Liz?' Nancy asked hesitantly.

'Not at all,' Liz said, although she hated the smell of smoke. 'I have an ashtray there beside you.'

'Oh, that's kind,' Nancy murmured, wishing her heartbeat would slow down and the nervous cramping she was having in her stomach would stop.

'These are good, aren't they?' Jessica held up a champagne-coloured invite with a beautiful flowing font. 'It's the same colour as my dress. I'll be colour-co-ordinated.'

'Oh! Did you go for cream?' Carol pounced on the snippet.

'Champagne actually,' Jessica said, remembering that was how the saleswoman had described it.

403

'Oh good. We won't be two peas in a pod. I'm going for the traditional white,' Carol informed her.

Bully for you! Jessica felt like saying at Carol's faintly superior tone, and then felt ashamed of herself for her pettiness.

'You know, you could have your invites in cream and I could have mine in white,' Carol suggested.

'And what about our mutual friends, all the gang from the club?'

'Oh, hadn't thought of that.' Carol wrinkled her nose.

'Are you inviting many?' Jessica asked delicately.

'Er . . . not too many, so far,' Carol hedged.

'I have some menus and price lists,' Liz said smoothly. 'I know the two of you are going to meet up with the wedding manager next week, but I have some figures here so you can be prepared. The average is between twenty-eight and thirty-eight euro per head for a four-course meal. And here's the prices for the tea and coffee reception and for finger food for supper.'

'Well, we can't have beef – mad cow and all that,' Carol decreed as she scanned the menu.

Jessica glanced at Mike. Typical of Carol's high-handedness.

'Steady on there, Carol,' Gary remonstrated.

'Some of us are prepared to take the risk.'

She glowered at him. 'Some people aren't, and how do we know who eats beef and who doesn't?'

'Lamb is always fairly acceptable,' Mike suggested diplomatically.

'Or the poached salmon,' Liz offered. 'There's chicken to consider too.'

'I wonder where is it sourced? You read so much about chicken these days,' Carol said gloomily. She looked at Jessica. 'What were you thinking of?'

'I'd go for the lamb with baby carrots and mangetout,' Jessica said firmly.

'Sounds good,' Garry said briskly.

'What do you think, Nancy?' Liz asked politely.

'It's up to them,' Nancy demurred.

'OK then,' Carol said. 'And how about the mozzarella and tomato leafy green salad for starters? It's a nice healthy option.' She eyeballed Jessica.

'Not dock leaves and nettles,' groaned Gary.

'*Gary!*' his fiancée exclaimed in exasperation.

'Sorry, sorry, just teasing.' He held up his palms.

'You OK with that?' Jessica asked Mike, hoping he'd say he preferred the deep-fried Brie.

'That's fine,' he said cravenly.

'And the carrot and coriander soup?' Carol pressed home her advantage.

'OK, and the pavlova for dessert?' Jessica had had enough.

'Lovely.' Mike rubbed his hands.

'That's that sorted,' Gary declared. 'Next.'

Jessica looked at Liz's list. 'What do you want to do about flowers in the church? Mam's doing my bouquet; she's good at that sort of thing. Just remember, Mike and I don't have a fortune to spend.'

'Who has? Pick a few tulips,' Gary suggested.

'Gary, will you be *serious*.' Carol rounded on him.

'I *am*,' he assured her.

'Tulips don't grow in September, you idiot—'

'If I could make a suggestion,' Liz interrupted. 'Gladioli look very well at that time of the year. I'll have plenty in bloom. You could buy ferns and gyp for dressing them up and it would look very nice. What do you think, Nancy?' She looked across at her neighbour, not wanting her to feel excluded.

'Gladioli are lovely—'

'I would have liked roses,' Carol said sulkily.

'They cost a fortune, Carol,' Jessica burst out.

'Well, couldn't you have two big vases of gladioli on the steps of the altar and two smaller arrangements of roses on the altar?' Liz negotiated.

'I suppose so,' Jessica said crabbily.

'Right, church music.' Liz moved things on briskly.

'I'm not fussy, we're not really churchgoers,' Carol sniffed. 'Jessica can choose whatever she likes,' she added magnanimously. 'I presume we will have the Wedding March.' She arched an eyebrow at Jessica.

'Of course.'

'We've had it once we hear that, buddy.' Gary shook his head at Mike. 'There'll be no escape.'

'Who wants to escape and miss the pavlova, not to mention the leafy salad?' Mike smiled at Carol, and she had the grace to laugh.

'OK then, Mike and I'll pay for the soloist, and we can share the organist's fees,' Jessica said. That way at least she'd be able to have the hymns she wanted played at her wedding.

'Agreed,' Gary said equably. 'Next?'

'Photographer?' Mike looked at Jessica's list.

'My brother's pretty good with the digital camera,' Gary said.

'I'd prefer a professional,' Jessica said firmly. 'Not casting aspersions on your brother's photographic expertise or anything,' she added politely.

'Vince's very good at photography, actually – we'd like him,' Carol insisted.

'Sure you two get him and we'll get whoever Jessica wants, no problems there,' Mike said matter-of-factly.

'No problem,' Gary agreed.

'The aisle in the church won't fit us all, it's too narrow. Would you like to go up first?' Jessica turned to Carol.

'No, you go.' The other girl shrugged. 'I don't mind.'

'OK, we're doing well.' Jessica tried to lighten the atmosphere. It wasn't a battle zone, she reminded herself.

'What about the band?' Carol asked. 'Do you remember we went to see the Righteous Rockers—'

'Yeah, they were brilliant,' Mike enthused. 'That was one of the best nights out I ever had.'

'What do you think? My brother drinks with them.' Gary eyed Jessica.

'Jessie?' Mike looked at her questioningly.

'Would they play for us? Do they do weddings?'

'Sure do, will I make inquiries?' Gary grinned at her.

'Yeah,' she agreed, delighted that they at least were all agreed on that much. 'They were fantastic, Mam, if we could get them we'd have a great hooley.'

'It *would* make the night,' Carol exclaimed, all tensions temporarily suspended.

'Why don't I put the kettle on for a cup of tea?' Liz suggested, relieved that so far the get-together had passed off without major friction and the important decisions had been agreed upon without bloodshed and with just a few compromises here and there.

Brona drummed her fingers on the table. She was agitated. Bill had taken no notice of her advice whatsoever. And that was troubling.

This stubborn, unreasonable, one-track-minded person was far removed from the man she had fallen in love with. He couldn't see her point of view on this issue at all and it grated. He'd suddenly become obsessed with Carol and her damn wedding and she felt excluded and very isolated. One of her friends had warned her when first she'd started seeing him that a married man with children would always have baggage that he couldn't offload. She had airily dismissed her friend's concerns, confident of her ability to cope with any difficulties that might arise.

She hadn't realized that a situation quite as difficult as this would occur or that Bill would behave the way he was behaving.

She sipped yet another cup of coffee. Ben was watching a *Bob the Builder* video. He should be walking on the beach with his dad, Brona thought bitterly. Bill had gone haring off to Arklow this afternoon despite her protests that no good would come of it, and she was furious with him. When it came to the crunch, her opinions, her advice and her feelings had not come into the equation. That hurt. It hurt like bloody hell. Resting her forehead on her arms, Brona cried her eyes out.

Arklow looked well, Bill reflected, noting the colourful, well-tended flowerbeds on the approach road into the town. Arklow had changed since his time. Apartment blocks were sprouting along the riverbanks, there was a big new swimming-pool and fitness centre near the wildlife reserve, and restaurants, bars and trendy boutiques dotted the narrow winding main street.

He'd liked living in Arklow, liked the friendliness of the people. He'd played tennis and bridge and had a good social life. He'd lost all of that and a lot more when he'd walked away from his marriage, he thought sadly. But worst of all, he'd lost the respect and love of his children.

Listening to Nancy's worries about Nadine's drinking, and aware that like every town in the country there was a disturbing drug problem, he admitted, reluctantly, that his wife didn't have it easy in that regard. Especially with such a strong-willed character as Nadine. She'd been wilful as a toddler, a real handful, he remembered, smiling at the memory of her marauding around the sitting-room before she could walk, creating havoc in her wake as she explored every nook and cranny. Nancy hadn't been able to handle her. She hadn't been able to handle anything. Things had got so bad he'd reached his breaking point. Everyone had a breaking point. Carol might find that out some time. Some day she'd understand.

The knots in his neck muscles tightened as he approached his former home. Dread enfolded him, as it always did when he turned down Nancy's road. There was a silver Passat parked outside the house. It probably belonged to one of the neighbours. He parked further along and switched off the engine. His hands felt clammy. Should he go and knock on the door first and then carry in the wedding present or should he bring it with him? He dithered.

He decided to carry it up the drive. The box was big and awkward and he was glad to lower it gently on to the path before ringing the doorbell. He never used his key now. He felt he didn't have the right. Felt it would be an invasion of Nancy's privacy. There was no answer and he pressed the bell again, keeping the pressure on a little longer than before.

How annoying, he thought irritably. He'd come all this way and no one was in. He peered into the sitting-room, which was empty but surprisingly tidy. He'd often arrived at the house to find it like a tip. It was such a lovely day; perhaps his wife was sitting outside. Nancy had liked sunbathing when she was younger. She found the sun comforting, she'd told him once when he'd told her he couldn't understand how people could sit for hours on the beach doing nothing.

Rigid with tension, Bill walked around the side of the house. The grass could do with cutting; the flowerbeds were choked with weeds. Surely she could make an effort to keep the place presentable? he thought sourly. It wasn't as if she were out working her butt off every day.

If she wasn't in the back garden and the gate was open he could wait for her there. It would be preferable than sitting in the car under the gaze of the neighbours, he decided, as he lifted the latch on the gate and pushed it open.

Nadine stretched languorously in the heat of the

sun. She hadn't felt so relaxed in a long time. Nancy was with Carol. The dreaded visit had turned out quite good, not the ordeal she'd been dreading. Her sister had seemed half-human, even inviting her to visit her in her new flat.

And Gary . . . She smiled, thinking about her future brother-in-law. He was not at all what she'd made him out to be in her head. He was fun and dishy, and best of all he treated her like an adult. No nagging and bossing. It was so refreshing.

The wedding might be surprisingly enjoyable after all. She was allowed to invite Mono and Lynn, so at least she wouldn't feel like a spare thumb. It was great that she hadn't to make a choice because her friend Lynn could get very thick about things and go into a snit that would last for days. She was hard going sometimes, but that was because she was spoilt rotten at home and expected the same treatment from everyone else.

Nadine's eyes drooped and a little snore escaped her lips. She hadn't fallen into bed until after five. A few of them had gone drinking down by the river after closing time. The dawn had been streaking across the eastern sky as she'd made her unsteady journey home.

She heard a voice call her name. A vaguely familiar male voice.

'Nadine. Nadine, wake up.'

Her eyelids fluttered, opened, saw the man looking down at her and closed again. It had to be a dream – more a nightmare, she thought crankily, annoyed that her lovely afternoon was being ruined with images of her father.

'Nadine!' The voice was louder, more insistent. She jerked awake. It wasn't a dream! He *was* there looking down at her. A living nightmare.

'What do you want?' she said sullenly, pulling her bikini top up higher. She should have locked the damn side gate. She'd remember to in future. What could be worse than having your father sneaking up on you?

'Where's your mother? I want to talk to her,' he said patiently.

'For what? You'll only upset her. She doesn't want to talk to you. Can't you get that into your thick skull?' she retorted rudely.

'That's between your mother and me, and don't be so rude and aggressive, Nadine. Show a modicum of respect, please. Now where is she? I need to talk to her. There was no answer at the door when I rang the bell.'

'That's because she's not in. Duh!'

Her father's lips tightened but he ignored her impertinence.

414

'Would you go in and open the front door for me, I have Carol's wedding present on the doorstep,' he ordered.

'Are you mad, Da? Carol won't take a wedding present from *you*! She *hates* you.'

'Just do as I ask, Nadine,' Bill said grimly.

'Keep your jocks on,' she muttered reluctantly, hauling herself up from the lounger.

'Is that smoke coming from the window?' Bill gazed in horror at the kitchen window as a cloud of smoke suddenly billowed forth.

'Oh my God!' screeched Nadine. 'She's set the fuckin' kitchen on fire with her fags. I knew she'd do it some day. I just knew it. You have to do something about her, Da. She's a danger to herself.'

Bill grabbed his mobile out of his shirt pocket and dialled 999.

'I need the fire brigade, urgently,' he said rapidly, as he watched Nadine struggle into her jeans and run yelling for help out of the side gate into the front garden.

31

'Who's that making such a racket?' Liz paused from refilling Gary's cup as the uproar intruded upon the indolent silence of a sunny Sunday afternoon.

'That's Nadine.' Carol jumped to her feet from where they were sitting around Liz's patio table and ran to the side gate, swiftly followed by the rest of them.

'Quick, quick, the kitchen's on fire, there's smoke everywhere!' Nadine, dishevelled and bare-foot, shouted frantically.

'Oh Gary, quick, do something!' Carol exclaimed, shocked, as a gust of smoke blew skywards.

'Liz, have you got a hose?' Mike asked urgently.

'It's in the shed,' she replied.

'Is that *my* house on fire?' Nancy asked shakily.

'Don't worry, it will be fine. Thank God there's

no one in it,' Liz assured her, dropping a comforting arm around her shoulder.

'You're after setting the place on fire, Ma. I
warned you about those butts that you don't put
out.' Nadine was pale with fright. 'Now look what
you've done.'

'Leave her alone, Nadine,' Carol chastised
sternly. Now was not the time to apportion blame.

'Look, it's all right for you. I have to live with
her; she's always doing things like this. No one will
listen to me,' Nadine exploded.

'It's OK, Nadine, take it easy.' Jessie tried to
calm the younger girl down as Gary and Mike ran
across the street with the hose to see what they
could do.

'What the fuck is *he* doing here?' Carol stopped
short when she saw her father.

'He brought you a wedding present,' Nadine
gulped, trying to regain her composure.

'He can stick it up his arse. I don't want any
wedding present from that bastard,' Carol fumed.
Nancy burst into tears. Neighbours were gather-
ing, and in the distance they could hear the fire
brigade siren.

Carol marched over to Bill, chin thrust out
aggressively.

'You take your present, buster, and stick it

where the sun don't shine. I wouldn't take tuppence from you and how *dare* you think I would. Go and give it to your fancy woman and tell her never to come near me again.'

Bill swallowed, shaken in the face of his daughter's naked aggression.

'Carol, don't talk to your father like that,' Gary chided, equally shocked by his fiancée's hostility. He had no idea that their relationship was so poisoned. Carol rarely spoke of her father.

'You stay out of it, Gary, you know nothing about it.' Carol was beside herself with fury. How dare her father come down to Arklow and act like a munificent benefactor? She was furious beyond measure that Gary should witness such a scene. It was bad enough that he'd seen her mother hungover and hardly *compos mentis*. All of this was excruciating. She feared that it might even put him off marrying her. She'd never let him know the extent of her family problems; today he'd seen them in all their glory.

'What are you talking about, Carol?' Bill demanded.

Fear lent bitterness to her tongue when she saw the effect her words had on her father. It was obvious by his reaction that he didn't know of Brona's little visit to her.

'Oh! Did you not realize that your mistress came to see me at work to insist that I let you walk me up the aisle?' she spat.

'What?' Bill said weakly.

'Oh yes. She thinks I'm being horrible to you. Well, I soon put her straight about who was horrible to whom . . . *Daddy*.' Her words oozed contempt. 'She's such a smug little bitch. It would be interesting to see how forgiving *she'd* be if you ever walked out on her and her child—'

The blare of the siren and arrival of the fire brigade interrupted her tirade. Moments later, hoses uncoiled and connected to the mains, the firemen got to work. It didn't take long to douse the fire. It hadn't caught hold and there was more smoke and water damage to the kitchen than anything else.

'Any idea how it started?' the chief fireman asked Gary.

'It was a cigarette butt. Hers!' Nadine said truculently, pointing a finger at her mother.

'For God's sake, Nancy!' Bill exploded. 'Look at the state of the place. Don't expect me to pay for doing it up if your drunken negligence caused this. I'm heartily sick of paying out, week in week out, with no thanks from any of you. What do you think I am? The Bank of Monte Carlo? You're a crowd of ungrateful bloody spongers,' he roared, beside himself with hurt and anger.

A gasp, half-horror, half-excitement, swept through the onlookers. This drama would keep the street going for months.

'Don't you dare speak to us like that!' Nancy pointed a shaking finger at her husband. 'How dare you come down here and make a disgrace of us—'

'Oh no!' Bill laughed bitterly. 'You don't need me to do that. You and that rude, ungrateful little brat,' he jerked his thumb at Nadine, 'manage to do that all by yourselves.'

He turned to Carol. 'So you're going to get married? I hope your marriage is a hell of a lot happier than mine was. I hope you never have to endure what I had to endure. And I hope your children bring you a lot more joy than mine brought me.' He turned to the crowd of neighbours. 'Clear off, you lot, the show's over. Bloody voyeurs.' Turning on his heel, he walked over to his car, did a U-turn and scorched down the street.

'If there's anything we can do to help, Nancy, give us a shout,' Johnny Kelleher, her immediate next-door neighbour, offered sympathetically, breaking the stunned silence.

'Thanks, Johnny,' Nancy said weakly.

'Mrs Logan, you've got to be very careful to make sure your cigarettes are completely extinguished before you put them into a bin. It's imperative that you check all your ashtrays at night also, or the next time you might not be so lucky,' the fireman warned sternly as his colleagues rolled up their hoses.

Nancy's face crumpled and she started to sob noisily. Nadine looked mortified.

'Come back over the road with me, and we'll let the lads sort out the place.' Liz stepped in quickly, taking Nancy by the arm. She led the distraught woman back to her house, away from the prying eyes of the neighbours.

'Come on, Gary, let's have a look and see what we can do to sort out the place,' Mike suggested.

'I'll help ye there, lads,' Johnny Kelleher said. 'First thing we'll need a couple of brushes to sweep up that glass there. I'll get mine.'

'I'll run down the town and get a couple of panes of glass; just let me measure up there,' another neighbour offered.

'Why don't you and Nadine and Jessie go back over to Liz's and have a cup of tea and we'll get on with the job,' Gary said to Carol. She could hardly look him in the eye, she was so humiliated.

'Go on, it's all right,' he said, in the gentlest

tone he'd ever used to her, and she burst into tears.

'Don't cry, Carol, come on – you too, Nadine,' Jessie said, feeling utterly sorry for the two girls. She put her arm around Carol and, trailed by Nadine, they crossed the road back to Liz's house.

'Fucking hell, I never knew it was that bad, mate,' Gary muttered to Mike, more shaken than he cared to admit.

'It will blow over,' was the best Mike could come up with. He didn't know what to say to the other man. It was clear Carol and he hadn't discussed the extent of her family difficulties. Did they communicate at all? he wondered as he rooted through Nancy's chaotic shed in search of a brush.

Would this contretemps have any effect on their forthcoming wedding? he couldn't help thinking. Would seeing the Logans in action make Gary back off?

Just when it looked like things were on an even keel again, it could all go very badly pear-shaped if the loony Logans were too much for Gary to handle.

What in the name of God have I let myself in for? Gary wondered miserably as he tipped the glass that Mike had swept into sheets of newspaper. He was thoroughly shaken by the events of the afternoon. He was marrying into a crowd of loopers. He'd made a big effort with them, just to try to get the afternoon over and done with as peacefully as possible once he'd sensed the unmistakable air of tension that permeated the household. The mother was off with the fairies, not on the planet at all. Carol had told him she *used* to drink when the husband had left her. She obviously still did.

The sister was a little skanger who was full of anger, and why wouldn't she be if that kind of carry-on was the norm? And the father certainly had issues. Carol had been really rough on him. He'd never seen her lose her cool like that before. She always liked to be in control. He'd felt very sorry for her, standing there berating her father. Gary hadn't realized the depth of her hurt at Bill's desertion of her. Even after all these years it still seemed very close to the surface.

She couldn't even look him in the eye. She'd been embarrassed. He'd never seen her so vulnerable. He didn't want to think of her as being vulnerable. He liked his tough, in-control, unruffled Carol. Vulnerable women needed emotional support. Giving emotional support could be hard going. He wasn't the best at it. It was too much of an effort.

Carol had kept her family very much at a distance all the time he'd known her. He could now see why. They were a major embarrassment. The neighbours had had a field day. What would his own family make of them? He'd introduced his mother and brothers to Carol and they'd socialized a couple of times, but generally they weren't in the habit of visiting. He wasn't great at keeping in touch with them either but at least they knew how to behave in public. Now in the light of the last couple of hours he was beginning to feel extremely apprehensive. He was certainly going to scrap his mother's suggestion of taking Nancy and Nadine to dinner so they could meet before the wedding day. Nancy would probably fall asleep in her soup. Another thought struck him . . . Did he really want to invite his friends to what could be an absolute disaster? He'd be a laughing stock. Gary could feel the beginnings of a headache. This was all the stuff of nightmare.

What kind of a wedding were they going to have? No wonder Jessie had been reluctant. Now he understood her hesitancy in agreeing to the joint celebration.

If he married Carol he'd be stuck with her family for life. What a thought. He groaned. It was bad enough having to get married in the first place. This was just the icing on the bloody cake.

Bill pulled onto the hard shoulder just off the Arklow bypass. His pulse was rattling. He took slow deep breaths, wondering for a moment if he was going to have a heart attack. What a dreadful scene. What a traumatic ordeal. Carol ranting and raving at him and calling him the most dreadful names. All the neighbours gawking and enjoying it, and the damn house going up in flames. The house he had paid the mortgage on for years. The house his wife now lived in rent-free, and all because of her damn stupidity it could have been a ruin. She'd have been on to him pretty quick to pay for alternative accommodation for her and Nadine if that had been the case. That's all they saw him as, a money machine. And he was the fool who paid out without a word of complaint, he thought bitterly, leaning back against the headrest.

And then there was Brona's totally unexpected intervention. At least it had been loyally motivated, if somewhat misguided. She had always been very protective of him. Her indignant protestations that his family took him for granted had always warmed him. Having a champion had helped more than she would ever know. But it was obvious that whatever Carol had said to her during their encounter had turned Brona away from him. She'd grown cold and sullen, no longer the loving companion he'd so enjoyed being with.

He'd have to sort it and try to get to the bottom of what was bugging her. He wouldn't tell her about the afternoon's events. Some things were best left unsaid, especially in the present pressure-cooker climate.

Feeling utterly beleaguered, Bill turned on the engine and waited for a gap in the heavy Sunday evening traffic.

'Oh Liz, I'm ashamed.' Nancy wept in the privacy of her neighbour's bedroom.

'Don't be, Nancy. It will be forgotten about soon enough,' Liz comforted.

'For it to happen in front of Carol's chap. What must he think of us?' She buried her head in her hands.

'That *was* unfortunate, but he'll get over it. If that's the worst that ever happens to him won't he be lucky?' Liz declared.

'It was my fault the house went on fire. And wasn't it just my luck that Bill called? I haven't seen him for months and he picks today to come. And did you see the way he turned on me? He

426

hates me, Liz. Can't bear the sight of me. And you know?' She rubbed her eyes with the backs of her hands. 'I loved him so much. I really loved him. I miss living with him. Why, Liz? Why did this all happen?'

'Look, Nancy,' Liz said firmly, having heard this many times before, 'don't you think it's time to put all of this behind you? Start afresh. Stop holding on to the past. Let him go. Why would you want to hold on to someone who doesn't want to be held on to? He's moved on, you have to as well. You'll never be happy otherwise.'

'It's very hard, Liz,' Nancy moaned.

'Do you want to be like this for the rest of your life? Look at the state of you, Nancy. You're shaking, you're smoking like a trooper, and you're not eating. Remember how you used to be, so vibrant and full of life,' Liz challenged.

'That was a long time ago. I'll never be that person again,' Nancy said mournfully.

'No, not that person, but you could become a happy, healthy person. Start again, cut down on the fags and the drink,' Liz said bluntly.

'Oh Liz, I don't drink that much,' Nancy protested.

'Now, Nancy, you know you do,' Liz pushed. 'Look, why don't you set yourself a goal for the wedding? I'll help you. We'll go walking, we'll eat healthy, and you cut down on the ciggies and do your best with the drinking. If you want to get professional help I'll come with you,' she offered kindly. 'I'm talking about AA.'

'No, no, there's no need for that,' Nancy exclaimed, horrified by the other woman's suggestion.

'OK, but let's make sure that Carol and Jessie have an unforgettable day. The loveliest wedding ever. They deserve it, don't they? And *we* deserve it. Both of us have had hard times.'

'I'd like that,' Nancy murmured. 'I'd like it very much. Will you really help me?'

'I will, Nancy. I *promise*,' Liz assured her. 'But you have to make the effort. Let's do it. Let's walk into that church and make our girls proud.'

'All right,' Nancy said shakily. 'Maybe some good will come out of this horrible day. I never want to go through a day like it again.'

'He's going to do a runner on me. He'll never marry me after this. Why would he want to?' Carol was in bits. Tears streamed down her face, which was buried in Jessica's shoulder.

'Stop bawling, will ya, Carol,' Nadine said uncomfortably.

428

'Let her get it out of her system,' Jessica said quietly. She pitied her friend from the bottom of her heart. What a horrible ordeal to have to endure. To have a family row was one thing, to have it in public with neighbours gaping open-mouthed, and, even worse, to have all of it witnessed by the man you were going to marry, was horrific.

Jessie had felt sick watching Carol scream abuse at her father. She hadn't realized the depth of Carol's hatred for Bill. It was very, very upsetting to view such naked hatred. She was so lucky to have known only love, she thought as she held Carol tightly. She wanted to reassure her and say that of course Gary would marry her and comfort and support her, but she wasn't at all sure that he would. That was the worst thing of all.

Wordlessly she patted Carol's back and wondered what other disasters could befall them. If they all got up the aisle at the end of September it would be an absolute miracle.

'Should we make a move, Carol?' Gary suggested, glancing at his watch. It was after nine and he was wrecked. If they left now he'd have time to go for a pint before closing time. He badly needed one.

'I think I'll stay the night, Gary,' she said

miserably. 'Jessie's staying the night, so I'll get a lift home with her in the morning.'

'Oh! Are you sure?' he asked, half relieved and half annoyed. If he'd known that she was going to stay he'd have left an hour ago. He and Mike had cleaned up the kitchen as much as they could and he smelt of smoke and sweat. He couldn't wait to have a shower and get out of his clothes. He couldn't wait to get out of this dilapidated, God-forsaken house and shake the dust of Arklow off his heels. If he never saw the place again it would be too soon for him, he thought grimly as he stood up to leave.

Nancy was in bed, doped out of her skull on the two Valium she'd taken. Nadine had gone to her best friend's house and he and Carol were sitting on the shabby sofa in mostly awkward silence. She stood up to walk him to the door. 'Are we OK?' she asked, more subdued than he'd ever seen her.

What could he say? That no, it was all off and he wanted out? He couldn't do it. He did love her, he supposed, surprised at the sudden rush of tenderness he felt when he saw her bowed head.

'Of course we're OK,' he said gruffly. 'Why wouldn't we be?'

'I wouldn't blame you if you wanted to break it

off after this afternoon,' she said unsteadily, unable to look him in the eye.

'Don't be daft, Carol, these things happen. Go to bed and have a good night's sleep and I'll see you tomorrow.' He gave her a hug and kissed the top of her head.

'OK,' she murmured wearily.

'Tell Nadine and your mum I said goodbye and I'll see them again,' he heard himself say as she opened the front door for him.

Heavy-hearted, he walked to the car. He'd had his chance to back out. She'd handed it to him on a plate and he just couldn't take it. He hoped he wouldn't regret it for the rest of his life.

Carol lay in bed, wide-eyed. Nadine had just come staggering in, pissed out of her skull. She could hear her thumping around her bedroom. Carol hadn't spoken to her; she didn't have the heart for it. One confrontation had been enough today, she thought miserably, as she tossed and turned, trying to get comfortable in her old bed.

Gary had come up trumps, that was one good thing, she tried to reassure herself. He'd treated her mother and sister kindly and he'd been un-usually gentle with her, especially when he'd said goodnight. Her heart had been in her mouth when she'd brought up the subject of him calling it off. She'd been all prepared for him to agree. And he hadn't. As far as he was concerned the wedding was still on track. Gary had stood by her. Right now that was all that mattered.

'We need to talk, Brona,' Bill said tiredly as he slumped into his favourite chair. He was whacked. The traffic had been bumper to bumper, single lane, for most of the way from the Avoca Handweavers until the Loughlinstown roundabout; the roadworks were an irritant he could have done without.

'I've a headache,' his partner muttered uncooperatively.

'What did Carol say to you that has made you so different towards me?' he demanded, determined to get to the bottom of their problem.

'What do you mean?' she stammered.

'I know you went to see her. Carol let me know in no uncertain terms. You've been very cold towards me for the past few weeks. Why? I want to know. I deserve to know. You owe me that much.'

'You don't want to hear what she said, Bill,' Brona said unhappily.

'Why? It can't be any worse than what she said to me today,' he said sardonically.

'Why did you leave them, Bill?' she burst out.

'But you know why I left, Brona, I told you all of that,' he said exasperatedly.

'No. No, I know why you left her. But why did you leave the kids? Why didn't you take them with you?'

'How could I? I couldn't take them away from their mother, from their home, their schools,' he argued, dismayed at her reaction.

'But you left them with an alcoholic, Bill. She couldn't take care of them. They had to take care of her. They were only children, for God's sake. What way did Carol put it? You left them physically, spiritually, morally and emotionally, she said. You left them to deal with her drunkenness. You deserted them totally and she can never forgive you for that. And I'm finding it hard to as well; they were only little kids. What do you expect them to do now, after deserting them, welcome you with open arms? Get real, Bill,' she said bitterly, before bursting into tears and running from the room.

The colour drained from his face. He felt he'd been kicked in the solar plexus. There was nowhere to hide. That dark thing he'd been running away from all these years had reared its ugly head and confronted him. Riven with guilt, he buried his head in his hands and wished he were dead.

'What a day,' Jessie whispered, snug in the crook of Mike's arm. He had stayed the night at her mother's. They had gone to bed early, tired after the drama of the day.

'Hard to beat, all right,' Mike agreed. 'Just when things were getting sorted too. Shame.'

'Do you think Gary will go through with it?'

'I don't know. He was fairly shaken. He never saw Carol like that before. None of us did. Plus it didn't help that Nancy was in a pretty bad way.'

'God, she was in an awful state. Mam said she's going to try and stop drinking for the wedding. Mam's taking her under her wing.'

'Good old Lizzie, she's got a heart of gold and if anyone can straighten Nancy out, Liz will,' Mike said fondly.

'What sort of a wedding are we going to have?' Jessie bit her lip.

'The best, Jessie. The best. Maybe the worst has happened. Nancy's going to get her act together. Bill's out of the picture. Nadine likes Gary so she'll behave herself.'

'And pigs will fly,' Jessica scoffed.

'Stop! I'm being positive,' Mike said sternly.

'And I'm being realistic.'

'And I'm horny.'

'Oh for God's sake,' Jessica giggled as she felt him grow hard against her.

'Come on, the worst that can happen is this antique of a bed will collapse,' Mike murmured, kissing her soundly.

She kissed him back and to her surprise felt her body respond.

'Hmmm,' he murmured, smiling against her mouth. 'This is just what we need, you know, and I'm not just saying it because I want a ride.'

'I know.' She slid her leg between his thighs. 'I love you,' she whispered, as his fingers began to do the most delightful things to her.

'And I love you and that's all that matters,' he whispered back. As silently and gently as they could, they made love tenderly, all memories of the last few hours pushed to the deepest recesses of their minds.

Afterwards, lying spooned together, they took comfort from their intimacy, its balming comfort a shield against all the uncertainties that lay ahead.

32

'We're really blessed with the weather this summer, aren't we, Nancy?' Liz observed as they walked down a small side street that led towards the wildlife reserve.

'The best since '95, I'd say,' wheezed Nancy breathlessly. Liz slowed her pace a little. Sometimes she forgot that Nancy wasn't able to match her pace. They had been walking together every evening for a month now, and she had to admit that she was more than surprised that Nancy had embraced the notion of starting afresh.

She felt a surge of admiration for her neighbour's frail but determined efforts to change her life. Nancy had cut down her cigarette intake, and was desperately trying not to drink as much. Sometimes she succeeded, other times Liz knew that drink had triumphed over her and she would be shaking and hungover. But she'd still gamely appear at Liz's gate at seven p.m., as if the walk was the lifeline that she clung to grimly.

Today, Liz was pleased to note that Nancy had a hint of colour in her cheeks. That awful, pasty grey hue that made her look so old and haggard was slowly disappearing. Liz had persuaded her to come to the hairdresser's with her one Saturday. She had entered the salon with shoulder-length lank, mousy hair liberally streaked with grey, and had left it with a chic strawberry-blonde bob that took years off her, highlighting her sculptured cheekbones and gold-flecked hazel eyes.

'It's hard to believe it's me,' she murmured, touching her hair as if she felt it was going to revert to its previous state of disarray at any moment.

'Yes, it is you. The new you.' Liz was thrilled at the transformation. She hoped with all her might that Nancy would keep it up. They walked past the swimming-pool and Liz suddenly had a brainwave. 'You should come swimming with Tara and me. We go twice a week. It's very invigorating.'

'I haven't swum in years,' Nancy replied. 'I don't know if I'd remember how to.'

'Ah, it's like riding a bicycle,' Liz laughed.

'Is it very expensive? I have to watch the pennies, you know. Bill never gave me a red cent towards doing up the kitchen. If it wasn't for your Mike and Johnny next door I don't know what I would have done. Can you believe that, Liz? Not a red cent. That man has a life of bliss up in Dublin with none of the worries I've got and it grieves me, Liz. It does my head in.'

Liz sighed. She should have known that 'Bad Bill' would come up in conversation at some stage. Not a walk passed that Nancy didn't launch into some sort of diatribe about her estranged husband.

'Let's make a pact, Nancy, as part of your new life. Let's not talk about Bill during our walks. Let's keep it a good and positive energy. Tara gave me great advice years ago when I was dumped by a rat, before I met Ray,' she said conversationally. 'I used to walk the streets with Tara saying, "Why did this happen? I loved him, I'll never get over him. What did he see in that other one that he dumped me for?"' She chuckled at the memory. 'I nearly drove Tara mad, so eventually she made me promise that I would only think about him and moan about him for ten minutes every morning. That's all I was allowed to keep him in my head for. It was really hard at the beginning, Nancy, but I stuck with it, and the funny thing was, I started to feel such a relief that I'd let go of him, I started to enjoy life again and then I met Ray and there was no comparison. Ray was solid, a real man, not like the other yoke.'

She sighed, thinking of Ray. 'I really miss him. I suppose I have some nerve telling you to let go of Bill when I can't let go of my Ray.' Tears suddenly spurted down her cheeks.

'Oh, Liz, poor, poor Liz, it's much harder for you,' Nancy exclaimed, jolted out of her introspection by her companion's grief. 'Why would you want to let go? He was the love of your life and you were the love of his.'

'I know.' Liz rubbed her eyes. 'But some of the spiritual books I've read say that you have to let go so that the person that you love can move on in the spiritual realms and I just don't seem to be able to do it. I'm so lonely for him.'

'Of course you are.' Nancy, the comforted, became the comforter. 'Why wouldn't you be? You had a great marriage. I used to envy you both, you were such companions to each other.'

'I know you probably think I'm horrible but I really envy Mike and Jessica,' Liz confessed. 'They have such fun and they can't keep their hands off each other. I don't know about you, and Tara's the only other one I'd say this to, but I miss sex. I really miss intimacy. Do you?' She eyed Nancy, curious to hear what she'd say. They were roughly of the same age, both were alone, and she felt comfortable enough with her now to ask her such an intimate question.

Nancy gave a wry smile. 'Liz, I've never told this to anyone, but I never knew what the fuss was about. I never had an orgasm; Bill wasn't a very tender lover. A few perfunctory kisses, a squeeze of the boobs and that was his idea of foreplay. Maybe he just didn't fancy me. Maybe it's different with the woman he's with. I torture myself about it sometimes, imagining them making love.'

'Oh, don't do that – why torment yourself?' Liz patted her on the arm.

'I know. I'm a sad specimen. Sometimes I pretend that I've met a gorgeous man and we're really happy and Bill comes back and gets mad jealous and tells me that it's me he's loved all along, and I tell him to get lost and it's *very* satisfying,' she said emphatically.

'I'm sure it is,' Liz laughed. 'And who knows, you might meet a gorgeous man. One of my books, I can't remember the name of it, but I'll root it out for you, says that when you let the energy of the past go, a door opens and a new energy comes in. Ask for a new man to come to you. Put that positive thought out in the Universe.'

'Are you mad, who'd look at me?' Nancy jeered.

'Stop that now, you're looking very well and you're doing great. You're a woman in your prime. Both of us are.'

'Do you think so?' Nancy asked, pleased.

'I know so,' Liz said warmly. 'Mid-forties is still young, Nancy, for God's sake.'

'I might meet a toy boy at the wedding,' the other woman laughed. 'Mike will surely have some nice friends.'

'Indeed he has.' Liz flicked a stone into the sea.

'He and Jessie are a happy couple, aren't they?' Nancy inhaled the balmy, sea-scented evening breeze. 'Happier than my Carol and her chap. Carol doesn't have a capacity for happiness, I don't think, after all that happened to her. I didn't help. I was drunk for so much of her childhood.'

'She should talk to a professional about it. Maybe you could persuade her. I think it would help her a lot,' Liz said tactfully.

'You should do counselling, you're very good at it,' Nancy remarked approvingly.

'Are you joking? I can't even get myself out of the bed in the mornings sometimes,' Liz scoffed.

'You hide it very well, Liz, and I'll never be able to thank you for the way you've helped me. You don't know what you've done for me.'

'You've done it for yourself, Nancy. Just keep it

up,' Liz encouraged, as they scrambled up over the rocks to escape the incoming tide and headed for the reserve to feed the ducks.

'I think it's lovely on you, Carol,' Amanda, her tennis partner and bridesmaid, said, trying to keep the weariness out of her tone. It was late-night shopping; this was the third bridal boutique they'd tried. And, after weeks of watching Carol trying on and discarding wedding dresses, she'd started lying through her teeth. If Carol decided on a sack, Amanda was now prepared to say it was gorgeous.

'I still like the one in Marian Gale's,' Carol dithered.

'I know, but it was very expensive. This one's half the price and it is lovely on you. It's so elegant.'

'I want it to be sexy, not elegant,' Carol retorted.

'It's sexy as well.' Amanda could have kicked herself.

'Do you not think it's a bit plain?' She turned and looked at the rear view of the simple white satin and lace sheath with the softly draped neckline and long white train that swirled around her feet.

'Oh no! It's you. Some of the ones you tried on

were a bit OTT. You know the meringue syndrome. It gives you a great cleavage and a lovely shape. Makes 'em stick out.'

'Really, do you think so?' Carol said eagerly, twisting and turning to get the best view.

'Absolutely,' Amanda said fervently, sensing that victory was in sight and congratulating herself for zeroing in on Carol's vanity point. 'Gary'd love it,' she added slyly. 'He'll be trying to slip his hand inside that neckline for a feel. Look at the way it shows the curve of your boobs. And yours are so firm. Very sexy, Carol. It's definitely the nicest one on you that I've seen.'

'Are you sure? I know the saleswoman will tell me it's fabulous but that's only because she wants a sale. Believe me, I've tried on enough of them to get to know the patter.'

'Look, we can go and look at a dozen more if you want.' Amanda backed off a little. 'I just really like that one on you. You've got great arms and the tan looks fantastic against the white.'

'Jessie's wearing cream so at least we won't clash—' The curtain to the cubicle swished open and a beaming saleswoman studied Carol approvingly.

'Much better than the last one on you. It's an ultra-classy style. Think Grace Kelly. Think

Audrey Hepburn. I suppose Alison Doody or Yvonne Keating would be the modern equivalent here in Ireland, if you wanted a contemporary comparison.' She studied her again, eyes flicking over Carol from top to toe. 'I like it,' she pronounced.

'I'll think about it,' Carol said, losing her nerve.

Amanda threw her eyes up to heaven behind Carol's back. The saleswoman gave her a sympathetic smile as she hurried forward to help Carol out of the precious creation.

'Let's go to the club and have a drink. I told Jessie I'd see her there,' Carol said tiredly as she stepped out of the dress.

'OK,' agreed Amanda. Her feet were killing her and a drink was just what she needed. 'And you know something, I'm damned if I'm waiting for a bus. Let's get a taxi. I'll pay,' she added exasperatedly when she saw Carol about to protest. It was a wonder she wasn't being asked to pay for her own bridesmaid dress, Carol was so mean sometimes, Amanda thought sourly as she plonked herself down on a chair and waited for the bride-to-be to get dressed.

'Hey, Jessie, I think I might have found us a house,' Mike said excitedly, the noise of the traffic behind him almost drowning out his voice. 'Hold on, I'll nip down a side street.'

'Where is it – what's it like?' Jessica felt excitement bubble.

'It's in Kilcoole, about two minutes away from the beach. I saw it in an estate agent's window the other day and I went to have a look. It's a little cottage, not very modern but it's spotless and I think you'll really like it. It's even got an Aga – you can cook great on an Aga,' he enthused.

'Well, seeing as you'll be doing the cooking, I'm very happy for you,' she teased.

'Could you drive down tomorrow night? I could meet you there. I've told the estate agent we'll take it. It's too good to let it slip through our hands.'

'You like it that much?' Jessica said in amazement.

'Yeah, I do. It's in a lovely place, real quiet, but only a few minutes' walk to the village. It's a good spot for commuting, it won't mean sitting in the car for hours for you. And we'll be able to walk on the beach. And it's only about twenty-five miles to Arklow. And there's a nice garden—'

'What's the bedroom like?' Jessica had her priorities.

'Snug and cosy, just the way you like it, and it's got a big brass bed.'

'Can't wait,' Jessica squealed. 'I'll take some time I'm owed and I'll leave work early. Friday evening rush hour on the N11 isn't for the faint-hearted.'

'That's my girl. Have to go. I'll talk to you later,' Mike said regretfully. 'Love you.'

'Love you too,' Jessica said happily as she carried her coffee over to an empty table in the bar. This was the best news that she'd had in ages. Maybe their luck was turning. It was a month since the nightmare Sunday afternoon meeting that had left her feeling edgy and worried. She and Carol had gone to meet the manager in The Four Winds and had sorted out the reception, but the other girl was distant and unhappy and it had put a damper on things. Carol had only gone home once since that afternoon, to help Mike and Nancy's next-door neighbour paint the kitchen.

She was a strange girl; she seemed to be able to switch off from her family just like that. If Nancy were Jessica's mother she'd be worried sick about her. But then maybe her friend had had to learn to switch off as a form of self-protection. It was easy for her to judge – she'd never experienced what Carol had. All she'd known in her childhood was love.

Shame washed over her. She'd been thinking

horrible bitchy thoughts about the other girl lately. Not even lately, she admitted ruefully. It was since Carol had suggested the double wedding. It was time to cut it out once and for all, she told herself sternly.

Liz had told her that Carol's mother was making a huge effort to straighten herself out. It would be great for her own sake if she did, but it would be great for Jessica's nerves too. A sober Nancy would be one less thing to have to worry about at the wedding.

'Hi, Jessie,' she heard Carol call across the bar. She looked exhausted.

'Hi, you look whacked.'

'I am.' Carol eased herself into the chair opposite her. 'Amanda and I were looking at wedding dresses.'

'Any luck?'

'I don't know. I saw one I kinda liked. Pity we're getting married together. I'd love your opinion.'

'I'll look at it if you want,' Jessica offered.

'Thanks, but I want to surprise you, just like Tara wants to surprise me,' Carol reciprocated.

'If you like it, buy it,' Jessica advised, ignoring the barb. 'That's what I did. It means you won't be going around annoying yourself.'

'I know, but it's my wedding dress. The most important dress I'll ever wear,' Carol wailed.

'I know that. And I would have been the same as you probably,' Jessica admitted. 'I just didn't have the money to go mad. It's as simple as that. So I said to myself, make up your mind fast and don't even look at anything else. Don't forget Mike's only started working, we'll be really skint once the wedding's over.'

'Poor but happy.' Carol smiled at her.

'Yeah. How are you getting on?'

'Since "the episode", do you mean?' Carol said caustically.

'Any word from your dad?'

'Nope, and I don't want there to be.'

'How are things with Gary?' Jessica arched an eyebrow at her.

'He's a bit subdued. I think it's all starting to hit home. Wedding, family stuff. He was fitted for his morning suit the other day. That was a panic-stricken moment for him, I can tell you. I was waiting for him to back out of it all day but he held his nerve, bless him.' Carol sighed. 'Nadine's coming to stay with me next week for an overnighter. We're bringing her to Temple Bar. If we survive that we'll survive anything.'

'He's doing fine,' Jessica comforted. 'He was

great that Sunday. He was very good with Nadine and your mam.'

'I know. I'll just be glad when we're married and settled down.'

'Speaking of settling down, Mike thinks he's found us a house,' Jessica said happily.

'Lucky wagon,' Carol said enviously. 'I'm not even bringing up the subject any more, he can only cope with so much at a time. We're going to live in his place or mine for a while. Once that ring is on my finger, I'll be looking for a house and if he doesn't like it he can divorce me.'

'I'm not going through all this hardship of trying to find you the right dress for you to be talking about divorce.' Amanda grinned as she plonked a Club Orange in front of Carol. 'We were this close, Jessie.' She held up her finger and thumb. 'And then she chickened out.'

'It will be worth it on the day,' Jessica assured her, glad that she'd been spared the trauma of helping to choose Carol's wedding dress. It was all starting to get exciting, though, and she was dying to see the house that Mike was so set on. Perhaps by the weekend they'd have a home of their own.

'Oh! Hi! What are you doing here?' Katie smiled to see a familiar if unexpected face in A & E.

'I'm badly in need of a country girl who likes looking at the stars and going to barn dances,' the man teased.

'Are you asking me on a date?'

'Yep. Are you coming?'

'Why not?' Katie agreed happily. 'I'm off duty at ten.'

'I'll be waiting,' he said.

'Why don't we get your mother to babysit and we'll go out to dinner?' Bill suggested.

'No, I'm not in the humour to go out,' Brona said coldly.

'Oh, for God's sake, Brona, give me a break here,' Bill said in desperation.

'Why? Why should I? It's always about you. You and your traumas. I'm in the middle of a trauma right now, so you give *me* the break,' Brona snapped viciously.

'Look, we need to talk at least—'

'You mean you'll do the talking and I'll do the listening. I don't think so, Bill. When I'm ready to talk I'll talk, but right now I'm so disappointed in you I don't want to talk to you.'

Utterly fed up, Bill slammed the door and walked out into the back garden. He was a disappointment to her. That hurt terribly. He'd

450

always liked the way she'd looked up to him. The worst thing was that he understood how she felt. Hell, he was a disappointment to himself, he thought glumly as he hauled the lawnmower out of the shed. He couldn't look himself in the eye any more. His guilt was so all-consuming he felt smothered by it. If Brona only realized how bloody guilty he felt she wouldn't be rubbing his nose in it.

Women were the most troublesome species that had ever existed. And he should know. All he'd had from every woman in his life was trouble. Poor innocent little Ben, he didn't know what miseries were in store for him when he grew up.

Gary groaned under the weight of the barbells as he pumped iron furiously in his local gym. He was spending a lot of time here, trying to dissipate the cloud of unease that assailed him of late. It was only pre-wedding jitters. All blokes went through it, he assured himself as he finished with the weights and headed for the bike.

He and Carol were treading water around each other and it was getting on his nerves. He'd nearly prefer for them to have a humdinger of a row and get it over and done with. He wiped the sweat off his forehead. It had been a scorcher all day, and the gym was stuffy. He saw that a treadmill was free and decided to do some running rather than cycling. He stepped on and set the programme. Steep incline, to really push himself. It was almost August, the summer was flying, and in a couple of months he'd be a married man. The thought filled him with dread.

He'd nearly lost his cool the day he'd been fitted for his morning suit. Alterations had to be made to the one he was wearing and he'd stood like a bloody idiot getting measured and pin-tucked like a mannequin. The hotel was booked, the menu agreed upon, band organized. It was all getting bloody serious.

Carol's father hadn't been in touch since the bust-up, and according to his bride-to-be, that was the end of it and things were back to normal. Well, as normal as things could be in that weird family, he thought despondently. Nadine was coming to stay with Carol next week. She wanted to go drinking and clubbing and Carol was having a fit. Carol was so uptight about drink. Now he understood why, but one of these days he was going to go on the tear and get hammered. He'd earned it, he decided, as he increased his pace and began to run in earnest.

* * *

Nancy sat on her lounger in her favourite spot in the garden. It was the corner at the end that faced the western sky and allowed the dying rays of the sun to bathe her in its benevolent, gold, warm light.

The grass could do with cutting, and the shrubs were terribly overgrown, she observed. It was a shame. The garden could be lovely. She'd let it go to pot, she chided herself, looking around at the sheltered private untidy garden that had been so badly neglected.

It was strange, she'd been sitting in this spot on and off for years and had never noticed how wild and untended it was. In the last week especially she'd begun seeing things with clear eyes. The shabby house in need of refurbishing and redecoration. The garden in need of tender loving care. She wasn't looking at them through drink-sodden eyes any more, she realized, and felt a rising sense of excitement.

That unbearable weight of depression she'd carried for so long seemed to be getting easier to carry. She felt stronger, healthier. She'd cut down her cigarettes from forty a day to twenty. She still drank, but only sips now. No more long slugs as if it were lemonade. She still felt the need to know that she had a bottle in her bag or by her bed if she needed it, but she was weaning herself off it and had only faltered badly three times since that soul-destroying afternoon.

She shivered, thinking of it. Seeing all those neighbours and, even worse, Carol's fiancé watch Bill roar and curse at her. She'd wanted to sink through the ground. That had been one of the worst experiences of her life. Her rock bottom, possibly. When Liz had thrown her the lifeline she'd been afraid she wouldn't have the courage or the willpower to keep holding it but so far she had, and it was getting marginally easier.

Liz was amazing, she thought gratefully. She'd always appeared so positive and together. Her tears earlier and her palpable grief over the loss of her husband had astonished Nancy. You'd never know by her outward appearance that she was still so bereft after all this time.

Liz had put her own troubles aside to help her, the least she could do was try and keep on the straight and narrow at least until the wedding. And even after it, Nancy decided. Liz was right, she *could* start afresh. Bill Logan was never going to see her in that state again. None of them were.

Feeling more peaceful than she'd been in many, many years, Nancy raised her face to the evening sun and felt the tension slowly leave her body.

Nadine buttered a slice of bread and butter and cut a chunk off a block of Cheddar. She was hungry. She stood at the kitchen sink, sipping a glass of milk and eating her snack. She could see her mother sitting at the end of the garden. She hadn't done that for such a long time, and now she was sitting out a lot. It was amazing, Nadine reflected. That haircut that Liz had persuaded her to have had made such a difference. It was like looking at a new woman. Even living with her was different. She was going for her walk with Liz every night. She had cut down on her cigarettes and she had cut down on her drinking.

She was still drinking; Nadine didn't fool herself there, but not as heavily at all. Her eyes were clear, and she was talking coherently, not in that pissed slurred dead way that Nadine had grown used to.

This was one of the best summers in a long time, she reflected, not only weatherwise. Her mother wasn't in a heap. Nadine had got a part-time job in a petrol station, and the money wasn't bad. She had a great new state-of-the-art hi-fi system courtesy of her father. Carol was adamant she didn't want it and Bill hadn't come back for it, so Nadine had appropriated it.

And next week she was going to Dublin to stay over and she was going to get to Temple Bar, the coolest place in Dublin. Even Lynn envied her that. Her friend didn't have family in Dublin and she'd never been allowed to stay over on her own. Nadine would love coming back home with tales of pubs and clubs that Lynn might not get to see until she'd finished school.

She wondered if she could persuade Carol to allow Lynn to come to stay some night. That would be brill. They'd really have a ball.

Nadine rinsed her glass under the tap and smiled. A month ago she'd been in bits, mortified by the carry-on of her parents and sister in front of the neighbours. Amazingly, today, it seemed like a bad dream.

And things were looking up.

33

The traffic was atrocious but at least she was getting off the N11, Jessica sighed with relief, as she indicated left to turn off at Delgany. She drove down the winding country road, admiring the big houses to her left and right. It was an affluent part of the county with a charm all of its own, a million miles away from the helter-skelter rat-race she had just left. She could feel herself relaxing already. She drove along until she came to the turn for Kilcoole and felt a carefree giddiness wrap itself around her. Soon she'd see Mike. She missed him like crazy.

She often looked at married couples she knew and wondered why they had let the intimacy of their relationship slide – the appreciation of being in each other's company, the pleasure of doing little things together, like watching the news or preparing a meal or going for walks and holding hands. She hoped the joy of such small things would always stay with her and Mike and that familiarity would not deaden their relationship. It all depended on the effort you put in, she reflected, remembering how, even after twenty years of marriage, Ray and Liz had delighted in each other's company. They were two of the lucky ones, and she hoped she and Mike would fare as well.

She drove along the narrow road gazing with pleasure at the panoramic coastal views away to the left of her. The sea was as blue as the Mediterranean. If she lived in the area she'd be able to walk to the beach from her house and watch the sun sparkle and glitter in summer and the waves swirl and pound in winter. She could smell the salty breeze and she very much hoped that this was to be her new home.

She bounced over the first of the ramps through the village and slowed to a more appropriate speed. She'd have to remember the ramps if she were going to live here, she grimaced, as she bounced over another one. She'd driven through Kilcoole many times, never thinking that she might live here. To her right she could see the church that had been made famous in a TV series called *Glenroe* that had been filmed in the village. She drove past the vegetable shop with colourful trays of bedding plants outside, and noted the Spar supermarket on her right. It would be her local shop, she thought happily. Following Mike's instructions, she took the left at the yellow pub and drove past a small well-kept housing estate for about half a mile until she came upon a narrow lane that led to a neat little cottage. This must be it, Jessica thought in delight, noting the freshly whitewashed exterior, the gleaming sash windows and the flower-filled garden.

It was just the way he'd described it. She rummaged in her bag for her phone and dialled Mike's number.

'Where are you? I'm here,' she said excitedly.

'I'm just coming into Newcastle, I won't be long. The estate agent gave me the key; he can't make it, so we have the place to ourselves.'

'Yippee,' she yelled exuberantly. What a fabulous way to start the weekend.

Ten minutes later Mike's red Volvo came rattling down the lane. Jessica flew into his arms. They kissed hungrily, touching each other's faces as though they had been parted for months.

'I missed you.' She drew away breathlessly.

'I missed you too. Do you like it?' He turned to look at the cottage.

'It looks gorgeous. Come on, let's have a look.'

'It's small enough now,' he warned. 'Small but perfectly formed.'

Hand in hand they walked up the path and Mike inserted the key into the lock. Impulsively he swept her up into his arms. 'I've a feeling this is going to be our place so I'm going to carry you over the threshold.'

He kissed her before carrying her into a small wooden-floored hall that had old-fashioned cream-painted wooden doors to the left and right. Mike carried her to the door at the end that led to the kitchen and pushed it open with his foot.

'Ohh!' she said appreciatively, looking at the neat little kitchen, dominated at one end by the big cream Aga. Cream and green fitted cupboards lined the walls and a big window faced on to a large tree-lined garden that had its own overgrown vegetable patch.

'We'll be able to grow our own cabbages and spuds,' Mike said cheerfully. 'We'll be able to have organic vegetables.'

'We'll be like Tom and Barbara out of *The Good Life*.' Jessica nuzzled in to him.

'You might need to lose a stone or two to be mistaken for Barbara,' joked Mike, easing her down to the floor.

'You stinker!' Jessica poked him in the arm before turning her attention to the kitchen. It was well fitted, with a fridge-freezer and microwave. In a little utility room that led out to the back there was a washing-machine and drier. A small archway led to a cosy dining-room with a cream table and chairs.

They moved on to the sitting-room, which was a bright, sunny room with an old-fashioned tiled fireplace, wooden floors and two squashy terracotta sofas made for sinking into. A low coffee table in the centre of the room held a trio of cream candles.

'It's been refurbished to let,' Mike explained when she remarked on how modern the interior was, belying its old-fashioned exterior.

The bedroom on the opposite side of the hall had a big brass bed, two bedside lockers and a fitted wardrobe whose cream doors cleverly matched the old-fashioned latch door into the room. It was a nice touch, in keeping with the cottagey feel, and Jessica was entranced.

'Oh, Mike, I love it. Imagine what it will be like when the bed is dressed.'

'And imagine us romping around in it *undressed!*'

'Yeah,' she agreed, eyes sparkling.

461

'And we have a guest room,' Mike said happily, leading her into the room next door which, though compact, held a double bed and two bedside lockers and a pine chest of drawers.

The bathroom was tiled from floor to ceiling in apple green and white and the bath was new.

It was perfect.

'Will we go for it? It's a thousand a month.'

'You bet, Mike.'

'Right. I'll drop the key back and confirm to the estate agent that he's definitely got two new tenants,' Mike declared, taking Jessica in his arms and kissing her hungrily.

Liz had the patio table set for tea. Chicken breasts stuffed with cream cheese and wrapped in bacon were cooking in the oven. The Caesar salad was prepared, and a bottle of wine was chilling in the fridge. Jessie and Mike had phoned to say that they were on their way and her heart had lifted at the sound of her daughter's happy voice.

While she waited she sat at her computer, logged on and opened her emails.

'This is lovely,' she murmured, reading an inspirational email Tara had sent her. The words were so loving, so kind, she felt a lump in her throat as she scrolled down to the final most comforting words of all. Pass it on, it said, and she sat thinking of all the dear friends who had helped, whose lives she'd like to enrich with the gift that had just been sent to her. She forwarded busily for ten minutes and then she thought of Nancy. It couldn't but help her, she decided, clicking on the print icon. The printer rattled into life and she picked up the pages that slid out and started to read the email again. It was called *The Interview With God*, and it was written in the form of a poem. Liz read it slowly, savouring every word.

the poem
The Interview With God

I dreamed I had an interview with God.
'So you would like to interview me?' God asked.
'If you have the time,' I said.
God smiled. 'My time is eternity.
What questions do you have in mind for me?'
'What surprises you most about humankind?'
God answered . . .
'That they get bored with childhood,
they rush to grow up, and then
long to be children again.
That they lose their health to make money . . .
and then lose their money to restore their health.

That by thinking anxiously about the future,
they forget the present,
such that they live in neither
the present nor the future.
That they live as if they will never die,
and die as though they had never lived.'
God's hand took mine
and we were silent for a while.
And then I asked . . .
'As a parent, what are some of life's lessons
you want your children to learn?'
'To learn they cannot make anyone
love them. All they can do
is let themselves be loved.
To learn that it is not good
to compare themselves to others.
To learn to forgive
by practising forgiveness.
To learn that it only takes a few seconds
to open profound wounds in those they love,
and it can take many years to heal them.
To learn that a rich person
is not one who has the most,
but is one who needs the least.
To learn that there are people
who love them dearly,
but simply have not yet learned

how to express or show their feelings.
To learn that two people can
look at the same thing
and see it differently.
To learn that it is not enough that they
forgive one another, but they must also forgive
  themselves.'
'Thank you for your time,' I said humbly.
'Is there anything else
you would like your children to know?'
God smiled and said,
'Just know that I am here . . . always.'

—author unknown

Tears slid down Liz's cheeks as she read the last line, but they weren't tears of sadness. It was as if her loneliness was being shared and she wasn't alone.

She sat peacefully looking out of the window, enjoying the way the sunlight dappled the patio through the leafy, fringed foliage of the Japanese maple that Jessica had given her a few years ago for her birthday.

Today was a good day, she told herself. She would live in the present, like it said in the poem, and make the most of it.

* * *

'I hope you didn't mind me not going on our walk last night, Nancy,' Liz said as they walked briskly down the road towards the town.

'Not at all – you had to be there for Jessie and Mike. Anyway, I did some gardening out the back and I enjoyed it, to be honest. Mind, my poor ass was aching after it from all the leaning into the flowerbeds. I'd like to have the place a bit tidy when Carol and Gary come down again. I got a chap to cut the grass for me and I'll be able to do it myself from now on.'

'I like cutting the grass,' Liz remarked. 'It's something that gives a very visible result, if you know what I mean. I always feel I've achieved something satisfying when I've cut the back garden. Sad, I know, but there you go.'

'I don't think it's sad, I felt a bit like that myself.' Nancy was privately chuffed that she was pacing her friend. Carol had promised to come down soon and she was looking forward to her daughter's reaction to her new health and fitness regime.

She'd gone swimming with Liz and Tara early one morning during the week and afterwards had gone for coffee and a fry-up with them in Anne's Bakery, something she hadn't done in years. It had been a real treat.

She'd been a little awkward and nervous at the beginning with Tara, not knowing her that well. But Liz's sister had soon put her at her ease with her outrageous sense of humour and devil-may-care attitude. She'd found herself laughing heartily at some of the other woman's witty asides and had wondered privately in amazement if it was really her, Nancy Logan, nervous, jittery recluse, sitting in public, eating and chatting and laughing and actually having fun. Sometimes she felt she needed to pinch herself.

The bad days came too, but she seemed to be able to deal with them more easily, not allowing herself to sink into the apathy of depression like she used to. It was a habit, she supposed, but habits could be broken and she found that these days she tended to go out into the garden if depression threatened to overwhelm her. The fine, warm summer had been her ally for sure, she thought gratefully.

At the beginning when she'd started walking with Liz, she'd been morose, finding it hard to talk; now she welcomed her chats with her neighbour and was careful not to talk about Bill or feel sorry for herself.

It must be starting to work, she reflected. Nancy noticed she didn't think of him as often, nor did she feel as sorry for herself as she used to. Liz was an inspiration to her. She was one of life's truly kind souls and Nancy counted herself lucky to have been befriended by her.

'I printed this off for you, it's an email I got from Tara. I thought you might like it – I certainly did.' Liz took a card out of the back of her jeans pocket and handed it to her. 'See you tomorrow.'

'See you, Liz, thanks for the walk,' Nancy said almost light-heartedly. She was looking forward to a cup of tea, a cigarette and a read of a lovely book that Liz had lent her. It was called *The Game of Life*, a spiritual book that was making her see life in a whole different way. It was all about thinking positive and not judging and seeing the good in every human being. She had a long way to go to see the good in Bill, she thought wryly, but at least she had made a start.

She made her tea, took her book and card and cigarettes and headed for the garden. This really was her favourite time of the day, this benign, soul-calming time with just the sound of the birds to keep her company. Nadine was working and probably wouldn't be in until all hours, but Nancy wasn't giving her grief. She was hoping that the change in her might rub off on her youngest daughter and she'd be happier to come home. She was certainly less abrasive these days and had complimented her a few times on her hair. One day she'd even done her nails for her.

That had been nice, a real mother–daughter thing, and Nancy hoped there'd be more of it.

She sat down, leaned back against her lounger cushion, took a sip of tea and lit up. Gratefully she drew the smoke deep into her lungs. Some day she'd give up the fags, but not yet. She needed her crutches.

She opened the card Liz had given her and smiled when she saw WELL DONE and a picture of a grinning Cheshire cat. Liz had written: *Just want to say you're doing great, and I enjoy our walks. Enjoy this. I did. Love Liz XXXX*

A page fell out and she unfolded it and read it slowly. As she read the last line a great lump came to her throat. A lump as big as a grapefruit. And then it was as if a knot of grief that had been stuck in her breastbone slowly came undone and she cried with abandon, all the sorrow of the years pouring out of her.

Nancy cried for a long time. She cried for herself, she cried for Carol and Nadine, and she cried for Bill and what could have been. She was shaking after the torrent of grief that had flooded out of her, and her first thought after her sobs subsided was to go inside and pour herself a stiff drink. It would calm her, soothe her. She lit another cigarette. She knew if she went inside to take that drink a sip or two wouldn't do. It would be a glassful, neat. And she'd be on a bender quicker than the blink of an eye.

Nancy took a few deep breaths and picked up the poem that had fluttered from her fingers. She read it again and lingered on the last line.

'*Just know that I am here . . . always.*'

'God! Don't let me drink, please, *please* don't let me drink!' she prayed aloud. 'Be with me and help me learn to forgive and not to hold on to the resentment.'

She picked up the little book Liz had given her and, holding it between her hands as her friend had instructed, asked for a message of comfort. She slid her thumb between two pages and opened it slowly.

'*God sees man perfect, created in his own image,*' she read, and for a fleeting moment had a memory of herself radiant and carefree as a young woman playing tennis before life's hard knocks had taken their toll. She hadn't smoked then or drunk, and while she knew she'd never be youthful again she could be carefree and healthy. The longing for a drink was still strong but she kept the vision of herself as she'd once been and gradually a composure of sorts descended on her and Nancy fell asleep, face raised to the evening sun, and dreamt she was bathed in a beautiful light.

34

'Jessie, I got a phone call from the estate agent's. The woman who owns the house has changed her mind all of a sudden and is letting it to someone in the family, so we'll have to keep looking. Talk to you later.' Mike's message ended, and Jessica wished she hadn't turned on her phone until after her lunch. She'd been in studio most of the morning and had turned off her phone, never thinking that she was going to hear such discouraging news. She looked at the quiche and salad on her plate and suddenly didn't feel very hungry. She was sitting in the big canteen in RTE, and all around the hum of chatter and laughter and the clinking of cutlery faded away as disappointment so intense that she could almost taste it swept through her.

She'd felt very at home in that cottage. It was so clean and well-furnished compared to the other two places they had viewed. It was completely disheartening.

'Back in a second, I just need to ring Mike,' she excused herself, and walked between the crowded tables to the relative peace outside. She dialled Mike's number dejectedly.

'What happened? They'd accepted us as tenants. The deposit was due tomorrow,' she demanded as soon as she heard his voice.

'I know. It's a bummer.' Mike sounded just as down. 'Seemingly some niece that was supposed to be going to Australia has changed her mind and she's going to rent it. I suppose we can't compete against family.'

'Well, I think it's very mean of the landlady. She'd agreed to let it to us,' Jessica moaned.

'We might have had a chance if she'd cashed the deposit. Anyway, there's no point in crying over spilt milk – we've just got to keep looking,' Mike said stoically.

'I know, I'm just pissed off. I really liked it.'

'Me too. Anyway, I have to go. I'll give you a call later, OK?'

'OK, bye.' She shoved her phone into her pocket and walked back into the canteen.

'What's wrong?' her friend Judy asked when she got back to the table.

'Ah, the house that we were looking at that we really liked has fallen through. So we're back on the hunt.' She sighed deeply. 'I *really* liked it, Judy, it was a lovely house.'

'Another one will come along,' Judy comforted.

'It would want to come soon. Time's getting on,' Jessica said despondently. 'The location was good for us as well as the house. It was about half-way in terms of commuting.'

'It's hard to find houses to let in the country, you'll probably have to come as far as Bray,' Judy observed. 'How about Greystones? And it's got the train service.'

'That's a thought.' Jessica perked up. 'I'll have a look on the internet and see what's on offer. Good thinking, Miss Judy. Well done.'

'So eat up your lunch there now and stop sitting there with a face on you like a smacked bottom,' Judy ordered briskly.

Jessica giggled. Judy was one of the most no-nonsense people she knew. Greystones wasn't too far from Kilcoole, and it was by the sea. It was a little further from Wicklow than she'd like for Mike's sake, but it was better for him than the trek to Bray.

Another two colleagues joined them at the table, so, making an effort, she pushed her housing worries to the back of her mind and turned her attentions to the gossip and chat of the day.

Nadine sat on the bus gazing out at the city traffic. They were driving past RTE, she knew, because she recognized the big TV mast from seeing it on the television. And she knew that Jessica worked there. It must be a very exciting and glamorous place to work, she thought enviously as they drove along the Stillorgan dual carriageway. She didn't know what she wanted to do when she finished school. She just wanted to get as far away from Arklow as she possibly could. A sliver of guilt flashed through her. Nancy had given her fifty euro to spend and told her to enjoy herself. She'd even given her an awkward sort of hug that had made Nadine feel embarrassed but pleased at the same time. Her mother was making a huge effort to straighten herself out, she acknowledged. Nadine knew that Carol thought Liz was a bossy-boots, but Nadine quite liked her. It was great the way she was going walking and swimming with Nancy and giving her books to read.

Her mother was behaving much more like a normal person, doing grocery shopping, keeping the house tidy, and doing the garden. She seemed a lot happier in herself. Nadine didn't dread coming home half as much as she used to. Nancy still took a drink, but nothing compared to the amounts that used to leave her comatose.

Seeing her dad yelling at her mother on that horrible Sunday afternoon had made her feel sick. When she'd seen Nancy dissolving into tears in front of everyone she'd wanted to scrab his eyes out. Living with Nancy, she understood her father's frustration and fury with her mother, but he shouldn't have made a show of her in front of the neighbours. Nadine had been petrified that Nancy would go on the mother and father of a bender, but the weird thing was, she'd never been on a bad bender since. It was like she'd hit rock bottom and could only go up. Whatever the reason, Nadine welcomed it. Things were different at home, different and better, and now she was going to Dublin to buy clothes and go clubbing. She couldn't wait.

Carol ran down the steps of the Civic Offices, glad to be out in the fresh air. It had been a busy day. Half her staff were on annual leave and the work was piling up. She had changed into her running gear and it was a relief to start jogging. She needed to clear her head. She was meeting Nadine wherever they connected on the quays. She'd told her sister to walk along the quays from Bus Aras on the north side until they met. The sun glinted on the gunmetal waters of the Liffey as it surged between the quay walls. The tide was higher than normal and the boats bobbed like corks at their moorings. Carol inhaled the salty, pungent smell as she weaved her way between the throngs of people homeward bound. She was looking forward to her sister's visit with more than a touch of apprehension. She didn't know Nadine very well. They didn't have a lot in common, and their encounters in the last year or so had been acrimonious because of Nadine's wild social life.

She'd spoken to her sister the day before, to make the arrangements, and Nadine was bubbling with excitement. She was dying to shop. Her targets included Top Shop and Miss Selfridge in Jervis Street, and River Island, Warehouse, Hairylegs and No Name, all recommended by her friends, and she was determined to sample them all, she informed Carol. They were then going to go back to the flat, change, meet Gary and head in to Temple Bar. Carol hoped it all went to plan.

She waited impatiently for the lights to turn green on O'Connell Bridge. It was impossible to jog, the crowds were so dense. She wondered how far down the quays Nadine was. She scanned the crowds along the bridge but didn't see her sister, so she crossed and turned right along Eden Quay. Then she saw her striding along purposefully, peering around on the lookout. Carol's heart softened at the sight of her bouncing along, listening to her Walkman. She was only a kid, despite the tough façade, she reminded herself. She waved to attract her attention and was rewarded by a smile of recognition. Nadine pulled her earphones down around her neck. 'Hiya, Carol,' she greeted her a little warily.

'Hi, Nadine.' Carol slid into step beside her, ignoring the slight tension. 'How are things? Did you have a good journey?'

'Traffic was crap.' Nadine shrugged. 'Can we have something to eat first? I'm starving!'

'Sure. We'll head up to the Jervis Street Centre and grab something there, and then you can go right into Top Shop and Miss Selfridge.'

'Deadly.' Nadine couldn't hide her excitement.

She wolfed down an enormous BLT, Coke and gooey dessert in short order. 'That was good, Carol, thanks. Could we start shopping now?' she asked impatiently.

'Yeah – what are you thinking of wearing to the wedding?'

'I don't have to wear a dress, do I?'

'You're not going to wear jeans, are you?' Carol asked in dismay.

'Could I?'

'No,' Carol said firmly.

'OK.' Nadine made a face.

'Let's see what's in the shops,' Carol suggested lightly. There was no point in starting a row.

Nadine's eyes lit up as they battled through the late-night shoppers to get into Miss Selfridge.

'Oh look! Oh, look at these tops. Oh, these are really cool,' she enthused, pointing to some skimpy off-the-shoulder belly tops.

Oh my God, Carol thought in dismay, as Nadine rampaged through the displays oohing and aahing and holding tops up against her.

'You'd just need to go a little more formal,' she explained as Nadine held up a pink halter. 'How about this and this?' She held up a little black vest top and a silver chiffony blouse with flowing sleeves. 'You could wear it with a pair of black trousers.'

Nadine looked at it critically. 'It's a bit fussy.' She made a face.

'OK.' Carol backed off.

Two hours later she was exhausted. They had traipsed up and down Henry Street; Nadine had tried on dozens of clothes, bought two pairs of jeans, three tops, two pairs of shoes, but no wedding outfit.

'Are you sure I can't wear jeans?'

'Aw, come on, Nadine, it's my wedding,' Carol snapped.

'OK,' she said sulkily. 'If you want me to get that gear in Miss Selfridge I will, but you'll have to give me some money for it. I've spent most of mine and I want to keep some for tonight.'

'I'm not the Bank of Ireland, Nadine,' Carol said crossly, feeling she was being more than a little manipulated.

'Well, I can't afford to get what you want me to wear,' Nadine declared airily.

'Oh, come on then,' Carol said grudgingly as they traipsed back down to the Jervis Street Centre.

Even Nadine had to admit the outfit looked very nice on. The chiffon top was dressy and Carol suggested a trip over to M & S to get some silver jewellery to accessorize it.

After much dithering Nadine selected a pair of silver diamanté drop earrings and a matching necklace.

'Perfect,' Carol said, trying to hide a yawn. She was whacked. Temple Bar was the last place she wanted to go. They trudged up to the bus stop laden with bags.

'That was brilliant, Carol. When you get your house I'll be able to come up for weekends. I might even get a job in Dublin next summer and stay for the whole summer,' Nadine announced cheerily as they boarded the bus.

Carol couldn't believe her ears. This was not the plan, under any circumstances.

'We'll see,' she murmured, wishing there was an empty seat, but there wasn't and they had to stand until they got to Phibsboro.

'Is that your local? And you've got a McDonald's.' Nadine stood gazing around after they got off the bus. 'Can I just go over to the newsagents and get a bar of chocolate? Do you want one?'

'No, thanks. Leave the bags, I'll wait here.' Carol sat on the wall and watched her sister lope over to Miss Mary's. Nadine's eating habits were atrocious. She might not be too happy living with Carol after a week or two on a healthy diet, she thought with a little glimmer of amusement. Even if she was out of pocket, the shopping had been a great success. She was relieved that her sister would be wearing a half-presentable outfit and Nadine was thrilled with all her new gear. Now all that had to be done was to take her out for the night and then she could send her home, happy in the knowledge that she had given her sister a memorable trip to Dublin.

Nadine had half the chocolate eaten as she rejoined her sister, and she grabbed her shopping and followed Carol up past Dalymount to the small side street where her flat was.

'Hey, this is nice,' Nadine approved, going from room to room. 'You're dead lucky having a place of your own and being your own boss.'

'Look, study hard, get a decent job and you can have the same,' Carol advised, pouring herself a glass or milk. 'Want one?'

'Uuggh!' Nadine wrinkled her nose. 'Do you have any Bacardi Breezers or Smirnoff Ices?'

'Get outta here!' Carol laughed. 'Do you want some orange juice?'

'I suppose so.' Nadine flung herself on to the sofa. 'What time is Gary coming?'

'He should be here any minute. Why don't you go and have your shower?'

'OK,' Nadine agreed. 'I'm going to wear my new jeans and the pink halter-neck.'

She practically danced into the bathroom. Carol tidied up the shopping bags that had been dumped in the middle of the floor. She'd wear her white jeans and black off-the-shoulder top, she decided, wondering which club would they manage to get into without ID for Nadine. She was under-age, no matter how sophisticated she liked to think she was. They could go to the Turk's Head and go downstairs to the club after a few drinks, that might do, or maybe Chez Tony – they weren't too strict about ID there.

Gary hadn't called since lunchtime, which was a little unusual. He'd told her he'd phone her while they were shopping to see what time they'd be home. She glanced at her watch. It was nine-thirty; she'd give him a buzz to see where he was. She dialled the phone in the flat but got no answer. Great, she thought, he's on his way. She dialled his mobile and got the out-of-range or switched-off message. That wasn't like Gary, he always had his phone switched on. A niggle of unease stirred, and she glanced outside to see if there was any sign of the familiar silver Passat.

'I'm finished – can I have a look through your make-up to see what you've got?' Nadine appeared, wrapped in a bathsheet.

'Help yourself, it's in the bedroom,' she said distractedly.

'Thanks, Carol, I'm having a great time,' Nadine assured her.

'That's good.' Carol smiled, glancing out the window again. She might as well have her shower, she decided. They'd be all ready to go when Gary got here.

'Another pint?'

'Ah sure, why not?' Gary agreed, glancing at his watch. It was after ten – he knew Carol and Nadine would be waiting for him, but he'd got side-tracked by a mate of his and had gone in for a quick pint, which had turned into a bit of a session.

Why couldn't Carol take her sister out on her own? Couldn't she have arranged to meet Jessie and had a girly night? He wasn't a bloody baby-sitter, he thought irritably as he checked to make sure his phone was off. The last thing he needed was Carol ranting down the phone at him. There was going to be hell to pay if he didn't turn up tonight, but he'd worry about that tomorrow; there were pints to be drunk and good company to be enjoyed. He hadn't been on the piss in ages; he deserved a night out, he assured himself.

'It doesn't look like he's coming, sure it doesn't,' Nadine said disappointedly.

'Something must have cropped up,' Carol said tightly. It was ten to eleven and she was raging. What a bastard Gary was, letting her down in front of Nadine and letting the poor kid down as well. Just when he'd been doing so well and behaving like a half-decent human being he pulled a stunt like this, she thought in disgust.

'At least he should ring you and tell you where he is,' Nadine grumbled. 'I suppose you don't want to go out now. I'll just have to make up a fib to tell the others when I get home.'

'No, come on, we'll go ourselves. I might just give Jessie a ring to see if she'd like to come.' Carol tried to ignore the heart-scalding disappointment at the knowledge that she just couldn't depend on Gary.

She picked up her mobile and dialled Jessie's number.

'Hi, where are you?' Jessie asked. 'Is Nadine having a good time?'

'She's all shopped out. We're still in the flat. We're just heading out, we wondered if you'd like to come?'

'No, I don't think so, Carol, I'm wrecked after my match. Dec and Anita ran us ragged.'

'Oh.' Carol couldn't hide her disappointment. It would have been a relief to have a moan to Jessie about what a shit Gary was.

'What's wrong?' Jessie knew her so well, Carol reflected.

'Umm,' she stalled, aware that Nadine was in the room.

'Gary,' Jessie said succinctly.

'Yep.' Carol was equally succinct.

'Hasn't arrived?'

'Got it in one.'

'Give me twenty minutes,' Jessica sighed.

'Thanks, you're a pal,' Carol said gratefully. The last thing she wanted to do was to put on a façade and pretend to be enjoying herself. It would be easier to have Jessie along for support.

Half an hour later, Jessie arrived. 'Hi, Nadine, you look great,' she greeted the younger girl, privately thinking that Carol's sister wasn't looking as much like a skanger as usual.

'I had a great time, I bought loads of clothes,' Nadine confided. 'Are we going clubbing?'

'I'm taking you to Chez Tony to see if we can get into the club downstairs. There's no point going to any of the others, it's too hard to get in without ID,' Carol said firmly.

'Oh, I wanted to go to Firecracker or Spirit. I heard they were brilliant,' Nadine declared.

'Forget it, sister.' Jessie smiled at her. 'You won't get into them without ID. Come on, Chez Tony is cool, and the music's great,' she assured her. 'We'll get a taxi, OK?'

'Just have to do a pee.' Nadine jumped up excitedly and hurried out to the loo.

'Where's Gary?' Jessica whispered.

'I don't know. His phone's turned off, the bastard. I'm sick of him, Jessie. Why does he do things like this to me? Does he not know how much he hurts me? And worse, does he not care? It's very hard. Why, Jessie, why?' Carol whispered back.

'I don't know, maybe he's feeling under pressure.' Jessica shrugged helplessly.

'We're all under pressure,' Carol retorted.

'I'm ready,' Nadine announced.

'Right then, let's go,' Jessica said brightly, seeing the tears in Carol's eyes.

Carol struggled to compose herself. Right at this moment she hated her fiancé.

Nadine was in her element. She slugged her VRB and lit up a cigarette.

'What are you doing?' Carol demanded. 'For God's sake, Nadine, cigarettes are the pits. You'll get lung cancer. Is that what you want?'

'Ah stop, Carol, don't be such a granny. You can't sit there drinking Club Orange. What sort of a wussy are you? We're having a night out, aren't we?' She turned to Jessica.

'I'm sitting on my fence, Nadine. Never take sides with sisters is my motto.'

'At least you're having a proper drink. The first of many, I hope.'

'Cut it out, Nadine. You shouldn't be drinking at all,' Carol growled.

'Chill out, for crying out loud. I know how to drink,' Nadine boasted.

'Listen, if you want to end up like Ma just keep on going. But I've no intentions of going down that road, OK?' Carol snapped.

'Neither have I,' Nadine protested hotly. That was a mean thing to say. One or two drinks didn't mean she was going to end up an alco.

'Stop fighting, you pair, or I'm going home,' Jessica warned.

Nadine took a slug of her drink. What a pair of grannies to go out with. She wished Lynn was here to share her night. Temple Bar was hopping. There were restaurants, bars and clubs everywhere you looked. You could feel the energy of the place. This was where she wanted to be every night of the week.

Gary fumbled with his key in the lock. He was hammered. He must have drunk at least twelve pints if not more, and all he wanted was to crawl into bed. The message light on the answering machine was flashing. It was probably Carol. Was he in for an earbashing, he groaned as he staggered into his bedroom. That was tomorrow's worry, he thought woosily before collapsing on to the bed and falling into a drunken stupor.

Nadine sat on the bus back to Arklow. Jessica had given her a lift to Bus Aras, which was very kind of her. It would be great to have your own car like Jessie. What freedom she'd have. She sighed, wriggling around in her seat to get the most comfortable position. She'd had a full day on her own shopping in town and her feet were sore. But it had been fantastic. She *loved* Dublin. She'd enjoyed her evening with Carol, in fact it had been a great evening until Gary had failed to show up and Carol had got all tight and tense.

It was a mean thing to do. She scowled. She'd gone right off him. She'd heard Carol crying in her bedroom after they'd got home. It was as bad as worrying about her mother, she thought frustratedly. He'd ruined her night and he'd certainly ruined Carol's. He wasn't going to get away with it.

'Am I in the bad books?' Gary asked penitently around lunchtime the following day.

'Fuck off, I don't want to talk to you,' Carol told him coldly and hung up. He hadn't phoned since.

She set out for her jog, looking forward to the relief of tension it always brought. She'd taken Nadine over to McDonald's at her sister's request when she'd asked her what she'd like for dinner before her trip home. She'd opted for the low-fat chicken and salad option while Nadine had tucked into a Big Mac meal and fries. Jessica had offered Nadine a lift to the bus and it was a relief to wave her sister off. At least she could be unhappy in peace, she thought sorrowfully as she ran in the direction of The Phoenix Park. She pushed herself hard, not allowing any thoughts of Gary to ruin her run. She liked The Phoenix Park, its great swards of green meadow and grasses a relief after the grimy, gritty noisy city streets.

She was exhausted as she jogged down her street a couple of hours later. A familiar silver Passat was parked outside the flat. So Gary was there, waiting for her. He had a key. She let herself in and wiped the sweat off her face.

'Hi, Babe. I'm sorry.' He put on his penitent little-boy look. A bouquet of red roses lay on the table.

Carol looked at him. He was such a prat if he thought some crummy roses were going to make everything all right. But she was an even bigger prat for thinking he'd ever change. He had no intention of changing. He was too self-centred. How long could she go on kidding herself?

'I'm going for a shower. Don't bother your arse waiting because I'm in no humour to talk to you. You're a selfish bastard and you might look down your nose at my family and I know you do, but you have nothing to feel superior about at all, Gary Davis. And if you think a dozen roses are going to make me feel better, you're even more superficial than even *I* know you are.' She turned on her heel and marched into the bathroom.

Gary could hear the shower running. He turned on the TV and surfed the channels. As tirades went, it certainly wasn't the worst, he decided. Although the crack about being superficial was well below the belt. At least she hadn't told him to get out. So things were salvageable enough. He settled back to watch the snooker, pleased that he'd got away with it.

'She's crazy to be marrying him. She'll never be happy.' Jessica dipped her spare rib into the barbecue sauce and ate it with relish.

'Give me one of those won ton things.' Katie took a slug of beer.

'And you know something, I told her we'd lost the house and she said, "That's awful," and carried on moaning about her bloody relationship with Gary.'

Katie laughed and took a portion of chicken satay out of the Thai special platter. 'Are you surprised? What did you expect? Anyway, I'm sorry that you didn't get the house too, but part of me is glad because it means you're still here for another while. I'm really going to miss you, Jessie.'

'Let's not think about it. Here, have a chicken ball,' Jessica offered. 'That will sort you.'

'You know me so well,' Katie grinned. She'd been on a diet for the past month and it was a great treat to break out.

'This is so relaxing.' Jessica stretched lazily. 'Honestly, I was like a referee between the other pair last night. They are so different. Carol who's so uptight and wouldn't have a drink or cigarette if her life depended on it, and the other one slugging VRBs and smoking like a chimney. You should have seen her on the dance floor. I thought Carol was going to freak. She'd be the one to sort Gary out.'

'Uuhh,' Katie shook her head. 'He's one joker that's never going to be sorted out by any woman. But you just look at it, Carol wanted to get engaged. She's engaged. Carol wanted a double wedding. She's having a double wedding. Don't feel too sorry for her. He might think he's the one with the upper hand in that relationship, but so far Carol's driving the pace. And I can tell you one thing – although Gary doesn't realize it, Carol Logan's the one who wears the pants in that relationship and always will,' Katie said shrewdly, pronging a fat juicy prawn.

'I still half expect him not to turn up at the church.' Jessica frowned. 'Can you just imagine the sort of wedding we're going to have if that happens?'

'Don't even go there.' Katie proffered a piece of sesame toast.

'I can't help it, Katie, it's just the kind of thing he'd do.'

'I know,' her friend agreed. 'All we can do is wait and see.'

35

'Have you farted or did you turn up the bubbles in the jacuzzi?' Katie demanded, and raucous laughter rippled around the group lolling in the foamy water. It was the morning after Jessica and Carol's hen night. A gang of them had gone to Kilkenny for an overnighter. They'd hit Kytler's Inn, had a meal and plenty of drink, before heading off to a club. They'd staggered back to the hotel in the early hours and were now relaxing in the jacuzzi after a leisurely swim.

Carol, who'd been persuaded to indulge in a fair few vodkas the previous night and some restorative glasses of wine over lunch, was suffering a massive hangover, being unused to copious amounts of alcohol. She'd gone very quiet, but the rest of them were in high spirits.

'It's hard to believe the summer's over and we're well into September.' Denise Hogan stretched luxuriously in the water.

'Don't talk.' Jessica shook her head. 'It's scary.' The past few weeks had been hectic and this was just what she needed.

'I couldn't imagine having a double wedding,' Orla Sinclair declared. 'I'd be afraid of my life I'd end up having a row with the other couple and I'd never speak to them again. You two are doing so well you're even having a double hen party.'

Jessica and Carol looked at each other. 'We've had our moments,' Jessica murmured.

'It's been OK once Jessie's been getting her own way,' Carol said drily.

Jessica's jaw dropped. 'That's not very nice or very fair, Carol!' she exclaimed.

'Well, it's true,' Carol said sulkily. 'You picked the church, the hotel, most of the menu and the flowers—'

'Calm down, girls, it's only wedding nerves,' Orla said hastily, wishing she'd never opened her big mouth.

'Carol! Stop that! You had every chance to do your own thing. You could have had your own wedding if what we were having didn't suit you. I told you that over and over, so don't give me that crap,' Jessie exclaimed indignantly. 'Don't forget you broke off the engagement and then you got engaged again and came back muscling in on our wedding. My mother was *raging*!' Drink had loosened her tongue and she gave vent to her feelings with reckless abandon.

'Your mother's a bossy cow—'

That was as far as she got. Jessie leapt to her feet in the jacuzzi and leaned over and gave Carol a slap on the jaw.

'Don't you dare talk about my mother like that! How dare you, Carol, my mum's been very good to you and your mother. If it were left to your mother we'd be going nowhere fast except to the off-licence for more drink.'

'Oh my God!' muttered Katie, aghast.

'You *bitch*!' shrieked Carol. 'That was below the belt! How dare *you* talk about my mother like that? She's had a very tough life; it's not her fault. This is going to be a crap wedding and I wish I hadn't agreed to it.'

'What do you mean *agreed* to it? *You* were the one that wanted it. Do you think in a million years that I wanted to share my wedding day with you pair?' roared Jessica.

'Girls, will you stop it! It's drink talking,' Amanda said in desperation.

'No, I won't. She's the one who wanted the double wedding, not me. All I wanted was to get married to Mike and have a beautiful day that we'd never forget, and I have to share it with that neurotic cow who's afraid if she doesn't have a double wedding with me and Mike she'll never get married. It's not fair and I'm sick of it.'

Jessica burst into tears and climbed out of the pool. Sobbing, she grabbed her robe and rushed out of the pool room.

'Jesus, Mary and Joseph, now look what you've bloody done,' Katie spat at Carol.

'You shut up, Katie Johnson, it's none of your business. Can't even get yourself a man,' Carol taunted her.

'Huh, that's all you know. You call what you've got a man! You had a real man and you didn't know what to do with him. Sean Ryan had a lucky escape,' Katie sneered as she got out of the jacuzzi and went to comfort her cousin.

A shocked silence descended on the group.

'Looks like the end of the party,' Carol declared coolly, stepping out on to the tiled floor. 'I'm going to my room.'

'Phew, opened a can of worms there, Orla.' Carrie giggled nervously.

'Poor Jessie, I never saw her losing the cool like that before,' Gina Dixon said sympathetically. 'She must be up to ninety.'

'I'd *hate* a double wedding – a single wedding's stressful enough,' Orla declared. 'Do you think they'll make it up?'

'Ah, it's only a tiff.' Carrie wriggled her toes and yawned.

'I don't know. Mothers were insulted. That's fairly high-grade weapons being unleashed.'

'I didn't think Jessie had it in her,' sniggered Gina. 'That crack about the off-licence was beyond.'

'Carol was just as bitchy. Did you hear what she said to Katie about not being able to get a man? Smug bitch. I hate that.' Carrie frowned. She was currently manless and not by choice. Carol had touched a nerve.

'Well, I think we should have our showers and go to the bar and fortify ourselves for the trip home. I'd say it will be fairly frosty,' Orla suggested. The others agreed with alacrity.

'The brides-to-be might not be talking but that shouldn't stop the fun,' chortled Gina, who thought the whole thing was hilarious.

'I suppose I should go and see if Carol's all right,' Amanda said dolefully. 'I *am* her bridesmaid after all, and Katie went to take care of Jessica.'

'It's like duelling at dawn – the protagonists always have their seconds. Does this mean you can't talk to Jessie and Katie?' Orla grinned.

'Ha, ha, ha! Very funny. Order me a double vodka – I'd say I'm going to need it,' Amanda groaned.

'Don't mind that ungracious cow,' Katie comforted, stroking Jessica's back. 'She was way out of line.'

'Did you hear her?' Jessica sat up, incensed. 'She *agreed* to a double wedding, as if Mike and I were down on our knees begging her to get married with us. And how dare she call my mother bossy!'

Katie hid a grin. Bossy was not an altogether unfair description of her Aunt Liz.

'And we were having such a nice hen party until she opened her big gob. I was really enjoying myself.' Jessica hiccuped.

'Me too,' Katie agreed.

'The poor girls, they must be horrified,' Jessica fretted.

'Don't mind them, it won't knock a feather out of them,' Katie declared. 'I bet we'll find them in the bar.'

'Carol's not able to drink – we shouldn't have persuaded her to. Look what's happened now,' Jessica said tearfully. 'How can we have a double wedding if we're not speaking?'

'It will blow over, you'll see,' Katie assured her kindly.

'Katie, it's Carol we're talking about,' Jessica said mournfully.

Katie chewed her lip. 'True,' she acknowledged. 'No better woman for holding a grudge after a row.'

'Oh God.' Jessica lowered her throbbing head into her hands. A row with Carol was the last thing she needed.

'The women are after having some sort of a row,' Gary announced irritably as he sat back down at the table beside Mike. They were in The Gravediggers, having a pint and watching a football match before heading off to Heuston to collect the girls off the train.

'About what?' Mike groaned.

'Don't ask, I didn't. Carol was yattering down the phone at me. Imagine ringing me in the pub when I'm trying to concentrate on a football match.'

'Terrible,' grinned Mike. 'These wedding nerves are getting bloody hard to handle. Jessie was bawling the other night because some cousin of hers sent a wedding gift and when Jessie folded up the wrapping paper a gift tag addressed to the cousin from someone else fell out. It was a recycled present. Of course she went spare and wanted to withdraw the invitation. This pair are loaded seemingly.'

''Course they are if they go around recycling presents. Forget them; let's enjoy our last hours of peace and quiet. When the girls get back this wedding stuff is going to take off in earnest. This time two weeks, my son, the pair of us will have rings on our fingers and nooses through our noses.'

'Where's Carol?' Katie demanded. They were in the foyer of the hotel, waiting for taxis to take them to the train station.

Amanda cast a sympathetic glance at Jessica. 'She got a taxi by herself. She wants to be alone.'

'Greta bloody Garbo,' snapped Katie unsympathetically. 'Come on, here's our taxis. It's going to be a tight squeeze, seeing as Madam Logan hogged a whole one to herself.'

'Ah, leave her alone, Katie. She was upset,' Amanda said loyally.

'So's Jessie, but you don't see her behaving like a prize prat.'

'Stop it, you two, it's bad enough that the brides aren't talking. We don't want the bridesmaids falling out too. You two have to hold it all together until the pair of them are safely down the aisle,' Gina ordered crisply as they piled into the taxis.

Carol sat in the back seat of her taxi, studiously ignoring the efforts of the driver to engage her in conversation. She was rigid with anger. Jessica Kennedy was a bitch of the highest order and for two pins she'd tell her to stuff her tacky, cheap, parochial little wedding and get lost.

But it was too late, much much too late, all the arrangements were in place. Invites sent out, flowers and cakes arranged, seating plans settled, dresses bought, honeymoons booked and paid for. Besides, she thought wearily, it had been a hell of a struggle to get this far with Gary. If she turned around and said to him she was cancelling the wedding she'd never get another chance. She was between a rock and a hard place for sure. She stared out of the window, scowling. The taxi driver prudently desisted from trying to have a conversation with her and concentrated on his driving.

She had two options as she saw it, Carol decided. Call the whole thing off and forget getting Gary to the altar, ever. Or swallow down her anger and pride, as usual, and get on with it. A thought struck her and she felt a flicker of fear. Jessica might call it off. She'd never seen her friend so wrathful. It had been shocking, actually, she reflected, remembering her friend's tirade.

'Oh God, what a mess,' she muttered.

'Sorry, did you say something?' the taxi driver said hopefully.

'Talking to myself,' Carol muttered, in such an intimidating tone that he retreated into silence.

'What's happened?' Mike asked stoically as Jessica got into the car beside him.

'Ah, Carol had a go at me and I had a go back and we ended up having a slanging match and then she went off on her own and wouldn't sit with us on the train. You saw the way she stalked off down the platform. I'm just sick of her,' she exploded. 'She had the cheek to say that my mother was bossy and that she was sorry that she'd *agreed* to the double wedding, as if *I'd* bloody asked her to have it. And then she accused me of making all the decisions. I was totally humiliated, Mike.' She burst into tears of frustration.

'Don't cry, Jessie,' Mike said in exasperation, glancing at Katie, who was in the back of the car. She threw her eyes up to heaven.

'I will cry, I was having a great hen party until she opened her big gob,' Jessie sobbed.

Mike's lips tightened into a thin line and he looked uncharacteristically stern as he started up the engine. This was a great blooming start to their wedding celebrations. Battling brides! What more could he ask for?

'If you're going to sit with a face on you all night, I might as well go to the pub,' Gary said irritably, as he sat in Carol's flat flicking through an old paper. 'I don't know why you wanted a double wedding in the first place, all you and Jessie seem to do lately is fight. I'm going for a slash, make up your mind what you want to do.' He marched into the loo.

Carol was fit to be tied. She couldn't tell him the ins and outs of the row. It would be the perfect excuse for him to call off the wedding. She was half surprised he hadn't suggested it. She'd better put on her 'everything's fine' act and get on with it.

'But everything isn't fine,' she muttered. 'I'm sick of them and I'm sick of him.' She stared out of the window, deeply unhappy and bubbling with resentment.

What a way to be preparing for her wedding.

She should be happy and excited. She was anything but.

'What are we doing?' Gary came and put his arm around her.

'Let's go to bed,' she murmured, cuddling in against him, desperate for comfort and a loving touch.

'Brilliant idea,' Gary approved, moulding her close to him. As he kissed and caressed her, Carol started to relax. In two weeks' time the wedding would be over and she'd never have to see Jessica Kennedy again if she didn't want to. Right now that seemed like a very good idea.

36

Mike glanced at his watch as he sat in the car. He'd give it another twenty minutes. If she wasn't home by then he'd have to talk to her on the phone. He'd prefer to talk face to face. What he had to say would be far more effective that way.

Dusk was settling on the city, the western sky washed with orange and pink hues. He hoped they'd be lucky with the weather on their wedding day. It had been a fantastic summer, and now an even more beautiful Indian summer was blessing them, with not a hint of autumn chill. Only the shortening of the evenings indicated the change of seasons.

A movement caught his eye in the rear-view mirror. His guess had been right. After all this time, he knew Carol quite well. He saw her jog steadily towards her flat, eyes forward, looking neither to the right nor left. She never noticed him sitting in the car as she sprinted past.

He uncoiled himself out of the car and called after her as she slowed down to walk up her path. 'Hey, Carol, can I have a word?'

'Oh! Oh, hi, Mike,' she said, surprised. She eyed him warily. 'What's up?'

'Will we go inside?' he suggested. He didn't want to have a slagging match on the front step.

Reluctantly she inserted her key into the lock and he followed her inside. Her new flat was far different from the hovel she'd been living in previously. Carol was such a strange girl. She could easily have afforded a decent place to live, but her insecurities were so great that she preferred to save a great chunk of her salary rather than have a good quality of life. He supposed it stemmed from her father walking out on the family. Money had been tight.

Mike chewed the inside of his jaw. When he'd made up his mind to confront her, he'd been gung-ho about it, but now he was less inclined. That was always the way with Carol. People were always making allowances for her. Jessica had had to cope with her father's sudden death, a huge trauma in anyone's life. She didn't spend her life making other people pay for her misfortune the way Carol did. His resolve strengthened again when Carol glowered sulkily at him as he followed her into her flat and closed the door behind them.

'I suppose Jessie sent you.'

'No, actually, she doesn't know I'm here. And I'd appreciate it if you didn't tell her. This is between you and me.' Mike cleared his throat. 'Look, Carol, I don't want to cause a row, there's been enough of those, but there's a few ground rules you should be aware of. We're all getting married in less than a fortnight. Now you know full well that the double wedding was your idea—'

'Well, you all agreed to it,' she interrupted sullenly.

'Be honest, now, Carol. You know in your heart of hearts that Jessie didn't or doesn't want a double wedding. You know she wanted for just the two of us to have our day. You took advantage of her soft heart. It's something you tend to do.'

She went to interrupt again, but he held up his hand and said sternly, 'Let me finish, Carol. Jessie's her own worst enemy. If she'd been a tougher nut you wouldn't be walking up the aisle with Gary as soon as you are and I think you know that. You told her when she said that she wasn't sure about the double wedding because of Liz, that Liz could organize it whatever way she wanted. Then you started to row back and make demands. OK, fair enough, it is your wedding too but it was a bit much insulting Liz to Jessie's face—'

'Jessie insulted *my* mother,' Carol raged.

'After you'd insulted hers,' Mike said calmly. 'But that's not the point and that's not why I'm here. The point is, Carol, Jessie made a sacrifice for you. I know sacrifice is a very strong word but that's what she did. And you've *never* acknowledged it. The whole lead-up to the wedding has been fraught. First yours was on, then it was off, and then there were huffs about morning suits, not to talk about your family problems. Jessie and Liz have enough to be dealing with themselves, especially emotionally, with Ray being dead, without all of what you're laying on them, so cut it out now, Carol. Fair is fair.

'Now whatever row the pair of you have had, get over it and you make the first move. It's the least you can do, because Jessie and I are going to have the happiest day of our lives on our wedding day and you and your problems are not going to interfere with that. Deal with whatever you have to deal with and get over yourself, Carol, because if you don't you're going to lose the best friend you've got,' Mike warned her.

Once he'd got going he'd let her have it fair and square and he was glad he had. Jessie deserved that much from him. It was only when he'd verbalized it that he realized just how much of a sacrifice his fiancée had made and just how little Carol appreciated it. She'd had this talking-to coming for a long time and he didn't regret one second of it, he decided as he eyeballed her. She dropped her gaze first.

'You certainly have a lot to say for yourself,' she muttered.

'Not for myself, Carol, for Jessie,' he corrected her coldly. 'And I hope you'll be honest enough for once in your life to acknowledge the truth of what I'm saying. You take and take from Jessie; it's time now to do a bit of giving. Think about what I've said – phone her and apologize or else pull out of the wedding and let us have our day. OK?' he challenged.

'OK,' she muttered.

'Fine. I'll be off.' Mike headed for the door. Right this minute it wouldn't worry him if he never saw Carol Logan again.

He sat in the car and gunned the engine; he wasn't sure what she would do. Would his home truths make enough of an impact on her for her to ring Jessica and apologize? Even better, would she get indignant enough to tell them to stuff their wedding so they could go it alone?

He sighed as he drove past Dalymount. He'd done what he should have done months ago, stood up to Carol and her bullying. It was probably too little and too late.

Carol's heart hammered in her chest. She felt sick. Confrontations always made her feel nauseous. Mike had been really horrible saying those things to her. The cheek of him! Where did he get off?

She slumped down on the sofa and curled her knees into her chest. The awful thing was that deep down she had to admit that he was right. She couldn't hide from the truth of his words, not that she'd admit it to anyone, ever . . . not even to Gary. It was even hard admitting it to herself, she thought, cringing inside. Mike was right, she'd known all along that Jessie didn't want a double wedding. From that very first night long ago in The Oval when she'd first mooted it, her friend had been completely resistant to the idea. It was only after Carol had done some serious 'pity me' stuff that Jessica had caved in.

Bloody wimp, she thought dismissively. Why didn't she just have the balls to say no? Jessica was never able to say no. Was *she* to be blamed for that too? Carol thought resentfully. Why didn't they just blame her for *everything*? How she'd love to tell the smug pair of them to go stuff their hickey little wedding. She chewed her lip. One whiff of this to Gary and he'd back out of it so quick you wouldn't see him for dust. Did Mike *really* think that she was dying to share her wedding day with them and that Katie and Liz and Tara shower? Well, she wasn't. If she never saw them again she wouldn't give a shite right now.

He'd some nerve if he thought she was going to ring Jessie and apologize.

But if you don't, Mike could involve Gary and that would be the end of that. The insidious little thought wouldn't go away. She groaned. Her head was throbbing; she was still toxic from all the drink she'd consumed at the weekend. Never ever again, she vowed, as she padded into the kitchen to drink a glass of water.

She couldn't tell Gary about this. She couldn't tell Jessie as she usually did, seeing as Jessie was the cause of it all. It suddenly struck her that she had no one to talk to, no one to confide in. A memory flooded back. Sean with his arm around her, comforting her as she confided her hurt and heartbreak to him. She'd let him go so easily and for what? A man who wouldn't ever stand up for her the way Mike had just stood up for Jessie. A man who wouldn't marry her without being pushed. A man she couldn't depend on. A man she would never be sure of.

It wasn't too late. She could back out of it. Sean had been very interested in her. At least he'd been kind to her and always would be if they got back together. The kindness of men was something she'd had little experience of. Why had she run away from it when it had been offered to her? Why had she preferred Gary's casual attitude and unreliability to Sean's dependable loyalty? Why did she accept Gary's bad behaviour? What sort of a sad basket case was she?

Impulsively she looked in her diary for his number and dialled it. She heard his voice, deep and comforting, with his attractive, western accent.

'Sean, hi, it's me, Carol. I was just wondering if I could see you,' she blurted. 'I think I made a mistake. Could we talk?'

There was silence along the line and then she heard him say a little awkwardly, 'Carol, I don't want to hurt your feelings, but I'm seeing someone, as it happens. And I really like her. I don't think it would be appropriate for us to meet.'

'Oh,' she said, her heart sinking like lead.

'Maybe it's wedding nerves,' he said kindly.

'Maybe it is. You're probably right.' She swallowed. 'Forget I called. Bye.' She hung up without waiting for him to answer. She felt humiliated beyond words. What had possessed her to make such a fool of herself? Tears smarted her eyes. He'd got over her pretty quickly. But that was men for you, wasn't it? You couldn't depend on any of them.

'Hi, Katie, Jessie not home yet?' Mike poked his head into the sitting-room.

'Nope, she was on an OB, wasn't she? She shouldn't be too late though.'

'Oh yeah, I forgot she was on an outside broadcast. I'll ring her mobile in a minute and see where she is,' Mike said distractedly. 'Katie, I don't know if I've done something I shouldn't have,' he said slowly, plonking down on the sofa beside her.

'What have you done?' she asked in alarm, turning to look at him.

'I had a word with Carol. I've just come from there.'

'What!' Katie eyed him warily. 'And?'

'When I saw how upset Jessie was after the weekend I just got mad. I called in on Carol tonight and told her where to get off. I told her she didn't appreciate how much of a sacrifice Jessie had made so that she could have her fucking double wedding. Basically I went to town on her. Maybe I was a bit over the top. A bit too heavy.' He rubbed his hand over his stubbly jaw.

'Mike, unfortunately, knowing Carol as long as I've known her, you could never be too heavy with her and that's saying a lot. But well done. That girl needed a good talking-to. I know she's got problems, but we all have and we don't take it out on our friends. She's hijacked your wedding; it's time she was told where to get off, so don't feel a bit sorry that you had it out with her. She had it coming.

'And you know something?' she said wryly. 'It's not going to make the slightest bit of difference. That's the nature of the beast unfortunately. Me, me, me.'

'Do you think I should tell Jessie?' he asked.

'Perhaps six months down the line, just so she'll know what a Sir Galahad you are, but right now, no. She has enough on her plate, and besides she's feeling a tad guilty for mouthing off about Carol's mother,' Katie advised. 'Look, just think – this day two weeks you'll be in Wales, riding each other ragged, with not a care in the world. Keep that thought for the next few days and you'll be fine.'

'You're a great old pal, Katie, thanks a lot.' Mike leaned over and gave her a hug. 'And you look a million dollars. Big date?'

'You bet. Here's Jessie. Mum's the word.'

'Hi, Mike. Hi, Katie.' Jessie greeted them wearily, kicking off her shoes. 'I'm whacked. Imagine, this is my last night sleeping here – it's sad, isn't it?'

'Sadder for me than for you,' Katie said. 'Eileen Kelly from work is going to move in after the wedding.'

'You don't look sad, you look fantastic. Another date? Who *is* this guy you've been seeing?'

'Yeah! Are you going to introduce us? I need to give him the once-over to see if he's suitable for you,' Mike teased. 'Are you going to bring him to the wedding?'

The doorbell rang.

'Good timing.' Katie jumped up, beaming.

'Bring him to the wedding,' Jessica urged.

'I don't think so.' Katie grinned. 'Be back in a sec.'

Moments later she walked into the room followed by Sean Ryan.

'Oh my God!' gasped Jessica. 'You rip! Imagine not telling me.'

'Hi, Jessie. How's things, Mike?' Sean looked somewhat embarrassed.

'Hey, buddy, good to see ya,' Mike exclaimed, delighted for Katie. 'So you finally got together.'

'What do you mean by that?' Katie demanded.

'I thought the pair of you were perfect for each other,' Mike declared matter-of-factly.

'It's funny the way things work out.' Katie smiled up at Sean, her eyes alight with happiness.

'I think you should come to the wedding,' Jessica said impulsively.

'I don't think so, Jessie. If it was just you and Mike I'd love to, but Gary and I didn't exactly part on the friendliest of terms. It might cause tension,' Sean said diplomatically.

'Tsk! It's an awful shame,' Jessica said crossly.

'We'll go out for dinner some night when you're back from your honeymoon and have a good night out,' Sean promised.

'We'll have plenty of nights out. You and Katie can come down and stay with us in Greystones,' Mike said, pleased at the unexpected turn of events.

'Yeah, Katie was telling me you're moving into a flat there. Nice part of the country,' Sean approved.

'We only got news of it last Friday – we went

down, had a look and decided on it. I moved in while herself was dossing in Kilkenny.' He grinned at Jessica.

'It wasn't our first choice, and the flat's not as modern as the cottage we loved, but it'll do us fine for a while,' Jessica explained.

'It sounds nice to me and at least it's near the sea,' Katie said, slipping her hand into Sean's.

'We'll have some great weekends there, all of us, won't we, Jessie?' Mike dropped his arm around her shoulder.

She snuggled in against him. 'We sure will,' she agreed.

'Look, Katie and I were going out to dinner. Why don't I ring the restaurant and change the booking for four and you could join us?' Sean looked at Katie. 'OK with you?'

'Yeah, come on,' she urged. 'Let's make your last night in Dublin one to remember.'

Jessica and Mike looked at each other and laughed.

'Why not?' Mike agreed. 'Go get your gladrags on, woman. And I'll have a quick shower and shave.'

'And we'll open a bottle of wine while we're waiting,' Katie proposed, delighted with the revised plan.

* * *

'Isn't it great about Katie and Sean?' Jessica said as she slid into bed beside Mike.

'They're perfect for each other,' he yawned, putting his arm around her as they spooned together.

'It was a terrific night, wasn't it? I really enjoyed myself. He's great fun.' Jessica stroked his arm. 'It was very relaxing in their company.'

'Hmm, compared to another couple I know,' Mike remarked acidly.

'It's a pity he can't come to the wedding. Carol will probably go mad when she finds out Katie's dating Sean,' Jessica murmured.

'Tough. She had her chance with him, she'll just have to get over herself,' Mike retorted. 'Go to sleep, we've a busy day tomorrow. I think we'll need a juggernaut to transport all your worldly goods.'

'Stop exaggerating,' Jessica said drowsily, but Mike didn't hear her. He was fast asleep.

Sean lay in bed wishing he hadn't refused Katie's invitation to stay the night. He'd been tempted, but he'd prefer to have her all to himself the first time they slept together. It had been a very enjoyable night out. All four of them had gelled together really well and there had been a lot of laughter.

Katie had been giving him the rundown on the events leading up to the wedding, and it was clear Mike and Jessica had needed to unwind and relax. Well, they had that, helped by gallons of beer and wine. Sean grinned in the dark.

His thoughts turned to Carol. Her phone call had been a real shock and totally unexpected. He wondered if he should have met her for a chat. If he was seeing someone other than Katie he might have considered it. But under the circumstances, it was all a bit complicated. Especially as Katie didn't want Carol and Gary knowing about them until after the wedding.

'Just for an easy life,' she'd said when he'd asked her why.

If Carol thought she'd made a mistake she should back out before it was too late. Maybe he'd just text her and say so. Cowardly perhaps, but he didn't want to get involved. Katie wouldn't be happy if he did.

He smiled, thinking of Katie. She was such fun and so uncomplicated, a far different kettle of fish from poor old Carol. With Katie you knew precisely where you stood and he liked that. Carol sounded so lonely and mournful though. He couldn't go behind Katie's back and meet her. She'd freak if she ever found out and Carol would surely let her know at some stage. The best he could do was text or phone. He'd do it tomorrow, first thing, and get it over with.

Troubled, Sean twisted and turned for ages until he finally fell asleep.

37

'Home sweet home,' Mike declared, as Jessica folded up the last of her black plastic sacks. Their new home was the upstairs floor of a large, red-brick Georgian house that had panoramic views of the sea and coast. The sitting-room was a fine airy room, with big sash windows that allowed the light to flood in. It was decorated in shades of cream and gold. A big chintz sofa, two armchairs and a coffee table completed the furnishing.

The bedroom at the front, which they had decided to have as their room, had a double bed with a pine headboard, pine wardrobe and dressing-table unit and, to Jessica's delight, a window seat in the big sash window. She could see herself curled up with a book in the winter, watching the mists sweep in off the sea, or watching the sun sparkle on turquoise waters on a hot sunny day.

They both liked Greystones, with its homely, seaside ambience, restaurants and shops. And while both of them would have to commute, it wasn't too daunting for either of them. Jessica would be able to take the train to the city if she wished, which was an option she certainly intended to use on Fridays in particular.

She finished placing her books on the shelves in the alcoves on either side of the fireplace, and that little personal touch made her feel much more at home.

'I can get some terracotta lamps for the sitting-room so we won't have to use that awful middle light. And a pair of yellow lamps would make our bedroom much more cosy, and I can get some yellow and blue quilt covers and throws to dress the bed.' Jessica planned happily as she moved into their bedroom. 'Pity the kitchen's pretty basic—'

'But you don't have to worry about that,' Mike joked. 'I'll be doing most of the cooking.'

'You'll probably be home before me most nights, you won't have to deal with as much traffic as I will, buster,' Jessica retorted. 'I'll *need* to be fed.'

'You will be, don't worry.' Mike put their tennis rackets up on top of the wardrobe.

'It was a pity about the cottage, wasn't it?'

Jessica said regretfully, staring at the by now bulging wardrobe. 'There was so much space in it.'

'We've a lot more space here than we would have had in the town house in Bray and that apartment we looked at in Loughlinstown,' Mike pointed out.

'It's definitely the best of what we've seen since,' agreed Jessica, filling the top drawer of the dressing-table with her underwear. 'And Greystones is lovely. That little coffee shop on the main street does fabulous soups and breads.'

'And we'll be able to go for walks by the sea, and maybe do some hill-walking. It will be great, we'll settle down in no time.' Mike pulled her down on to the bed and kissed her.

'We haven't time for this.' Jessica pushed him away breathlessly a few minutes later.

'Come on, let's christen the bed and make ourselves really at home.' Mike slid his hand up under her T-shirt and began caressing her breasts.

'Aw, Mike, that's not fair,' Jessica murmured. 'You know I can't say no when you start to do things to me.'

'Don't say no then,' he said huskily, silencing her with a kiss, his hands tracing a feathery path up along the inside of her thigh, making her ache with want.

'Mike, Mike,' she whispered, unbuckling his belt. 'Don't stop . . .'

'I don't want to get up now,' Jessica said sleepily half an hour later as she lay nestled in against him. It had started to rain. The weather had broken, and they could see through the big sash window that the sea in the distance was a choppy, churning pewter. The rain lashed against the windowpane and the wind whistled and keened outside.

'We could have a snooze and go out to dinner later,' Mike suggested. 'After all, it's our first day in our new home, what better way to spend it than making love and cuddling? We've put away all your stuff, what else did you want to do?'

'We were going to drive over to Mam's to collect the wedding presents that are at home.' Jessica gave a jawbreaker of a yawn.

'We'll go at the weekend,' he suggested.

'OK, I'm knackered anyway – I don't want to go anywhere.' Jessie curled in closer and was asleep in seconds.

Sean sat in his car and stared at his mobile phone. He should call Carol; he'd been putting it off all day. She deserved that much friendship from him. He'd brushed her off too casually yesterday, he thought guiltily.

Taking a deep breath, he scrolled to 'received calls' and found her number. He selected the dial option and waited, half hoping it would go into 'message' and he could get away with leaving one.

'Hello,' she said briskly.

'Carol, hi, it's Sean. I was just wondering how you were? I was thinking about you last night and I just wanted to say to you, if you really do feel you've made a mistake don't go ahead with it. It would be much better to back out of it now rather than further down the line. And much less expensive too,' he advised, hoping he didn't sound as rattled as he felt.

There was a strained silence.

'I'm fine, Sean. It was pre-wedding nerves like you said. Sorry for troubling you,' she said, her tone as brittle as cracking ice.

'It was no trouble, Carol. I was glad that you felt you could phone me,' he said quietly.

'Look, I have to go, I'm having a fitting for my wedding dress. Thanks for calling, bye.' She hung up, not waiting for him to answer.

Sean stared at his phone. 'That was a disaster, mate,' he muttered. Why did he feel so guilty? Why did he feel that he had let her down? *She* had dumped *him*, for crying out loud. Annoyed, he started up the engine and headed for home.

* * *

'Patronizing git,' Carol muttered, putting her phone back in her bag. Who did Sean Ryan think he was, ringing her up and pretending to be concerned about her? He'd been pretty quick to let her know he was seeing someone. She didn't need his sympathy or advice. As far as she was concerned he could get lost. She'd never be contacting Garda Sean Ryan again.

'Now, dear, here's your dress. You look as if you've lost some weight since you bought it, not surprising, most brides do, all the arranging and so on,' the bridal assistant twittered as she pulled the curtains across the cubicle and hung Carol's dress on the hook.

She fussed around Carol, tweaking and arranging the dress so that it fell in elegant folds around her feet. 'Perhaps get it taken in at the waist. It's a little loose,' she murmured, stepping back to have a critical look at the bride-to-be. 'Hmm,' she murmured. 'I'll just go and get a few pins.'

It was a relief to be on her own, and Carol stared at her reflection in the mirror, marvelling at how different she looked in the white duchess satin creation that clung to her supple body in a subtly sexy way that delighted her. In spite of herself a frisson of excitement raced through her. She was getting married. Something she'd always wanted. In less than two weeks' time she'd never have to worry about dating or men again. She and Gary would have a good life together; they'd buy a nice house. She had enough for a deposit. It would be a chic and elegant house, far different from what she had grown up in. In time she'd give up work to have children and they would be the most loved children, she vowed. They'd never suffer the way she had. They'd be sure of a mother's and father's love. They'd never know the kind of scrimping and saving she'd known. She lifted the veil and placed it on her head, arranging its pristine folds around her. She looked fabulous, she decided, her heart lifting a little. Gary would be gobsmacked. Spending the extra money on her dress was well worth it. At least she wouldn't be trotting up the aisle in a homemade dress, she reflected snootily, thinking of Jessie.

She sighed. She should ring Jessie and make sure she wasn't still in a snit, she supposed. After Mike's humiliating rebuke she wasn't particularly eager to have any contact with her friend. But she didn't want to risk his wrath again.

She left the bridal boutique twenty minutes later, happy that her dress was the perfect dress for her. She was pleased that she'd finally selected the elegant duchess satin model that Amanda had so liked on her. Her bridesmaid had selected a pale lilac halter-neck dress that suited her tanned sallow skin and black shoulder-length wavy hair. She looked very well in it, but most importantly, in Carol's view, Amanda didn't outshine her. All eyes would be on her, very definitely. She'd better sort the situation with Jessica, she decided, rooting in her bag for her phone.

Can we meet for a chat?

She keyed in the text message, deciding it was the easiest way to make contact. The ball was in Jessie's court. It was up to her. Mike couldn't accuse Carol of not making the first move. She saved the message before sending it. Just in case she needed proof.

'Carol's sent me a text,' Jessica informed her fiancé as they tucked into a Chinese takeaway. They'd decided against going out for a meal and were curled up snugly on the sofa in their new sitting-room, slathering plum sauce on to pancakes and filling them with spring onions and crispy duck.

Mike took a draught of Bud. 'What does she

say?' he asked offhandedly, secretly pleased at this development. He'd been waiting all day for Carol to contact Jessie. He'd been all prepared to phone her and tell her the double wedding was off if she hadn't got in touch.

'She wants to meet for a chat.' Jessica nibbled on a prawn cracker while she made up another selection of pancakes and duck.

'Good!' he said succinctly. 'Sort out your tiff and forget it and let's enjoy the wedding.'

'Yes, boss,' Jessica scowled. 'It means if I meet her after work tomorrow, I'll be late getting home.'

'It would be worth it though, wouldn't it?' Mike helped himself to a chicken ball.

'Yeah, you're right. Once the wedding's over and done with I don't give a hoot what she does or says.' Jessica started keying in her reply.

Thank God for that, Mike thought gratefully, hoping against hope that this was the final hurdle and that they could all walk up the aisle in relative harmony.

'Carol rang me and told me she thought she'd made a mistake. She wanted to meet me,' Sean confessed as he and Katie sat in Eddie Rocket's waiting to be served.

'What!' Katie couldn't believe her ears. 'I don't

believe it. What did you say?' she asked uncertainly.

'I said I was dating someone that I really liked and that it wouldn't be appropriate,' he told her evenly.

'And do you want to see her?' Katie asked, staring at him.

'No, I don't, Katie, not the way you mean. I just wanted to make sure she's OK. She sounded so miserable.'

'For fuck's sake.' Katie scowled.

'It's not going to happen, don't worry,' he assured her hastily. 'I rang her today to tell her that if she was having doubts she should call off the wedding.'

'And did she listen to you?' Katie said crossly.

'Nope. She told me in a very frosty voice that she was having a fitting for her wedding dress and then said goodbye and hung up. And do you know something?' He took her hand and stroked it gently. 'I felt bloody guilty, Katie. Why did I feel that way? She was the one that dumped me, after all.'

Katie laughed at the perplexed expression on his tanned face.

'Sean, honey, you've just been well and truly "Caroled". Don't worry about it. It happens to us all. In fact,' she glanced at her watch, 'as we speak, Jessie will soon be experiencing the exact same feelings. Making people feel guilty is darling Carol's forte.'

Jessica parked the car along Merlyn Park, and hurried across the train tracks just as the red lights began to flash in preparation for the barriers to come down. She hoped the Dart was heading for town rather than Bray. She raced into Sydney Parade station and bought her ticket just as the train came clattering along the tracks. What a bit of luck, she thought with satisfaction as she shoved her way on to the packed train.

She and Carol had arranged to meet close to a Dart station so that she wouldn't be stuck in traffic trying to get into the city from RTE. They'd decided on Clontarf. All arrangements had been made by text. She would have to apologize to Carol for insulting her mother, she thought ruefully. She'd gone too far and she was ashamed of herself. That barb had been well below the belt. Carol had plenty to apologize for too, though. It wasn't all one-sided.

The train drew into Lansdowne Road and a woman in the seat she was standing next to got out. Jessica sat down gratefully; she was tired. She was working flat out to clear her desk before she took her wedding leave. She'd spent the afternoon chasing guests who hadn't got their bank account codes or PPS number filled in on their payment dockets. It was a pain in the ass. The previous payments system had been much less hassle. Some guests got very tetchy being asked for such personal details, and she'd had to be at her most diplomatic.

The train pulled into Pearse Street, and for a moment a welcome breeze wafted through the carriage as the doors slid open and a good number exited the train. It was a temporary respite. As many people boarded as had left, and the carriage was full in seconds, the smells of perspiration, smelly feet, perfume and garlic breath inter-mingling with the stale smells of the upholstery on the seats. A toddler fell into her lap and guilt got the better of her, so she offered the grateful mother her seat and stood once more as the train swayed along the winding tracks.

She was mighty glad when the train doors closed at Amiens Street and it gathered speed for Clontarf. As soon as she saw the sun glinting on the sea and the cars winding bumper to bumper along the Alfie Byrne Road, she weaved her way through the throngs to the door. It was very possible that Carol was on this Dart, she thought, as she stepped on to the platform and let the welcome breeze wash over her.

She watched the alighting passengers hurry past her down the steps and saw no sign of Carol. Perhaps she'd arrived already. They'd arranged to meet in Bar Code, the airy, spacious restaurant attached to the Westside Fitness and Leisure Centre, just minutes from the Dart station. The weather had picked up again during the day and the sea breeze blowing in from the bay was cool and refreshing, lifting her hair from around her face. She inhaled deeply. She'd be glad when this ordeal was over. She was longing to get home to Mike and their new home.

Carol was already seated in a booth when Jessica made her way into the cool, spacious, dimly lit restaurant.

'Hi,' she said cautiously, not sure of what sort of reception she was going to get as she slid into the booth.

'Hi.' Carol was equally wary. 'I asked for a booth, it's more private,' she said awkwardly.

'Good thinking,' Jessica murmured as the waiter arrived with menus.

'Drinks, ladies?'

'Pity I've got the car. I should have come in on

the Dart from Greystones this morning. I wasn't thinking straight,' Jessie remarked after she'd ordered a white wine spritzer.

'It's so handy that you have the Dart option.' Carol thawed, fiddling with her cutlery.

'I'm sorry about what I said about your mam.' Jessica bit the bullet.

'It was very hurtful,' Carol said quietly.

'I know, I'm sorry. It was way out of line,' Jessica repeated.

'I'm sorry as well. I suppose I said things too,' her friend acknowledged to Jessica's relief. For a minute or two it had looked as though the apologies were going to be one-sided.

'Let's forget it, will we?' Jessica said warmly. 'Let's have a meal and enjoy it, because the next meal we have together will be our wedding feast.' She grinned.

'It's hard to believe, isn't it?' Carol murmured. 'Are you sorted?'

'More or less.' Jessica sighed. 'We'd better order, the waiter's hovering.'

She ordered the pâté for starters and the shank of lamb for her main course, while Carol went for the fish cakes and Caesar salad.

'So what's it like living together?' Carol asked when the waiter had taken their order.

'Great, so far.' Jessie laughed. 'We spent all yesterday afternoon in bed. I took a day off to move my stuff. Has Gary moved in with you yet?'

'At the weekend. I'm telling you, Jessie, he's not going to know what's hit him once we're married. I'm going to put the deposit down on a house so fast his head will spin. Would you believe he still wants to go to the Octoberfest! He's got another think coming . . .'

Jessica sat back with a little sigh of relief as Carol continued in full flow. Things were back to normal.

Carol let herself into the flats, pleased with the way the evening had gone. Jessie had apologized first, that was the important thing. It had been nice to enjoy a meal with her and she'd been most sympathetic about Gary's utterly unrealistic and selfish plan to go to the Octoberfest in Munich. It had been just like old times, pouring out her woes and Jessie reassuring her that everything would be fine.

There were two bills and a letter with vaguely familiar handwriting on the hall stand. She picked them up and let herself into her own flat. She kicked off her shoes, ambled into the kitchen, poured herself a glass of milk and tore open the envelope. It was a letter from her mother, she saw with surprise, noting the signature. What on earth was Nancy writing to her about?

Dear Carol,
I've been thinking about us as a family a lot lately and just want you to know that if you would like your father to walk you down the aisle I won't object. Liz has given me some beautiful books to read which have helped me to change my attitudes a little. Forgiveness is very hard but not impossible. Liz has been so helpful to me and she gave me this beautiful poem which I enclose and think you would like. I hope you like it as much as I did and that it helps you as much as it helped me.

Your loving Mother x

The poem was written on a separate page, and as Carol read it, her lips tightened in fury. How *dare* Liz Kennedy interfere in their family business? How dare she infer that it was up to Carol and Nancy to forgive Bill and give Nancy a smarmy poem about God and forgiveness? She had such a nerve! This was one thing that bossy cow wasn't going to get away with, Carol fumed, as she tore the poem in strips and shoved it in the bin.

Her mother must be mad if she thought for one moment that she'd even consider the idea of Bill walking her up the aisle.

Liz had interfered once too often in her life. Carol flung the glass into the sink in a temper. She was sick of the Kennedys. Once the wedding was over that was it, they were never going to interfere in her life again.

Bill,
I just want you to know that if you want to walk Carol up the aisle next Wednesday that's entirely up to you and her. I won't interfere. I'd prefer if you didn't come to the house. The wedding is at two p.m. in Kilbride church.

Nancy

Bill couldn't believe his eyes as he read the letter that had been top of the pile of post that Brona had left on the hall table for him.

'Anything interesting?' his partner queried as she tossed a salad to accompany their salmon steaks. She had relented a little in the past week, and things weren't as tense between them.

'Not really, just bills and charities looking for donations,' he fibbed, shoving the letter into his pocket. He wasn't going to risk their fragile peace by even mentioning his other family or the contentious wedding.

Nancy had offered a *huge* olive branch, he thought with a rising sense of excitement. Had she discussed it with Carol? She must have to make an offer like that. Could it be possible that his daughter wanted him at the wedding and wanted him to give her away? Should he ring her at work and make the arrangements? he wondered.

But Carol didn't like being contacted at work; she'd let him know that in no uncertain terms. Perhaps not. He'd get his best suit cleaned, take a day off work, tell Brona he was going on a golf trip and be at Kilbride church waiting for his eldest daughter.

Finally, at long, long last, there was light at the end of the tunnel. Everything was going to be just fine, Bill thought happily as he swung Ben up in his arms and started to tickle him.

The Wedding

38

At least the sun was shining, Carol thought sleepily, as she stretched out in the narrow divan that she'd slept in on her last night as a single woman. This small, shabby bedroom of her childhood held no happy memories for her and she hadn't slept well.

She didn't feel very well, either, she thought in dismay. Usually she was as healthy as an ox, but for the past two days she had been feeling queasy and grotty. There was a terrible bug going round at work; what rotten bad luck to have been stricken with it on her wedding day.

She dragged herself out of bed and stood looking out of the bedroom window. The back garden looked well tended, she noted in surprise. The grass was cut, the flowerbeds were weeded, there was even a bed of Busy Lizzies flowering voluptuously down in the corner where Nancy liked to sit.

And Nancy . . . . it wouldn't be an exaggeration to say that her mother was a changed woman. She looked clear-eyed and healthy. Her hands no longer trembled and she had an energy about her that she hadn't had for years. There was a calmness about her that Carol had never seen in her before. It was as if she had made a decision to let go of the past and was bravely moving on, even if it was with some trepidation. She'd actually had a meal cooked for Carol when she'd arrived home the previous evening, and rather than hurt her feelings, Carol had forced it down even though she didn't feel a hundred per cent. Gary hadn't stayed long once they'd unpacked the car. He'd kissed her on the cheek and gone to check into the hotel. He still had to face Nadine after letting her down about her night out and wasn't particularly anxious to hang around.

She, Jessica and Mike had gone to the hotel later, sorted the seating arrangements and met him for a drink in the bar. It had been a relaxing end to a stressful week. She and Jessie were agreed that there was nothing more they could do, so they might as well enjoy themselves. She hadn't said much to Mike. In fact she'd been quite cool with him. His confrontation with her still rankled.

'Mam's made tea and toast if you want some.'

Nadine poked her head around the door. 'God, you look rough,' she declared. 'Were you on the sauce last night?'

'No, I wasn't,' Carol exclaimed indignantly. 'I only had soda water. I think I've got some sort of a bug or something.'

'Better a bug than a bun.' Nadine grinned.

'A bun! What sort of a bun?' Carol looked at her younger sister, perplexed, wondering what she was wittering on about.

'In the oven. A bun in the oven. Duh!' Nadine explained patiently.

Carol felt she had been hit by a sledgehammer. Pregnant! She couldn't possibly be pregnant. Could she? She sat on the bed in shock.

'Hey, you look like you've seen a ghost. I was only joking,' Nadine said, exasperated.

Carol licked her lips. That night when she'd had sex with Gary after the row in Kilkenny he'd wanted to make love a second time. They'd used the only condom he had the first time, and even though he'd withdrawn she'd felt instinctively that he hadn't pulled out soon enough. With all the trauma of Mike's outburst and then the disastrous phone call to Sean, as well as the frantic toing and froing of the past week, she'd forgotten about it, until Nadine had made her most unfunny joke.

There were two scenarios to deal with, she reasoned. Either she had a bug or she was pregnant. If she had a bug she could take Imodium to sort out her tummy. If she was pregnant, there was nothing she could do about it. She needed to know . . . and fast.

'You're not pregnant, are you?' Nadine faltered when she saw the expression on Carol's face.

'I don't know.' Carol's mouth was so dry she could hardly talk.

'Aren't you on the pill?' Nadine asked, aghast. 'I am.'

'What!' Carol was shocked.

'Look, Carol, I don't sleep around but when you're pissed things happen. I've slept with Mono.'

'Oh, Nadine, you're so *young*!' Carol exclaimed, dismayed.

'But I'm not pregnant,' Nadine retorted drily.

'Would you do me a favour?' Carol said shakily. 'Would you get me a packet of Imodium and a pregnancy test kit from the chemist?'

'I'll go to one down the town. I don't want that one up the road gossiping about me getting a pregnancy tester to all her cronies.'

'Good thinking,' Carol said distractedly, taking a fifty-euro note from her purse. 'Will you go now?'

'OK, stay calm. I'll get Mono to give me a lift on his bike.'

'Wear a helmet,' Carol warned.

'I will.' Nadine grimaced. 'I'm not a total idiot.'

'But I am,' Carol said, burying her face in her hands.

'Hey, hey, it will be OK,' Nadine said awkwardly, patting her on the back. 'It's probably a bug. I'll go and get the test now and put you out of your misery.'

'Thanks, Nadine. I appreciate it. Not a word to Ma.'

Nadine gave her a pitying look and threw her eyes up to heaven. 'As if,' she said in exasperation as she hurried out of the room.

Carol watched her go. This day she had looked forward to with such anticipation was starting out to be an absolute nightmare.

'Mono, don't ask questions, just get here quick. It's an emergency,' Nadine hissed into her mobile. 'I'll be waiting outside in five minutes.' She threw on a T-shirt and a pair of jeans and ran a brush through her hair. Her stomach tightened in knots. Poor, poor Carol. Imagine if she found out she was pregnant on her wedding day. How gross was that? She'd never seen her sister so unsure of herself. It made her feel nervous. She much preferred the bossy, in-control Carol, she decided.

'Have to go somewhere with Mono. I'll be back in a minute,' she yelled to her mother, who was in the kitchen eating her breakfast.

'Have a cup of tea, Carol,' Nancy urged, thinking how peaky her daughter looked.

'I'll just have tea, I'm not really hungry,' Carol murmured.

'Are you nervous? I know the feeling. I'm not feeling hungry either,' Nancy confessed. To tell the truth, she had elephants not butterflies in her stomach and she'd hardly slept. She'd even taken a couple of slugs of vodka, she felt so nervous. 'Er, have you been talking to your father at all?' she ventured as she passed the milk jug to Carol.

'No,' Carol said shortly.

He won't be at the wedding so, Nancy surmised, feeling a huge sense of relief. He wouldn't be able to blame her that he hadn't been at their daughter's wedding. She had done what she had to do, sending him that letter. After that, it was up to him and Carol.

'I really like your outfit, and your hair suits you like that.' Carol perched on the edge of the table.

'I like it myself. Liz was a great help to me

getting the outfit. We went to Gorey and went into that boutique down the side road opposite the supermarket after doing all the ones on the main street. I got the trouser suit there. She got a lovely jacket and dress in Wicklow. It looks terrific on her.' She put her hand in her dressing-gown pocket and pulled out an envelope.

'I don't know how to use the internet for your wedding list, so here's something to buy whatever you want off it. And, er . . . Carol, I'm sorry that I wasn't a very good mother to you when you—'

'It's OK, Ma,' Carol interjected hastily, clearly uncomfortable with the way the conversation was going.

'Er . . . right. I'll just go and have my shower.' Nancy tried not to feel snubbed. She'd been trying to apologize for being such an inadequate mother. Carol just didn't want to know.

They had no real relationship, Nancy thought sadly, unlike Liz and Jessie, who were as close as could be. It wasn't Carol's fault. It was hers. She had let both her daughters down, badly. A lump rose in her throat. She felt terribly sad today. Carol was getting married and starting a new life with Gary, and Nancy knew that the tie with home which had grown looser and looser as the years went by would for all intents and purposes be well and truly severed. Carol and Gary were not the type of couple who would be coming to visit regularly for afternoon tea.

Nancy went into her bedroom and sat on the side of the bed. She was going to get her hair done with Liz in the next hour or so. The way she was feeling now, she wished she could get back into bed and stay there and pretend the day wasn't happening.

She pulled open the drawer of her bedside locker. Just for this day she needed a little help to get through it. Tomorrow she'd be good, she assured herself, as she uncapped the bottle of vodka and took a big slug.

Gary filled his plate with bacon, sausage, pudding, mushrooms, hash browns and two eggs. He might as well get his money's worth, he reflected, as he smiled at the young foreign waitress who refilled his coffee cup. His family were arriving around twelve, and he felt at a bit of a loose end.

Today was D-Day, he thought wryly, as he dipped some sausage and hash brown into the runny egg before slathering on the brown sauce. Now that it was here he felt surprisingly calm. There was no point in getting agitated. He'd moved his stuff from the apartment in Christ

Church to Carol's pad in Phibsboro. Although his place had been new and modern, it really was the size of an egg-box and not big enough for the two of them. Carol's place had big rooms, and more storage space, even though it was an old redbrick house.

He hoped she wouldn't bang on about getting a house. A house meant you were really settled . . . trapped even. The thought chilled him. Besides, he had every intention of going to the beer festival with his mates and he'd need a decent wad of cash for that. Once you were paying a mortgage, you could forget having any spending money worth talking about. A mortgage was not on his agenda for a long time to come.

A good workout in the gym would do him all the good in the world, he decided. He'd walk to the Leisure and Fitness centre along the beach, pump some iron and be back to have lunch with his family when they arrived.

Gary ate his breakfast with relish, making the most of his last hours as a single man.

Mike gave the wedding rings one last polish and laid them carefully in their blue velvet boxes. His brother and best man, Tony, had stayed the night with him in Greystones and they'd gone for a couple of pints the night before. Tony, making the most of a wifeless night and morning, had enjoyed a drink or four too many and was groaning and berating himself in the shower. Mike grinned as he slapped the bacon on the grill and turned the sausages.

Now that his wedding day was upon them he felt surprisingly apprehensive. Not about marrying Jessie, he was really looking forward to that. He just hoped that everything went smoothly, especially with Carol's family. She'd been cool with him the previous night, and he knew it would take her a long time to forget the ultimatum he had given to her. Carol held grudges, unfortunately, but he still felt it was worth it to have confronted her so that Jessie could have the best day of her life.

It would be difficult for her and Liz, especially walking up the aisle and during the speeches. Ray's absence would be very keenly felt. There was nothing any one of them could do about it, they had to get on with it the best they could. All he could do was hope the day would go as smoothly as it possibly could.

'Oh Mam, the flowers are gorgeous,' Jessica exclaimed, as she saw the great vases of scarlet and white gladioli, stunning against the backdrop of gypsophila and greenery. She had just arrived at the church, where Tara and Liz were busy tidying up after their flower-arranging marathon.

'And the roses are gorgeous. Carol should be pleased.'

'I should think so.' Tara sniffed. 'Could she not even be bothered to come and see them?'

'She's not feeling the best. She thinks she's got a bug,' Jessica said hastily. 'I was talking to her on the mobile.'

'Huh! She'd better keep it to herself.' Tara was still not impressed.

'Ah, don't be like that, Tara. Carol's never sick. She's amazingly healthy. I feel sorry for her,' Jessica protested.

'It's probably nerves,' Liz said kindly.

'I know. I'm so nervous I feel pukey too,' Jessica confessed.

'Stop that nonsense right now,' Tara instructed. 'We haven't time for nerves. Come on, Liz, we have our hair appointments and we've to collect Nancy. Give me those buckets and I'll take them out to the car.'

She marched down the aisle, buckets and secateurs swinging briskly at her side.

'She'd have made a great sergeant-major,' Liz observed, as she stood back to observe her handiwork.

She fussed and tweaked until she was completely satisfied, and smiled at her daughter. 'Might not be able to sew but I can arrange a vase of flowers.'

'It's gorgeous, Mam. I can't believe we'll be walking up this aisle in a few hours. I love this church.' Jessie gazed around at the worn, polished wooden seats, rainbow-dappled as the morning sun shone through the stained-glass windows. The simple altar, dressed with pristine linen and Liz's flowers, was glorious. The scent of beeswax polish permeated the air and the silence was broken only by birdsong. It was a most peaceful place.

If her father had been walking her up the aisle it would have been perfect, she thought sadly. Liz caught her eye and knew exactly what she was thinking. She saw her mother's eyes well up with tears and felt a lump rise in her own throat.

'Don't cry, Mam,' she whispered, putting her arms around her.

'I'm sorry. I can't help it. He'd be so proud of you, Jessie. I'm so proud of you,' Liz said brokenly, as the tears overflowed. They held each other tightly, grief pouring out of them. They never even heard Tara come to the door to see what was delaying them. Instant understanding and pity swept over her. Discreetly she stepped into the porch, leaving them alone, and wished with all her heart that things could be so different.

'Give it to me, I'll hold it,' Nadine ordered, taking the white wand from Carol's shaking hand. 'Count to sixty.'

'I can't. Quick, let me see it.' Carol jumped up off the side of the bath. Nadine pushed her down again.

'Stay calm, Carol. What does it matter anyway? You're getting married today. How far gone would you be?'

'Nearly two weeks,' Carol said miserably.

'Is that all? Well, that's no problem if you're afraid of the gossips. It can always be two weeks early.'

'It's not that, Nadine. It's just we don't have a house. Gary didn't really want to get married so soon. He doesn't want to have children for ages. He'll go mad.'

Fuck him! Nadine's lips tightened as a heart-stopping double blue line grew stronger and more unmistakable in the little window.

'I'm pregnant, aren't I?' Carol said weakly when she saw the expression on her sister's face. Wordlessly Nadine handed over the wand.

'Oh, my God. Maybe it's a mistake,' Carol muttered in dismay.

'I bought two, just in case,' Nadine admitted, taking another kit out of her bag. 'Can you go again?'

'Yeah, I was drinking water all morning,' Carol muttered.

The second test was just as positive as the first. 'Look, don't think about it. Just get through the day as best you can and worry about it in a couple of weeks' time,' Nadine advised, feeling absolutely helpless. The more she was hearing about Gary, the less she liked him. She wanted her sister to be happy. Carol's getting married had meant there was one less person to worry about, or so she'd hoped. Nadine felt a flutter of apprehension in her tummy. Carol's marriage wasn't going to have a fairytale ending – far from it, she thought disconsolately, wondering bitterly why God was always picking on their family. Surely for once He could give them a break?

She wasn't ready for a baby. Nothing was going to plan. How could she have been so careless and so stupid? Gary would absolutely freak. She wasn't going to say a word to him until after the honeymoon. She could always say she got pregnant on their honeymoon, Carol thought miserably, as she changed into her running gear. She needed to go for a jog, badly. It would help clear her mind, which was racing like a train. She pulled on her trainers, laced them up and headed for the door.

'Where are you going?' Nadine asked worriedly when she opened the front door.

'Just going for a jog. Don't panic, I'm not going to do anything silly,' Carol whispered, touched by her younger sister's concern. Nadine had really turned up trumps today, she acknowledged, giving her younger sister a faint smile. 'Just need to have a think.'

'Don't forget, Amanda will be here soon and we've all to go to the hairdresser's,' Nadine fretted.

'We've loads of time. It's not even half ten yet. I'll be back in twenty minutes,' she promised, surprised that Nadine was getting so involved. 'It's a pity you're not my bridesmaid,' she added impulsively.

Nadine actually blushed with pleasure. 'I'm not good at that sort of stuff,' she muttered awkwardly. 'But thanks anyway.'

'The baby's only going to have one aunt. That's going to be you. Gary only has brothers. I'll be depending on you, Nadine,' Carol said fervently. She didn't see the expression on her sister's face as she took off down the path and headed towards the beach.

What would she do when she couldn't run? she thought in a panic. Would jogging harm the baby? When should she stop? Would Gary start seeing other women when her body became swollen and heavy? The thoughts crowded in on her relentlessly. Carol swallowed hard. She felt scared, really, really scared.

'I don't want to be depended on,' Nadine groaned as she watched Carol running down the road. She'd had enough of people depending on her. She just wanted to have to worry about herself for a change. At least her mother had cut down on the booze; how would Nancy feel about becoming a granny?

Where was her mother, anyway? She hadn't seen her around since before she'd gone out for the pregnancy test. There was no point in telling her Carol's news and spoiling her day. Carol could tell Nancy when and where she wanted to, she thought grumpily.

'Ma, where are you? I'd say Liz will be over in a minute. I've just seen them drive into their drive,' she called.

Nancy appeared at the door of her bedroom,

bleary-eyed and unsteady. 'I'm nearly ready,' she slurred.

'Ah, *Ma!*' Nadine couldn't believe her eyes. 'Ah, Ma, what the fuck did you do that for? You're a stupid bitch! Just when Carol needed you most!' she yelled, and burst into tears.

39

'Liz, Ma's pissed, and we can't let Carol see her like this. And I don't know what to do,' Nadine blurted in desperation, barrelling through Liz's back door like a tornado. 'And her friend Amanda will be here any minute and I don't want her to know that Ma's an alco. None of Carol's friends know.' She burst into tears of frustration and anger.

'Ah, no, Nadine!' Liz couldn't hide her dismay. 'And she was doing so well.'

'What will I do, Liz?'

'I'll come over with you. Come on. Don't be crying now,' Liz said firmly, trying to hide her consternation.

'Will I come with you?' Tara asked.

'No, boil the kettle and make a pot of strong coffee,' Liz instructed. 'Stop worrying, Jessie, it will be OK,' she comforted her daughter, who was speechless.

'I knew it, I just bloody well knew it,' she swore as Liz followed Nadine out of the back door.

'It's just a hiccup, dearie,' Tara said briskly, filling the kettle. 'Stop panicking – if anyone can sober up Nancy, Liz will. And I'll tell you one thing, I'm feeling the teeniest bit sorry for poor Nancy already!'

Jessica giggled nervously. 'I hope you're right.'

'Of course I'm right. I'm always right. Trust moi,' Tara said confidently, wishing she could believe it herself.

'Is she very bad?' Liz asked Nadine as they hurried across the road.

'Not totally blotto, but pissed enough,' Nadine said defeatedly.

'Chin up, Nadine, we'll sort her. There's plenty of time yet,' Liz soothed.

'That's not all,' Nadine burst out, totally fraught. 'Carol's just found out that she's pregnant and she's gone off jogging and I'm afraid she won't come back.'

'Oh Lord,' murmured Liz. 'You're having a tough day, lovey, aren't you?' she said sympathetically as they closed the side door behind them. Nadine burst into loud sobs.

'I'm sick of them all, Liz. I have to do all the

worrying and it's not fair.' She wept, fraught. 'Just when I thought things were getting OK. I should have known better.'

'Ah, you poor old dote.' Liz put her arms around the teenager and rubbed her back comfortingly as she cried.

Nadine rested her head on Liz's shoulder as years of pent-up fear, grief, anger and sadness erupted out of her. It had been so long since she had been held and comforted, she couldn't even remember a time as a child when her mother had put her arms around her the way Liz was doing.

'You know, when the wedding's over I think you and I might go and find out about Al Anon. None of this is your responsibility, pet, you need to understand that. You don't have to mind the family, you just have to mind yourself. Now come on, let's get your mam straightened out and we'll get back on track. OK?'

'OK,' Nadine gulped, trying to compose herself. 'Don't say anything about Carol, sure you won't?' she hiccuped.

'Not a word,' Liz promised. 'Don't worry.'

She led the way into the kitchen and found Nancy trying to light a cigarette from a butt. Her hand was shaking.

'Hello, Liz,' Nancy tried hard to focus.

'Ah, Nancy, look at the state of you. How much did you drink?' Liz demanded.

'Just a little drop.' Nancy gave a little titter.

'It's not one bit funny and you were doing so well. Into the shower with you this minute,' Liz ordered, taking the other woman by the arm and manhandling her to the bathroom.

'Stop, Liz, I don't want a shower,' Nancy protested drunkenly.

'Nadine, get me some towels and a tracksuit for your mother,' Liz ordered.

'OK.' Nadine scuttled off, glad to have someone else take charge of the situation, embarrassed yet strangely relieved that she had confided in Liz.

Liz, being far fitter and stronger than Nancy, had no trouble bundling the other woman into the shower, having managed to remove her dressing-gown but not her nightdress.

Nancy yelled as the cold water cascaded over her, but Liz kept a firm hold of her even though she was getting drenched herself. She kept her under the cold shower for a couple of minutes before turning on the hot water and withdrawing.

'Take off your nightdress and wash yourself, Nancy,' she ordered in a tone that brooked no nonsense, handing her neighbour a bar of soap.

Five minutes later she opened the door of the

shower cubicle and handed in a bath towel that Nadine had given her. 'Get dressed, quick,' she said brusquely.

The brusque tone got through to Nancy. 'I'm sorry, Liz. I just lost my nerve,' she muttered, ashamed.

'Well, you're going to get it back again.' Liz softened. 'Come on, quick, before Carol gets home. You don't want her to see you like this.'

'Where is she?' Nancy asked, perplexed, trying hard to concentrate.

'Gone for a jog. Come on now, Nancy, we've to sober you up and get ourselves to the hairdresser's.'

Liz badly needed a shower herself – she was drenched to the skin.

'Finish getting dressed, I just want to have a word with Nadine,' she instructed, slipping out of the bathroom. Nadine was hovering around anxiously.

'Do us a favour, Nadine. When I take your mother over to my house, have a look around for that bottle she was drinking from and get rid of it, OK?'

'OK,' Nadine said, subdued.

'She's much better already – stop worrying.' Liz smiled kindly at her. 'These things happen on the road to recovery. After all, it's a big day and a lot of pressure and your mam's been doing very well.'

'I suppose so,' the teenager sighed.

Ten minutes later Nancy was sitting in Liz's kitchen drinking a mug of strong black coffee. Liz was in the shower and Tara was making more coffee.

'Just get it down you, Nancy, and have some of those sandwiches I made up for you. They'll soak up the alcohol, and anyway it's not good for you to be going around on an empty stomach,' Tara said matter-of-factly, trying to make the other woman feel less ill at ease.

'I've let everyone down,' Nancy muttered.

'No, you haven't,' Tara said stoutly. 'Just put it behind you now and best foot forward for the rest of the day. Right.'

'Right,' Nancy agreed, ashamed and disgusted with herself.

'Nancy's plastered!' Jessica whispered, opening the door to Katie.

'Oh shit!' Katie groaned.

'Don't go into the kitchen, Tara's sobering her up. Let's go up to the bedroom.'

'OK, is Carol in bits?'

'I don't know. Poor Nadine was bawling her eyes out.'

'Aw, the poor kid,' Katie said sympathetically as she followed Jessica into her bedroom.

'At least it's a lovely day. Are you organized?'

'Yeah, everything was going fine until this happened,' Jessica said dolefully.

'Is she very pissed?' Katie made a face.

'I don't know – I kept out of the kitchen. I was afraid I'd give her a puck in the jaw.' Jessica scowled.

'Stay calm, breathe deeply.' Katie flung herself onto the bed. 'I can tell you one thing. I'm going to pig out for the rest of the week once this wedding's over. If I never see a Ryvita and cottage cheese again I won't be sorry.'

'You've done great,' Jessica praised. 'Your dress is going to look stunning on you.'

'Pity Sean won't see it. I'd like him to see me looking my best,' Katie said regretfully. 'Still, I've lost ten pounds at least – when we do the biz I won't be worrying about my spare tyre.'

'When are you going to do it?' Jessie asked eagerly.

'The sooner the better. I just didn't want him to think I was too easy, you know, after the way Carol went on about me being manless.' Katie frowned.

'He's gorgeous. I'm mad about him and I think I've waited long enough. Carol was an awful eejit to let him slip through her fingers.'

'I know. There's no contest between him and Gary,' Jessica said caustically.

Katie glanced at her watch. 'We'd want to be getting a move on – are we supposed to be collecting Carol and Amanda?'

'Yeah, I expect we'd better get going,' Jessica said reluctantly. 'I wonder how's Nancy?'

'Forget Nancy – Mam and Liz are on the case. Just concentrate on yourself. Let's go and get the girls.' Katie hopped up off the bed and gave her cousin a comforting hug.

'Is Ma gone to the hairdresser's?' Carol wiped her brow with her towel as she marched into the kitchen. The run had steadied her nerves and she felt physically better, if not mentally so.

'Yeah,' Nadine fibbed.

'Amanda phoned me, she's in Rathnew, she won't be long. I'd better get my ass into the shower.'

'Good idea,' Nadine said tiredly. She was wrecked. She'd found a half-empty bottle of vodka in Nancy's bedroom and had stashed it at the back of her wardrobe. She needed to have a shower herself, and she was supposed to be going to get her hair done with the girls.

She tidied up the kitchen, not wanting Amanda to think the house was a tip. After her trip to Dublin she'd been quite looking forward to the wedding, but so far it was turning out to be a complete disaster. Not only was Carol pregnant and Nancy pissed but she'd had a row with her friend Lynn over money the other girl had borrowed from her weeks ago and hadn't paid back. She wanted the money for Carol's wedding present.

She'd told Lynn over and over that she needed her cash but the other girl had ignored her pleas. Nadine was really bugged about it. Lynn was much better off than she was. She was only a user, she'd decided, and had sent her a text telling her to get lost and not bother coming to the wedding. Lynn hadn't even responded. That was infuriating. There was nothing worse than being ignored.

She knew Carol had a wedding list but she didn't possess a credit card, and although there was an internet café on the main street she hadn't even tried to open the site. Instead she'd gone into a jeweller's and bought Carol a gorgeous little Waterford Crystal clock.

Now would be a good time to give it to her while

they had the house to themselves, she decided. She waited until she heard Carol come out of the shower and knocked on her door.

'Here's your wedding present,' she said gruffly, thrusting the wrapped gift into her hands.

'Oh! Nadine, thanks, I wasn't expecting one. You didn't have to.' Carol was taken aback.

'I *am* your *sister*,' Nadine said indignantly. 'Of course I'd get you a present.'

'Can I open it?' Carol asked, sitting on the side of the bed.

'Sure. I hope you like it.' Nadine shrugged.

'Oh, Nadine, it's gorgeous. Aw, thanks very much,' Carol said, clearly touched as she looked at the delicately designed clock nestling in its velvet resting-place. 'I'll treasure it,' she said quietly, reaching out to give her sister a hug. Nadine managed a hug back; hugging was not something she was used to, but for that brief moment she felt a kinship with her sister that she had never felt before. It felt good.

Bill took one final look at himself in the mirror and was satisfied with the image he saw reflected back at him. He looked very smart, he approved, flicking a piece of lint off his freshly cleaned, charcoal-grey, fine-wool suit. His hair was neatly cut; he'd bought a new white shirt and a tasteful maroon tie.

He planned to take his time, stop in Chester Beatty's in Ashford for lunch and be at the church by one forty-five. The fact that Nancy had given her imprimatur to his attendance at the church gave him confidence. At last bygones were going to be bygones and he had to give his wife all credit for that. He'd make sure to thank her sincerely, he decided magnanimously, as he checked his wallet to make sure he had cash for the trip.

He felt bad going behind Brona's back but he didn't want to upset their uneasy truce. Maybe in time he might be able to tell her of the day's happy events.

With nervous but happy anticipation, Bill Logan left the house and set out on the journey to his daughter's wedding.

40

'She did a lovely job on your hair, Jessie. The rose is gorgeous,' Amanda enthused. 'And I love yours swept to the side, Carol.'

'I hope the blinking thing stays in, I keep wanting to fiddle with it—'

'*Don't!*' Amanda, Katie, Carol and Nadine said in unison.

Jessie laughed. 'I won't, I won't.'

'We all scrub up well, don't we?' Katie declared, delighted with her shining copper tresses. 'Nadine, you look a million dollars. Mono'll be mightily impressed.'

Nadine blushed. She wasn't used to compliments. 'Give over,' she said gruffly, but she was pleased. Her hair was sleek and shiny and the rat's tails at the end had been cut and tidied. It was quite sophisticated, she thought, secretly pleased. It was a pity Lynn wasn't coming to the wedding to see how well she looked in her new gear.

'God, isn't he a fine thing?' Amanda declared, as they overtook a cyclist who was booting along the slip road from Arklow heading for Dublin. He had his shirt tied at his waist, and was drinking from a bottle of water as he pedalled furiously. He looked foreign. Sallow-skinned, tanned, hard-muscled, hairy-chested, he was a fine specimen of manhood and they all ogled him unashamedly. He grinned and waved at them, showing even white teeth.

'Ooh, he's gorgeous! I wish he was riding me, not his bicycle,' Amanda sighed as the others guffawed. 'I love hairy chests.'

'Sean's got a hairy chest,' Katie said dreamily, the sight of the fit, lean cyclist putting a longing on her.

'*Sean Ryan?*' Carol demanded from the front seat. 'My Sean?'

'Er . . . umm—' Katie came to with a start. What a blabbermouth she was, she thought in dismay, as she caught Jessie's horrified gaze in the mirror.

'Are you dating Sean?' Carol turned to look at her. And Katie knew that the old saying 'If looks could kill you'd be dead' described perfectly the expression on the other girl's face.

'As it happens, yes, actually.' Katie decided to go for broke. Carol would know about it some time; there was no point in lying.

'I never thought you'd take my leavings. You're welcome to him,' Carol said coolly, and a tense silence descended on the car.

'What time are the beauticians coming?' Amanda babbled hastily when she saw the flush of temper rise to Katie's cheeks.

'Soon,' Jessica said, putting her foot down on the accelerator, not caring whether she got points for speeding or not.

Katie sat in the back seat, incandescent with rage. Carol Logan was a wagon of the highest order. A walking bitch. If it wasn't Jessie's wedding day she'd pull the bloody head off her, she raged. How *dare* she speak of Sean like that. The unmitigated cheek of her. Once this wedding was over she was never having anything to do with that bitch again.

Carol clenched her fists in her lap as waves of humiliation and nausea swept over her. That bastard Sean Ryan was dating that stupid cow! Had he no taste? How could he? She hated him. Why, oh, why had she made that totally mortifying phone call? She cursed herself. The pair of them had probably been sniggering at her behind her back. Bile rose to her throat.

'Stop . . . stop the car, I'm going to be sick,' she urged as beads of sweat broke out on her forehead.

Jessie pulled onto the hard shoulder and stood on the brakes, earning herself an angry beep from the car behind. Carol hurled herself out the door and bent double into the ditch, retching. Jessie reluctantly got out to assist. She didn't want to catch Carol's bug.

'Are you OK?' she asked, handing her a tissue.

'No, no, I'm not OK, Jessie. I'm pregnant!' Carol retorted and burst into tears.

'It's good enough for her, sarky cow.' Katie was not to be pacified as she sat in her dressing-gown watching the beautician apply Jessica's make-up.

'Ah, don't be like that. She's in shock. Imagine finding out that you're pregnant on your wedding day!' Jessica retorted. She was still stunned at her friend's news. 'Carol of all people. She was always paranoid about getting pregnant. I just can't believe it. I feel really sorry for her.'

'Jessie, I'm sorry, you can say what you like, *I'll* never feel sorry for Carol Logan and I wish I'd asked Sean to the wedding so I could really rub her nose in it. How dare she refer to him as her "leavings"?'

'Forget it, will ya?' Jessica groaned.

'If she said something like that about Mike, would you be able to forget it?' Katie demanded.

'Well, so far it's just been the perfect bloody day,' Jessica snapped. 'What more could I ask for than for you pair to be fighting?'

'Sorry.' Katie had the grace to look ashamed. 'At least Nancy's sober again,' she murmured, casting around for something positive.

'Yeah, but for how long?' Jessie sighed, sinking into gloom.

'She'll be fine,' Katie declared, with more conviction than she felt. 'Just think, in a few hours you'll be Mrs Mike Keating and you won't give a hoot about anyone or anything. And your dress is out of this world.'

'Yeah, it is lovely, isn't it?' Jessica cheered up, looking at the creamy gold ensemble hanging on the back door. 'Tara did a terrific job.'

'I'm dying to see Carol's designer gear,' Katie said cattily. 'And I'm dying to see her face when she sees you. She really looks down her nose at dressmaking. Or "home-made" dresses, as she so disparagingly refers to them.'

'Will you forget her!' Jessie growled.

'Sorry, sorry, won't mention her again,' Katie said sourly.

'Huh! And pigs will fly,' came back the tart rejoinder.

'I'm only going to the loo, Nadine,' Nancy snapped. 'Will you stop following me around? Aren't you supposed to be getting your make-up done with the girls?'

'She'd not finished with Amanda yet,' Nadine retorted sulkily.

'I won't drink, if that's what you're worried about. I promised Liz.'

'Are you sure?' Nadine said doubtfully.

'Yes, Nadine. I am,' Nancy said quietly.

'I took the bottle out of your locker,' Nadine confessed. 'Just so you wouldn't be tempted.'

'That was kind, Nadine. And I'm sorry you had to do it,' Nancy said unhappily.

'Look, why don't you take this packet of Polo mints and if you feel shaky and want a drink, suck one,' Nadine suggested agitatedly, pulling a packet out of her jeans pocket.

'That's a really good idea, Nadine. Thanks.' Nancy took the sweets. 'I'll put them in my bag. Now go and get ready, the car will be here in another three-quarters of an hour.'

'OK,' her daughter agreed, and went to join Carol and Amanda. Nancy bit her lip as she looked at the packet of Polo mints. Poor Nadine, too old for her years and all because of her and Bill. Guilt engulfed her yet again. She'd let everybody down today. And her bottle was gone out of her drawer. The only crutch she had was her Polo mints, she thought wryly.

A thought struck her, and she slipped into her bedroom and sat on the bed. Her little spiritual book lay on her locker. She picked it up, closed her eyes and said simply, 'Help'. Slowly she opened a page and read the words that awaited her. *I cast the burden on the Christ within, and I go free.*

Nancy read it again just to make sure.

What a perfect message, she thought in amazement. And for the first time in her life she felt as though she was not alone and that some Divine Being was minding her. She sat quietly, repeating the words, letting them sink in, as the knots in her stomach loosened and the headache that had pounded her temples began to fade and a measure of calm descended on her.

'How are you feeling now?' Amanda asked anxiously. The last thing she wanted was to be trotting up the aisle after a barfing bride.

'How would you feel?' Carol said miserably.

'I know.' Amanda frowned. 'I meant physically. Your tummy?'

'Once I was sick I felt better.' Carol shrugged.

'Would you have a drop of brandy and port?' her bridesmaid suggested. 'Just to keep it at bay.'

'I'll see how I'm getting on. It wouldn't exactly be PC to be reeking of alcohol up at the altar.'

'You wouldn't be the first,' Amanda scoffed, stepping into her lilac dress.

'I wonder have my boobs got bigger?' Carol murmured as she slipped her dress carefully over her head.

'Ah, come on, Carol, it's only two weeks.' Amanda laughed at the notion.

'I supposed it's wishful thinking. I always wanted bigger boobs.' Carol managed a wan smile. 'Don't tell any of the gang in the club, sure you won't?'

'Don't worry. I wouldn't dream of it. They'll all think you got preggers on the honeymoon,' Amanda assured her, helping her to slide the folds of the dress over her hips.

'Gary'll probably divorce me when he finds out.'

'Indeed and he won't. Stop being dramatic,' Amanda chided as she arranged the soft neckline over Carol's bosom. 'He certainly won't divorce you when he sees you,' she said in admiration when she stood back to admire her friend. 'Look at yourself,' she urged.

Carol looked at her reflection in the mirror. She looked beautiful, she acknowledged without conceit. Her dress sculpted her body in a classical, sensual way that was almost Grecian in style. If Sean Ryan saw her he'd never look at Katie Johnson again, she thought defiantly, squaring her shoulders and lifting her chin. She was going to walk up that aisle, head held high. Gary Davis didn't know how lucky he was.

Bill paid for his meal, tipped the waitress and walked out of Chester Beatty's happy in the knowledge that he was in plenty of time. The traffic was heavy, granted, he noted as he stood waiting to cross the road to where his car was parked outside the pharmacy. It was a lovely day. He squinted up at the sun. It was hard to believe it was the last week in September. It had been a hell of a summer and the heat in the sun gave lie to how late it was in the year. Kilbride church was the perfect wedding setting on a lovely autumn day such as today, he reflected, as he eased himself behind the wheel.

He felt very optimistic that Carol's hostility

would fade when she saw him. After all, blood was thicker than water when all was said and done. Almost jauntily he started the ignition and pulled out into the traffic.

'I can't remember the way to the bloody church. I know we were to turn right at some pub,' Gary said bad-temperedly as they drove down a winding country road that had no sign of a church to the left or right of it.

'Are you sure it was Jack White's?' his brother Simon asked irritably. 'Ask that old lad over there.'

'I'm not asking,' Gary muttered.

'Tsk.' Simon tutted and rolled down his window. 'Excuse me – could you tell me are we on the right road to Kilbride church?' he shouted across the road at an old man who was walking his dog.

'No, you're on the way to Brittas Bay; go back the way you came and take the right turn at Lil Doyle's pub,' the elderly man instructed.

'Thanks very much.' Simon did a U-turn with difficulty.

'You plonker.'

'I knew there was a pub involved. I wish I was in it. Don't hassle me. I'm getting married.'

'Poor bastard!' grinned Simon, scorching back on to the N11.

'Here's Dad with the car,' Katie called, as Peter's maroon Vento swung into the drive.

'Right, time for a quick glass of champers,' Tara announced gaily, popping the cork on a bottle of Moët.

'Nice touch, Ma,' Katie approved, whipping some champagne flutes out of Liz's drinks cabinet. She looked sexy and voluptuous in a slinky ruby gown with a fishtail frill. She exuded glamour.

Jessica laughed as the bubbles tickled her nose. All her nerves had disappeared. She was excited and happy and longing to see Mike, and she felt gloriously special in her bridal dress.

'Look at our girls, Tara,' Liz said proudly. She was wearing a smart, chic navy and cream dress and jacket.

'Stop that, Liz, and don't get maudlin,' Tara said crisply. 'Otherwise we'll all start bawling and our make-up will be ruined.'

They all laughed and sipped their champagne, glad the moment was finally upon them after all the fraught tensions of the past weeks.

The photographer arrived and took over, and the next twenty minutes were spent posing as he instructed, with Tara making witty asides that kept cracking them all up, much to his annoyance.

* * *

'Tell me the minute you see Jessie coming out,' Carol instructed out of the side of her mouth as she stood in the back garden getting her photo taken with Nancy. Gary's brother Vince snapped away, checking the results on his digital camera every so often.

'Come on, get in the photo with your mam and sister,' he invited Nadine.

'I hate getting my photo taken,' Nadine protested.

'Me too, come on.' Carol held out her hand.

'Oh, all right,' Nadine agreed with bad grace. 'But I'm not doing any more at the church or in the hotel.'

'OK.' Carol didn't make an issue of it. She was feeling terribly nervous. She wondered if Gary was at the church yet. Just say he jilted her and left her standing at the altar. She'd die. *Stop it! Pull yourself together!* She drew a deep breath, trying to compose herself, hoping her turmoil didn't show in her face.

Her Aunt Freda and Uncle Packie arrived to take Nancy to the church, and Carol was thrilled when she saw the flash of surprise and admiration in the older woman's eyes. Freda and Packie had notions about themselves and thought they were leaders of Arklow's high society. They'd always looked down their snooty noses at the Logans. She'd show them all that she was just as good as they were, she thought bitterly, remembering how her relatives had left Nancy to get on with it when Bill had walked out on them.

Despite their affluence, they'd ignored her wedding list and bought a duvet set that had come out of a catalogue. They were as mean as misers and always had been.

'Will you be all right coming up the aisle on your own? I could ask Packie,' Nancy murmured.

'That mean old walrus, no, thanks,' Carol whispered back. 'You look lovely, Ma,' she said awkwardly. Nancy's taupe trouser suit with the little black camisole was very elegant on her mother's slender frame.

'Thanks, Carol. You look lovely too. Really beautiful.' Nancy's face broke into a rare smile. And Carol caught a flash of the old Nancy as she had been before depression, stress and drink had taken their toll.

Impulsively she leaned down and kissed her mother's cheek. 'See you at the church,' she said, squeezing her hand.

'We should go,' Freda said bossily. 'We want to get good parking. Can't see why you didn't have it in Templerainey where there's a decent car park.'

'Jessie's father was buried from that church. It has sad memories for them,' Nancy said coldly. Freda looked taken aback at her sister's tone. It was most unusual for Nancy to argue with her.

'Ma, would you like to come in the limo with us, there's loads of room?' Carol asked, flashing a look of disdain at her aunt.

'No, I'll be fine with Freda and Packie, but thanks. You three enjoy it.' Nancy gave her the tiniest wink.

'Ma, don't forget your handbag,' Nadine reminded her, handing her the elegant black clutch that Nancy had left on her lounger.

'Oh, thanks, Nadine, enjoy your trip in the limo.'

'I will – and, Ma, I got you another packet of Polo mints. They're in your bag,' Nadine whispered.

'They're a great help,' Nancy whispered back, and felt a wave of love for her youngest child. 'Thanks, hon, I don't know what I would have done without you.'

Nadine watched her mother follow her aunt and uncle out of the side gate and hoped against hope that just this one day she'd manage to get through the rest of it without a drink. Nancy looked so smart. As smart as Liz. It would be great if she could look like that all the time.

Carol was having a photo taken with Amanda when Nadine spied movement across the street through the gap in the half-open side door.

'Here's Jessie. Ooh, she's gorgeous!' she exclaimed, completely dropping her cynical façade about weddings, brides, and all the palaver.

Amanda and Carol hastened into the house and peered eagerly out of the window in the front room.

'Her *aunt* made the dress?' Amanda exclaimed in wonder. 'It's awesome.'

Carol couldn't believe the vision across the road. Jessica's champagne wedding dress looked as expensive and exclusive as her own, if not more so.

'Nice dress Katie's wearing,' Amanda observed.

'Huh, she looks like J-Lo!' Carol sniffed. 'Oh good, here's the white limo,' she exclaimed, her confidence restored when she saw her big car glide up the road. It looked so swanky compared to Katie's dad's ordinary maroon Vento. *She* would certainly make the most dramatic entrance, Carol thought, satisfied with that small victory.

'Posh car, pretentious wagon,' Katie derided as she watched the white limo pull up across the road.

'Stop it. If it's what Carol wants, let her have it. It's her wedding day,' Jessie chided.

'I don't care if she gets to the church on her broomstick,' Katie retorted huffily.

Jessica laughed as she got into the car beside her. 'Cow.'

'I can't help it,' grinned Katie. 'She just gets right up my nose.'

'Right, girls. Have you got everything?' Her father got into the driver's seat and turned to look at them.

'I think so,' Jessie said.

'Wave at the neighbours, then, and let's hit the road,' Peter chuckled, starting the engine.

Jessica beamed broadly at the neighbours who had gathered around to wave her off. She wondered if Mike had arrived at the church yet. She had promised him that she wouldn't be late and it was a promise she was determined to keep. She couldn't wait to walk up the aisle to him. She knew she was the luckiest woman in the world.

'Ma and Da are just ahead of us in Ashford. I told them to wait and we'd catch up with them,' Mike told his brother as they bypassed the Cullenmore Bends and drove on to the new stretch of road that he was so familiar with. He was tense with nerves.

It was weird not having any contact with Jessie. He'd picked up the phone a dozen times this morning to call her before remembering that it wasn't allowed.

He loosened the knot in his tie and swallowed hard. The journey to Kilbride seemed to be taking for ever. If anything had gone wrong, Jessie would have had to phone him, so he decided to assume that all was well.

'Relax – enjoy the ride. You'll be making your speech before you know it,' his brother teased.

'Thanks. I'd forgotten about that,' Mike groaned, taking his well-thumbed speech out of his inside pocket and reading it over for the umpteenth time.

His phone beeped and he saw that he had a message.

See you soon. I love you.XXXX

His heart lifted. It was from Jessie. All was well, and he couldn't wait to see her.

'Nearly there,' his best man announced cheerfully fifteen minutes later as Lil Doyle's appeared to the right of them. Their parents were in the car behind.

'Some poor bugger's got a puncture,' Mike

observed, as he saw a car bounce slowly across the meridian line and turn into the pub's car park.

'Don't mention the P word,' his brother warned. 'Remember my wedding? I was half an hour late because I got one and I thought Val was going to clobber me. How are we doing for time?'

'Loads of time, it's just around the next bend.' Mike stretched, very glad to have reached the church at last.

'For crying out bloody loud.' Bill swore with frustration, struggling to keep the car under control as he swung into Lil Doyle's car park. A fucking puncture was the last thing he needed. He jumped out of the car, took off his jacket, rolled up his shirtsleeves and rooted in the boot for the jack.

The sun was beating down as he struggled with the nuts on the tyre and he could feel the perspiration between his shoulder blades. He badly wanted to be at the church before Nancy and Carol got there.

'Just concentrate,' he muttered, puffing with the exertion of trying to loosen the last nut. He saw a maroon car with white ribbons flapping in the breeze turn to the right at the crossroads. Was it Carol or Jessica? He didn't know.

'Why?' he muttered as he finally managed to

loosen the last nut and eased the wheel off the axle. What a disaster it would be if he arrived at the church and Carol had already walked up the aisle.

'You look really terrific, Nancy, that colour is fabulous on you. I'm so glad you bought it.' Liz embraced her friend warmly. 'Are you feeling OK?'

'Not bad,' Nancy murmured. 'Sorry about earlier.'

'Forget it. You're here, you look great. And it's going to be a happy day.' Liz smiled.

'Poor old Nadine told me she'd confiscated my bottle of vodka,' Nancy said ruefully. 'She told me to suck Polos if I got the urge for a drink. I've eaten half the packet already.'

'If it gets too much for you, just tell me and I'll help in any way I can,' Liz said earnestly.

'You've helped so much already,' Nancy assured her. 'I opened my little book and got the most amazing message, about casting the burden.'

'Oh, that's a great one. I've got that many times when I've been on my knees in despair missing Ray.' Liz nodded.

'Today must be hard,' Nancy said sympathetically.

'I'm trying not to let it be,' Liz admitted. 'It's

hard for you too. It's such a special day for the girls, they don't need wobbly mothers.'

'No, you're right. Come on, we'll go up and say hello to our future sons-in-law,' Nancy said, firmly linking her arm in her friend's and walking up the aisle with her.

'Could you get a smell of drink off her?' Freda hissed, digging her husband in the ribs.

'I could smell mints off her but I wouldn't say she's been hitting the bottle. She looks very well,' Packie answered.

'That's an expensive-looking suit. And where did they get the money for that limo? And that wedding dress was expensive, too,' Freda said crossly. Nancy had surprised her with her finery, and she'd seemed very calm and in control, not the shaky, fidgety nervous wreck she knew so well. She watched her younger sister walking up the aisle laughing at something Liz Kennedy had said to her.

'She'll be drinking before the evening's out. You mark my words,' she said caustically, turning around to study the finery worn by the rest of the guests.

'Here's Jessie.' Tara walked up the aisle to her sister, who was chatting to some of Jessie's friends.

'Excuse me, girls. I have to walk my daughter up the aisle.' She smiled.

She walked down the aisle into the porch, where Jessica was posing for a photograph with Katie.

'Excellent,' Frank, the photographer, said. 'Liz, get in there now and seduce the camera.'

Liz, Jessica and Katie guffawed. And Frank snapped away, delighted with their response. That would be a jolly photo that would bring back happy memories for years to come.

Five minutes later Carol's limo swept up the road.

'Oh Carol, you look beautiful,' Jessica exclaimed warmly when the other girl joined her in the porch.

'So do you,' Carol said enviously, eyeing her friend's cleavage. 'That bustier is gorgeous.' She ignored Katie.

'Are you feeling OK?' Jessie asked, as Amanda arranged the other girl's long floaty cathedral veil.

'Yeah. I don't feel as grotty. It's wearing off. That's why it's called morning sickness, I suppose,' Carol said ruefully.

'You always wanted a baby,' Jessie comforted.

'I know, but not exactly like this. I'm not saying a word until after the honeymoon.'

'Good thinking,' Jessica agreed, as the two of them stood together for their photographs. 'Nadine, you look brilliant. Mono's inside, half-way up your side of the church.'

'Thanks, Jessie. Your dress is really cool.' Nadine couldn't hide how impressed she was. She preferred it to Carol's, but she wouldn't dream of saying it.

'Pop your head in the door and see if Gary's here?' Carol whispered tersely, half afraid her fiancé hadn't shown up. Nadine did as she was told, peering up the aisle until she found him. She gave her sister the thumbs-up.

Carol felt herself relax a little. 'Thanks, Nadine, are you going in?'

'Yeah, enjoy yourself, Carol,' she said kindly, giving Carol a pat on the arm.

'You too, and thanks for all your help.' They smiled at each other, then Nadine clattered up the aisle in her high heels, leaving Carol to her solo entrance.

'Are you all right, Jessie?' Liz smiled at her daughter.

'Yeah – did you see Mike?' she asked eagerly.

'I did, and he looks dead dishy,' Liz assured her as she gave the nod to Tara, who gave the signal to the organist.

The notes of the organ filled the church and Jessie felt her heart leap in her chest.

'Best foot forward,' whispered Liz as she gave her daughter a little squeeze and they began their walk up the aisle.

Jessica was aware of Mike turning slowly to look at her. She saw his eyes widen in amazement and pleasure and couldn't hide her joy as her face creased into a huge grin.

'You look radiant,' he whispered as he leaned down to kiss her.

'That's because I am,' she whispered back, wishing she could throw her arms around him and never stop hugging him.

Gary gave her the thumbs-up and they turned to await Carol's arrival.

Carol took a last deep breath as Amanda adjusted her veil over her face. 'Ready?' she said briskly.

'As ready as I'll ever be,' Amanda assured her, and turned in surprise as a car skidded to a halt at the church gates and a man jumped out.

'Carol. Carol, I got here just in time,' Bill said breathlessly, hurrying up the path.

Carol couldn't believe what she was seeing. After all she'd said to him, Bill had ignored her wishes completely. Why did he continue to treat her as though her feelings meant nothing? Fury erupted.

'What the fuck are you doing here?' she shrieked. 'How dare you? How *dare* you ruin my wedding day, you arrogant bastard!' She was shaking with anger.

Amanda gazed at the pair of them in shock. What the hell was going on?

A gasp of excited horror rippled through the guests as they turned to face the door at the sound of raised voices.

'Oh, no!' Nancy raised a hand to her mouth.

Jessica stared at Mike in dismay as Carol's profanities carried to the altar. Tears welled in her eyes.

'For God's sake!' Katie exclaimed in disgust.

Gary looked down at his hands, mortified.

Freda and Packie looked at each other in triumph.

Nadine jumped to her feet and raced down the aisle. She closed the doors viciously and turned to face her father.

'Why are you here? You're not wanted. Why don't you listen to her?' she shouted. 'Why won't you do what she wants?'

'She's my daughter. I want to make my peace with her,' Bill explained weakly. He couldn't believe Carol's reaction.

'Well, guess what, Dad? It's not all about you. And she doesn't want you here. None of us do. Now leave us *alone*!' Nadine spat. 'Go on. Get lost!'

Dazed, Bill backed down the path. How could he have misjudged things so badly? If Nancy could put the past aside, why couldn't they?

'Are you OK, Carol?' Nadine asked her sister, who was trembling like a leaf.

'Could you get me a drink of water?' she whispered, gutted.

'There's a bottle in the limo,' Amanda said weakly. She felt sick at what she'd just witnessed. 'I'll get it.'

She got the bottle of still water and passed it to Carol, who took a couple of sips.

'Well, we'll be the talk of the parish as usual,' she said shakily to Nadine.

'And why not?' said her sister stoutly. 'I bet Freda and Packie are wetting themselves, boring old farts – we needed to liven them up. Come on, take another drink, fix your veil and let's march up that aisle with our heads high.'

'You're quite amazing, Nadine. And you're a great sister,' Carol said slowly.

'So are you. Come on. I'm walking you up the aisle. You're not going up there on your own.'

Nadine linked her arm into Carol's. 'Open the door for us, Amanda, we're coming through.' Carol managed a weak grin as her bridesmaid opened the porch door for them and the Bridal March issued forth with gusto.

41

She could see Packie's ruddy face and his little beady eyes glinting at her. She could see her mother, pale and concerned, at the edge of the seat. She could feel Nadine's arm in her own and that gave her courage.

Carol paused beside her mother's seat. 'Are you OK, Ma? It was Dad – I didn't want him here,' she murmured, conscious that every eye in the church was on her.

'That's up to you, Carol. Are *you* all right?' Nancy was very shaken.

'I'm fine, Ma. Honest.'

'Have a Polo,' Nadine urged, and in spite of herself Nancy had to smile at her youngest daughter's naïvety. If only it were that simple.

'I will,' she said. 'Go on now, don't keep them waiting.'

'Are you OK, Carol?' Jessie asked as she

slipped into place beside her in front of the altar.

'Good to see you, Carol.' Mike held out his hand to her.

It was a heart-warming gesture and she took it. Mike was a decent sort. He'd only been looking out for Jessie when he'd taken her to task. It would be churlish to hold the row.

'Thanks, Nadine.' She turned to her sister and smiled at her before handing her bouquet to Amanda.

Finally, she turned to Gary.

'Hello,' she murmured a little apprehensively, unsure of her reception.

His eyes were like flints. 'Well done,' he muttered. 'You really made a disgrace of yourself.'

It was as though he'd slapped her hard in the face. Her mother, Nadine, Amanda, Jessie and Mike had all been concerned for her. But the one whose concern she needed most had withheld it and judged her harshly. Distressed, she turned away from him and looked straight ahead.

The priest cleared his throat. 'Will we begin?' he suggested as the soloist began to sing 'Perhaps Love'.

The leaflet in Carol's hand shook and the words jumbled up in a blur. She could hear Mike and Jessie making their response with fervent sincerity.

This whole ceremony meant so much to them. They had put their heart and soul into it.

Gary hadn't cared what form the service took. The shorter the better, he'd told her.

He was sitting stiffly beside her and was making no effort at all to get involved.

It was her own fault, she acknowledged flatly. She'd pushed and pushed until he'd agreed to the double wedding. In her heart and soul, Carol knew full well that Gary would not be here if he really had to make a choice. Maybe he did love her in his own odd way, but it wasn't the cherishing, enriching love that she saw between Jessie and Mike or other couples of her acquaintance.

And today, just when she'd so badly needed the proof of his love and concern, he'd withdrawn from her and uttered words of condemnation. It was totally disheartening.

Jessie's left hand shook slightly as she held it out to Mike so he could slide the ring on to the third finger. He smiled down at her, his blue eyes full of love. It was as though no one else existed at that moment. The music, the coughing and shuffling of the congregation, all faded away as Mike made his vows to her. Slowly, tenderly, he slid the narrow gold band on to her finger.

Then it was her turn, as she repeated the priest's words in a clear, calm voice that brought tears to Liz's eyes. She kissed the ring before she slipped it on to his finger, and they smiled in delight at each other as the priest pronounced them man and wife. The congregation burst into applause and, not even waiting for the priest's permission, Mike wrapped his arms around her and kissed her. It was a day Jessie would never forget, for many reasons, but this was the memory she'd hold close to her heart.

Carol swallowed hard as she watched Mike and Jessie embrace. It was almost her turn now. The moment she had always longed for was at hand. She turned to look at Gary. There was no happiness in his expression, no anticipation. Just sullen resignation. He couldn't even make the effort. Any kissing that they'd do would be purely for show.

Was this what she wanted? Did she need to be married so badly that she was prepared to marry a man who wasn't even half-way committed? As if in slow motion she saw the priest turn and walk in their direction. *You don't want to be a single mother*, she thought in desperation as he placed her hand in Gary's. *You don't want to be an unhappy wife for the rest of your life.* The thought was clear and unsullied.

'Carol and Gary, we are gathered here today in the sight of God to—'

'No!' she heard herself say as she pulled her hand out of Gary's.

The priest looked at her, perplexed.

'No, I'm not doing it. I don't want to marry him,' she said with certainty. She could hear the collective gasp of horror behind her. She didn't care. If she married Gary she'd never be able to look herself in the eye again. She would have settled for second best and she deserved much more than that.

'For crying out loud, Carol, this is ridiculous!' Gary exploded. 'First you cause a rumpus in the porch and now you pull a stunt like this. What the hell are you playing at?' he demanded angrily.

'I'm not playing at anything, Gary,' she said wearily. 'I just can't do it any more. You don't want to be married. You don't want to make a proper commitment. You still want your bachelor life. Well, you've got it. Enjoy it.'

She turned to Jessica and Mike, who were looking on in stunned dismay.

'I'm really, really sorry,' she apologized. 'I mucked up your wedding big time, but at least the two of you know that your vows really mean something. Believe me, that's the most important thing of all.'

With great dignity she turned to the shocked guests and said quietly, 'I'm leaving now. Please enjoy the rest of Jessie and Mike's wedding and give them all the love and support they deserve. I'm sorry for all the upset.'

Silence descended on the church as she walked briskly down the aisle followed by a thoroughly shaken Amanda, who assured herself that she was never, *ever* going to be a bridesmaid again.

Nancy stood up and turned to leave. Liz hurried over to her.

'Would you like me to come with you?' she offered.

'No, Liz, you stay with your daughter and I'll go and look after mine,' she said firmly.

'Maybe it's all for the best. It was a brave thing to do,' Liz murmured.

'I think you're right, actually. We'll talk tomorrow,' Nancy agreed, kissing her on the cheek. 'Go and have a proper wedding now and enjoy it.'

Nadine joined them.

'Come on, Ma, Carol needs us,' she said, glaring around defiantly.

She caught Gary's eye and marched up to the altar.

'You're only a prick and she's well rid of you,' she hissed before hurrying after her mother.

Puce with mortification, Gary turned to his family. 'Let's get out of here,' he snapped. There was a side door to the right of him, which saved him from having to make the humiliating trip down the main aisle. His family and guests followed him awkwardly.

Jessica and Mike watched them leave. Jessica was shaking like an aspen.

'Could I say something, Father?' Mike asked calmly.

'Of course,' the flabbergasted priest agreed.

'Sorry for all the fuss, folks. Try not to let it spoil your day because Jessie and I aren't going to. So please join us in celebrating the rest of our wedding ceremony and we'll see you all at the hotel.'

'Well done,' said the priest, as the remaining guests applauded warmly.

Mike put his arm around Jessie and they turned to face the priest.

'Let us now say a prayer for the newly married couple,' he invited, and with audible sighs of relief the congregation knelt and sent up a heartfelt prayer.

'I'm sorry, Ma. I just couldn't go through with it.' Carol looked at her mother, not sure what sort of a response she'd get. They were in the limo heading back to the house.

'I'm very proud of you, Carol. It took a lot of guts to do what you did, and don't for one minute feel bad about it,' Nancy said, unexpectedly.

'Thanks, Ma.' Carol's lip trembled. Her mother's response touched her deeply.

'Yeah, it was real brave,' Nadine agreed. 'Especially with you being pregnant an' all.'

'You're *pregnant*!' Nancy couldn't hide her shock.

'Sorry, Carol.' Nadine's hand flew to her mouth. 'It just slipped out.'

'Yes, Ma, I am,' Carol said in resignation.

Nancy was silent for a minute. 'Well, Carol, I've even more admiration for you if that's the case. And for what it's worth I think you've done the right thing.'

'Hear, hear,' Amanda chipped in. 'Better to nip it in the bud now than spend your life rueing it.'

'I hope I'll feel like that in nine months' time,' Carol said shakily.

'We'll all help out.' Nancy patted her hand.

'I'm starving!' Nadine exclaimed. 'It must be all the excitement.'

'I'm glad you thought it was exciting.' Carol grinned at her younger sister. 'It's the kind of excitement I could do without. But you know, I'm kind of peckish myself. Ravenous in fact. It's weird.'

'Are you getting cravings already?' Amanda teased.

'We could always get the driver to drop us into Ashford for something to eat and get a taxi home,' Nancy said slowly.

'In all our gear?' Carol said, surprised by her mother's suggestion.

'Why not? You can take the veil off. You know what we should do, Carol? We should *celebrate* your great escape.' Nancy sat up straight and looked around at the others.

'I wouldn't mind something to eat either. I think that's a great idea, Mrs Logan,' Amanda declared good-humouredly.

Carol looked at her travelling companions in amazement. They were being absolutely gung-ho and supportive. She felt a cloud lift from her. 'Right then,' she said briskly, tapping on the glass that separated the driver from them. 'Could you drop us in Ashford, please?'

'Whatever you want,' said the driver, who'd never had a job like this before. One minute he'd been having a nice doze, the next minute the bride, bridesmaid, her mother and sister had all come trooping out of the church demanding to be taken home. Now they wanted to go to Ashford. It was no skin off his nose. They could go to Timbuktu as long as he was paid.

Twenty minutes later, the four of them were seated at a pine table in the little Italian restaurant perusing the menu.

Nancy lifted her glass of mineral water. 'To Carol,' she said supportively.

'And all who sail in her.' Nadine grinned affectionately, clinking her glass against her sister's.

'To family and friends.' Carol raised her glass. Although it had been the most traumatic day of her life, she felt as if a weight had been lifted off her shoulders, a weight that had bowed her down for a long, long time.

Already she was making plans. She was going to put a deposit on a house and get a mortgage, that was her first priority. And one of the rooms would be a guest room for two very important people: her mother and Nadine. She might have lost a fiancé but she'd found her family. That was the most positive thing of all.

Gary changed out of his morning suit, gathered his belongings and brought them down to Vince's car. He was in total shock. Carol had literally ditched him at the altar. Made a laughing stock of him in front of their friends, in front of his family. She'd walked away from him. And this time she meant it.

He was angry, he was relieved, and he was pissed off. He wanted to get the hell out of here and never set foot in the place again. He strode back into the foyer and asked for his bill. What a pity the wedding meal had been paid for in advance, he thought nastily as he proffered his credit card. She could pay him back for all of the wedding expenses.

A thought struck him. He couldn't stay in the flat with her. Now he was bloody homeless. What a pain in the ass having to go looking for a flat when he'd just let go of a perfectly good one in Christ Church.

'Ready to go?' Vince asked. 'The others have all checked out.'

'Yeah. Let's get the hell out of here, let's get home to Dublin and go and get hammered.'

'I'm with you all the way, Gary.' Vince slapped him on the back sympathetically. 'For what it's worth, I think you had a lucky escape. She was a bit neurotic, to say the least. All that healthy eating and no drinking. Not your type at all, mate, not your type at all.'

'You're dead bloody right,' Gary growled, wondering why he felt a sudden pang of loneliness.

'Well, it wasn't your boring old run-of-the-mill wedding, that's for sure,' Mike remarked good-humouredly as he lathered soap down Jessie's back. They were having a shower before joining some of the others for a crack-of-dawn breakfast. They'd been up all night.

'It was a *great* reception – I feel sorry for Carol and Gary that they missed it. That band is fantastic.' Jessie yawned and choked on a mouthful of bubbles.

'I'm glad she didn't marry him. I really admire her, even if she did muck up our day.' Mike rinsed his hair.

'I'm glad she didn't either. He never treated her right. He'd no respect for her. I never thought she had it in her. We saw a different Carol for sure.' Jessie reached out through the door and found a towel as Mike turned off the steaming jets.

'And a different Nadine, and a different Nancy.'

Mike wrapped a towel around his waist and proceeded to towel his wife dry.

'They've all sort of gelled, haven't they? They've become a family again. Even though they don't realize it, Bill and Gary have done them a favour,' Jessie observed.

Mike smiled down at her. 'Hey, wife, let's forget about Carol and Gary and all the rest of them and let's just think about us,' he murmured, cupping her breasts in his hands.

'Whatever you say, husband,' Jessica giggled, sliding his towel down over his hips. 'Whatever you say . . .'

42

Nine months later

Nancy felt her mobile phone vibrate silently in her pocket. Discreetly she slid it into her hand and opened the message from Carol.

'Excuse me, I'm afraid I'm going to have to go,' she said. She smiled at the people gathered around in a circle. 'Hi, my name is Nancy and I'm an alcoholic. And my daughter's in labour...' Everyone at her AA meeting clapped and wished her well as she grabbed her coat and bag and hurried to the door.

She'd been staying with Carol for the past week, awaiting her grandchild's birth, and now it was imminent. She felt flutters of excitement as she hurried to the bus stop.

It was hard to believe that almost nine months had passed since that crazy day of upheaval that had ended Carol's relationship with Gary.

They had all come a long way. It had actually been a very positive time for them as a whole, she acknowledged. With Liz's help she'd finally admitted she had a problem with drink and had gone to her first AA meeting.

It was a hard struggle and she was learning a lot about herself, but she was persevering. Nadine was going to Al Anon and was much less abrasive and aggressive. Carol's troubles had brought them all closer, and it gave Nancy great joy to watch the bond between her daughters strengthen and grow.

She saw the bus hove into view and rooted in her purse for the correct change. Sometimes she had to pinch herself to see if it really was her hopping on to buses in Dublin, going to AA meetings in the city, shopping, eating in cafés and restaurants and generally being 'normal'.

If someone had told her eighteen months ago that her life was going to change completely she would have accused them of fantasizing. But it *had* changed since that terrible Sunday when she'd set the kitchen on fire and Bill had hurled abuse at her in front of all her neighbours. That had been the lowest point in her life, the turning point. Hearing the various stories at her AA meetings had led her to believe that often you had to be on your knees before you made the decision to change your life.

She was surely glad she'd changed hers. Nancy stepped on to the bus and paid her fare, relieved that she hadn't been waiting too long. The sooner she got Carol to the Rotunda the better. She slipped a Polo mint into her mouth. Thanks to Nadine she'd become addicted.

'Carol's gone into labour.' Katie yawned, nearly breaking her jaw. Jessie had just sent her a text to tell her the news. She snuggled against Sean in the big double bed. They were both working night shifts, which meant they could have an early breakfast together before falling into bed, bog-eyed with tiredness. As often as not their shifts clashed so the past few weeks it had been a rare treat for them to spend a lot of time together. Katie was as happy as she'd ever been in her life.

'Well, at least her family seems to have rallied round, from what you've been telling me, so that's good.' Sean smiled at her and tucked her in closer to him. 'Should we visit?'

'You must be mad, Sean!' Katie exclaimed indignantly. Since she no longer shared a house with Jessie she had little or nothing to do with Carol and that was just how she liked it.

'Look at the mad head on you, would you calm down, my dear woman?' Sean laughed at her. 'It wouldn't kill us to show the girl a bit of kindness, she's had it tough.'

'Listen, mister, you go if you want to. I'm not. Not after the way she insulted you.' Katie was hopping mad.

'She never insulted me that I can remember.' Sean looked at her, surprised.

'I just never told you about it, but she was a right wagon.' Katie's cheeks reddened at the memory of Carol's insult to her precious darling.

'Why? What did she say?' Sean leaned up on one elbow and twirled a russet curl around his finger as he smiled down at her, amused at her indignation.

'She called you her "leavings". She told me I was welcome to her "leavings"! The absolute cheek of her.' Time had not lessened the insult in Katie's eyes.

Sean whistled. 'Way to go, Carol.' He grinned at her, blue eyes twinkling. 'And imagine she survived to tell the tale,' he teased.

'Huh! I couldn't say much. It was the day of the wedding and there was enough drama going on,' Katie said regretfully.

'Just as well.' Sean leaned down and kissed her

slowly. 'You know we only ever snogged,' he said reassuringly.

'Am I a much better kisser?' Katie demanded.

'Much better. Far superior! The best kisser in the universe,' Sean assured her.

'Are you going to visit her?'

'Perhaps not. I wouldn't like to be murdered in my bed. A red-headed Scorpio is not to be tangled with, as I've found to my cost,' he murmured, nuzzling her earlobe.

'Sensible boy.' Katie sighed with pleasure. 'This Scorpio is all yours . . .'

Carol mopped the kitchen floor, glad that her waters had broken on the creamy tiles rather than in the sitting-room or bedroom. It had been such a strange sensation, that sudden hot wet gush. Her heart had lurched in excited terror. Her baby was ready to come. Who would have thought that the night of its conception was the last time she and Gary had slept together? What an irony, she thought, as she gazed out into her sunlit patio, which, thanks to Nancy, was full of tubs of colourful petunias and Busy Lizzies and scented stocks and geraniums.

This time last year she'd been living in a flat in Phibsboro, feeling beleaguered and unhappy, wondering if Gary was ever going to marry her. Now she had her own smart new townhouse high on a hill in Glasnevin, overlooking the Botanic Gardens and the Tolka River. A small second-hand Fiat Uno was parked outside. She'd taken a refresher course in driving and bought a car. She'd done a lot with herself once she'd walked away from Gary and realized that she had to get on with things, she thought proudly.

It hadn't been easy going back to the flat a couple of days after her wedding drama. She'd wondered if Gary would be there. It was with a stomach-lurching sense of shock that she'd realized when she opened the door that all his stuff was gone. He'd left a curt note and she could still remember it.

Carol,
I expect to be reimbursed for all wedding expenses,
Gary.

Had she not been pregnant she would have coughed up. After all, fair was fair. She had called off the wedding at literally the last second. But she needed every penny she could lay her hands on, she reasoned – she had her baby to think of. In a temper at his mercenary attitude she'd phoned him.

'What do you want?' His surly reply stiffened her resolve.

'Gary, I'm pregnant. I'm looking for a house for our child. If I have any money left over I'll be delighted to give it to you,' she snapped.

'You're *pregnant*!'

She could sense his shock in the silence that followed and then he'd uttered the ultimate insult. 'Are you sure it's mine?' he asked nastily.

Disgusted, she'd hung up. That was low, even for Gary. She knew there and then that she was on her own and that he wouldn't have any involvement in their child's life. Once Carol knew what she was facing she got on with it.

Fortunately the lending agencies were dishing out loans right, left and centre and interest rates were low. She'd secured her mortgage with very little hassle and had got the keys to her new home by Christmas. Even though it was still a building site she didn't care. She and Nadine and Nancy had spent quite a jolly Christmas shopping for bits and pieces to furnish the place. Mike and Jessie had come and spent a weekend with her, and for the first time in her life she'd truly appreciated Jessie's friendship. She'd been so encouraging and full of admiration for her new house. It had been fun having them to stay, and it had been almost like old times when they'd gone for a drink in the tennis club.

People had been surprisingly kind to her. Her friends in the tennis club had clubbed together and given her a substantial gift voucher for Arnotts at her house-warming party. She'd bought her kitchenware and bathroom essentials and bedlinen for the two divans in her guest room with it. Their support had meant a lot to her. Even when she'd no longer been able to play tennis she'd still gone to watch the matches and keep in touch, a couple of times a week. Gary had stopped playing there and it was a relief knowing that she wouldn't bump into him. She'd heard on the grapevine that he was renting a place in Smithfield and dating a solicitor. Carol didn't care any more. He'd stepped over a boundary that there was no going back from. He was history and she was looking forward to her future. A future that she was perfectly capable of providing for herself.

She loved putting the key into her own front door. It gave her a great sense of security and a great sense of pride. She'd done it on her own. She didn't need Bill and she didn't need Gary – she'd proved that to herself well and truly. If she ever had a relationship with a man again, and she hoped that she would, she wouldn't be coming at it from neediness. Her next relationship would be a relationship of equals.

But best of all out of those turbulent few days last year was the knowledge that when she needed them most, Nancy and Nadine had been there for her.

She heard her mother's key in the lock and hurried out to greet her.

'Are you ready to go?' Nancy's eyes were sparkling with anticipation. She was really looking forward to the birth of her first grandchild. Carol was thrilled about that.

'Yep, I've got my case.' She looked at her mother. 'Ma, I'm scared,' she admitted as a contraction gripped her.

'Breathe deep like they showed us at your class. You'll be fine – take whatever they give you, no need to be brave.' Nancy gave her a comforting hug.

'Ouch, it hurts!' Carol yelled indignantly as hot pokers of pain gripped her.

Nancy laughed. 'Of course it does. I'll phone for the taxi.'

The next morning at seven a.m., after a long, tiring labour, Carol lay in bed holding her newborn daughter. She had a shock of black hair and the tightest little grip. She was gorgeous, and Carol felt an overwhelming sense of love and happiness infuse every cell in her body. This beautiful child made up for every hurt, grief and pain she had ever suffered. This was perfection, she thought as she kissed her baby's downy cheek.

'We're going to take her now so you can rest,' the nurse told her firmly.

'Just let me hold her for another little while – we have to bond,' Carol pleaded.

'The pair of you are well bonded,' the nurse laughed understandingly, 'but all right then, another ten minutes.'

This was the best, the greatest, moment of her life and she wanted it to last for as long as it possibly could.

43

The Anniversary

It was hard to believe that a year had passed since Carol had left him at the altar. Gary eased himself out of the bed, not wanting to disturb the tousle-headed young woman sprawled asleep beside him.

Why was this day bothering him so much, he wondered gloomily. He'd been dreading it for the past week. It was just another day to all intents and purposes.

It was knowing that he had a daughter that bothered him and made him feel like a heel. He knew he'd behaved like a bastard. Asking Carol if the baby was his was beyond the pale. It was shock that had made him say it. The shock of hearing that she was pregnant. He knew in his heart of hearts that the baby was his. Carol had had a period the week before she went to Kilkenny;

he remembered her saying she was glad it was over before she went away for her hen night. It had to have been the night they slept together when she was upset over the row with Jessica. How ironic that Carol, who had kept him at arm's length because of her fear of getting pregnant, should get caught just before the wedding. If she'd known about it on their wedding day, he had to admire her guts in walking away from him.

One of his mates on the tennis circuit had told him that he was a father. Carol hadn't got in contact. He didn't know whether to be sorry or glad. He was as free as a bird, he was having a great time socially, and he was dating a hot babe, who didn't want any strings. How lucky could a guy get? His life was so different from what it had been a year ago when he had made that interminable journey to the church, dressed up like a dog's dinner, wanting to be a million miles away and feeling utterly trapped. It was good to have closure on that chapter of his life. There was no point in hanging on to the past.

He didn't want to be facing maintenance and visiting rights and all the responsibilities that having a child entailed. Sometimes when he saw small babies he wondered what his daughter looked like. But he never lingered on those thoughts. It was only sentimental foolishness and he was far from sentimental. He missed Carol, though. He missed their sparring. He missed the way she used to chivvy him to eat properly. He missed their humdingers of tennis matches when neither would give an inch. He missed knowing that even though she pretended not to be, she'd been mad about him.

His new girlfriend loved parties and clubs and drinking as much as he did, but there were times he wearied of the same old thing. One thing about Carol, he'd never been bored with her.

Gary sighed deeply and went into the kitchen to get a glass of water. He had the life he wanted, he reflected ruefully, why on this day of all days did he have the horrible feeling that it wasn't enough?

'Daddy, why are you sad?' a little voice asked anxiously.

'I'm not sad, Ben. Why did you say that?' Bill came to with a start.

' 'Cos you look sad!" his son said perceptively.

They were watching cartoons on TV while Brona had her shower.

'I wish I didn't have to go to the crèche today,' Ben announced, flicking the pages of his favourite book of dinosaurs.

'Why not?' his father asked, wiping Coco Pops off his chin.

'Just wish,' Ben sighed.

'I wish I didn't have to go to work,' Bill declared, kissing the top of his son's head.

'Can we stay home, Dad, just you an' me an' have a boys' day like Mom likes us to?'

'On Saturday,' Bill told him.

'Aw, Dad, is it not Saturday today?' Ben was crestfallen.

'No.' Deep, deep sighs followed this pronouncement, and Bill felt a pang as he looked at his son's despondent face.

He was feeling pretty despondent himself. It was a year ago today that Carol and Nadine had firmly and viciously closed the door in his face, and he had to face the hard fact that he was no longer part of their lives. They didn't want him and he didn't see that changing in the future. His only hope was that Carol might in time soften her attitude towards him now that she had a child of her own.

Nancy had phoned him at work to tell him the news. She felt he should know that he was a grandfather. They'd chatted awkwardly at first, but at least there was no longer huge animosity between them. He'd phoned her about six weeks later just to see how things were and they'd had quite a civil conversation. Nancy seemed much calmer in herself. She'd told him that she was in AA. He was delighted for her. That was a big step, and a brave one.

A thought struck him. This day last year had been an absolute disaster; he should do something today to counteract the bad memories.

'Hey, pal, you're right. Let's have a boys' day,' he said impulsively.

'Yeah, Dad.' Ben launched himself on him gleefully.

'What's going on?' Brona demanded. 'Look, you haven't even put his shoes on, we'll be late,' she tutted.

'It's OK, Brona, I'm going to take a day's leave. We're going to have a boys' day today.'

'Why? What's brought this on?' She was perplexed.

'I just want to spend some quality time with my son and I've built up a lot of flexi time. I need to take some.'

'What about me?' she pouted.

'Dinner in Wongs tonight?' he invited.

'Sure!' She brightened up. 'See you later, and have fun.' She kissed him on the cheek, rumpled Ben's hair and click-clacked her way across the wooden floor to the front door. Bill watched her leave. At least they were back on a fairly even keel. He'd never mentioned the events of Carol's wedding day to her, and she'd never brought up the subject of his daughters again. It was best to leave it at that.

'Let's go to Dollymount when I've had my breakfast,' he suggested to his son.

'Deadly, Daddy,' the little boy exclaimed, and Bill hid a grin. The expressions he picked up at the crèche were a constant source of amusement.

Two hours later they were building sandcastles on the beach. Ben shrieked with delight as the waves washed over the toes of his wellingtons.

It was a warm, breezy day. Fortunately the wind was from the south, protecting them from the autumn chill. He watched his son playing with carefree exuberance and wondered how his grand-daughter was faring. On impulse he took his phone out of his fleece pocket and scrolled down to Nancy's number.

'Hello,' she said, cheerfully enough.

'It's me,' he said awkwardly.

'I know, your name came up in my screen. What's wrong?'

'Nothing, I was just wondering how everyone was. How's the baby?'

'She's a dote. I've just finished feeding her.'

'Oh! Is Carol in Wicklow?'

'No, herself and Amanda and Nadine have gone for a beauty day and a meal in a leisure centre in Clontarf and I'm babysitting.'

'So you're in Glasnevin?'

'Yes. It's the anniversary. Carol wanted to do something positive so I said I'd come up and mind my precious dote,' Nancy said almost gaily.

'I'd love to see her.' The words were out before he realized it.

There was silence on the other end of the phone. Then Nancy asked, 'Are you at work?'

'No,' he responded. 'I'm on a day off. I'm with Ben on the beach.'

'I was going to go for a walk in the Botanics,' Nancy said slowly.

'Ben loves the Botanics,' Bill said with a rising sense of excitement.

'I suppose we could always bump into each other. But don't ever let on to Carol, Bill, she'd never forgive me if she thought I'd gone behind her back,' Nancy warned.

'OK, ditto. Brona wouldn't be too happy either. We'll just keep it between us.'

'You know the little shelter in to the right, at the gates? I'll wait for you there. Say, in half an hour?'

'Nancy, thank you,' her husband said earnestly.

'It's OK, Bill. I'd like you to see her. See you soon.'

Bill couldn't believe his luck. It wasn't all a total disaster. He and Nancy were talking and he was going to see his grandchild. It was better than nothing.

'Now, darling Charlotte, you have to look your very best,' Nancy crooned as she dressed her granddaughter in a snug little lilac and cream trousers and top. The baby cooed at her, her rose-bud mouth widening in a big smile.

'You're so beautiful, Baba,' Nancy declared happily. She was having the best time of her life. It was like she'd been given a second chance with her new grandchild. She'd never been so content. She'd heard the longing in her husband's voice and found enough compassion in her heart to feel sorry for him. His daughters had turned away from him. That was hard. He'd never have the joy of Charlotte that she had, and that was a big loss.

She felt no bitterness any more. AA had helped her to release that and take responsibility for her own behaviour. She'd made his life a misery and it was time to try and make amends. She could only work on her own relationship with him.

Nadine and Carol had to deal with Bill their own way.

'Now, Baba, give Nana a big kiss,' she urged, nuzzling into her granddaughter before laying her in her pram. It was a lovely day; she could see the Dublin Mountains very clearly. The trees of the Botanics in the distance were showing a hint of golden autumn. She was looking forward to her walk in the Botanic Gardens. It was a most beautiful place. A haven from the city.

Nancy set off briskly, enjoying the breeze against her cheeks.

Where was she? Bill wondered, peering around to see if he could see Nancy.

'I'm here.' He turned again and looked. That slim, healthy woman with the blondish short hair and smart trouser suit was hardly Nancy. But she was smiling at him and she had a pram.

It was her. He didn't recognize her. The last time he'd seen his wife she was shaking with drink, unkempt and, grey-faced. This Nancy looked twenty years younger.

'You look very well . . .' he stuttered.

Nancy laughed. 'Don't look so shocked. Here, have a look at your granddaughter.' She pulled back the covers of the pram and he leaned in to have a look.

'Oh my God!' he exclaimed as a lump rose to his throat. 'She's a miniature Carol.'

'Isn't she?' Nancy smiled. 'The very image of her. Come on, let's bring your little lad for a walk – he's trying to drink out of the fountain over there. He's a lovely little fella.'

'Yeah, he is,' Bill said, moved beyond belief at the sight of his grandchild.

They walked for an hour, and she showed him Carol's house from the banks of the river. Later they had coffee in the tea-rooms.

'I'm just going to say I met an old friend from work, because Ben will surely say something and, er . . . Brona . . . er—'

'It's OK, Bill, say what you have to. I don't have to say anything, well, not until Charlotte starts talking, anyway.'

'Do you mean we can meet again?' he asked eagerly.

'I don't see why not, if I'm up here babysitting.' Nancy shrugged. 'As long as we keep it between ourselves. I wouldn't dream of hurting Carol.'

'Absolutely. Whatever you say,' Bill agreed, cuddling Ben, who had fallen asleep on his knee, with one arm and holding his granddaughter's tiny hand with the other.

Nancy smiled at him. 'Thank God we've come out the other side, Bill.'

'Thank God, and thank you, Nancy,' Bill said quietly, leaning across the table to kiss his wife's cheek.

'Isn't this the life?' Carol stretched luxuriously in her fluffy white terry-towelling robe. She smelt of lavender and rose and had had the most relaxing full body massage. Amanda had just gone off to have a pedicure and she and Nadine were relaxing before their next beauty treatments.

'Thanks for inviting me.' Nadine yawned. She wasn't used to being pampered. It was deliciously exhausting.

'I wanted to share my day with you. This day last year I was so unhappy and you were so supportive of me. I really appreciate all you've done for me,' Carol said quietly.

Nadine blushed. 'Stop! I did nothing.'

'No, Nadine. You stood up for me and stood beside me and you've been so good to the baby. I don't know what I would have done without you.'

'She's gorgeous, isn't she? I can't wait to come and live with you when I go to college next year,'

Nadine said eagerly. 'I really hope I get that course in DCU.'

'Just keep on track. You're doing well,' Carol encouraged.

'Are you sorry you didn't marry him?' Nadine asked out of the blue.

Carol's brow wrinkled in thought. When she'd woken up this morning she'd lain in bed watching Charlotte in her cot and remembered how she'd felt a year ago. Stressed out, sick, apprehensive and unhappy. It was as if she'd been a different person.

Now, even though she still felt very hurt by Gary's treatment of her, she had accepted her part in the failure of the relationship and so her bitterness was tempered by self-knowledge and acceptance of her own behaviour. She had her baby to thank for that, she admitted. If she'd been on her own she might have turned in on herself and allowed bitterness to eat her up. But all her energies were concentrated on her daughter and she didn't spend time regretting the past.

It was a futile, pointless exercise. Her mother had wasted years of her life in bitterness; Carol wasn't going to make the same mistake. Gary was the loser. He didn't see Charlotte's toothless gummy innocent smile first thing in the morning. He didn't get the sweet talcy scent of her after her bath. He didn't know what it was like to feel her fall asleep snuggled against a shoulder. He had none of that.

She didn't miss the angst. She didn't miss the unreliability. She didn't miss the resentment and irritation that had pervaded their relationship.

Carol smiled over at her sister. 'Am I sorry I didn't marry him?' she repeated slowly. 'No, Nadine, I'm not sorry,' she said. 'I'm not sorry in the slightest.'

'But why are we up so early? And why have I to go with Katie?' Jessie demanded sleepily. 'And where's my card and present? Did you forget our anniversary?'

'No, I didn't,' Mike said indignantly. 'You'll get your prezzie later, and if you got me one keep it for later too. Now go and wake Katie up and get going, we're on a tight schedule,' Mike ordered.

'Tell me what's going on or I'm not getting up,' she said truculently.

In response Mike rolled her across the mattress and hauled her out of bed.

'Hey, mister!' she protested, half amused and half annoyed at him.

'Really, Jessie, trust me,' he said earnestly. 'It's a

surprise for you for our anniversary and that's all I'm telling you.'

'Oh, all right then,' she grumbled.

'Katie, tell me what's going on,' she pleaded with her best friend, who was sprawled limbs to the four winds in the double bed in their guest-room.

'I can't. I'm sworn to secrecy,' Katie muttered crankily. 'I'm sorry I agreed to it – it's too early for civilized people to be getting up. Go and make a pot of coffee and stick a rasher on the grill.'

With a mounting sense of excitement, Jessica did as she was bid. What had Mike organized for their wedding anniversary? She'd just been told to take two days' annual leave and that Katie was staying the night and that she was to do whatever her cousin told her to do.

An hour later, after a satisfying bacon and mayo sandwich, she and Katie were on the road in Katie's car. They were heading south.

'Tell me,' she begged for the umpteenth time.

'Jessie, please don't ask me. I promised Mike,' Katie said sternly.

'All right then,' she exclaimed in exasperation as they whizzed through the Glen of the Downs.

'Why are we going to the hairdresser's?' she

asked an hour later as Katie led her into the hair salon in Arklow.

'For dinner tonight. Now *don't* ask any more,' Kate retorted, winking at the stylist.

An hour and a half later Katie pulled up outside Liz's house. Jessie's mother greeted her with a bear hug. She was in her dressing-gown but had her hair done and her make-up on. Her eyes were sparkling with mischief.

'What's going on?' Jessie demanded.

'Is she here?' Katie asked.

'In the front room,' Liz said mysteriously.

Tara appeared out of the kitchen, dolled up to the nines.

'Better hurry, time's getting on,' she declared.

'Will someone tell me what's going on?' Jessie demanded as she was bustled into the sitting-room.

'Hi, Jessie, sit down there for me and let me put this around you,' Jenny, the beautician from the beauty salon, invited, waving a gown.

'This is crazy. Where are we going?' Jessie murmured.

'Lunch,' Tara said succinctly.

'I thought you said dinner?' Jessie said accusingly to Katie, who was standing grinning at her.

'Lunch and dinner,' her cousin said airily.

The three of them were so giddy and giggly it was driving her crazy.

Eventually, her make-up applied, Jessie was instructed to put the kettle on and make a pot of tea for them all while Katie had her make-up done.

After tea and home-made quiche, Katie took her by the arm. 'Right, we just have to get changed,' she said.

'But I didn't bring anything with me to change into,' Jessie wailed.

'It's all sorted,' Katie soothed. 'Your dress, Cinderella, is on the bed.' She opened Jessie's bedroom door and Jessie gasped when she saw her wedding dress flat out on the bed. Beside it lay Katie's ruby fishtail gown.

'What's happening?' she stammered.

'You're getting married,' grinned Katie, followed by Liz and Tara.

'But I am married. I got married this day last year.'

'Well, you're getting married again, properly this time, with no dramatics and tragedy – just your own little wedding all to yourselves,' Tara declared happily. 'Mike and Katie have arranged it all. Father Henry's going to officiate at the renewal of your wedding vows—'

'And Sean's coming,' Katie giggled. 'And if you're not careful I'll ask you can we have a double wedding,' she teased, waving her diamond solitaire. She and Sean had got engaged in August.

'Oh my God! *Oh my God!*' Jessica was completely overwhelmed. Tears brightened her eyes.

'Don't cry!' they all yelled. 'Your mascara!'

Jessie laughed and cried at the same time. Imagine Mike planning all of this behind her back. No wonder she was crazy about him, she reflected as she stepped out of her jeans and shirt. Getting married again with no drama. How blissful.

Dizzy with happiness, she stood still as Liz and Tara slipped the champagne skirt over her head, followed by the beaded bodice. Opposite her Katie pulled her dress over her ass.

'Still fits, thank God,' she announced. Triumphantly. 'I'm never ever eating lettuce again. The next time you renew your vows you're on your own.'

'Sorry, honey. The next big do you've to slim for is your wedding, so there,' Jessie riposted, and was gratified to find her cousin speechless for once.

Ten minutes later, Katie announced, 'Here's Dad with the car.' And Jessie had the strangest sense of *déjà vu*. Was this all happening or was she dreaming?

She was still pinching herself when she stood in the porch of Kilbride church and heard the organist begin the Wedding March. Liz, wearing the lovely navy and cream suit she'd worn a year ago, turned and smiled at her daughter.

'Best foot forward,' she murmured, just like before.

In a dream Jessie walked slowly up the aisle on her mother's arm. Mike's family were there, and Sean, smiling broadly at Katie, and two of the girls from work and some of her relations. And waiting for her with a smile of pure happiness was Mike in his smart, grey suit.

'Hi.' He smiled down at her. 'You look radiant!'

'That's because I am.' Jessica smiled back and reached up and kissed her husband with all the love she possessed.

THE END

TWO FOR JOY
by Patricia Scanlan

Oliver Flynn's wedding is the social event of the year, and the *crème de la crème* of Kilronan are happy to boast of being invited.

Noreen, his new wife, has finally outclassed her two sisters, who think they are better than her in every way. Not any more! But there is one nagging doubt: does Oliver *really* love her? Would he have married her if she hadn't done the proposing herself?

Wedding guest Lorna Morgan can't wait to shake the dust of Kilronan off her shoes. She's destined for bright city lights, unlike her stick-in-the-mud cousin, Heather Williams, who was only invited to the 'afters' with her clodhopper boyfriend, Neil. But then, in Lorna's eyes, Heathers' just an 'afters' sort of person and always will be.

But worms turn, and what a difference a year makes. In Dublin, London and New York there is no respite for Noreen, Lorna or Heather. Only in Kilronan can the Pandora's box that was opened at the Flynns' wedding finally be closed.

A Bantam Paperback

0 553 81391 9

BANTAM BOOKS

FRANCESCA'S PARTY
by Patricia Scanlan

After years of being the perfect wife and mother, Francesca
Kirwan finds her life has changed irrevocably one dismal
autumn morning when her husband Mark forgets his
mobile phone. In the space of ten minutes her comfortable,
safe, uneventful existence is completely shattered. With her
life turned upside down and an extremely uncertain future
ahead of her, she has two choices . . . sink or swim!

Francesca decides to get a life, but first she must deal with
razor-sharp international banker Nikki Langan. Super-babe
is ten years younger and two stone lighter than Francesca.
Sculpted, toned and dressed to kill, Nikki wants it all and
she doesn't intend to let anyone, least of all Francesca, stand
in her way. But youth and beauty aren't everything, and
Francesca proves to be a far tougher adversary than the
glamorous career girl had anticipated.

After a shaky start, Francesca's life takes a decidedly upward
turn. New job, new friends, new lifestyle – and when dishy
journalist Ralph Casson shows more than a professional
interest in her, Mark is not at all pleased.

Francesca decides to throw a party, and that's when the fun
really starts. Revenge is a dish best served cold . . . *especially*
if you've been on a diet.

A Bantam Paperback

0 553 81292 0

BANTAM BOOKS

A SELECTED LIST OF FINE NOVELS
AVAILABLE FROM BANTAM BOOKS

81305 6	VIRTUAL STRANGERS	*Lynne Barrett-Lee*	£5.99
81400 1	THE HOUSE OF FLOWERS	*Charlotte Bingham*	£6.99
40615 9	PASSIONATE TIMES	*Emma Blair*	£5.99
81256 4	THE MAGDALEN	*Marita Colon-McKenna*	£5.99
81394 3	MIRACLE WOMAN	*Marita Colon-McKenna*	£5.99
81397 8	DISTANT SHORES	*Kristin Hannah*	£5.99
81625 X	DIARY OF A C-LIST CELEB	*Paul Hendy*	£6.99
81186 X	NADIA'S SONG	*Soheir Khashoggi*	£6.99
81410 9	MOSAIC	*Soheir Khashoggi*	£6.99
40732 5	THE JEWELS OF TESSA KENT	*Judith Krantz*	£6.99
81641 1	ANGRY HOUSEWIVES EATING BON BONS	*Lorna Landvik*	£6.99
81605 5	THE GIRL IN THE GREEN GLASS MIRROR	*Elizabeth McGregor*	£6.99
81338 2	A WAY THROUGH THE MOUNTAINS	*Elizabeth McGregor*	£6.99
50719 2	THE LAZARUS CHILD	*Robert Mawson*	£5.99
81251 3	SWAN	*Francis Mayes*	£6.99
81477 X	BACK AFTER THE BREAK	*Anita Notaro*	£5.99
81478 8	BEHIND THE SCENES	*Anita Notaro*	£6.99
81287 4	APARTMENT 3B	*Patricia Scanlan*	£6.99
81290 4	FINISHING TOUCHES	*Patricia Scanlan*	£6.99
81286 6	FOREIGN AFFAIRS	*Patricia Scanlan*	£6.99
81288 2	PROMISES, PROMISES	*Patricia Scanlan*	£5.99
81289 0	MIRROR, MIRROR	*Patricia Scanlan*	£5.99
40943 3	CITY GIRL	*Patricia Scanlan*	£6.99
40946 8	CITY WOMAN	*Patricia Scanlan*	£6.99
81291 2	CITY LIVES	*Patricia Scanlan*	£6.99
81292 0	FRANCESCA'S PARTY	*Patricia Scanlan*	£6.99
81391 9	TWO FOR JOY	*Patricia Scanlan*	£6.99
81393 5	A BEND IN THE ROAD	*Nicholas Sparks*	£5.99
81431 1	STRIKING POSES	*Kate Thompson*	£5.99
81373 0	PERFECT ALIBIS	*Jane Wenham-Jones*	£5.99